THE
NANNY

ALSO BY GILLY MACMILLAN

What She Knew

The Perfect Girl

Odd Child Out

I Know You Know

GILLY MACMILLAN

THE NANNY

A NOVEL

wm

WILLIAM MORROW
An Imprint of HarperCollins*Publishers*

THE NANNY. Copyright © 2019 by Gilly Macmillan. All rights reserved. Printed in the United States of America. No part of this book may be used or reproduced in any manner whatsoever without written permission except in the case of brief quotations embodied in critical articles and reviews. For information, address HarperCollins Publishers, 195 Broadway, New York, NY 10007.

HarperCollins books may be purchased for educational, business, or sales promotional use. For information, please email the Special Markets Department at SPsales@harpercollins.com.

FIRST EDITION

Designed by Bonni Leon-Berman

Library of Congress Cataloging-in-Publication Data has been applied for.

ISBN 978-0-06-287555-6 (hardcover)
ISBN 978-0-06-291458-3 (international edition)

19 20 21 22 23 LSC 10 9 8 7 6 5 4 3 2 1

To Helen Heller, agent extraordinaire, fashion guru, family accent coach, and friend. This book is most definitely for you.

THE
NANNY

PROLOGUE

WATER CLOSES OVER THE BODY. Swallows it. The rocking of the boat subsides quickly. Its occupant waits until the surface of the lake is still. Her breathing sounds shockingly loud. She takes the oars and rows away from the site with determined strokes. Her arms ache and she thinks: *I can't believe I had to do this. I hate to have done this.* When she reaches the boathouse, the boat glides in gently. She walks back to Lake Hall in silence, taking care where she steps. She is very tired. *The water was extremely cold. It's such a bad end for a person,* she thinks, *so unfortunate, but so necessary.* As she slips into the house, she doesn't notice the breeze moving the tips of the weeping willow branches, encouraging them to dance in the dark on the water's surface.

I STARE AT MY REFLECTION, transfixed by it. I am a grotesquely made-up version of myself, distorted like everything else. Which is the real me? This painted creature or the woman beneath the mask?

I no longer know whom or what to believe.

The door opens behind me and I see my daughter's reflection in the mirror, her face hovering behind mine, round as a coin, with bright cornflower-blue eyes. Unblemished.

I don't want her to see me now. I don't want her to become me.

"Get out," I say.

ONE

1987

JOCELYN IS DISORIENTED WHEN SHE *wakes up and her mouth is sticky dry. It's light outside and she feels as if she's been asleep for a very long time. She studies the hands on her bedside clock and concludes that the time is exactly twenty-six minutes past eight. Usually, her nanny wakes her up at seven.*

She yawns and blinks. Curvy, dancing giraffes cavort in pairs across her wallpaper, and soft toys carpet the end of her bed. Hanging on the door of her armoire, where Nanny Hannah left it yesterday, is an empty padded clothes hanger. It's supposed to be for Jocelyn's special dress, the one her mother bought for her to greet their guests in, but the dress got ruined and now it's gone. Jocelyn feels guilty and sad about that, but also confused. She knows what happened was bad, but she can only remember little flashes from the evening, and she pushes those out of her mind because they come with sharp feelings of shame.

Usually Jocelyn's bedroom is one of her favorite places to be, but this morning it feels different, too quiet. The door of the armoire is ajar and she imagines a creature lurking inside it, with talons and long limbs that will snake out and grab her at any moment.

"Hannah!" she calls. There's a band of light underneath the door that separates her room from her nanny's, but no sign of the moving shadows that usually tell her when Hannah is up. "Hannah!" she tries again, stretching out the vowels. There's no answer.

She gets out of bed and runs the few paces across the room to Hannah's door, slamming shut the armoire as she passes by. The

clothes hanger falls, the clatter it makes startling her. Jocelyn is sup-
posed to knock and wait for Hannah to answer before she enters her
nanny's bedroom, but she throws the door open.

She expects to see Hannah in bed or sitting on her chair in the cor-
ner, wearing her red dressing gown and fluffy slippers, but Hannah
isn't there. She expects to see a glass of water and a fat dog-eared
paperback on the bedside table. She expects to see Hannah's hair-
brush and makeup, her two porcelain figurines of kittens. But there
is no trace of Hannah or her belongings. The bed is neatly made, the
candlewick bedspread smoothed out with hospital corners, the pillows
are plump, the curtains are open, and every surface is bare.

"Hannah!" Jocelyn shouts. It's not just the shock of the room's
emptiness but also a sudden terrible feeling of loss that makes her
scream so piercing.

MARION HARRIS, the housekeeper at Lake Hall, pulls open every drawer
and door in Hannah's room. Lining paper curls in the base of the
drawers and empty metal hangers jangle in the wardrobe. She flips
up the edges of the bedspread to peer under the bed and checks the
bedside table. The girl is right—there is nothing of Hannah's to be
seen. She marches down the corridor to the box room. "She's taken
her suitcases. I can't believe it." The light cord swings in a wild
trajectory.

"I told you," Jocelyn whispers. Her chin wobbles. She's been hold-
ing out hope that Marion would be able to explain the situation or
fix it. Marion huffs. "It's so unlike her! She surely would have said
something or left a note. She'd never have dumped us in it like this."

Church bells begin to chime. Marion casts an eye out of the win-
dow toward the top of the spire, just visible above the dense band of
oak trees surrounding Lake Hall's grounds.

"Stay here and play," she says. "I'll fetch you a bit of breakfast, then I'll speak to your mother and father."

Jocelyn stays in her room until lunch. She works on a picture for Hannah, painstakingly selecting colors and being careful not to go over the lines. By the time Marion calls her down, she is bursting to know what's happening, but Marion says, "I don't know any more than you. You'll have to ask your parents." Her lips are set in a tight line.

Jocelyn finds her parents in the Blue Room with two friends who stayed the night. Newspapers and color supplements are spread out all over the sofas and the coffee table. The fire is lit and the air in the room is thick with wood and cigarette smoke.

Jocelyn wants to attract her daddy's attention, but he's deep in his armchair, long legs crossed and face hidden behind his pink newspaper. Mother is lying on one of the sofas, her head resting on a pile of cushions, eyes half shut. She's stubbing out a cigarette in the big marble ashtray balanced on her tummy. Jocelyn takes a deep breath. She's trying to work up the courage to speak. She doesn't want to attract her mother's attention if she can help it.

The lady friend turns from the window and notices Jocelyn in the doorway. "Hello, there," she says. Jocelyn thinks her name is Milla. Milla has brown hair backcombed to look big. "Hello," Jocelyn says. She tries to smile but blushes instead. She knows she was bad last night, but not if Milla knows.

Virginia Holt's attention is caught by her daughter's voice. "What do you want?"

Jocelyn flinches and glances at her father. He's still behind his newspaper.

"Hello!" her mother snaps. "I'm talking to you; he isn't."

Jocelyn swallows. "Do you know where Hannah is?"

"She left." Two words, and Jocelyn feels as if the bottom has *dropped out of her world. Hannah is her everything. Hannah cares. Hannah listens. Hannah has time to explain things to Jocelyn. Hannah is better than Mother. Hannah loves Jocelyn.*

"No!"

"Don't stamp your foot at me, young lady. How dare you?"

"Hannah didn't leave! Where did she go?"

"Alexander!"

Lord Holt puts down his newspaper. He looks very tired. "Mummy's right, darling. I'm sorry. We'll find you a new nanny as soon as possible. Mummy will make some calls after the weekend."

Jocelyn screams and her mother gets to her feet instantly, the ashtray falling to the carpet, its contents scattering. Virginia grabs Jocelyn's arms and leans down so her face is only inches from Jocelyn's. Her eyes are horribly bloodshot. Her hair falls across her face. Jocelyn recoils, but her mother's grip clamps her in place.

"Stop it this instant! Hannah left and you may as well know she left because of you. You are a bad girl, Jocelyn, a very bad girl. Is it any wonder Hannah couldn't stand to look after you anymore?"

"But I'll be a good girl, I promise. I'll be the best girl if you get Hannah back."

"It's too late for that."

JO

THE HOTEL TEAROOM HAS HIGH ceilings and pastel walls. In a far corner, the plasterwork is in need of patching. Rain is falling so hard outside it seems to liquidize the windowpanes. The room is almost full, and humming with chatter. Crockery and cutlery chink. Live light piano music and occasional laughter provide cheerful high notes. The room is warm but too large and formal to be cozy. I expect the glowing chandelier bulbs are reflected prettily in my eyes, but behind them, my state of mind can be summed up by that famous painting by Munch: *The Scream.*

However, I'm making a big effort, because it's Ruby's birthday.

"Salmon and cucumber, Jocelyn?" Mother says.

There's no point in reminding her yet again that I prefer to be called Jo now. I must have told her a hundred times already since Ruby and I got here, and still she refuses to accept it. I wish she hadn't overdone the rouge today. Her cheeks are as pink as a picture-book piggy, and her steel-gray hair is teased into a smooth quiff and fixed immovably under a velvet hairband.

Mother reserves the corner table in this tearoom every time she comes into town. It has the best view of the room. She tells me the food has gone downhill since she brought me here when I was a child, which is, she says, a shame. I get the impression the only reason she comes now is because she enjoys talking down to the employees. I hated coming here with her when I was little, and I don't feel any different thirty years later.

"Thank you." I take one of the limp white triangles and place it neatly in the middle of my plate.

"Ruby, darling?" Mother has launched an unexpected charm offensive. Her target is my ten-year-old daughter, Ruby. They met for the first time a month ago and I thought they would be like oil and water.

My mother: a seventy-year-old relic of the English aristocracy, cold, old-fashioned, snobbish, selfish, greedy, and fluent in the Queen's English.

Ruby: a kid who was born and has been raised in California, whip-smart, kind, an Internet gamer, an ex-member of a girls' soccer team, and a lifelong tomboy.

I was so wrong about their compatibility. I have been the absolute center of Ruby's world since her dad died, but I have acquired some serious competition from my mother now. A bond between them is forming right in front of my eyes. I feel as if my mother is maneuvering herself, uninvited, into the void Chris left in my and Ruby's lives after his death, and I'm not even a tiny bit comfortable with it.

"Thank you, Granny." Ruby treats my mother to a blinding smile and takes a sandwich from the four-tiered cake stand. It's the tallest in the room. On the menu it's described as "Decadent Afternoon Tea." My mother ordered it with relish, although the cost per head is eye-watering. I think she's done it to shame me for not making Ruby a birthday cake. I did buy one, but it was from the budget range at the supermarket. Needs must.

Ruby's eyes are bright with excitement and she's nibbling the edge of her sandwich in an affected way. I don't like it. Ruby is a gulp-it-down-so-you-can-run-back-outside sort of girl. Or she used to be. I have been amazed by the way she has thrown herself into English life since we arrived here. It's as if she's using all the new experiences to fill the gap her dad's death has left. I wonder how long the novelty of it will last, but for now at least, she fills her

Instagram feed with photos of Lake Hall and the surrounding countryside, of curiosities and objects she finds in the house and the people who work there. Since we've been in the tearoom, she's already posted several close-ups of the cakes. She tags her pictures as if they're curiosities in a museum or props at a British theme park. "Sooooo cute!" her California friends respond.

I guess I shouldn't fret about such harmless stuff. I should feel grateful she's coping at all, especially as today is special: not only is it the first birthday Ruby has had since her dad died, it's a milestone birthday.

"How does it feel to be ten?" Mother asks.

"Same as being nine." Ruby speaks with her mouth full, and automatically I brace myself to defend her if Mother tells her off, but she doesn't. She smiles instead. "You look very pretty in that cardigan," she tells Ruby.

We arrived here after spending an arduous length of time in a department store, where Mother bought Ruby two bags full of clothes and insisted Ruby take off her favorite hoodie and wear her new red cardigan to the Swallow Hotel for her birthday tea.

"I love it," Ruby says. "It's so retro."

"What?" Mother says, and I wonder if she has become a little hard of hearing.

She has aged remarkably well since I last saw her. The only obvious impairment the years have brought on is arthritis. Her knuckles are noticeably swollen on both hands. It is the only sign of physical weakness, of diminishment, I have ever noticed in my mother. I admit it makes me feel as if I have won a small victory, because when somebody has bullied you for your entire life, when you've felt driven to put an ocean between you and your upbringing to try to forget it, then you can't help it. I'd be lying if I claimed I was above this petty brand of schadenfreude.

Ruby doesn't repeat her comment because she's distracted by figuring out how to use the strainer provided for pouring the loose-leaf Assam tea, which she and my mother ordered; they're sharing a pot.

"You're almost a proper young lady now," Mother says. Her fingers aren't so bent she can't efficiently swipe a pistachio macaroon from the top tier of the cake stand.

"La-di-da," Ruby sings. Little finger extended, she sips her tea in a parody of gentility.

Again, I expect my mother to scorch Ruby with a reprimand, as she would have done to me, but she laughs, showing gums and long teeth. A macaroon crumb is stuck between her incisors. "La-di-da," she repeats. "What a funny little thing you are." It's her highest form of praise for a child.

"Excuse me," I say.

In the tearoom bathroom, surrounded by suffocating chintzy wallpaper and chilled by a draft, I get my phone out. The last texts Chris and I exchanged were two and a half months ago. It was a beautiful California morning. He was at work. I was standing in our light-filled kitchen watching a hummingbird at the feeder in our garden. The blur of its emerald wings was mesmerizing.

Got you a present, he texted.
Thank you! Exciting!!! What is it?
Wait and see . . . Back by 7 xx

It was a small Japanese ceramic vase. It had a beautiful deep crackle glaze. I'd been longing to add it to my modest collection for ages. The vase survived the impact that took Chris's life. As he drove home, a delivery van ran a red light and rammed into the driver's side of Chris's car as he pulled out of a junction. The van driver was drunk. A police officer handed me the vase the next day along with Chris's messenger bag. "It was in the passenger-seat footwell," she said. The vase was gift wrapped.

I scroll back through the texts Chris and I exchanged multiple times every day when he was alive. It's a compulsion I can't resist, even though I shouldn't do it because it always hurts. If anybody else looked at the texts they might seem banal, but I can vividly reconstruct moments from our shared life when I read them. They allow me to imagine Chris is still alive. When I've finished looking through them I do what I always do. I send a message to his number saying "I love you so much," and within seconds I get one back: "Unable to deliver."

Sometimes my grief for him is so intense it feels as if I'm bleeding out. When that happens, I am seized by the fear that if I'm this broken, how can I possibly be the mother that Ruby needs me to be? And that thought leads inevitably to the next: If I can't, does that leave room for my mother to try to take my place? The idea of it is unbearable.

"WOULD YOU like me to hang your things up for you?"

Anthea, my mother's housekeeper, has regularly asked me the same question since Ruby and I arrived at Lake Hall a few weeks ago. She is troubled by the fact that I'm still living out of a suitcase. My clothes are a messy heap, half in the case and half all over the rug. She must think I'm a lazy slob. Normal me would have unpacked as soon as we arrived, but inertia has crept into my bones since Chris died.

It's grief, a friend advised me over email when I described how I felt. Don't be too hard on yourself. Let yourself feel it.

She was right, but I know it's denial, too. Unpacking would

mean accepting the reality of my situation and admitting to myself that Ruby and I are stuck living here at Lake Hall for the foreseeable future, and I can't bear to do that. Not now. Not yet.

"No, thank you," I tell Anthea. "I'll do it later."

"Should I do Ruby's?"

"No. I'll do hers, too."

Anthea has a terrific poker face, but even so, I sense her disapproval and her pity. Both wound my pride, because as soon as I could leave home, I did. I walked away from Lake Hall and my parents and I distanced myself from them as much as I could. I changed my name from Jocelyn to Jo and refused to accept a penny from them. It's why it hurts so much to be here now, dependent on my mother's charity.

I go downstairs to get out of Anthea's way. I had forgotten what it's like to have a housekeeper, and though I accepted it as a child, I've found it deeply uncomfortable since we arrived here.

In the kitchen, there's an empty sherry bottle on the side, waiting to go out to the recycling bin. Mother and I got tipsy on sherry last night. I don't even like the stuff, but I was making an effort because the local priest dropped around unexpectedly to offer snippets of commonplace advice about grief as if they were rare pearls of wisdom.

Mother and I are both widows. My father died of a heart attack two months before my husband died. It came out of the blue. He was only sixty-nine. I didn't return home for his funeral. I considered it, but I hadn't seen him for over a decade. His death blindsided me. I loved him very much. I didn't come back to bury him because I couldn't face being an extra at his funeral while Mother played leading lady and owned all the pain.

While the priest droned on last night, Mother refilled our glasses too often and I drank to alleviate the boredom. By the time he left, the sweet heat of the evening had been sent on its way by a breeze coming up off the lake and gusting through the open windows, and the sherry had loosened my tongue.

"Do you ever feel awkward about employing people in the house?" I asked Mother. My father's Labrador, Boudicca, shifted on the rug and stared at me. It's what she does if she hears a harsh tone of voice.

"The Holts have always employed people from the village. It's expected. Honestly, darling, you sound like a bloody communist."

Her gibe needled me, as she intended. What I took away from the conversation was that the class bubble Mother lives in remains, in her mind at least, intact. I felt incredulous and disappointed. Most of all I felt an intense claustrophobia.

I'll never be able to change this place, but if we stay here long enough, I'm afraid it will change my daughter and me.

ALMOST NOTHING inside Lake Hall has altered since I left. Accompanying Ruby while she explores drives this home. She has almost free rein, though I warn her off taking the steep back stairs up to the attic where the nursery rooms are. She races around the place, otherwise. Rare Chinese vases and elegant Hepplewhite chairs quiver in her slipstream.

I feel strangely spooked when I watch her run her fingers along the pitted stone walls or the yards of dark wood paneling or when she examines the antique objects strewn through the house like badly tended museum exhibits. Lake Hall feels stagnant and obsolete to me now, especially in the absence of my father. The walls seem to harbor a cold, uncomfortable energy, pervasive as damp. Sometimes the hairs on the back of my neck stand up unaccountably. I don't want Ruby to acquaint herself with every detail of this place, because this is not the backdrop I want her to grow up against.

The only things in the house that feel like old friends to me are the artworks. I didn't pay much attention to the Holt Collection of paintings and drawings when I was a child, but at university I took an option to study art history and was immediately hooked. As my interest grew, I began to understand and appreciate exactly what my family were custodians of. I studied hard in the hope of becoming a connoisseur like generations of Holts before me. It's about the only family trait I inherited that I'm not ashamed of.

As I wander around Lake Hall with Ruby happier memories sometimes pierce my darker feelings. They feel like respite. I remember when my nanny, Hannah, was my world and Lake Hall felt like our private, perfect domain. That sweet nostalgia never lasts long. The memories inevitably sour when I recall it was my behavior that drove Hannah away and how in the aftermath my relationship with my mother took a downward spiral we haven't recovered from.

Even before Hannah left I avoided contact with Mother. When my parents were at Lake Hall—usually only at weekends—everything here felt different. I longed to spend time with my father but was so desperate to avoid Mother that I steered clear of the formal rooms they occupied, my heart thumping as I crept through corridors and up and down stairs from nursery to kitchen to garden: safe places where Hannah and I would be undisturbed.

Ruby knows very little of what my life was like then, and I hope she never has to.

AS THE honeymoon period of Ruby's love affair with England comes to an end, and the reality of Chris's death bites more with each day he's absent, Ruby withdraws into herself and begins to spend more time online.

I'm struggling, too. I am afraid I'm losing Chris all over again as my memories of him threaten to fade with each passing day. And it's not just memories of what we did; I fear I'm losing his face.

It seems impossible. Chris and I met in London and fell in love when I was just twenty-two years old and he was twenty-four. It was a coup de coeur. We moved in together almost immediately. Joining my life to his was the best decision I ever made. We became soulmates and best friends, we were inseparable, but there are times now when I panic because I can't precisely picture his features and I scroll frantically through my phone to revisit photographs so I can study them.

My memory isn't perfect, I know that, but some things should be sacrosanct. I want it to provide me with a perfect image of Chris forever; I shouldn't have to rely on my imagination to color in the forgotten bits. I get my favorite photograph of Chris, Ruby, and me printed and framed: one copy for her room and one for mine. It helps a bit.

I try to distract Ruby from her absorption in her iPad. One night, when she won't even answer basic questions, I ask her to put it down and look at me.

"What's wrong, honey?"

"I just want to play."

"You don't want to talk?"

A tight shake of her head.

"Are you sad?"

"A bit, but this helps."

"Are you sure?"

She nods, and I haven't got the heart to take the iPad from her.

I can't deny that her closed expression is new, though, and I feel terrified she's starting to drift away from me.

After our talk, I message her with a penguin emoji, even though I'm sitting right beside her. It's a joke she and I and Chris shared: you get a "well done" penguin if you've done a good job. Ruby's iPad pings when the penguin appears on her screen, and she smiles. A few seconds later, she sends one back to me.

She pushes me away at times, but at others she still needs me fiercely. We have slept together almost every night since Chris died. Most nights she starts off in her own bed but later creeps in with me. I always wake before her in the morning and the sight of her beautiful, innocent little face on the pillow beside mine cracks my heart. I love her so much. I can't bear to see her hurting. I can't bear to see her here.

I monitor her use of the iPad and her phone and decide that the elaborate online worlds she spends time in are not harmful. The gaming communities she joins are a form of company, at least, and contact with kids her own age. Mother notices the increased screen time and snipes at both of us about it. She believes it will "rot Ruby's mind."

When Ruby and I ignore her, Mother tries more actively to distract Ruby. She offers to show her how to prune the roses in the walled garden. Ruby says no in a rude tone of voice. Her manners have slipped as her boredom increases. I don't correct her. Let my mother have a taste of her own medicine.

Mother offers to teach Ruby how to play bridge. They start well, but Ruby loses interest quickly. "She's too young," I say and Mother says, "Well, at least I'm trying."

At lunch, Ruby asks, "Can we sail a boat on the lake, Granny?"

"That's a good idea!" I'm thrilled there's something she's enthusiastic about.

"No. I'm afraid not," Mother says. "The boats aren't fit for purpose any longer. They're rotten and very dangerous. It would be like going out in a sieve. Do you remember the charming rhyme about that, Jocelyn?"

"They went to sea in a Sieve, they did / In a Sieve they went to sea . . . ," I dutifully quote. The lines come back to me instantly. I can clearly remember every inflection of my nanny's voice as she read them aloud to me.

"You used to love that poem when you were a little girl," Mother says.

"How would you know? You never read a book to me in my life!" I didn't mean to raise my voice. Ruby stares at me and Mother blinks before she says, "No. I suppose I didn't. Somebody must have told me."

"Can't we fix the boats?" Ruby asks.

"I would love to if we can. Can we ask Geoff to open the boathouse?" It's been locked for as long as I can remember, certainly since I went to boarding school.

"Don't bother. Nobody is to go out on the lake," Mother says, "and that's a rule."

Disappointment drags Ruby's expression down. Her chair scrapes sharply across the floor and she runs from the room.

"Don't run up the stairs!" I shout. I look at my food, but I've lost my appetite. I'm furious with Mother for putting a damper on the idea. Mother, with pursed lips, hacks a slice of cheddar cheese from a huge hunk, hardened at the edges. I wonder if I could afford to fix a boat or buy a secondhand one.

My financial situation is dire since Chris died, because every penny we had was invested in his business and it will take time to get the money released. Chris and I rented the sweet little home we had in California and we had no life insurance. We also had an overdrawn current account. That wasn't the end of my troubles, because my immigration status wasn't secure either and I was prohibited from staying on in the United States after Chris's death.

When Chris died, Ruby and I were not just shorn of him but of every single other thing she had ever known.

I put my cutlery down. "I'm going to see if she's all right," I say.

"It's not good for children to have too much attention."

My fingers clench into fists. "Don't ever tell me how to raise my daughter."

"In my home, I'll do and say whatever I want."

I FELT it was too late in the year to enroll Ruby at school when we first arrived back in the UK. There were only a couple of weeks of term left and I wanted to give her time and space both to grieve and to settle in. To make sure she doesn't get too much of a shock when school starts in September, I contact them and arrange for her to spend a day there in the last week of their summer term. I hope she'll meet somebody she likes, someone we can arrange playdates with during the summer holidays. Ruby needs friends and she needs fun. Most important, she needs somebody her own age to dilute Mother and me.

The teacher is waiting for Ruby at the school gate. A warm breeze whips her hair around her face and makes her voluminous shirt balloon. I'm horrified to hear Mother's voice in my head: *shapeless*. I think she looks lovely.

"You must be Ruby? I'm Mrs. Armstrong. Welcome to Downsley Primary School. We're all so excited you'll be joining us next year."

Ruby manages a half smile. I'm proud of her because I know how nervous she is.

When I get back to Lake Hall, it feels strange to be without her, as if I've lost a piece of myself, or my armor. She has been a Velcro child since Chris's death, and I feel as if I haven't had time to experience a single thing alone or process any of my own emotions.

I know precisely what I want to do, even though the thought of it fills me with nerves. I can't help it, I feel drawn to do it in the same unhealthy way you can't look away from a car accident. Some urges are impossible to resist.

I climb the main staircase to the first floor, where its threadbare crimson carpet bleeds onto a wide landing overlooked by a stained-glass window.

To get to the attic floor you take the back stairs, the original servants' stairs, which go all the way from the bottom to the top of the house. I access them at the far end of the landing. The narrow treads are stone, worn shiny from centuries of footfall. The hand rope is saggy and not securely fixed onto the wall. I climb carefully, holding on gingerly. I have never liked these stairs.

At the top, I flick a light switch, and three out of the four ceiling bulbs illuminate weakly along the length of the low-ceilinged corridor. The light shades are stained and crooked. The doors to the nursery suite, where Hannah and I had adjoining bedrooms, are halfway down the corridor. The door handle to my old room has a smooth familiarity as I turn it. My old bed and armoire are covered in dust covers, but the dancing giraffes on the wallpaper are brighter than you might expect after all these years and somehow they don't look quite as I remember them.

I moved out of this room after Hannah left. I didn't want to be up here alone without her, and anyway, Mother insisted I take a room downstairs. That was one of the rare times we have been in agreement.

I open the door to Hannah's bedroom. In here, the furniture

is also covered in dust sheets and moth-eaten blankets, but the curtains are closed. Floorboards creak as I cross the room and dust snowflakes tumble from the rail when I move the curtains, making me cough. As light fills the room, it's clear there's nothing to see apart from the same horrible emptiness I discovered on the morning Hannah left.

I feel bereft all over again. I shouldn't have come up here. It brings back too much, none of it happy. I was hoping to reconnect with the gorgeous warm feelings I had for Hannah when I was a child and the positive memories: all the wonderful times we did things together, the way she made me feel safe and loved, the absolute devotion I had for her. Instead, I feel nothing but the same coruscating hurt and confusion that assaulted me on the morning I first found her room empty.

I want to get out of here. I move to reclose the curtains so I can get out of here, but as I do, I notice something: this room has a view into my father's study. I never knew that before. I guess I wasn't tall enough to notice when I was little, because the sill is high and I wouldn't have been able to see out at the right angle. I wonder if he knew he could be observed in his sanctum. The thought makes me feel uneasy.

I ARRIVE late to collect Ruby from school because I misread the email her teacher sent. By the time I get there, I've missed the opportunity to meet any of the other parents. Ruby is waiting with her teacher on a bench on the playground, head down and kicking. The soles of her shoes scuff the tarmac. My heart sinks, but I try to sound bright: "How did it go?"

"Ruby was brilliant," the teacher says. "Hasn't she got beautiful handwriting?"

In the car, Ruby says, "They said I sounded stupid because of my accent and they said I was stuck-up because I live in Lake Hall. They hate me!"

I could murder the kids who spoke to her so cruelly. I should reassure her, tell her everything will be okay. Instead, shamefully, I begin to weep uncontrollably, and Ruby looks scared. She tells me it wasn't that bad really because the teacher was nice and they have a class hamster and a cool system for looking after him where people take turns to bring him home. She says she thinks it'll be okay. I pull myself together and apologize and tell her how brilliant she is and how everything will be fine and feel like the worst mother in the world.

"Please don't tell Granny you didn't like school," I say as we park at Lake Hall.

I'm afraid my mother will try to take over Ruby's schooling and get her into the local private school I went to and hated. It prides itself on preparing children to go to boarding school. I'm afraid Mother will try to shape Ruby the way she tried to shape me. She will train my daughter for a life of snobbery and privilege; this will involve crushing Ruby's spirit until she learns to repress every single raw and healthy emotion she ever feels.

I will not let that happen.

IN AN effort to help her with friendships, I dip into my dwindling pot of cash and enroll Ruby in a tennis course. While she's out, I seek the help of Mother's gardener, Geoff.

"What does your mother say?" he asks when I tell him I want to get into the boathouse. He's tending the rows of geraniums in the greenhouse. Their smell has a velvety intensity.

"She wants Ruby to be happy. I think this would be a lovely surprise."

"Haven't seen Ruby smile for a while."

"Exactly." His expression tells me he knows I'm being economical with the truth about Mother, but he agrees to help.

"Don't fancy our chances of finding the key to the padlock, though," he says.

He's right. He has to bust open the lock in the end. We do it while Mother is out at a bridge game.

Inside, the boathouse is dark and matted with cobwebs, though the decking floor feels sound. We find a small wooden rowboat, but it's rotten and half submerged. The name on its prow is crudely hand painted: *Virginia*. I have a sudden memory of my father painting it on a hot afternoon.

"She's had her day," Geoff says.

"Can we do anything?"

"No. But if you want to get Ruby out on the water, I can lend you my brother's kayak. It's been in my garage for years."

I feel my excitement rise. Chris, Ruby, and I went on a kayak trip in California. It was one of the best holidays we had.

Geoff and I work together, behind Mother's back, for the next couple of days. Once everything is ready, I can't stop smiling as I collect Ruby from tennis. When we arrive home, I beckon her to follow me around the side of the house.

"What are we doing?" she asks.

"It's a surprise."

I take her hand and lead her to the boathouse.

"Help me," I say and she puts her whole weight into pulling open the doors. She's tense with excitement.

Geoff and I have removed the broken rowboat and replaced it with the inflated kayak.

Paddles, two life jackets, and all the other kit we'll need lie on the decking beside it.

"Wow!" Ruby says. "Can we do it now?"

We get kitted up and cast off. The surface of the lake is glassy and we float smoothly out onto it.

"I want to go to the island!" Ruby shouts from the front. She has a lovely paddling technique her dad taught her and I'm happy to sit behind her and let her take the lead. It feels, for the first time since Chris died, as if we're doing something together that we can truly enjoy without thoughts of what we've lost or where we might end up. Our paddles slice the water easily and we move swiftly toward the island, which is small and circular and crowned by a lone tree.

"Can I go on it?" Ruby shouts as the nose of the kayak nudges the island's shore. She starts to clamber out and I hold the kayak steady against the bank. Tree roots delve into the water, tangled with flotsam and other debris. "Careful," I say, but she's too hasty and her foot slips. I lunge for her and catch her by the back of her life belt before she loses her balance. The kayak rocks but doesn't tip.

"I'm stuck," she says. Her foot is tangled in the roots just below the surface of the water.

"Hold on!" I say. "Hold the edge!"

She clings on as I climb out of the kayak and onto the spongy edge of the island shore.

"Pull your foot up gently," I say.

She tries, but it's well and truly stuck. Her chin wobbles.

"It's okay. Don't panic. Just stay really still."

The lake isn't clear enough for me to be able to see Ruby's foot, so I sink my hand into the water and run it down her leg until I can feel where her foot is stuck. The tree roots are tangled like spaghetti down there, but I manage to dislodge some sticks and an object that's wedged above her ankle.

"There!" I say as she pulls her leg up and I help her onto shore. "Well done. You were so brave!"

She gives me as tight a hug as you can when you're both wearing life jackets. We sit side by side on the shore of the island, facing Lake Hall.

"I don't think this view has changed for hundreds of years," I say.

"What's that?" Ruby gets up to examine an object being gently tossed against the shore by the lapping water. It's about the right size and shape to be the thing I dislodged to free her foot. She picks it up, and as she turns to show it to me, I freeze.

"It's really weird," she says. She can't see what it is yet, but I can.

"Ruby, put it down! Now!"

She catches the fear in my tone and drops the object as if it were scalding her hands.

It lands at her feet with a moist thump. It is a human skull. The deep orifices where its eyes and nose would have been gaze blackly at me. Even though it's dirty I can clearly see fracture lines tracking across the dome of the skull like ancient pathways through a landscape.

Ruby peers at it.

"It's a skull!" she says. "Oh my gosh. That's so cool. I wish I had my phone so I could take a picture!"

She crouches down to take a closer look at it. "It's broken on the top," she says.

"Don't touch it!"

"I'm not! But can you see it's broken?"

That's not just broken, I think. *Whoever this is, they almost certainly didn't die naturally.* I feel a cold, visceral fear. I want to get as far away from it as possible.

"Do you think it's, like, from history times?" Ruby asks.

"I don't know, Rubes. Most likely it is. Step away from it."

"Why?"

"Because we have to report this to the police."

"No . . . way."

I nod. "It's human remains. That's what you have to do. Come on. Step away. Let's go now. We'll leave it where it is."

"Can't we take it with us?"

"No!" I don't mean to snap at her, but I can hardly bear to look at it. The fractured skull is a horrific thing, tangible proof of a dark current running from past to present.

Ruby sits behind me in the kayak on the way back to shore and forgets to paddle because she keeps looking back over her shoulder, even when we're too far away to make out the shape of the skull any longer. I chivy her to pick up the pace. I want distance between us and the island. When we reach the shore, she jumps out, discards her life belt, and sets off across the lawn.

"Hey!" I call after her. "Where are you going?"

She stops and turns. Excitement lights up her face. "To tell Granny what we found!"

I shudder involuntarily as I watch her go.

1976

HELP REQUIRED.

Four hours per day for busy family household.
Cleaning, ironing, other household tasks as required.

THE ADVERT ITSELF DIDN'T STAND out much from the others pinned around it on the bulletin board in the newsagent. The difference was that Linda saw the person who pinned it there. He was a man she guessed to be in his thirties. Quite old, she thought, but not too old. He wore a beautiful suit and quality shiny shoes, and his thick hair was neatly cut around his ears, showing off a lovely profile.

Linda lurked behind the humming refrigerator until he was gone, pretending to consider the latest issue of Jackie, even though she couldn't afford to buy it. She watched him take the notice out of his inside jacket pocket—a thrillingly intimate place—and unfold it. He took his time to find a good spot for it before placing a pin carefully in each of the four corners, making sure it wasn't crooked. She fell a little bit in love with him.

She watched as he picked up his briefcase, chose and paid for a packet of cigarettes (Benson & Hedges, no tips—she considered them a gentleman's choice), and left the shop with the bells on the door jangling in his wake. Then she approached the bulletin board and read the advert. The job was just the sort of thing she was looking for. When the shopkeeper wasn't looking, she unpinned the advert and slipped it into her pocket.

LINDA STARTED *work a week later. An advance on her wages enabled her to rent a tiny bed-sitting room in a redbrick terrace in Chapeltown in Leeds. She shared with another girl to save money. Her roommate was a runaway, too. Her name was Jean.*

Jean worked in Woolworths and brought home stolen makeup and magazines. They got on well from the first moment.

Linda could walk to work from her lodging, passing from her own neighborhood, where the only greenery was dandelions growing through cracks in the pavement, into better areas, where cultivated hedges and shrubs marked property boundaries, and on farther still, into his neighborhood, where fine specimen trees, heavy with scented blossom or bright green buds, bordered wide avenues.

His house was a handsome detached property, tall and wide. It suited him, she thought. It was the sort of place he should live. A Silver Cross pram nestled in a corner of the porch and a black Ford Granada was parked under a carport. She imagined what it would be like to push the pram or to ride in the car.

Whenever she arrived at work, she thought of where she'd come from originally: the tiny cottage on the moors, where her filthy siblings ran riot underfoot; the bruises on her late mother's face after her dad spent his paycheck at the pub; the way her father loved his racing pigeons more than any of them; the manner in which he took the birds out of their cages as if they were precious objects, cradling them and stroking their heads with a filthy finger, making kissing noises that seemed to mesmerize them.

Linda wrung the neck of his favorite bird before she left home, slung its body onto the floor of the shed. "Let's see how much he likes you now," she said to the limp carcass.

THE WORK *was easy enough if you didn't mind getting your hands dirty, and Linda didn't. It was all she'd ever known apart from desultory,* disengaged hours she'd spent in overcrowded classrooms. In the man's house, she scrubbed bathrooms and floors and dusted and polished surfaces and banisters and ornaments just the way his wife told her to. She was a clever girl and a quick learner. The wife increased her hours some days.

He was hardly ever there, which was disappointing. She studied photographs of him that were around the house and fingered the objects on his desk, but the next time she saw him in person was the summer holidays. He wore shorts and a T-shirt. His hair looked sunbleached. He backed the car out of the carport onto the drive and washed it while Test match commentary played on the radio. She decided to learn the rules of cricket.

Linda was never jealous of his wife because she thought the woman was spineless: too old for him and incompetent. The wife bought clothes that never looked right on her; she tried to make a Black Forest gâteau one day and wept when the tiers slid, one off the next, into a creamy, red-streaked mess. The wife didn't care much for their children, either—twins, one of each—but he seemed devoted to them on the rare occasions he was home.

One afternoon that summer he lay on the carpet and played with them, tickling them, making watery popping noises like a cartoon fish, laughing when they laughed. They curled their bodies toward him, their little fingers clutched at their little toes, and he blew raspberries on their tummies until the babies' nanny, whom everybody called Nanny Hughes, cleared her throat and said it was naptime. Linda tried not to stare, but the father with the babies was such a lovely sight. It thrilled her. She told Jean everything about him.

"Isn't he a bit old for you?" Jean said. She and Jean had begun to share clothes and secrets and to go out together on Saturday night. Jean was dating the boy who worked in the ticket booth at the cinema. He couldn't smoke without coughing.

"He's just right," Linda replied.

"I'd take his money," Jean said. "But you can have his horrible old body." Their landlady said Jean had a "dirty laugh" and she needed to "learn to keep it down."

When she was at work, Linda watched Nanny Hughes closely and felt twitchy with envy. Nanny Hughes wore a uniform, which sometimes included a hat and white gloves, because she was a Norland nanny. She had trained for three years at the prestigious Norland College and graduated the previous summer. Nanny Hughes enjoyed telling anybody who would listen that one of the girls who recently left the college was working for a member of the royal family and that she herself had hopes of a similar position once she'd gained some experience. Nanny Hughes never raised her voice and had won a prize for her excellent posture.

Linda watched and listened very carefully, taking note of everything, but especially the way Nanny Hughes spoke to the babies, the way the babies gazed adoringly back and clung to their nanny when the wife held out her arms to take them. When Linda emptied her buckets of filthy water out in the drain at the side of the house, she sometimes lingered to watch Nanny Hughes pushing the big pram up the driveway, with shoulders back and confident steps. Linda was interested in power, and she recognized that in this family, Nanny Hughes had it in spades, because the man loved the children and the children loved their nanny. When Nanny Hughes was out of the room, Linda mimicked her. Soon the babies grew to love Linda, too.

VIRGINIA

THE ADVANTAGE OF SITTING IN the front-row pew in church is that nobody can see you cry.

But what about the vicar? you might ask. Surely he surveys his flock as he preaches and, like his predecessors for centuries, pays particular attention to the reception his words are getting in the Holt family pew? Chantry roofs don't repair themselves, after all.

You're right, of course. The vicar does peer at me frequently, but I happen to know our current representative of God is extremely shortsighted, too cowardly to try contact lenses and too vain to wear spectacles. I could replace my nose with a carrot and he would still press my hands between his and tell me I was the very picture of elegance. A tear shed during his sermon will certainly go unnoticed by him; I shall not draw anybody else's attention to it by wiping it away.

I should be at a bridge game, but I wasn't in the mood and came here instead. Once a month there is an early evening communion service, so tonight I'm seeking refuge, since I need a reprieve from being in my own home. I am sitting alone, as I have done in church since Alexander died. The empty seat beside me belonged to my late husband and all of the Lord Holts who came before him. My Alexander didn't attend church regularly because it bored him—he preferred to walk the dogs—but it is his seat nevertheless and it would be presumptuous of anybody from the village to take it.

The tear tracking down my cheek feels as viscous as a snail

trail. My shoulders, back, and buttocks ache, but I force myself to maintain good posture. A widow in my position must be careful if she is to retain the authority she previously held as half of a couple. My hands are gloved and folded neatly on my lap. I tune out on the sermon and stare at my interlinked fingers. My gloves are made from the softest, scarlet calf leather. They were a gift from Alexander and are a devil to put on over my arthritic joints, but are too beautiful not to wear. I wish I could slip off one of my gloves and reach for his hand, as I used to. I imagine feeling once again the warmth, contours, and textures of his palm, his fingers.

Widowhood is lonely, and the responsibility of being the sole representative of this family is a heavy one. My daughter, Jocelyn, thinks I feel nothing, but she is wrong.

Behind me the pews are sparsely filled, though not as sparsely as you might suppose. Tradition runs strong through the veins of many people who live in this area, and attendance at this small church built hundreds of years ago by our family is a part of that. The Holts and other local families have lived cheek by jowl for centuries and know each other well. We have been mutually dependent at times, in the old circle of employer and employee. As far as attitudes toward us go, there are both sycophants and haters amongst this congregation and the residents of our local village.

To some, the Holt family is an essential part of the landscape here, as unchanging and important as the ancient cluster of trees in the dip on Downsley Hill. Some consider that to lose the Holt family from these parts would be to lose some essence of this landscape—this land, even. To others, we are entitled, exploitative, and undeserving of our status and our financial fortune. We deserve to be taken down a peg or two or three. The worst of these people used to line the lanes and hold placards if we hosted a fox hunt. "Fascists," they chanted, or "Hunt scum!" or worse.

"Let us pray," the vicar says. Behind me, they lower themselves onto their knees; I hear the muted groans that elderly joints can tease from the mouths of even the most faithful. I bow my head. If I go down, I will not come up again without help. My kneeler hangs uselessly in front of me. A woman from the village has made a tapestry cover for it: the Holt coat of arms. It's rather botched, but of course I appreciate the effort.

I close my eyes, but not before another tear has escaped. If anybody behind me was to notice, they would probably assume I'm grieving for Alexander, but they would be wrong, because it's my daughter who has brought me to tears.

When I agreed to Jocelyn and Ruby's moving in, I had a fantasy that Jocelyn and I might, for the first time in our lives, get along with each other, or at the very least offer each other some comfort and support in widowhood. It turned out to be nothing more than wishful thinking. Jocelyn has missed no opportunity to make it crystal clear that she is back at Lake Hall only because she has nowhere else to go. Any port in a storm, as they say. It fills me with sadness, though I know better than to let her see that. To do so would risk her contempt.

The final prayers seem to go on forever, as the vicar mentions every unfortunate you can imagine and describes their physical ailments in excruciating detail. *What about the invisible afflictions?* I think. *How many people are suffering in this church at this very moment?* I know I am.

To have a child whom you love but who does not love you back is a particularly intense and unrelenting source of pain. Jocelyn has never loved me, not even when she was a very little girl, not even when she was a baby. In that situation, it can only be the fault of the parent, but I have never worked out what I did wrong.

But—and this is an important *but*—there is a silver lining, and her name is Ruby.

Ruby is a true gem, an absolutely darling girl, full of whimsy and confidence and potential. She sparkles. When Jocelyn first bothered to let us know she'd had a daughter, I hated Ruby's name. I thought it sounded very common, but I've changed my mind since meeting her. Now I believe it's just the right name for a girl like her. I have so many hopes and dreams for Ruby, if only Jocelyn will allow me to get close to her.

I join in with the "Amen" at the end of the Lord's Prayer and open my eyes. I tilt my head back, stretching out my sluggish muscles. I think my tears have dried well enough to permit me to face even the most sharp-eyed congregation members.

Boudicca, Alexander's Labrador, is asleep on a blanket on the back seat of the Land Rover. Alexander brought her to church with him on the rare occasions he came, so I keep up the tradition. Like me, the dog misses him.

The car windows are open, and I keep them that way as I drive home. I enjoy being buffeted by the warm evening air. The Land Rover gears crunch as usual when I make the turn between the gateposts and glimpse Lake Hall at the end of our drive. The acid-green leaves on the beech trees form a lush canopy overhead and are attractively sun-dappled, even this late in the evening. The sight of them lifts the heart in summer, though in winter I feel the branches resemble the bare bones of a leviathan.

Boudicca stirs on the back seat as I try to negotiate the potholes on the drive without jarring us both too severely. I expect she and I have the same thing in mind: we are wondering what Anthea has left for supper.

What neither of us expects to see is a police car in the drive.

DETECTIVE ANDY WILTON

ANDY WATCHES HIS MEN LAUNCH their boat into the lake.

"Your gardener said it's very deep out there," he says.

The daughter of the house stands beside him. She introduced herself as Jo, to be fair, but he couldn't help smirking because he'd read her full name on his colleague's notes: Jocelyn Camilla Frances Holt. She's the only child of Lord and Lady Holt.

"Apparently," she says. "I wasn't allowed to swim in the lake when I was a child, so I don't know for sure."

Her accent is Queen's English, but mellowed a touch around the edges. Transatlantic, he realizes when she explains she's been living in the United States for over a decade.

Posh people make him feel self-conscious about his own accent. He grew up twenty miles and a world away in Swindon Railway Village, where three generations of his family had employment at the engineering works. He is working class through and through and proud of it, and his hackles are quick to rise if he thinks anybody is looking down on him because of it.

"Holy shit," he said when Lake Hall first came into view that day, "it's got more chimneys than the street I grew up on."

"Don't exaggerate," Maxine said. "It's not Downton Abbey."

On first impression, Lake Hall was more medieval manor house than Buckingham Palace. Maxine was right, it wasn't Downton Abbey, but it was mighty impressive.

Jo has her arms wrapped around herself. She's thinner than looks healthy.

"Why weren't you allowed to swim?" Andy asks.

"My mother insisted it was unsafe. I remember being taken out in a rowboat once or twice when I was a child, but that's all. Nobody went out on the lake when I was a teenager so far as I can remember. The boathouse was kept locked. You'll have to talk to my mother or the housekeeper or the gardener if you want to know what's been going on more recently."

They have staff, he thinks. *Of course.* He glances at Maxine and she rolls her eyes.

Jo is shivering even though the air is warm and the sun just high enough still to glint off Lake Hall's windows. "It's got to be an old skull, though, right?" she asks, though she must know he can't answer that yet.

"Who's that?" he asks. An old woman is making her way across the lawn toward them, walking briskly. She reminds him of his old headmistress striding into the playground to break up a fight.

"My mother," Jo says. "Good luck."

Lady Holt starts to interrogate him before he's had a chance to introduce himself. "What the hell is going on? Why are there men out on the lake? Who gave you authorization?"

He's not impressed with her attitude. He's not going to be barked at by her. He stares her down and offers her his hand in lieu of a reply. She glances at it before shaking and does so using only limp fingertips.

"Detective Constable Andy Wilton," he says, "and this is my colleague Detective Constable Maxine Flint." Maxine offers her hand, too, but Lady Holt ignores it.

"Your daughter made a discovery." He's interested that Jo has backed off a bit. He'd expect her to be gagging to share the news.

"What discovery?" Lady Holt's voice falters momentarily as she asks the question. It interests him.

"She found a human skull out by the island."

She blinks rapidly and covers her mouth with her hand. The stones in her rings are rocks. "Out there?" she asks.

"On the edge of the island."

"I see. Well, carry on, then. Jocelyn will tell you where to find me if you need me."

She pulls herself upright, as if trying to look composed, but he doesn't think that's how she's feeling. Not at all. She walks back to the house without saying a word to her daughter.

"Trouble in paradise?" Maxine mutters so the daughter can't hear.

"I'd say so," he says. He'd be lying if he said the thought of shaking things up here at the big house didn't give him a bit of a kick.

JO

IT'S ALMOST DARK BY THE time the police divers drag their inflatable off the lake and go home for the night. As I wave them off, bats are emerging one by one from their roost above the stables and disappearing into the solid darkness of the oak canopy.

The divers retrieved the skull. It looked yellowed, grotesque, and somehow ancient through the silt-smeared evidence bag. They recovered other bones, too, and plan to continue their search in daylight tomorrow.

The surface of the lake looks tranquil, reflecting the dying light, the bulrushes silhouetted against it. You would never know anything had happened here this afternoon, but I have a churning stomach and I feel a strange, creeping sense of inevitability. A hideous idea arrives out of the blue:

What if this skull belongs to my nanny, Hannah?

The thought makes my heart feel as if it is caving in a little. It destabilizes me, as if the world around me has tilted a few degrees.

Earlier, when I stood vigil beside the lake with the detectives while the divers worked, I felt calm. Detective Andy Wilton doesn't do small talk. He has a leanish build and a five o'clock shadow and looks to be about my age. Before he introduced himself, I noticed him surveying the house and grounds. He made no effort to disguise his disdain.

Please don't judge me by what you see here, I was desperate to say. *This house doesn't represent me. I am not my mother.*

In clipped sentences, he told me the bones would be sent for

forensic examination. I got the message loud and clear that whatever they find out, they will be sharing it with me only on a need-
to-know basis.

Now, I think, I want to know everything about the bones, but
at the same time I don't, because what if I'm right about it being
Hannah? And what if she was killed? That skull had a nasty fracture on it.

I turn to head back to the house. These are crazy runaway
thoughts, and I need to pull myself together and collect Ruby from
Anthea's house, where we sent her while the search was under way
because I didn't want her to witness it. She threw a fit when I insisted she go, because she was desperate to stay and share in the
drama of it all, but there was no way that was going to happen.

As I make my way across the lawn I see lights blazing in the
Blue Room, the kitchen, and my mother's sitting room. Mother is
in there. We haven't discussed the skull yet. As I watch, she moves
to the window and looks out, one hand pressed on the window-
pane, her palm pale against the glass. I raise my hand to wave, but
she doesn't react. I don't think she can see me in the gloaming. The
skin on the back of my neck prickles.

RUBY'S MORBID fascination with the skull grows swiftly until she is
brimming with it, and it doesn't help me keep my own thoughts
about it under control. She asks countless questions, some of which
I can't begin to answer: *Who died? How old were they? Why didn't
the skull dissolve? Did they drown or were they killed by a murderer, or did they die of old age? Do you think the person was nice
or horrible?*

Then, finally, a question I can answer: "Can Stan come and play?"
"Yes! Who is Stan?"

"I met him at tennis. I told you."

"Did you get his mum's number?"

She looks at me as if I'm a dinosaur. "Stan's got Snapchat. We message all the time."

I make contact with Stan's mum and arrange a playdate. I'm thrilled Ruby has a new friend. Stan gawps at the house after his mum drops him off.

"Do you want to explore?" Ruby says. "I'll show you where they found the skull!"

"Ruby!" I say. "I'm sure Stan's not interested." I forgot to warn her not to talk about the skull. I don't want to terrify her new friend and get off to a very bad start with the other mums.

"It's okay," Stan says. "I know about it already. I'm not scared or anything."

"He likes ghost stories," Ruby says.

Stan nods. "I know about decomposition. And did you know you dissect an eyeball in biology class in Year 7? My brother did it."

"Well, okay, then, I suppose. But you have to keep away from the lake if you go outside. Don't go past the edge of the lawn. And be careful in the house. Don't be running up and down the back stairs or going where you shouldn't, and don't get in Anthea's way."

I watch them go and smile at the conspiratorial angle of their heads and the way their shoulders rub together. This is why Ruby needs to spend time with kids her own age. She looks lighter than she has for ages.

ANTHEA IS polishing silverware at the kitchen table. The radio is on low, but she turns it down further.

"Please don't turn it down on my account."

"That's all right."

"Can I help?"

"No need, thank you."

While the kettle boils, I watch her buff a candlestick. She works methodically and painstakingly. You can tell she's done this many times before.

"Would you like a cup of tea?" I ask.

"No, thank you."

"How long have you been working here?" I know she probably doesn't want to be my friend, but it would be nice if we were at least on chatting terms. I could do with an ally.

"Fifteen years now. I took over the position when my mother retired."

"Marion is your mother?" I can't believe I didn't realize this before, and now that she says it, I can see a resemblance.

"She used to tell stories about you and that nanny of yours."

"Hannah and I spent a lot of time with Marion."

"So I heard."

"She taught me how to make flapjacks using her secret recipe. How is she?"

"Not too bad, not too good." I get the impression I shouldn't pry.

"Please send her my regards." She nods. I try my luck with a different subject. "Ruby told her new friend about the skull," I say. "I hope it doesn't freak him out."

She stops polishing. "People will be talking about it. You can't have the police calling in without people noticing. There'll be gossip spreading already, if I know anything about Downsley."

I wonder what she believes and how much she's shared.

There's a sharp rap on the back window. We weren't expecting more divers today or I wouldn't have let the children out, but a man half dressed in a wet suit is standing outside and has Ruby and Stan with him. "Caught them spying on us down by the lake.

Not the best place for youngsters," he says. Ruby and Stan don't look repentant in the slightest.

"We just wanted to see," she says.

MOTHER REFUSES to talk about the skull. She's been unusually quiet since the police came.

"There's absolutely nothing to discuss," she says when I raise the subject.

"Aren't you at all curious about it?"

She clips a rose stem and places the bloom into a rose bowl. She considers it for a moment before selecting another.

"You are like a dog with a bone," she says. "Let it go."

"Mother! I saw the skull! It was fractured. That person didn't die a natural death. Why doesn't that mean anything to you?"

"I don't know what you want me to say! People have been living on this site for nearly a thousand years. You know that as well as I do. The skull probably belongs to some poor stable lad who fell off a horse hundreds of years ago and hit his head on a rock or some unfortunate who lost a drunken fight. We might never know who it is, so why is it obligatory that I emote about it?"

"But what if it is more recent?" She ignores me and titivates the flower arrangement. "Do you think it could be Hannah?" Her lips purse. "Did you ever hear from Hannah after she disappeared?" She gives a small shake of her head. "Do you think it could be her?"

"Of course it's not Hannah!"

"How do you know?"

She ignores me again, just as she always did whenever I tried to talk about Hannah. Within hours of Hannah's leaving, her name was completely taboo. The sense of powerlessness it makes me feel is horribly familiar. Mother clips another stem and takes her time inserting the final rose. They smell sickly sweet.

"There," she says once she's finished. She turns the rose bowl around to admire it from all angles. "Doesn't that look lovely?"

I hope they all die.

VIRGINIA

EVERYTHING FEELS FRACTURED. I WATCH from inside as the divers extract more bones from the silt and tangled roots and sticks. They wrap the remains as carefully as if they were fine pieces of porcelain and remove them from our grounds. It takes a few days. It feels as invasive as Jocelyn's endless questions about the skull.

The detective calls at the house on the last day. I don't invite him inside. The porch shelters him well enough from the rain.

"Yes?" I say.

"We're done for now."

"I see."

"I'll keep you updated as and when."

"This will be a very old skull, you know. Very old. So I don't know why you're bothering to string up that horrible yellow tape everywhere and make such a fuss about it."

"We have procedures to follow when human remains are discovered."

"Well, procedures can be very dull, don't you think?"

He runs his tongue over the front of his teeth while he's thinking, making his lips bulge. It's very unattractive.

"I would say that procedures are necessary, Mrs. Holt."

"Lady Holt."

"We'll be in touch."

"Thank you," I say.

I try not to let the dread I'm feeling show.

I MET Jocelyn's father in 1975. I was invited by my brother to join him and some friends on a ski trip. Alexander met us for lunch one day, though I didn't notice him until after we'd eaten and were putting on our skis. Somebody proposed a race to the base of the mountain and bets were placed.

"Join us?" Alexander asked. If he ever told this story in later years he claimed he already had an inkling of how good a skier I was, but I swear he was expecting me to bat my eyelashes and state a preference for clapping on the boys from the sidelines. I lined up with them instead. The sky was bluest blue and the snow-capped mountains seemed to float on the horizon.

Alexander and I were neck and neck near the bottom of the piste and a good fifty yards ahead of the others when a grand French madame appeared from nowhere and cut across us with stately momentum. I swerved and missed her, Alexander didn't. Snow, French curses, and her large fur hat tumbled through the air around them.

"Nobody has ever beaten me in a race before," he said afterward. "Especially a girl. Rematch?"

I brushed a bit of snow off his hat. "I'd rather have a drink."

He was the most beautiful man I'd ever seen.

"GRANNY," RUBY says.

"You're a sight for sore eyes, darling. What have you been doing?"

"Do you know any good ghost stories?"

"No, but I know a very good book which will frighten you just as much as a ghost story, if you like a good scare. It's called *The Night of the Hunter*."

"Can you show me?"

I find the volume on my shelves and give it to her. She takes a quick look at the book and her expression tells me she's impressed.

"Stan says I should come to his house for a bonfire and we should tell each other ghost stories."

"What a good idea, darling. My sister and I used to do the same."

She is just like me, I think, and the thought brings me such a warm feeling.

RUBY SEEKS me out wherever I am in the house or garden. Her questions are as relentless as Jocelyn's, but usually a great deal easier to answer.

"How old is your house, Granny?"

"There has been a house on this site since the eleventh century, and it could have been even earlier. Do you know how old that is? It's about a thousand years ago. That's when they carved our family motto over the door. Have you seen it?"

How Alexander would have loved to see the expression on her face. She is rapt. He cared so much for this place it would have made his heart sing. It's a tragedy that he never met her.

"A thousand years!" she says.

"The first house built here was smaller than the one we have nowadays. People added bits onto it as the years went by. Once, a fire destroyed some of the rooms and your great-great-great-great-granddaddy had to rebuild them."

"Anthea told me a king had a sleepover here once."

"That's what they say, though I'm not sure if it's true."

"I wonder which bedroom he stayed in."

"The best one, don't you think? For a king? And you know, darling, you said this was my house, but it isn't really. I'm just looking after it for the family. It'll be yours one day and you'll do the same."

"Will I?"

"I hope so."

"Then I'll get rid of the ghosts!"

My heart skips a beat. "What do you mean by that?"

"Stan says the person in the lake probably died from something bad, and they're going to haunt the house now they've floated up. They'll probably be a poltergeist because they're angry."

"That's silly talk." I hope she can't hear the wobble in my voice.

"If I see a poltergeist, I'm going to karate-chop them or . . ." She thinks for a moment. "Granny, do you know the vicar?"

"I do."

"Stan says vicars can do a ceremony to get rid of ghosts. We could ask him."

I burst out laughing at the thought of Reverend Whittard's face if I should ask him to exorcise a ghost, but Ruby frowns.

"It's serious, Granny." She takes my hand. She is the only person who touches me these days. She meets my eye with a very serious gaze. "Ghosts can harm you, especially poltergeists."

Something about the way she looks at me makes me ease my hand away. There's an echo of the way Jocelyn used to stare at me, studying me, after Hannah was gone. I couldn't stand it. I felt as if she was trying to see through me to the truth of things. If I had ever imagined things would be better between Jocelyn and me once Hannah was gone, I was proved very wrong. Jocelyn's ability to trust was amputated that night and the breach between us became irreversible.

"Can you be an absolute angel and go and ask Anthea if I could have a cup of coffee, please?" I say. I need urgently to be alone.

I sit down heavily once she's left the room and feel my energy drain from me.

Alexander was the only person I could confide in. Now I have no one.

If he had been sitting here with me now, I would say, "You know, there is only one person that skull could belong to."

1977

LINDA IS HAPPY. SHE LIKES *her job, and she and Jean are getting to know each other better and having a laugh. The only day Linda doesn't like being at work is Monday, because that's Nanny Hughes's day off. One Monday is especially bad. When Linda arrives, the baby girl is already fretting. Linda gets on with her work, but she can't help staring as the mother tries and fails to settle the baby. "I think she's getting a tooth," the mother says when she catches Linda looking. Linda thinks the mother's wrong. Neither of the babies behaves like this when they're teething. They can be grumpy and fractious, but this baby looks feverish and she's impossible to soothe. Linda daren't say anything, though. It's not her place to.*

The mother's frustration builds as the day wears on and the baby refuses her milk and won't settle. Linda plucks up her courage. "Would you like me to telephone Nanny Hughes?"

"No!" the mother says as she botches a nappy change. "I'm perfectly capable of looking after my own children!" The little boy is screaming in his crib. The nursery is chaotically messy in a way Nanny Hughes would never allow. "Haven't you got work to do?"

"Yes, Mrs. Burgess," Linda says. As she lowers her eyes, she notices a red mark on the girl's thigh. The mother follows her gaze. "It's just a heat rash. I'm going to settle her and take my own nap now, so please shut the door quietly when you leave." She places the girl in the crib beside her brother's. "Settle down, both of you," she says to the babies, as if they are schoolchildren. "Mummy needs her rest, too."

The babies cry for what seems like forever, but the mother doesn't respond. Linda considers phoning the husband or their doctor, but she doesn't know their numbers. She lifts the red phone receiver in the hallway and dials Nanny Hughes. She lets it ring and ring, but there's no answer. She goes back upstairs. She doesn't want to leave while the babies are distressed.

The boy has settled now, so she picks up the fretful girl and the baby's hot little head flops heavily onto Linda's shoulder. The baby settles quickly in Linda's arms, and it makes Linda feel good. She'd like to check the rash on the baby girl's leg, but she daren't, because her mother has put her in a sleep suit, and removing it might wake her. Linda puts the girl back in her crib and carefully unfastens just three snaps at the neck of the sleep suit and pulls the window open a little wider to help cool the baby down.

Linda shuts the door quietly behind her as instructed, and as she walks home, she feels uneasy about the baby girl, but she thinks she did all she could without risking losing her job.

Her dad grabs her by the scruff of the neck just as she turns her key in the door of her flat. He yanks her backward, then throws her inside. She sprawls across the floor and scrambles away from him, picking up a frying pan that had gone skittering across the floor when she did. She can smell the booze on him.

"How did you find me?"

"It weren't difficult." I bet it was, *she thinks. He must have really wanted to find her, because what has she ever been to him apart from a mouth to feed?*

"I need you to come home and look after the little 'uns. It's where you belong."

"I won't."

He punches her in the face and the pain is breathtaking. He raises his fist to do it again, but Mr. Pebworth from the bedsit next door drags him off and blocks him from coming back in. "I'll be back!" he shouts from the stairs. "I'll keep coming back until I get you."

"*Fuck off!*" *she tries to shout, but she chokes because her mouth has filled with blood, and when she tries to spit it out, a tooth falls onto the linoleum.*

LINDA GOES *into work the next day, anyway. The missing tooth isn't too noticeable if she doesn't smile. She has an excuse ready if anybody asks about the injuries to her face, just as her mother used to. Jean didn't ask too many questions and she cleaned the blood from Linda's face tenderly. "We'll get you right," she said. There was understanding in her eyes.*

When Linda arrives at work, she lets herself in as usual. She's forgotten all about the baby being poorly. She remembers as soon as she walks into the kitchen. He is sitting at the table wearing only pajama trousers. She doesn't know where to look. He doesn't notice her injuries. He looks at her with empty eyes and says, "Baby Hannah is dead."

He sobs so hard it's frightening.

LINDA CONTINUES *to turn up for work as usual in the days that follow because nobody tells her not to. Nanny Hughes turns up as well. "Somebody has to be there for Oliver," she says. Linda isn't sure if she's referring to the husband or the baby boy. They're both called Oliver. The babies were named after the husband and his sister who died.*

"They were touched with tragedy already," Nanny Hughes says, cradling the baby boy, eyes welling with tears. She shows Linda a photograph of the husband with his sister, who looks much younger than him. "To lose a daughter and a sister in such a short space of time," Nanny Hughes says. Linda watches the tears slide down her cheeks. She doesn't cry herself, but she misses the way things were.

Linda keeps the house nice, but everything feels different now. The mother shuts herself in her bedroom all day and the husband isn't what he used to be. He doesn't go to work. He sits at his desk and draws horrible dark things on his blotter. He spends hours in a lawn chair staring at the sprinkler. It's like working in a morgue.

LINDA'S DAD *returns. Once she spots him in her neighborhood and flattens herself against a doorway to avoid him. The second time he's outside her house when she gets back from work, hurling foul abuse up at her window. She ducks away and walks for hours. By the time she gets back he's gone, but she's terrified.*

What if he finds out where she works and turns up there? She could get dismissed without a reference. Or worse, what if he hurts somebody? Jean could be in danger, or the family. She knows what he's capable of.

She needs to move on, she thinks, and she needs to work out how to do it without his finding her again.

DETECTIVE ANDY WILTON

ANDY IS BUYING LUNCH. A new girlfriend means a new daily limit on calories because she doesn't like his "teeny little potbelly." Her words, not his, and mildly insulting, he feels, but he hasn't had a long-term girlfriend since school, so he's taking the view that beggars can't be choosers. In pursuit of his weight-loss goal, he has chosen falafel and hummus in a plastic tub with a nest of julienned carrots and other matchstick-shaped healthy things. The sight of it makes him feel glum.

He picks at his food at his desk and thinks about the body in the lake. An email from the lab has given him some information based on their preliminary observations. She's female; she has fillings in her teeth made from an amalgam that was introduced to the UK in the mid-sixties; she was probably over twenty-six years old when she died and was around five foot four inches tall.

More tests are ongoing and he'll have to wait longer for the results of those, but he's happy to have something to work with. He thinks of the way Lady Holt behaved when they talked beside the lake. He feels there's a distinct possibility the owner of the skull could be known to her, which makes things much more interesting.

He is fascinated with Lake Hall. It's a throwback to another century. He's familiar with the expression "how the other half lives," but he's never stepped into their world before.

"It is absolutely disgusting how much money some people have," he says to Maxine.

"Are you talking about your country house case, Monsieur Poirot?" she says.

"Hilarious." His colleagues have taken to calling him Poirot since he's taken the lead on the Lake Hall case; not one of them seems to have a problem with flogging the joke to death. "It is disgusting, though." He wants her to share his outrage. "It's the way they treat you, as if they're better than you."

"Don't let it get to you. They probably can't help themselves."

"I'm not letting it get to me. I'm just saying."

He gives up on his lunch and dumps it in the bin. On the way to the canteen to buy something he actually wants to eat, he makes a detour to see Richard Price, a detective sergeant who has been around for as long as anybody can remember. He's known for his encyclopedic memory of old cases.

"Lake Hall," Andy says, "just outside Downsley in the Pewsey Vale. Owned by Lord and Lady Holt. Do you remember any old cases or cold cases involving the house or the family, or the village?"

"I remember we went to see the daffodils there once. They used to open up the garden once a year."

"That's not helping me."

"I think Rob worked on something down there back in the day. A nasty bit of business around a shooting."

"Rob?"

"Rob Mostin. He's retired now, but the file should be in the archives. I'd say it was early eighties."

The archivist can't locate the file immediately. "I can request it from the storeroom."

Andy feels impatient about the delay. He should probably be doing something else until he gets more specific forensic results in, but when an Internet search doesn't turn up anything relating to Rob's information, he decides to visit the local library. It's a long shot, but there's no doubt Lady Holt was rattled when the skull was found and he wants to know why.

THE LIBRARY in Swindon town center was rebuilt ten years ago. Andy feels nostalgic for the modest 1960s building they demolished because they said it was unfit for purpose. He disagreed. He used it and loved it when he was a kid.

"Uh-oh. Here's trouble," Lizzie says when she sees him. "Hello, Detective Constable." Lizzie has known Andy since he got his first library card. She peers over half-moon glasses sternly before cracking a smile and raising the counter so she can give him a hug and plant a kiss on him, pinking up his cheek with lipstick. "Can I kiss you when you're on duty? Or have they kicked you out yet?"

He flashes his badge at her. It never gets old for him.

She sets him up at the microfiche machine and he searches through old editions of the *Swindon Evening Advertiser.* He starts at the beginning of the 1980s.

He's not really sure what he's looking for. It's more a hunch than anything else, but he reckons that any case relating to the Holts might have been newsworthy. At first all he finds are one or two articles about the annual summer fete held at Lake Hall. He studies the grainy black-and-white photographs illustrating them. Lord and Lady Holt stand there looking like bloody majesty. He shakes his head.

He scrolls through more editions of the *Evening Advertiser* and comes across the Holts in another photograph from the fete a few years later. The daughter, who looks around three or four years old, appears for the first time. She is standing near her parents but holding the hand of another woman and pressed closely against her legs. As before, Lord and Lady Holt look every inch the part.

She's got a Lady Diana haircut and wears a floral dress, and he's in corduroy trousers and a checked shirt with a vest over *it*. *Handsome couple*, Andy thinks. *There's something off about the daughter, though. She looks sullen and grumpy.*

The woman whose hand the girl is gripping is dressed less formally in a blousy shirt tucked into belted trousers. The nanny? he wonders. They surely had one. She's attractive, with big eyes and dark shoulder-length brown hair. She has the advantage of looking normal, unlike the Holts.

He keeps searching and is rewarded when he reaches the edition dated 2 February 1984.

"Bingo!" he says once he's read the article.

A prissy-looking woman sitting nearby shushes him, and Andy flicks her the finger. He's not in uniform and old habits die hard. What was it an actress said on TV recently? *I have a problem with compliance.* That's how Andy feels more often than he should.

JO

I HAVE A JOB INTERVIEW. I applied for a position advertised at the local nursery before they found the skull and I forgot about it in all the drama, but they emailed and invited me in. It's a menial job: duties include watering, pruning, deadheading, and general helping out where required. I really want it. It would be perfect to ease me back into things.

Ruby and Mother go strawberry picking at the nursery while I have my interview. I wanted to go alone, but Mother insisted they come. "We'll keep out of your way, darling. We'll make a lovely afternoon of it. Don't worry about us." I could have forbidden it—it felt like a bad omen, somehow—but Ruby was enthusiastic and I didn't want to disappoint her.

"You seem a little overqualified," the manager says. He is looking at my résumé on an iPad, stabbing at the screen with grimy fingernails. His desk is heaped with earth-streaked paperwork. He has weather-reddened skin, a slab of a face. A small rise in the corner of his lip seems to pass for a smile.

"I'm a very hard worker."

"What's your gardening experience?"

"I'm a keen amateur gardener. I don't mind getting my hands dirty and I'm a quick learner."

"You're staying over at Lake Hall, are you?"

He knows who I am and where I live because my name and address are plain to see on my application. "I'm a very good worker. I'd love to show you if you'll give me a chance."

"And you're Lady Holt's daughter, are you? You have a strong resemblance."

I realize with a sinking heart that this deliberate stating of the obvious means my employment chances here are probably doomed. "I am."

"Right," he says. "The thing is, we can't pay more than minimum wage. This is more a job for somebody who has just left school. That sort of person."

Not a Holt is the subtext. *Not you.*

"I heard they found a skull in the lake," he adds as I leave.

"You heard right." I can see he wants to know more, but I'm damned if I'm going to tell him anything, because I don't like the way he's looking at me.

"Got some murderous ancestors hidden away, do you?" His tone is snarky, verging on mocking.

"Not that I know of," I say. I close the door behind me before he says anything else.

In the strawberry field, Mother is sitting on a seat cane at the end of a row while Ruby picks. The strawberries grow on raised beds and Ruby looks a picture of concentration as she sifts through the dangling leaves.

"Any luck, darling?" Mother asks. The brim of her hat is wide and floppy, casting shade over her eyes. A full basket of strawberries is at her feet. I shake my head.

"Well," she says, "I told Janet you should be getting a better job than that. Something in London would be far more appropriate, or even Swindon if you were desperate."

Janet does the flowers in the church. She is the sister-in-law of the manager of the nursery. The message from my mother that this wasn't the job she wanted me to have will have gotten through loud and clear and in double-quick time.

"When did you tell Janet that?"

"I'm not sure I remember, exactly. Perhaps it was yesterday."

My frustration levels are at peak. I might have had a shot at getting this job if Mother hadn't interfered. I want to empty the basket of strawberries over her head, smash the fruits into her face, and rub them into her hair, but I keep control.

"Let me ask you, if I work in London, who will look after Ruby? The commute would be seventy-five minutes each way."

Clearly Mother hasn't thought about that. The minutiae of childcare have never been a concern for her: they were something other people dealt with. Nanny gone and can't find a suitable replacement? Send the devastated child to boarding school. Never mind if she's only just turned eight.

"If you took a job in London, I could ask Anthea to pick Ruby up from school and make her something for tea," Mother suggests. "And I suppose I could drive her to school, if you just worked a day or two a week."

"That won't work. You know it won't. You've never looked after a child."

"I looked after you."

"Did you?"

"Why are you so angry all the time?"

I want to answer but Ruby is skipping toward us, smiling. Her smile has been a rare sight since her school visit. The basket in her arms is brimming with fat red fruits, and strawberry juice is all over her T-shirt, face, and fingers.

"I filled it up!" she calls.

"Well done, darling," Mother and I reply simultaneously.

RUBY AND I are hiding out in the Blue Room because Mother has friends over for a bridge game. I heard them talking on the driveway when they arrived.

"Remember, don't mention the police business in front of Ginny," one of them said.

"I heard she's very touchy about it," her friend replied.

"Well, you would be, wouldn't you?" They cackled like harpies but I felt no sympathy for Mother. She reaps what she sows.

Ruby and I talked Mother into a Netflix subscription, and it's been a success. All three of us have watched *The Crown* together, although Mother constantly annoys me by claiming to have met some of the characters in real life. I don't call her out on it because Ruby laps up her stories.

Ruby and I are curled up on the sofa watching *SpongeBob* reruns. Ruby is giggling, but I feel sad because I'm awash with memories of how we used to do this with Chris at home. Our move here seems to have robbed us of all those small, relaxed domestic moments where nobody asks anything of anybody, except that they know they're loved.

"Mom?" Ruby says.

"Yes?"

"Why do you call your mom 'Mother'?"

"I don't know. I can't remember why. I think I always have done."

"It sounds weird."

"Maybe. But it's a bit late to change now." Actually I like the distance it creates between my mother and me. "Mum" would suggest an intimacy that never existed.

Once I called Hannah "Mummy" in my parents' earshot. Everybody froze.

"I don't think you meant to say that, did you, Jocelyn?" my father said.

Shame rose so quickly and powerfully that I stuttered my reply. The look my mother gave Hannah could have started a fire. Hannah kept her head bowed. She had no words to save me on that occasion.

"It was a mistake," I said. "Sorry, Mother."

"Are you addressing me?" Mother said. "Or her?"

"You. I mean you." But I didn't run and hug her like I would have if I'd wanted to make something up to Hannah.

"Very good," my father said. "That clears that up, then." He nodded at Hannah, who led me away, and as we walked down the corridor, we heard Mother and Father talking behind us in low, intense tones. Mother shouted, "My own daughter doesn't even like me!"

Hannah squeezed my hand tight.

THE DOOR to my father's study opens soundlessly. It's not a large room. Two worn wingback armchairs flank the fireplace, and floor-to-ceiling bookshelves line the walls. I spy familiar books on fly-fishing and a set of Kipling first editions that my father treasured.

There's a gap on the bottom shelf where the Holt Catalogue used to be kept. I feel a twinge of regret. How I would love to be able to handle it now and pore over every detail of my family's art collection. The Holt Catalogue was a meticulously kept ledger compiled over hundreds of years, a valuable resource for art historians. The entries recorded every work of art added to our collection, its dimensions, where it was bought, and for what price. I deeply regret not studying it more closely when I was younger.

One of the most memorable conversations I had with my father in the last decade, probably because we were both too emotional for it to be as stilted as usual, was one in which he told me the Holt Catalogue had been destroyed by flooding. We were both devastated.

I sit at my father's desk and ease open one of the drawers. It releases a smell that reminds me so powerfully of him that it feels like an emotional punch. The drawer is cluttered, yet everything in it is familiar to me, even the ink-stained lining paper. I remove a battered Kendal Mint Cake tin and remember him slipping little pieces to me at the weekends. "Don't tell your mother or Hannah," he would whisper, and I would slip the white sugary shard into my mouth and suck every bit of flavor out of it until it dissolved.

I take out his cigarette lighter, which is strangely warm to the touch. It's a beautiful object, solid gold and engraved with his initials. I flip the lid back and spark it up. A tall flame flares, then dies away. I replace it. Tucked at the back of the bottom drawer, wrapped in an old yellow dust cover, is his cigarette case. I pause before I unwrap it. Even though my father isn't here anymore, I feel as if I'm intruding on his privacy because this was his most prized possession.

"It was a gift from a very important man," he told me the first time he showed it to me, holding it on the palm of his hand, letting me run my fingers over its surface, "to my grandfather, your great-grandfather, for his services in the First World War. Do you know how special that is? There probably isn't another one like it."

"Is it precious?" I asked.

"It's very valuable, but its true worth is much more than money because it has a special place in this family. It's a noble part of our history. *Precious* is actually a very good word for it."

The case is as tactile and beautiful as I remember it. It is made from gold, with inset enamel so richly dark you could be staring into the deep water. The Fabergé mark is on the base. I open it and inhale. It still smells faintly, nostalgically of cigarettes. I wrap it back up carefully and replace it where I found it.

For my whole life, I have had the feeling that my father and I lived with our hands stretched out toward each other but were never able to touch.

Mother got in our way.

She always came first, and he was loyal to her to a fault. I remember his hand on the small of her back when they entered a room for dinner, the way he lit her cigarettes for her, the way his eyes fixed on hers, and his perfect manners when he thanked her—as he often did—for running the household "so marvelously well."

If Mother hadn't been here, I sometimes wondered, would I have become his princess instead?

DETECTIVE ANDY WILTON

MAXINE SQUINTS AT THE COPY of the newspaper cutting Andy has given her and reads out loud:

"'Police are appealing for help locating a witness to an incident that took place during a shooting party in the grounds of Lake Hall, Downsley, Wiltshire. Fifteen-year-old Barry Toogood, from Downsley, sustained a bullet injury to his head and is being treated at the Princess Margaret Hospital in Swindon, where his condition is said to be "critical." The potential witness is said to be in her late twenties or early thirties, with long brown hair and brown eyes. She was wearing shooting attire. Her name is not known, but it is thought she may have formed part of the shooting party. Police are appealing to anybody who may have seen her or a blue Volkswagen Golf parked in the area on the morning of Sunday 29 January.'"

"They never found her or the car," Andy says. "The Holt family claimed they couldn't confirm whether she came out on the shoot or not. One of the beaters said they'd seen her arguing with a man in the shooting party, but he didn't know who. He said the pair of them appeared to have strayed away from the main group and were near the spot where Barry got shot."

"Do you think the Holts did in the witness and dumped her in the lake to get themselves out of trouble? That's a bit of a stretch, isn't it?"

"Either them or one of their guests, and I don't think it's a stretch. That's how people like them sort out problems. Always has been. They think they're above the law."

. . .

THE COUNTRYSIDE makes Andy uneasy. There's no shelter from the elements, and you can take one wrong step and find yourself sunk in inches of mud. He prefers clean urban lines, where if trouble's coming, you can hear footsteps on the hardstanding.

The cottage they've come to visit is in the heart of the village. It's an old worker's home, part of a row of six, built from redbrick and linked by a thatched roof.

They've come to visit an older gentleman called Fred Toogood. Fred is the uncle of Barry Toogood, the lad who got injured on the shoot. Fred was also working as a beater on the day of the accident.

Fred is wizened and stooped and sinks back into his armchair with a groan after showing Andy and Maxine through to the back room. Andy guesses he spends most of his time in that chair. He's got it all set up with the TV remotes and a jug of orange cordial in reach, and there's an oily patch on the back of the seat where his head rests.

The houses are tiny inside. Andy can see that each has a tight patch of land out back, one separated from the next by low stone walls. In the garden next door a big kid bounces on a trampoline. The rhythmic squeak sets Andy's teeth on edge.

They ask Fred about the shoot.

"I had a good dog with me that day, my favorite, a bitch called Jessy, and I remember it was bitter cold. Frost as thick as your finger, and it lasted all day. I only saw the shooting party at lunch, and that was from a distance, because we ate separate from them. The rest of the time we were beating from the edges of the woods, just like we were supposed to. They would have drunk a lot at lunch. They always did. You always had to be extra careful in the afternoons."

"Do you remember this woman at all? The one they said might have been a witness?"

He shakes his head. "Lady Virginia will know who she was, if anybody does. She was one for knowing every detail. Marion used to respect her for it. I'm sorry I don't remember more."

"And Marion was?"

"The housekeeper at Lake Hall. She still lives here in the village. Her daughter took the job over from her eventually. Marion did that job her whole life. They say she's losing her marbles a bit now, though."

"How is Barry?" Andy asks. It's been difficult to find out what became of the lad who got shot in the head.

"He wasn't the sharpest tool in the box before the accident, but he's good for nothing now. Shame. He was a lovely lad with a gentle soul. Last I heard he moved to Wales with his mum."

"I'm sorry," Andy says.

Outside, the boy on the trampoline begins to make shapes as he jumps, arms and legs forming crooked angles like a scarecrow. He is silhouetted against the granite sky. Behind the gardens, the deep furrows of a plowed field comb the landscape all the way to the horizon.

"How were the Holts as employers?" Andy asks.

"I'd say fair," Fred says. "I never had no bother with them. There's others might disagree, mind you, but you'd have to ask them about that if you can find anybody still alive." He laughs so hard he almost chokes.

They write down the names of a few people Fred remembers being employed by the Holts at the time. Andy looks at the list in the car. "One of this lot has to know that family's secrets," he says.

VIRGINIA

THE SILENCE FROM THE POLICE is unbearable. I wonder constantly what they're doing.

Each day when I wake the first thing on my mind is, Will it happen today? I try to keep close to Jocelyn when she's home. I want to know what she's doing. I don't want her to learn anything without my knowing.

I jump when the phone rings. I am fidgety. The waiting is excruciating, so I find excuses to leave the house. The church flower committee and the parish council have both been surprised to have my attendance at their meetings this week, though they didn't provide much of a safe haven.

"What's happening about your body in the lake?" Marjorie Eastlake asked when we were filling the tea urn. Such barefaced cheek, but she comes from a long line of interfering busybodies.

"The police are looking into it."

"No news, then?"

"Not yet. Sorry to disappoint!"

The expression she makes does nothing to enhance features that long ago settled into pinched disapproval.

"I expect you feel funny knowing someone's body has been in the lake for all that time." She mimes a theatrical shudder.

"Not at all."

"You're made of sterner stuff than I am."

One of the other council members creeps closer, as if to listen better. Have they really nothing else to think about? I start to lay out teacups and saucers, and I don't bother to reply to Marjorie. I decide I won't come again.

AT HOME, I watch Jocelyn closely, and I continue to deflect her questions. It's obvious the skull is preying on her mind almost as much as it is on mine. She is more than capable of becoming unnecessarily dramatic about things like this, but I must be careful there isn't more to it, that she isn't nurturing suspicions that could be damaging if they're allowed to grow.

I begin to think I shouldn't have meddled in her application for the nursery job. Perhaps it would be better if she was out of the house. Memories are less likely to return if they're not prompted.

I offer to look after Ruby while Jocelyn searches for work. Of course she acts surprised and is prickly about my being supportive, as if I have a hidden agenda, but we both know beggars can't be choosers.

JOCELYN AND Anthea are out and it's too drizzly and foul to go outside, so Ruby and I have come up with a plan to entertain ourselves indoors. Ruby wants to do a fashion show and plunders my wardrobes with abandon.

My bedroom has become such a lifeless place since Alexander died, a widow's room, too quiet and tidy. I can't remember the last time I saw my bed covered in dresses and my shoes cradled with tissue paper in their open boxes. Ruby even gets my silk scarves out and hangs them on the bedstead and mirrors like bunting.

She examines my dresses closely. I show her the different fabrics and explain how they've been cut; she listens and looks with fascination. She delights in beautiful covered buttons and intricate beaded detail. It's absolute bliss. Jocelyn was never interested, no matter how much I tried to share my joy in fashion with her or treat her to nice outfits.

Ruby picks out things to try on and I sit on my bed, surrounded by the mess of it all, and watch her watching herself in the mirror. Of course the clothes are far too large for her—dresses fall off her shoulders and drag on the carpet, their waistlines only just above her knees, and her feet slide to the front of my heels—but it is so much fun.

"I like this one best," she says.

"That's one of my favorites, too. I once wore it to a fabulous party at Annabel's. And do you know what I wore with it?"

"What?"

"Can you keep a secret?"

She nods.

"Come here."

She totters over in my shoes and I open the drawer of my bed-side table. "Watch this." I pull the drawer out completely and place it on my knee. I press the bottom of the dovetail joint that connects the front of the drawer and its side. A secret box pops out, and she gasps when she sees the necklace inside.

"Diamonds," I say.

"Real ones?"

"Naturally! Your grandfather gave this to me."

I put the necklace on Ruby. It suits her. "Would you like me to do your makeup?" I ask. I shall try not to be hurt if she refuses— Jocelyn always used to—but Ruby doesn't hesitate. She sits straight-backed in front of my mirror.

"I'm only putting a little bit on you," I say, "because you're too beautiful to need much."

I stop, mascara in midair, when I hear the crunch of gravel on the drive. I know Jocelyn will hate this if she discovers us. I hurry to the window, but I'm too slow to see who has parked.

"Is it Mom?" Ruby says. "Can I show her?"

"No," I say. "Stay here and I'll talk to your mummy and you must change back into your clothes and wash your face before you come down. I don't think Mummy will like you dressing up."

"Why not?"

"It's a feeling I have. Please, darling. Do it for Granny."

I am halfway down the stairs when the doorbell clangs. Has Jocelyn forgotten her keys? She can't have done if she's taken the car. And why doesn't she just come around the back? I open the door. The detectives are standing there.

"Hello again," the woman says. "Would this be a good time for a chat?"

I can hardly refuse, so I let them in, though my instinct is to slam the door in their faces. I lead them through the hall, feeling as if my feet have turned to lead. Ruby appears on the half landing. She hasn't got changed. Instead, she has finished making up her face with buckets of mascara and a slash of red lipstick. She looks like a miniature courtesan.

"Hello," she says to the detectives.

The male detective ignores her, but the woman says, "Nice dress."

I would tell Ruby to go and clean her face off and get changed immediately, but nerves have parched my mouth and I'm afraid if I say anything, my fear will be heard by all.

DETECTIVE ANDY WILTON

LADY HOLT HERSELF OPENS THE door to the detectives. Andy is surprised she lowers herself. He'd have thought she would have had somebody to do that for her.

"Please. Do come in," she says.

A girl is standing on the landing looking down at them. She looks like something out of a David Lynch movie.

Lady Holt takes them down a long corridor and Andy rubbernecks unashamedly. The ceiling is domed and fussy with plasterwork. The walls are half paneled with dark wood and hung with dead-eyed portraits and other paintings. He's never seen so much art in one place outside of a museum.

Lady Holt shows them into a room she describes as her private sitting room. The windows must be eight feet tall, and the furnishings show signs of wear and tear. The beige carpet is so old it has turned pink in places, and the dimly glowing lampshades are watermarked.

Andy could do with a coffee, but they are not offered anything. He raises the topic of the shooting accident.

"What on earth has that got to do with anything?" Virginia Holt asks. "It was donkey's years ago. I barely remember it."

"A young man was very badly injured that day."

"He was. It was very unfortunate and very sad, but some sports come with risks."

"A potential witness disappeared. People thought that odd at the time."

"*Allegedly* disappeared. Isn't that what you say? And there was never any proof she witnessed anything or that she even came out on the shoot with us. That was pure conjecture on the part of your colleagues."

Bollocks, he thinks. *According to witness statements in the file, at least one person described seeing her near the boy who got shot. She saw something.*

"I'm interested to know how it came about that you had a guest who you treated to a shoot and a meal, but who you didn't know. Allegedly."

She arches an eyebrow. "We had big parties in those days. Certain close friends were invited to bring a plus-one. It's not for me to pass judgment if they bring somebody they met for the first time the night before and whose name they didn't learn until breakfast. Our friends liked to enjoy themselves, Detective. Haven't you ever done something similar? I'm sure a red-blooded young man like you has had some adventures."

She smiles condescendingly and it infuriates him.

"I do remember seeing the woman you're referring to at breakfast before the shoot, though," Virginia Holt adds. "I may even have been introduced to her, but I couldn't say for sure. The shooting was an accident—a very unfortunate accident, but an accident nonetheless. We had a very experienced team and we ran our shoots like clockwork, but sometimes people do foolish things. The young man who got hurt was where he shouldn't have been. It was very sad, but that's all I have to say on the subject, so if you've no further questions, I'd like to get on. Honestly, this skull is certain to be an ancient one. They found plague pits near the village, you know."

Maxine flips a few pages in her notebook. "One of the things we're here to tell you," she says, "is that we've ascertained the skull belonged to a woman. We believe she was around five foot four inches tall. She was probably over twenty-six years old when she died, and she had fillings in her teeth that weren't available in the UK until the sixties, which makes her very much of your time, don't you think?"

"Does that help jog your memory at all?" Andy asks. He watches her closely. Her expression betrays almost no reaction. She has an extraordinarily good poker face, but he thinks her reply comes a few beats too late to be authentic.

"Is that *all* you've managed to find out so far?" she says. "I thought you people could do extraordinary things with science nowadays."

Nice try, Andy thinks, *but I'm not buying into this show of bravado.* She already knew whom the skull belonged to. "Don't you worry," he says. "There's more to come."

Back in the car, Maxine says, "How the other half lives."

"Unbelievable. If she thinks she's above the law, she's got another think coming."

"You're reading her wrong because you don't like her. She doesn't think she's above the law. She's not arrogant, she's scared."

"She's both."

JO

MOTHER IS DRIVING ME NUTS, hovering around Ruby and me like a pesky fly, and I have no idea why. For the first time in my life, she tries to involve me in decisions about the house.

"I think I might close up the attic floor for good," she says. "It's so expensive to keep it heated."

"Whatever you think." I refuse to get involved because I'm not going to be here long term.

She bothers me with this kind of stuff, but still she refuses to discuss the skull. I don't understand her. The more she stonewalls me, the more obsessed I become.

One morning I'm so frustrated I say, "Honestly, Mother, you're so bloody reluctant to talk about this, you'd think you had something to do with it."

The look she gives me is so black it startles me.

"That's a terrible thing to say," she says. She stalks from the room.

"You made Granny feel sad," Ruby says.

"She's overreacting. It was just a joke, but she took it the wrong way," I say, but I think, *That was some overreaction.* It gives me goose bumps. It makes me wonder.

MOTHER STARTS to eat her breakfast with Ruby and me in the kitchen instead of having a tray in her bedroom. Anthea's eyebrows disappear under her fringe when Mother appears one morning and announces this will be her new routine. "I've taken up a tray every morning for fifteen years," Anthea mutters when she puts Mother's empty crockery in the dishwasher. "Deliver the tray, turn on the electric fire. She eats first and dresses when the room is heated up warm enough. I know where she is and what she's doing, and she doesn't come bothering me in here first thing."

I wonder if Anthea thinks Ruby and I are bothering her, too.

Mother has invited a few people to lunch. She offers to show Ruby how to set the table correctly. "It's a very important skill," she insists. I sit on the window seat and push linen napkins into silver rings.

"The detectives came back," Mother says.

"Really? When?"

"Yesterday."

"You didn't say."

"There was nothing important."

"There must have been something if they came all the way out here."

"Just something about an old shooting accident."

"Do I know about this?"

"You were very young. It was nothing to do with you."

"Shouldn't I be told about it now if the police are asking about it?"

"I don't see how that makes a difference. Anyway, I think they've decided to persecute me because the detective has a chip on his shoulder. Ruby, darling, you've done a marvelous job. Do you want to come and help me choose what to wear for lunch?"

"Did they have any more information about the skull?"

"No."

"Can I put makeup on for lunch?" Ruby asks.

"No!" I say. "You're far too young!"

Ruby starts to reply, but Mother cuts her off briskly. "Come on, darling."

They leave the room hand in hand. I check my emails. There are two job application rejections.

OVER THE soup starter, Mother and her guests talk disparagingly about mutual acquaintances. I haven't met Rory the surgeon and his rake-thin wife, Julia, before, but I know they're fairly new to Downsley and this is their first invitation to Lake Hall. Rory fawns over Mother while Julia not so surreptitiously clocks every single detail of the house.

Elizabeth, the third guest, I do know. According to Mother, Elizabeth has found significant success as an artist over the years and is represented by a prestigious London gallery. It's amazing news. I remember Elizabeth drawing sketches of our pets when I was a girl, as a hobby.

Today Elizabeth is exuberant and braless in a saggy sundress, her tousled hair barely contained in a topknot and paint on her forearms. Hairgrips protrude at all angles, as if they were torpedoed there. She looks and behaves like an unlikely friend for Mother, but they have been close for as long as I can remember.

"Virginia, would you like me to carve?" Rory asks when we're seated. Anthea has prepared the lunch, but we are serving it because she's gone home to feed her own family.

"Darling, that would be marvelous. Alexander used to do it. I wouldn't know where to start." Mother squeezes Rory's arm. Her rings glint. Rory's wife strokes her eyebrow with a fingertip. Mother's ability to dominate other women is second to none. Julia shouldn't worry, though. Mother would never shack up with a surgeon. And of course she can carve. In the back of a kitchen drawer there is a fabric wallet containing a set of Sabatier knives from the Cordon Bleu cookery course she took before she married my father.

"Sprouts, Ruby?" Mother asks.

"No, thank you," Ruby says. "They taste like the devil's balls." I try to quell a snort of laughter. She's quoting her father.

Rory's brow gathers in folds and Julia looks aghast. Elizabeth and Mother laugh like quacking ducks.

"You've got a live wire on your hands there, Virginia," Elizabeth says.

"Isn't she darling?" Mother coos. I was never her darling. I would have been reprimanded right there at the table if I'd spoken up like Ruby did.

"I hear you're after a job, Jocelyn?" Elizabeth asks.

"Yes. Probably not until September, though, when Ruby's settled . . ." I want to add "in school," but I let the sentence peter out because Ruby hasn't yet recovered from her disastrous visit to school and doesn't need reminding of it.

"Did you hear from those office people?" Mother asks.

"They said no. Wrong qualifications."

"I think you should be a detective," Ruby says. "You could solve the mystery of the skull. Or you could be a sidekick. You could have a Ouija board. Then we could ask the ghost of the skull who they are!"

"I think you mean *psychic*, not sidekick," I say, "and no, thank you, it doesn't appeal."

"Somebody at the golf club was talking about the skull," Rory says. "It sounds very mysterious. Do tell all, Virginia."

"There's nothing to tell. The police are overreacting terribly. You'd think they've nothing better to do. I have absolutely no doubt it's a very old skull." Mother looks flushed and sounds snappish, and there's an awkward beat of silence.

"Well, I expect this place has seen its fair share of history," Julia says. "It really is the most remarkable place. A national treasure! What these walls must have seen! You could write a book about it. Or perhaps there's already a book?" She laughs at her own joke.

Mother almost manages a smile. She can't stand sycophants. She dabs her mouth with her napkin and I know it'll be twisting underneath.

Elizabeth defuses the tension: "What about the art industry, Jo?" she says. She at least has respected my wish to be called Jo now. "Have you thought about trying to get a job in a gallery? You can brush up your art history in a jiffy, I'm sure."

I'm surprised to find I feel a flicker of real interest at this idea. I left a good job in a commercial art gallery when Chris and I moved to the United States. I wasn't allowed to work legally in California, so I had to shelve my ambitions of a proper career in the art world, but I took a volunteer position as a docent at a small local art museum to keep my hand in and dragged Chris and Ruby to exhibitions in the city on the weekends, when they would let me.

There's a kicker, though, to Elizabeth's suggestion: "That would be amazing, but I would have to find a gallery close to here to take me on. I couldn't commute to London and leave Ruby."

"Oh, don't be so *pathetic*, Jocelyn!" Mother's voice cuts across mine.

"It's not pathetic to want to raise your own child yourself."

Rory and Julia stare, hardly managing to hide their excitement at witnessing the rising tensions.

Elizabeth saves us again. "Well, my exhibition opens next week," she announces, "and I'm hoping for lots of red dots. So how about a toast to me?"

We drink to her success. Elizabeth goes on: "Jo, darling, why don't you come up to London for the opening? I'd love it if you did."

"I'd love to, but I can't leave Ruby."

"Nonsense! I'll look after Ruby," Mother says. "We can do that computer thing you were telling me about, darling."

"I'm going to teach Granny to play Minecraft," Ruby says.

"Oh, I say, how modern!" Julia says.

"Please come," Elizabeth says. "We'll have some fun!"

She directs a teasing smile at me and her eyes sparkle. I give in. "I'd love to." Fun sounds good. It's been in short supply for a long time, and even if the evening isn't all that she promises, at least I'll be able to escape this place. There's only so much harm Mother can do in a few hours.

THE SEARCH for work doesn't get any easier. I send my résumé out far and wide and interview for office work at several agencies. So far nothing suitable has come up, and I'm not getting any encouraging noises about future possibilities. Everything seems stagnant.

Phone calls with Chris's business partner become tense. He is beginning to sound embarrassed about the money. Apparently he cannot extract our share of it from the business without the whole thing's going under, and he has been struggling to find alternative sources of funding. I sense that he's becoming more cagey each time we speak, but he assures me I'm imagining it. I try to give him the benefit of the doubt but my sense of claustrophobia worsens.

RUBY AND I take daily walks around the estate, just as I used to do with Hannah when I was a little girl. She's always ahead of me, jumping over fallen branches, racing down slopes. She climbs like a mountain goat. I have to warn her away from the taller trees and walls. She has more ambition than sense when she chooses what she wants to scale. She got her recklessness from her father.

As we walk, we see Lake Hall from every angle: its uneven stone walls; the ancient mossy roof tiles, some chipped, some slipped out of place; the steeply pitched gables; here and there a weather-beaten, crumbling gargoyle glowering from beneath a parapet; and the small windows set deep in the walls on the upper floors of the house, with larger ones below, claiming the best views of the lake and the countryside.

Chris once said I should take more of an interest in Lake Hall because it would be mine one day. In our small, sunny little kitchen over a Sunday-morning coffee, I told him exactly where he could put his idea that he and I would eventually become the new lord and lady of the manor one day, and he replied wryly that it was a good thing he loved me with or without my inheritance. "Anyway," I said, "I'll probably be forced to sell it because of death duties."

"But wouldn't it be nice to know that for sure?" he asked.

"I won't know until both my parents die. End of story."

As we walk, Ruby often asks about the skull. She is as obsessed as I am. I make up stories to hide my suspicion that it might be Hannah.

"It's the skull of a very wise old man who lived here and took care of the creatures of the lake," I tell her. "He loved them so much that when he died he wanted to be buried in the lake so he could watch over all the little creatures that lived here."

"But that's a bit gross, isn't it?"

"Why?"

"Because Stan said bodies disintegrate in the water and creatures eat them all the way down to the bones." Her nose wrinkles. "So gross."

I can't think of a good way to spin it. Honesty might be the best policy. "When you put it like that, it's totally gross."

"I'm still not scared."

I am, I think, but I say, "I'm glad."

"Can we go out in our kayak again soon?"

"Not just yet, darling. The police will tell us when we can."

"Granny was scared when the police came," she says.

"Was she? Why?" Out of the blue, my heart skips a beat, as if something I've been fearing has come to pass.

"Because she thought it was you coming and she thought you were going to tell her off because I was dressing up in her clothes and she put makeup on me!"

She smiles and takes off running down the path before I can answer, a glow of light around her from the late afternoon sun. I tell myself to settle down, to be less jumpy, but questions about the skull prey on my mind again immediately: When will the detectives know how old it is? Could it really be Hannah? And if it is her, what happened?

The past is such a frustratingly slippery thing. You try so hard to cling to your memories of someone, but they slip away anyway. It's funny, but as memories of Chris fade unstoppably, the only reminiscences that are crystal clear in my mind are recollections from early childhood, lovely times spent with Hannah. I've thought of them almost daily since we've moved back here, but even they aren't complete. I come up blank whenever I trawl my memory for clues as to whether something sinister went on the night she left.

"LOOK AT this," Ruby says later. She turns the iPad to show me an article. It makes my stomach drop because it's about us. The headline is:

MYSTERY BODY FOUND IN COUNTRY HOUSE LAKE

"Where did you find this?" I ask.

"Stan sent it to me! He made a Google alert for 'Lake Hall' so we can follow developments. Isn't it cool? We're famous now!"

I scan the article. It just describes the discovery of the skull, that's all. There's nothing in it that's new information to me, but what it means is that the news is spreading beyond Lake Hall and beyond Downsley. The thought of others being able to read about it widely makes it all the more horrible. I feel spotlit. Tainted. I desperately don't want Ruby to be judged because of this.

VIRGINIA

THE CHINESE LANTERN PLANTS IN the pot outside my sitting-room window are flourishing. Later this autumn, once the fruit pods have turned a deep orange, I'm going to cut them and dry them and show Ruby how to varnish them. I think she'll enjoy it.

I know I'm not perfect, but I want to pass on to Ruby all that is good about me while I can and I want to do it before things happen that will sully her view of me. If the police do their job, it is not difficult to imagine such a time, and it could be very soon, when I shall disappoint and even horrify her.

I already knew the skull belonged to a female before the detectives told me. I knew her height and I know better than the police what age she was when she died. Of course I wasn't going to share the news with Jocelyn, even though it won't be a secret for long now. I will shield her from everything I can for as long as possible.

I hold myself partly responsible for what happened to Hannah. Her position was right at the heart of our family, it was intimate by its very nature, and that should have made me vigilant, but I let my guard down because Alexander and I wanted the very best for Jocelyn, and by that I mean we wanted her to feel the most loved and most cherished child in the world.

I simply couldn't imagine that Hannah wouldn't want the same, and I thought I saw nothing to suggest otherwise. I must have had my eyes half shut.

While I played my role of bright-eyed and bushy-tailed young society wife and mother, Hannah deftly moved her major pieces into checkmate position. Being so confident in my position as I was, I was too stupid to notice anything more than the incremental advance of her pawns.

She would bombard me with fussy, trivial questions all the time; the sheer number of them was enough to drive you up the wall, and how harmless they seemed, but what Hannah understood is that an accumulation of them would give me the illusion that she was both well-meaning and trustworthy. Clever Hannah.

"Jocelyn wants a SodaStream for her birthday. Would you like me to pick one up for you to give her when I next go into Swindon?"

"Jocelyn needs new ballet shoes. She wants pink ribbons on them, but I wondered if you would prefer white?"

"Jocelyn and I have sewn these lavender pockets. She wants to hang one with Lord Holt's shirts, but would you rather I put them in the linen cupboard?"

Bloody hell! I used to think. *I employed you to make most of these decisions for me!* But as complaints about nannies go, I knew mine were mild—trivial, even. My friends were jealous of Hannah and her competence and reliability. I couldn't deny that Jocelyn, who was difficult with me right from her first colicky weeks, thrived in Hannah's care. She was devoted to her nanny, more devoted than I cared to admit to myself for a long time.

I played straight into Hannah's hands when I sat her down one day to put things straight. "Hannah," I said, "I'm happy for you to be more independent. You don't need to consult me on every tiny decision where Jocelyn is concerned. I trust you to come to me with important things *only.*"

"I understand," she said. She had a disarming way of appearing bovine when she was with me. I dismissed her and moved on to the next bit of household administration without giving it a second thought.

What a fool I was.

I didn't realize those eyes looked placid only when they engaged with mine. For others, she made them sparkle. She used them to seduce and to control, and she did it right up until the day the life went out of them for good.

JO

WHILE I'M ON THE TRAIN to Elizabeth's private viewing in London, Ruby texts me a series of updates on her efforts to teach Mother how to play Minecraft.

> Uh-oh Granny keeps pressing the right key whenever I tell her to press the left one
> Granny takes forever to find each key on the keyboard 😖
> Whenever I tell Granny to look up in the game she looks up with her real head 🙄
> We're going to make brownies instead 😎

The texts make me laugh. Through the window beside me, rich golds and greens blur as we shoot through the countryside. I feel rising excitement as I leave Wiltshire behind me, and the urban shock of arriving in London feels thrilling.

Emerging from the Tube, I walk slowly down the broad, crowded pavements of Piccadilly and pause to admire the displays in the bijou shop fronts of the Burlington Arcade: towers of macaroons, jewelry to rival my mother's, leather bags in all colors of the rainbow.

I leave the arcade to find myself just a short distance from where some of London's finest private art galleries are located. I'm nervous because I've been such a recluse since Chris died. I make myself pick up my pace and walk briskly, hoping momentum will help me quash the urge to turn and run.

Elizabeth's party has spilled out onto the street and she is right in the middle of it, holding court. "You came!" she says. "I wasn't sure if you would! Everybody! There's somebody I need you to meet."

I take a glass of fizz from a tray, suck in a deep breath, and slap on my best smile.

It goes well. Elizabeth's paintings are richly colorful but compact abstract oils in chunky black frames, some of which are also painted. They're stunning and exuberant, they reflect her personality, and at least half are sold by the time I arrive. She looks after me like a perfect hostess and I find I'm actually having fun, just as she promised.

"Come to dinner with us," she says as the last of the guests leave. "Don't worry. We'll make sure you get on a train home tonight."

We walk arm in arm to the restaurant. "It's nice to see a smile on your face," Elizabeth says. "Do you know, I think it might suit you to come and work in town a few days a week. You could really do well."

I start to rehash the reasons it wouldn't work for me to take a job in London, but she shushes me. "No talk of boring practicalities tonight, please! You can dream instead! Think big; be brave. There's no harm in it. Now, there's somebody very interesting I'd like you to meet at supper. He knew your father. I'll make sure you sit by him."

The man's name is Jacob Faversham, but everybody just refers to him as Faversham. He has a gravelly voice, thick-rimmed glasses, and a silk handkerchief protruding from his jacket pocket.

We chat easily about Elizabeth's paintings and his personal collection of art. He is urbane, erudite, handsome, and well preserved for a man of my parents' generation. As the wine flows, he becomes conspiratorial, too. We are breaking the caramel on our crème brûlées when he mentions my father.

"A lot of us looked up to Alexander. He had an effortless charm. Do you miss him?"

"I do." I don't tell him how much distance I put between my father and me. I don't know how much he knows.

"I do, too. He was a proper old school gentleman. They don't make them like that any longer. He was proud of you, you know."

"Was he?" I feel myself tensing up. This isn't easy to hear.

"He had hopes of your coming back and taking over Lake Hall one day. He hoped the drawings collection would lure you back even if he and your mother couldn't."

"I should like to see the drawings," I say. "The best ones are still kept under lock and key."

"You should. I hear they're exceptional. I'm sure you'd enjoy them greatly. Now, if you'll excuse me, I need a smoke. Please don't disapprove."

"I don't disapprove."

"You look like him, you know. I expect everybody says you're the image of Virginia, which is true up to a point, but I see him in you, too."

I watch Faversham walk away. He has a slight limp. He stops halfway across the restaurant as if a thought has occurred to him and returns.

"You don't want to come and work for me, do you? If you're interested, I think you'd be absolutely perfect."

He doesn't give me time to answer, nor does he mention it again when he comes back to the table reeking of smoke, but at the end of the evening he presses a business card into my palm.

"The job offer stands. You could come and do a trial. I think we'd work well together. Phone me."

The evening leaves me buzzing with optimism and energy that last all the way back home on the late train. As I get out onto the platform at Downsley, a handful of other passengers do the same. Most of them head to the car park. I wait beside the sign that says TAXI. I have phoned ahead to book the local service, but it hasn't showed up.

A lone woman remains on the platform. She has a suitcase at her feet. She is absorbed in looking at her phone. There is something familiar about her. I wonder if she is from the village or if she's waiting for a connection and if there even is one this late at night.

A car swings into the taxi area, headlights raking the station building. "Sorry I'm late, love," the driver calls. "Lake Hall, was it?"

"Yes, thank you." I turn back to where the woman was because I want to ask if she is okay and if she would like to share the taxi or ask the driver to come back for her, but she's gone.

1977

LINDA WRITES A LETTER GIVING *notice and hands it to the husband at work the following morning. He's a shadow of his former self, but even so, she splurged out on a nice envelope and a pad of Basildon Bond paper and wrote the letter out three times, each time forcing her handwriting to make less babyish shapes. She didn't want him to think she was thick.*

He doesn't even open it. He puts it down on his desk as if it's meant for somebody else. She tells him what's in it and he looks through her. "Right" is all he says. It hurts her feelings. He's lost his shine, she thinks as she polishes the parquet in the hall. He's a broken man. It's going to be easier to leave him than she thought possible. She wonders what she ever saw in him.

On her last day she sees two sheets of paper laid out very precisely side by side: death certificates. She scans the information on them. The first is the baby girl's:

NAME: HANNAH JULIA BURGESS
DATES: 11 December 1976–3 September 1977
CAUSE OF DEATH: MENINGOCOCCAL MENINGITIS

She thinks the second one relates to his sister:

NAME: HANNAH MARIA BURGESS
DATES: 7 November 1957–1 February 1973
CAUSE OF DEATH: SELF-ASPHYXIATION

His sister was only six months older than me, *Linda thinks. She wonders if she ever reminded him of Hannah Maria, but tells herself it doesn't matter now, because he's become a broken man, so what does she care? Linda thinks about something she heard: that if you want a new identity, you can create one easily if you can find a dead person who was born more or less at the same time as you. And what she could do just now is exactly that: create a new identity. Good luck to her dad finding her if he doesn't know what her name is.*

Hannah Maria Burgess. Hannah Burgess. She repeats the names to herself as she walks home. It's brilliant, she thinks. Much more classy than being Linda Taylor. Linda No Middle Name Taylor. Linda No Hope Taylor. The next day she asks her landlady if she can borrow the phone book and funnels ten pence into the pay phone in the hall. She requests a copy of a birth certificate for Hannah Maria Burgess, born 7 November 1957. "Yes," she says, "I've lost the original." She provides her current address. It's that easy.

A few days later the replacement certificate arrives in the post. Linda packs it and most of the rest of her belongings into her bag and hides it under her bed. She leaves a few things out for now, because she doesn't want Jean to know what she's planning. She likes Jean, but it's safer to slip away alone.

She pops out to the shop to get a few bits to take on her journey and a ticket for the first coach heading south in the morning. It's going to Bristol.

When she gets home, Jean is sitting on her bed, holding the birth certificate. Linda's packed bag has been pulled out from under the bed and is open on the floor at Jean's feet.

"Are you leaving without telling me?" Jean asks. "I thought we were friends."

"I was going to say goodbye."

"Whose is this?" Jean holds up the birth certificate.

Linda knows how clever Jean is, and now she's seen the name on the birth certificate, it's probably better to let her in on the whole secret. She describes her plan.

"You bloody genius!" Jean says. "But you aren't going without me. I'm sick of it here. Help me pack."

They wait until the middle of the night, when they're sure the landlady won't hear them. They slip out the front and post their keys back through the door.

They walk briskly and silently down the street, thrilled with their own courage, and start to run as soon as they've turned the corner. It's hard to run and laugh and carry suitcases at the same time. They head into the city center and spend the rest of the night huddled together on a bench in the bus station. They board the Bristol bus first thing the next morning.

JO

RUBY IS IN MY BED when I wake up, and for once she's awake before me, reading a book.

"You were talking in your sleep," she says.

"Was I? What did I say?"

"Hannah."

"Really?"

"I heard you."

"What else?"

"You said other stuff, but I couldn't understand it."

"What are you reading?" I've just focused on the cover of the book she's holding. It's an old hardback called *The Night of the Hunter.* The image on the jacket is terrifying: a lanky man preparing to snatch up a small girl and her doll; a young boy's terrified face hovering above them.

"Granny gave it to me. It's *very* scary."

"Could I have a look?"

I flick through the book. The word *hangman* jumps out; the prose is vivid and chilling.

"Did Granny let you pick this yourself or did she recommend it?"

"She told me I *have* to read it. It's her favorite book. I'm nearly halfway through."

"I'm sorry, but it's not appropriate." I sit up. I'm fully awake now.

"But I love it."

"No. You're too young for this stuff. Granny shouldn't have given it to you."

Ruby's expression darkens. "But I want to!"

"We can't always get what we want."

"Granny says you're horrible sometimes, and she's right!"

"Okay, that's enough!"

"And Granny saved me last night, so you need to say thank you to her!"

"What do you mean? Saved you from what?"

She clams up as if she's realized she's gone too far.

"Saved you from what, Ruby?"

"I got stuck."

"Where?"

She bites her lower lip. "In the barn."

"What were you doing there?"

"Geoff said Sally cat had her kittens in there. I shut the door to be safe, but the latch fell down on the outside."

"Where was Granny?"

"She found me and let me out."

"After how long? And how come she let you go outside exploring on your own anyway?"

"It's not her fault! I did it on my own."

"She should still know where you are. That's the point of looking after you. There are all sorts of hazards in that barn. Honestly!"

She storms off, and I am left with the book and a tension headache. I lie down and ask myself why it is that I can never trust Mother.

OVER BREAKFAST, I tell Mother I've been offered a job. I don't want to confront her about the barn incident in front of Ruby.

"That's wonderful!"

"Well, don't get too excited. I don't have any details yet, the offer was only made in passing, and I'm not sure about traveling to London, but if I can negotiate something part time."

"Don't look a gift horse in the mouth."

"I won't. But I have responsibilities."

"That's me," Ruby says. "I'm your responsibility, aren't I? You should take the job, Mom. Granny can look after me."

Mother beams when she hears this but checks herself when she sees me looking. "I'd love to look after Ruby, and before you say anything, I know you think I'd be useless at it, but Anthea can help."

"Can Stan come and play when you're looking after me?"

"Of course. We could get the tennis court tidied up for you both."

They're getting carried away. "If this is a real job offer, I am not accepting it unless I can make other childcare arrangements. You had Ruby for six hours last night, Mother, and things happened that I'm not happy about."

"What on earth do you mean?"

"Ruby's getting stuck in the barn, maybe?" I'm so irritated that it pops out.

"Ruby's fine! You weren't in the slightest bit upset about it, were you, darling? I found her curled up with the kittens. No harm was done."

"Really? You didn't think about what might have happened?" I feel my temper rising further, but I mustn't get into a row. I take a breath. "I don't want to talk about it now. We'll discuss it later."

"When I'm not here?" Ruby asks.

"Yes, actually! Now I need to phone Faversham to see if the offer was a real one, or if it was the alcohol talking."

"Did you say Faversham?" Mother says. She pauses, marmalade-filled spoon hovering.

"Jacob Faversham. He wants me to work at his gallery."

She taps the spoon on the side of the plate to transfer the marmalade and attempts to spread fridge-hard butter onto her toast before replying. "Faversham has a lovely gallery, but are you sure it's not a bit stuffy for you? Wouldn't you rather work in one of those lovely bright new spaces with modern art in them?"

"It's a potential job offer. Just a second ago you were pleased for me. What's wrong with Faversham and his gallery?"

"Nothing. You're right. I suppose hearing his name shocked me because he was a very close friend of your father's. It caught me off guard, that's all. Actually, I think my eyes were bigger than my stomach this morning." She pushes her plate away. "Let me know what Faversham says when you phone him, won't you? I have an appointment in Marlborough at ten, so I think I'll leave now and call in at the butcher on my way to order the joint for Sunday."

I nod. I feel deflated, as if everything that happened in London wasn't real. I won't let Mother get me down, I tell myself. I will pursue this. I decide to wait a few hours before I call Faversham, though. I don't want to seem needy.

AFTER MOTHER has left I go online and try to find out what a typical salary might be at a commercial art gallery these days. Still not much, is the answer, but you can do well on commission. I click through to Faversham's website. The styling is very luxe.

I'm browsing the impressive stock list and thinking how much I want this job when the doorbell chimes.

The dog's claws clatter on the stone floor as she accompanies me to the door. I open it and the sun shines directly in my face, silhouetting our visitor. I shade my eyes.

"Hi," I say.

She smiles. It's a lovely smile. Soft skin crinkles around kindly brown eyes. She is an older woman, nicely dressed in a navy blue dress with a belted waist, a lime-green cardigan over her shoulders, and a pair of well-worn red moccasins. Her hair is brown, well colored and cut in a neat bob.

"Jocelyn?" she asks. "Is that you?"

I don't recognize her. I shift to get the sun out of my eyes. She sticks out her hand, so I return the gesture and we shake. The intensity of her squeeze feels somehow meaningful, as though I'm meant to have a significant response.

"Goodness!" she says. She covers her mouth with her hand. Is she blinking back tears? "I didn't think you would be here. What a wonderful surprise."

"I'm so sorry," I say, "but . . ."

"You don't recognize me?"

I shake my head.

"I'm Hannah. I was your nanny."

Shock makes me stare at her openmouthed as I try to take in what she says. I realize I would not have recognized Hannah if I had walked past her in the street and it astounds me. When you have thought about someone regularly for almost thirty years since you last saw her, you don't imagine you won't recognize her. Not when you were as close as she and I were. Not when she is imprinted on almost every happy memory you have from your childhood.

I feel my chest tighten and my heart thumps hard within it. Is it her? It could be, but is it? I search her features for something recognizable, something that tugs at my heart and tells me: *This is Hannah. It really, actually is her.*

"Why don't I leave you with one of these?" She pulls a card

from her bag and hands it to me. "Would you mind giving this to your mother?"

The card says:

CHANGE OF ADDRESS

HANNAH BURGESS

has moved to

HILLSIDE COTTAGE, DOWNSLEY, WILTSHIRE, SN9 4NZ

I read it, but it's hard to take in. I have a brief flash of memory. "Did I see you at the station last night?" I ask.

"No, dear. That can't have been me. I was at home last night. I'm so sorry. I can see I've shocked you. I'm back in the area, probably permanently, so I called in on impulse, but I should have phoned first."

I'm speechless as I try to take in the fact that Hannah is not only standing in front of me but has apparently moved back to Downsley. She smiles graciously and makes to leave, and I feel a startlingly strong wrench. "Please don't go!"

Ruby arrives beside me as I'm still working out what to say next. "Hi," she says, and sticks her hand out.

Hannah shakes it formally. "Hello," she says. "I'm Hannah. What might your name be?"

"Ruby Black."

"What a glamorous name! And do you happen to have a fondness for cupcakes?"

That's the moment it feels as if I am actually standing in front of Hannah—really, truly my Hannah. The way she phrases the question and smiles at Ruby melts away the years and causes a lump to rise in my throat.

"A big fondness," Ruby says, rubbing her tummy. She's still

wearing her pajamas. They are covered in a cupcake print. "Especially red velvet."

"Well, you've got very good taste, because they're the best kind. It's so nice to meet you, Ruby, and lovely to see you, too, Jocelyn. You look so well, it's just marvelous. A really wonderful surprise. I won't keep you now, but I'd love to see you and your mother if it's ever convenient."

"That would be lovely," I say reflexively, although I have no idea how to feel.

My heart says this reunion is something I've been longing for for thirty years; my head reminds me Hannah was driven away by my appalling behavior but also celebrates the fact that the skull in the lake cannot belong to Hannah if she's alive and well and standing in front of me. Elation, shame, and relief all course through me at once.

"Who was that?" Ruby asks as Hannah walks away.

"My old nanny."

"Your actual old nanny from when you were little? The one you loved a lot?"

"Yes."

"I thought she disappeared?"

"She did. It was a horrible shock."

"Aren't you happy she's back?"

"I can't believe it."

VIRGINIA

WHILE I'M IN MARLBOROUGH, I try to phone Faversham a couple of times using my mobile phone, but he doesn't answer. He's canny beyond belief, but we both know he can't avoid me forever. I'm not sure what he's playing at in offering Jocelyn a job, but I have a good idea.

I feel worn out by the constant rowing with Jocelyn. I'm more snappish with her than I would like to be, but the way she snipes at me over every little thing wears my patience very thin.

My beautician knows I don't like to chat, so she works on my face in silence, removing rogue hairs and working her magic to coax a semblance of vigor back into my skin. Needs must. Appearances matter. There'll be no flies on me when I emerge from here.

Strangely, I feel brave enough only now, eyes shut, prone on the paper-lined bed with my neck and shoulders exposed, to face up to a question I have been avoiding:

When the police identify the skull as belonging to Hannah Burgess—and they will, it's only a matter of time—what shall I do?

I consider my options.

I could write a confession that explains everything. It would result in scandal, of course, but Jocelyn might be able to ride it out. She is stronger than she thinks and everybody knows she distanced herself from us as soon as she was able to. She could do that again. Sell the house and start over. The house would be hers because once I had written my confession I would sign Lake Hall over to her and disappear completely. By which method, I'm not sure yet, but that's just detail, shades of finality.

I think it through again.

My plan is a good one, but it's not perfect.

Ruby is a problem. Ruby, Ruby, Ruby. I love her too much to leave her and I want Lake Hall to be hers one day.

And Jocelyn. If I disappear, what might she remember? I cannot leave that to chance. I must be here so I can try to limit the damage.

Perhaps it would be best to give in to the police process instead: interviews and possibly arrests. I could deny all knowledge of what happened and cross my fingers. It's worked for Alexander and me in the past.

The beautician starts on my shoulders.

"There's a lot of tension here today, Lady Holt," she says. "Let's see what we can do about that for you."

If only she knew. Her fingers mash into my muscles.

Alexander, my handsome gambler, my risk-taking lover, once told me this: "You have to know when to play a long game, and when you decide that's what you have to do, you must be patient. Bide your time and don't panic. If you must panic, you never let it show. Hold your nerve and eventually you will know what the right move is."

Brave words, and my goodness, how I wish the strategy had worked for him, but he lost money hand over fist at the card tables. Even so, I think it's just the advice I need now. I'm willing to sacrifice myself for my family if necessary; it's a matter of timing.

Nobody is in when I get home. I go directly to my sitting room and try to phone Faversham again. He still doesn't answer. I hang up and sit alone with my panicky thoughts.

The carriage clock above the fireplace ticks loudly. I feel as if it's counting time until the police arrive, even though I know that's ridiculous. It could be days or even weeks until they've got enough test results back to focus their investigation. Still, the sound of it is unbearable. I insert the key that winds up the mechanism and try to turn it the wrong way to make the ticking stop. I rattle it, then force it. I shouldn't. It's a rare, valuable clock, but I don't care. My hand is trembling.

"Can I help you with that?" Anthea startles me.

"Goodness! I thought you were out!"

"Something wrong with the clock?"

"Yes. No." I put the key down.

"There's a card for you on the side in the hall."

"Thank you." It's a relief to have an excuse to escape her gaze. Sometimes it's pregnant with judgment. Alexander had a word with her about it once, but it made no difference.

I find a change of address card on the table, just as she said, and I have to read it a few times before I can take it in. When I do, my skin crawls. Somebody must be playing a sickening practical joke.

"Anthea!" I call. I have to sit down.

"What's wrong? Are you unwell?"

My hand trembles so much the card quivers when I try to hold it up and my chest feels as if something is cinched tightly around it.

"Where on God's earth did this come from?"

TWO

1980

"WELL?" LADY HOLT ASKS.

Nanny Hannah leans over the crib. Baby Jocelyn is tiny. She has a scrunched-up expression, a slightly misshapen head, what looks like the remnants of a nasty forceps dent on one of her temples, and red scratches on both cheeks. She's no oil painting. "May I?" Hannah asks.

"Yes, yes, of course."

Hannah reaches into the crib and picks up the swaddled infant. Lady Holt gazes at her child adoringly. Hannah has seen it before: the smitten mother. They never notice how ugly the baby is. It's one of nature's miracles. Hannah examines the baby's face close up: "She's absolutely beautiful," she declares untruthfully, and Lady Holt's face lights up.

Hannah has been briefed by the outgoing night nanny: Jocelyn is a grisly, colicky baby, and her mother is finding it hard to bond or establish a routine. At three weeks old, Jocelyn is to have a dose of Infacol and a feed every three hours, and not a minute sooner or later. Lady Holt is not to be allowed to have the baby sleeping with her, although she will try to. Hannah didn't particularly like the night nurse, but she was in agreement with the suggested routine. Letting the mother get too involved disrupts everything. Better to break that pattern earlier rather than later.

Lake Hall is everything Hannah dreamed of. It's like a set for a film or TV. Hannah has never been anywhere so grand. The thought of having her own room here and being an official member of staff is intoxicating. People in the village and in town will have to look up to her when they know whose baby she's caring for. Everybody has heard of Lake Hall and the glamorous Holts. She feels as if she has struck gold.

"I'll leave you two to get to know each other," Lady Holt says. She looks nervous.

"That would be perfect," Hannah says. She takes a seat in the rocking chair by the window and coos at the baby, who opens her eyes and gazes toward the light, unfocused but mesmerized. "She's a real doll," Hannah says to Lady Holt to encourage her to relax and bugger off from where she's hovering in the doorway, her fingers twiddling the string of pearls at her neck as if they're worry beads.

Once Lady Holt's footsteps have died away, Hannah shifts so she's holding the baby upright, the little face only an inch from her own.

"Hello," she says. "It's just us now. Your mama has gone away. What a stupid fuss she made. We'll be okay, won't we? I can tell already that we're going to be the best of friends."

She rubs the tip of her nose on Jocelyn's, then cradles her so she can examine the baby's fingernails. They are too long. Hannah knows they shouldn't be cut with scissors at this age because they are attached too closely to the wafer-thin skin. She leans over and takes one of Jocelyn's fingers in her mouth. She nibbles at the nail. When she's finished, she admires the result: the long, sharp edges are gone. After she's done the rest, there will be no more scratches on the baby's face and she'll look so much prettier.

Hannah smiles. She plans to look after this baby as if she were more precious than the crown jewels. Jocelyn is, after all, her key to a better future. She leans her head back and gazes out at the grounds of Lake Hall. She rocks the chair in a steady, gentle rhythm and softly sings a lullaby.

VIRGINIA

ANTHEA SAYS SHE DIDN'T SEE the woman who dropped off the change of address card, so she can't describe her. "I never knew Hannah when she was here before, anyway," she says, "but your Jo looked fit to faint afterward."

I can visualize Jocelyn's expression. My daughter used to treat Hannah as if she were some sort of deity.

I ask Jocelyn about it when she gets home.

"It was Hannah. She's moved back here."

She sounds as if she's trying to mute her excitement, and she can hardly meet my eye. It's as if she doesn't want to share the news with me. It was always like this. I employed Hannah, but Jocelyn was terribly possessive of her, shutting me out of their relationship whenever she could. But this can't be Hannah. Hannah is dead.

"Did you recognize her?" I ask, trying to sound casual.

"Yes. No, well, she's changed a lot, obviously. But I knew it was her."

"How?"

"By the way she was and the way she spoke. It was her."

"Did she say why she's come back here?"

"No! She was only here for a few minutes. I wasn't going to interrogate her. Why are you even asking?"

"I'm curious."

"I'm surprised you care."

I don't rise to the bait. If she ever understands how much I care, then I will have failed her.

I keep the card. I push aside the rest of my correspondence and place it in the middle of my desk.

I phone Elizabeth, who makes it her business to know everything that's going on in the village, and I ask about Hillside Cottage. She tells me she heard an older woman had taken over the tenancy, but she had no idea it was Hannah.

"She's got a nerve calling at the house," Elizabeth says. "Did she apologize for upping and leaving?"

"She spoke to Jocelyn."

"Did she say why she'd come back to Downsley?"

"Not that Jocelyn mentioned."

"Well, that's certainly a turnup for the books."

She tells me Hillside Cottage is owned by a couple from London, who have plans to renovate and expand it but haven't yet acquired the relevant permissions, so they're letting it in the meantime. The information gives me pause for thought. Who bothers to print such a formal change of address card if she's merely a temporary tenant? Certainly not the practical, sensible Hannah I used to know.

On the other hand, I can't help thinking that Hannah missed nothing. She would know I value a weighty board, fine calligraphy, raised printing, a gilded edge. I know it's impossible, it has to be, but even so I wonder if the quality of the card is meant to be a message to me: the start of a new conversation between old foes.

I'm curious as to where it was printed. There is only one possibility locally.

I drive to Marlborough and take the card to the Kwikkest Copy shop and inquire whether it's one of theirs. "It's so lovely," I say. "I'm thinking of doing something similar." The youth who serves me snaps gum and has a greasy fringe, but confirms it wasn't a job they did. "I'd remember it," he says when I ask if he's certain.

Back at home I avoid Jocelyn and Ruby and replace the card on my desk. I must clear my head. I must think this through. The card cannot be from Hannah. Hannah's skull has just been pulled out of our lake. It is fractured in all the right places.

I rip up the card and throw it away, but it doesn't help. I don't think I can afford to ignore it. I get it back out of the bin and reassemble the pieces on my desk.

Daylight is dying outside and my room is darkening. I don't switch on a lamp. I want to watch the landscape outside lose its resolution. I want the lake to be swallowed by darkness and I want it to absorb me, too, erasing my physical self until only the sharper ridges of my mind remain. I need every ounce of concentration and clarity I can muster because I have an extraordinary question to answer:

How can a dead woman come back to life?

DETECTIVE ANDY WILTON

MAXINE SMILES AND LEANS BACK in her chair as Andy walks through the office. "And how are you this morning?" she asks. Last time she saw Andy was when she left the pub at a sensible hour the night before. He was still at the bar.

"Don't ask." Andy's hangover is the biggest he's had for years, and so was the row with his girlfriend it provoked. "Get me a coffee, will you?"

"Get your own. We've got good news, though. Do you want to hear it?"

He manages the tiniest of nods.

"They radiocarbon-dated the tooth enamel from the skull and got a year of birth. Well, a range, but it's small. They reckon she was born in 1958, and that's accurate to within eighteen months."

"So she could be born in 1957, '58, or '59?"

"Exactly."

"Does that match with our shooting witness?"

"It would make Jane Doe approximately twenty-six or twenty-seven years old in 1984."

"Young enough."

"I think so."

A FRIEND of Marion Harris answers the door at Marion's home and lets them in.

"Marion's lovely," she says, "but I warn you she's a bit prone to oversharing and sometimes using bad language as her mind goes, but there's no offense meant. I'll need to serve her lunch in a few minutes."

Andy likes the sound of oversharing. It will make a change from the many taciturn interviewees he's faced, so he's keen to talk to Marion. He reckons the housekeeper must have known more than most about the Holts.

Marion is wheelchair-bound and frail but cheerful. A tartan rug is neatly tucked over her knees and she wears velour slippers with pompons on the toe. Her chair is pulled up to a table and she's working on a jigsaw puzzle.

"It's my daughter's house," she says. "I live here with Anthea and her husband. They've no children. Alan was shooting blanks."

"We've come to talk to you about Lake Hall," Andy says. "And Lord and Lady Holt."

"There's not much I don't know about them," she says. "But it was a while ago now when I was their housekeeper. You'd be better off asking Anthea about them nowadays."

"We're interested in the early 1980s, specifically the time of a shooting party the Holts had in 1984, when one of the boys from the village was injured."

"I don't know nothing about that. I was having an operation at the time. Women's problems."

Andy feels disappointed.

"Mind you, the things I did see, though," she says. "They'd make your hair stand on end. The parties they had. I wasn't invited, of course, but when you do the clearing up there's not much you don't know or can't work out."

"We'd love to hear about it," Maxine says.

"They're different from the likes of us, the Holts. He loved her, he was devoted to her, you could see that, but there was so much temptation for him, even out here, and London must have been worse. Men like him don't think anything of having an affair. In their circles it would probably be frowned on if you didn't take up with a girl who threw herself in your way."

"Who are we talking about?" Andy asks. "The girl at the shooting party?"

Maxine shakes her head. "You're talking generally about Lord Holt, aren't you, Marion?"

Marion doesn't react to their questions. She's in full flow, in a world of her own. "I never saw Lord Holt betray Her Ladyship, mind you, but it would have been so easy for him. He was catnip to the women. That fellow was so handsome you'd drop your own husband for him in a heartbeat if you thought you had a chance. Nanny Hannah used to stare at him as if the sun shone out of his backside."

"Was Lady Holt aware of this?" Andy asks.

"Lady Holt was a stunner, but she had a quality to her that made her seem distant to people. If she noticed Hannah Burgess making doe eyes at Lord Holt, she wouldn't have shown it. It wasn't her way. She'd have dealt with it in private."

"Did anybody who worked on the shoot at Lake Hall talk to you about the day of Barry's injury?"

"They all had their story, just like when Nanny Hannah went."

"And when did Nanny Hannah leave?"

"A year or two after the accident, I reckon. Something like that. She upped and left one night without a word of warning. Little Jocelyn was only seven. Jocelyn's back at Lake Hall now and all, and you know that's hard for Anthea because she doesn't have the help I had in the house. They work her to the bone, and bless her, she looks after me and Alan so well, too. Anthea and Alan never had children, you know. He was shooting blanks."

Andy looks at Maxine and she flips her notebook closed.

"Thanks so much for your time," she says. "I think we've got everything we need."

"Are you clearing off now, you buggers? Will I have my dinner now?"

"You will." Andy can't help laughing. "Pleasure to meet you, Marion."

"I expect even you'd drop your pants for Alexander Holt!" she says and winks at him.

"Marion!" Her friend sets a lunch tray on the table. "That's quite enough talk like that."

JO

I AM ON MY WAY to Jacob Faversham's gallery for a trial day. Apparently the job is mine if I enjoy it. I am not as nervous as I thought I might be.

On the train, Hannah is on my mind. I can't stop thinking about her since she showed up. It was the most extraordinary feeling to be standing there in front of her. How does she even feel about me now? I wonder. Will we be able to have a relationship? Where would we start after all these years and after the way she left because of me? The countryside rushes past as I grapple with my feelings about it. I don't come up with any answers.

When I arrive at the gallery, Jacob introduces a woman called Clemency, who is the gallery manager. I am immediately in awe of her poise and style: she has dark hair in a pixie cut, green eyes, lips painted a pert red; she manages to look effortlessly chic dressed all in black. I wish I had dressed better, but I haven't had a working wardrobe for years.

Clemency is polite but muted. The vibe I get from her is a curious one. Her welcome smile doesn't quite reach her eyes.

The hours I spend at the gallery are exhausting and a rush. There is so much to learn that apart from checking in now and then by text I don't give home a moment's thought.

"How do you fancy a trip out with Clemency and me this afternoon?" Faversham asks after lunch. "There's somewhere I think you might like to see."

We take a cab to the Burlington Club, located on a square in

St. James's favored by embassies. Every building has a columned facade and an elegant spiderweb fanlight above its entrance. Most have doormen.

"Women aren't usually allowed in," Faversham says as we climb the steps. "But I've pulled strings, so please try to behave as if you are venerable experts."

"I'm sure they allow women in to serve the tea and do the cleaning," Clemency mutters as we enter the building in Faversham's wake.

Inside, the proportions and decor are far more elegant than Lake Hall but no less expensive and ornate. The place has the quiet, confident feel of a power base. You could dazzle with luxurious hospitality here, or you could plot and swap secrets in a private corner.

Faversham nods to the porter as we climb the stairs and surprises me by taking me by the elbow and pulling me to a halt beside him as we come to the first-floor landing. We look down at the floor below. "You have to see it from up here," he says. "It's the best view." The staircase loops elegantly below us, and the mosaic floor in the entrance atrium looks dazzlingly complex. "Your father was a member here. And your grandfather and great-grandfather before him."

"I didn't know." I wonder if that's how he got Clemency and me in here. The Holt name opens doors in certain circles.

The painting we have come to assess is in an intimate dining room where long curtains drape in swags across the tall windows and wall lights reflect dimly on the polished tabletop. The painting has been removed from the wall and put on an easel so we can examine it. It's luminous, complicated, and mysterious.

"What do you think?" Faversham asks. He looks at me intently.

"It's sensational. Won't the club be devastated to lose it?"

"They need the money, darling. It's always about the money. And I believe they're commissioning a reproduction to replace it."

"I don't suppose many of their members will notice," Clemency says.

"Indeed."

I examine the painting. It's of a type called a vanitas. Typical subject matter: a still life including skulls, fruit crawling with insects, wilting flowers, and other reminders of death.

"'As shadows wait upon the sun,'" Faversham says. "Isn't it beautiful and chilling?"

"Who is it by?"

He points at a signature hidden within the painting.

"Rachel Ruysch," I read.

"She was working in the eighteenth century, and she rarely painted anything other than floral still lifes. It makes this work all the more special."

"What's the provenance?" I'm interested to know how the painting arrived here.

Faversham looks at me, a teasing look in his eyes. "Don't you remember it? It used to hang in your parents' house in Chester Square. In the dining room."

I don't remember it, but I can't deny the painting tugs at me somehow. I had put this effect down to its strange beauty, but perhaps it's something to do with recognition, too.

When Clemency steps out of the room, Faversham says, "Help me sell it, Jocelyn. I can tell you love it."

"How did it get to be here?"

"Your father used it to repay a debt, I believe."

"But it must be worth, I don't know, a small fortune."

"Alexander didn't gamble for small change. That wasn't his world. You know that about him, surely?"

I nod but I didn't know. I'm starting to understand there might be a lot I'm ignorant of.

"Think of it this way," Faversham says. "I can't get this painting back for you unless you want to buy it from the club, but if you *sell* it for me, your family gets to be a small part of the painting's history once again and you get to make a very healthy commission on it."

"How much commission?" I ask.

He whispers a percentage in my ear that feels more than generous to me.

"Can I work a four-day week?"

"You drive a hard bargain."

"My daughter needs me."

He offers me his hand. "Done."

I can't believe it was so easy.

ON THE way back from London, I think about my father. It's strange to hear about him from a friend of his when I've only ever really seen him through the lens of the family. I never properly considered before what the world thought of him, or who else apart from Mother really knew him.

What's also on my mind is how to tell Mother and Ruby I've accepted the job. Mother *should* be pleased, and Ruby and I will need to talk about who will look after her because having Mother and Anthea covering childcare is not going to work as anything more than a temporary solution. If I take this job, it will be the first time I've had to rely on other people to care for my daughter. I feel nervous about it, but I remind myself I had the best childcare when I was growing up and I had a nanny.

I yawn as the train pulls into Downsley, even though it's only early evening. I'm back earlier than I said I would be and I have an idea that makes my heart beat a little faster. I text Ruby.

> I'll be home in half an hour oooxxx
> Cool 😎 Granny is showing me her favorite paintings and then she wants to show me how to walk with a book on my head 📚 so I can get a goodhusband 😵

I remember perfectly the address on the card Hannah gave me.

I pull into the Coop in Downsley. I grab a few treats for Ruby and wait my turn at the checkout.

Eileen—whose checkout aisle I favor because she is reliably dour and taciturn—attempts a smile. "Heard the police was up at the hall," she says. I'm not quite sure if it's a question or a statement. I glance at the person waiting behind me. It's one of the lads who work at the pub. "All right?" he says. He makes no pretense that he's not listening.

"They found a skull in the lake," I say. "And some other bones." They obviously know already, so there's no point in fudging it.

Eileen looks pleased to have confirmation from me, and the lad looks impressed. "Do they know if it's a modern skull?" he asks.

"They don't know yet."

"It'll be archaeological," Eileen says. "They might get that *Time Team* fella back to come and do a dig. I'd make that fella a cup of tea any day. Lovely, isn't he?"

"There's probably a whole pile of bodies in that lake," another cashier chips in.

"Hopefully it's some toff from one of their posh parties who got drunk and fell in," a man's voice contributes from behind a display. "Good bloody riddance. Mind you, you wouldn't put it past the Holts to have a murderer in the family, would you?"

I freeze for a moment. I wonder if he knows who I am. It's probably best to make a quick exit. I've no desire to fuel this particular fire by answering back. Confrontation with the villagers never did anybody any good. "Thanks," I mouth to Eileen as she hands me my receipt. She looks embarrassed for me.

The young lad leaves the store almost on my heels, and I ask if he knows where Hillside Cottage is.

"Past the pub, turn right, make a left opposite the cricket club. It's a narrow lane, mind you."

On my first pass I miss the entrance to the lane and have to double back. The hedgerows haven't been trimmed, and leaves and tendrils whip the car windows as I make the turn. The lane is single-track and so little used that grass grows along a ridge down the middle. The car lurches on the uneven surface.

I find the cottage is a quarter of a mile down the lane. It's not the picture-perfect place I'd imagined, but an ugly modern bungalow in need of some TLC. I think I see why Hannah wants to live here, though. While there's a steep wooded bank behind the house, at the front is a pretty, mature orchard. I spot apple, pear, and plum trees, some heavy with unpicked fruit, a mess of dropped flesh beneath.

Hannah always enjoyed bringing order to things, and she especially loved the pleached fruit trees in the walled garden at Lake Hall. "Try this," she would say, handing me a fruit picked straight from the tree, "and tell me if that isn't a bite of heaven." *She's going to tame this orchard and this house,* I think. *She's going to make both of them beautiful.*

I park across Hannah's driveway, blocking her modest little car in. On the way here I imagined I might call in and say something, but my nerves ambush me now. I still haven't worked out what to say. How do you pick up a conversation with somebody you were close to when you were seven years old, especially when the relationship ended the way it did? When she left because I was so vile? My doubts escalate. What am I even doing here? I ask myself. What if she sees my spying on her? What will she think?

I put the car into gear and drive on. There was no sign of life in the house, so hopefully she didn't see me. Very soon, the lane narrows, and I'm afraid if I don't turn around, I'll get stuck or lost. I do a clumsy six-point turn by a gateway into a field and almost land a wheel in a ditch. I'm hot and flustered and wishing I'd gone straight home.

As I approach Hillside Cottage again, Hannah is standing at her front gate. I keep my foot on the accelerator and my eyes straight ahead and pretend I don't see her—even though that's ridiculous—and hope she won't recognize me. I sit rigid in the driving seat until I reach the bend in the lane where Hillside Cottage will disappear from view behind me. Only then do I dare to glance in the rearview mirror.

Hannah is waving.

VIRGINIA

I FEEL SUCH A FOOL. I forgot how bad the terrain is in this part of the woods. It looks so docile in spring when a carpet of bluebells spreads as far as you can see, but now I find myself wading knee-high through ferns and nettles and I can't see the ground beneath them.

I'm climbing the bank behind Hillside Cottage, where this woman calling herself Hannah Burgess is supposed to be living. I want to try to see her for myself.

I swing my walking stick ahead of me as I take each cautious step. The dog is searching for rabbit holes. I hope she doesn't start barking. My breathing has become labored and loud. I consider heading back to the car, but I'm too close to give up now.

At the top of the incline, I'm grateful to see a fallen branch I can sit on. It is well shielded by trees, but I have a decent view of the back of the cottage. It's frightfully small and ugly. I couldn't bear to live somewhere like it. I see a car parked beside it, which makes me confident that this woman, whoever she is, is home.

I sit on the branch for so long that I have pins and needles in my ankles before I see her. She comes around the side of the house and the car yelps electronically as she unlocks it. I can't quite see her face, because of the angle she's standing at, but the deities intervene by sending a rabbit to dart through the field beside us. Boudicca, who has been panting on the ground, springs to life with a deep bark and takes off in pursuit.

The woman's head whips around and she peers into the woods toward us. I freeze. Sunlight slants between tree trunks. I can only hope it makes me hard to see in the shadows. She squints and scans the woodland, but she doesn't see me.

I am transfixed by the sight of her. She is more or less the right height and build to be Hannah, and she stands in a way I find familiar. She puts up a hand to shade her eyes and I get a flash of memory: Hannah, on the lawn at Lake Hall, in the same pose, calling for Jocelyn. Her features are hard to discern precisely from this distance, and though I know in my mind that it cannot be her, my instincts tell me loud and clear that it might be. I feel an uncontrollable urge to flee.

I stand. She detects the motion and looks right at me. I try to climb over the branch I've been sitting on, but it's too high. I teeter on the top of it and know that I'm not going to be able to save my-self. The tree canopy rushes away from me as I fall onto my back and pain explodes in my head.

HER FACE appears out of focus at first.

"You're back!" she says. "You fell unconscious, but only for a few seconds. You've got a nasty gash on the side of your head, though."

She's talking just the way Hannah used to talk to Jocelyn: a "mother knows best" tone of voice. I am on the ground where I fell and she is sitting on the tree branch I was on earlier, staring at me with an expression that appears benevolent and caring, as if I were a child who had grazed her knee. I search her face for features I remember, but so much time has passed and my vision is swimming and I can't be certain of anything except that I think she has big brown eyes, just as Hannah did. I try to move, but my head and neck feel as if they are trapped in a vise. The pain is vicious and incapacitating.

"Help me," I say. "Call Jocelyn."

She laughs.

I black out.

WHEN I come around, I'm still lying on the ground and a blanket has been put over me. I hear the woman's voice: "We're over here!" I don't know if it's Hannah. She spoke to me nicely before I blacked out but does that make it less likely to be her, or more?

Two paramedics work on my body as if I'm a piece of flesh. "She might not be who she says she is," I say when one of them bends over me, but I can hardly get the words out. He says, "Don't you worry, love, you'll be all right. Don't try to talk. Deep breaths now. That's it." They give me gas and air, which only partly dull the agony of being moved onto a stretcher and carried down the hillside.

"Her family members haven't arrived yet," I hear her tell the paramedics as they load me into the ambulance. "May I ride with her?"

"No!" I try to say, but I have a mask over my mouth, so my words are garbled and the paramedic strokes my arm and talks to me as if I'm deaf. "It's best if you can stay calm, Mrs. Holt. Try to relax. Now, we want to try to put a cannula in so we can give you some better pain relief intravenously, okay? Are you ready for a sharp scratch?"

I try to tell him again.

"She's a little agitated," he says. "Perhaps you could hold her other hand. It might help calm her down."

"Of course," Hannah, or whoever she is, says. I feel her fingers around mine. Have you ever tried to recoil from something, but you physically can't? It's the most helpless, terrifying feeling in the world. She sticks to me like glue all the way into the hospital. Once they've transferred me to a bed, she pulls up a chair beside it. I am woozy and nauseous and I feel as if I'm looking at her face through a pane of swirled glass.

"How are you alive?" I ask. "Who are you?" But she smiles and pats my hand and says, "Try not to talk. Get some rest."

My eyelids droop. The drugs are powerful.

I WAKE up shaking. They're lifting me, swaddling me. "Alexander!" I say. A face comes into view. "Don't worry, Mrs. Holt. Your temperature dropped a bit lower than we were happy with, but we're warming you up. You've got heated blankets around you. Would you like somebody to call Alexander for you? Your daughter's here. She's just outside in the corridor, do you see? It'll be easier if I raise the bed up a bit?"

Jocelyn and the woman who calls herself Hannah are standing in the corridor, face-to-face, talking, but I can't hear what they're saying. They embrace and I want to scream at Jocelyn not to touch her. The woman leaves and Jocelyn watches her go.

When Ruby and Jocelyn come in I can't help it, I start to cry.

Ruby makes it better. She doesn't stand and look at me from across the room like Jocelyn does, as if I'm something to be embarrassed by. Ruby hugs me with her tanned, slender arms and I feel as if they're restoring some life to me.

But what kind of life is it now?

I am not so bombed on the painkillers that I don't realize I made a grave mistake by putting myself in danger today. Whoever this woman is, she wants something from me and I cannot afford to let myself be vulnerable to her.

Worse, if this is Hannah Burgess—and after seeing her I think it could be, I don't know *how*, but it *could*—I believe none of us is safe.

What if she wishes to take revenge for the violence she suffered?

JO

WHEN I WAS A CHILD, I used to fantasize about Hannah adopting me. They were idyllic fantasies in which she and I stayed together for life. I never dreamed she could be my real mother—I had enough physical characteristics inherited from both parents that this would have required an extraordinary level of denial—but I wished Hannah could become my new mother.

I had only one problem with the scenario: I couldn't imagine Hannah being with my father. Hannah and Father would never have fit together like Father and Mother did. My fantasy solution to that: Hannah and I should find a new home for just us. We could visit my parents—or my father, at any rate. I had it all planned out in my head.

I have had bad news this morning. I got an email from the solicitor handling Chris's probate:

> Your husband's business partner has provided documents confirming what he told you informally. The money your husband invested in the business has been used as a guarantee against a loan the business took out. It cannot be extracted from the business until another backer is found. They assure me they are making efforts to do this, but until it is done, they are unable to release any funds.

I was hoping for better news, that I'd misunderstood the situation, or that there was something we could do. My job offer is an absolute godsend.

Stupidly, I complained in front of Mother about my lack of appropriate work outfits. She offered me the use of her closet and got offended when I said I'd rather not because it would be ridiculous to turn up looking like a clone of her. Ruby looked disappointed, too. They lay together on Mother's bed and made an odd couple, with Mother in a lace-edged white nightgown and a dressing on her head and Ruby in sweat pants and a T-shirt but wearing a turban Mother had fashioned from one of her silk scarves.

"Do you want to come with me to Marlborough, Rubes?"

"No, thanks."

I leave Ruby reading *Harry Potter* to Mother and try not to feel offended, but not before extracting a pile of thrillers Mother has on her bedside table. "These aren't suitable for Ruby," I say.

"Those are jolly good books!" she protests. "Don't limit her reading. Her imagination needs to grow. And I'm in the middle of that one!"

I hand her the book she wants but keep the others.

"She can read them when she's old enough," I say.

Mother and Ruby look disconcertingly alike when they glower.

Anthea is dusting the furniture in the corridor. "Do you mind if I go out?" I ask. "They seem fine up there."

"You can do what you like."

She's right, but I resent her tone because I was trying to be courteous. I want to be sure she doesn't feel put-upon because Ruby and I are here.

"Anthea?"

"I'm here."

"Are you sure you're happy to help Mother with Ruby when I start work? It really shouldn't be too much bother and we'll make sure you're paid for any extra time and work."

"If Lady Holt wants it, I'll do it."

"But . . ."

"It's not ideal, but I expect we'll manage."

"Are you sure?"

"The shops will be shut if you don't hurry."

I take the hint and leave. In Marlborough I allow myself to go into one boutique that has a sale rack. I can't afford a whole new outfit, but I see a beautiful blouse in my size and I'm tempted.

"Would you like to try that on?" The sales assistant is peering at me from behind the till.

"May I?"

"There's a lady in the changing room but you can go in as soon as she's finished."

The dressing room curtain whisks back and a woman steps out. She's wearing a full-length formal dress. She turns halfway to one side to look at herself in the floor-to-ceiling mirror. The dress is gorgeous: formfitting, flattering, and just the right amount of daring. She bends one leg and points her bare toe. My eyes travel upward until they reach her face and we both startle. It is Hannah, but looking as I've never seen or imagined her before. In the world of my childhood, it was me that was to be the princess and Hannah the courtier, never the queen.

"Oh!" she says.

"The dress looks lovely!" I don't know what else to say.

"Thank you. I need something for a wedding. It's probably too much."

"It's not too much. It looks stunning. Did my mother used to have something similar?" The dress looks familiar.

"I don't think so, dear, not that I remember, anyhow. How is your mother?"

"She's doing okay, thank you. Well enough to milk being a patient at any rate. Ruby discovered that the original servant's bells still work and Mother's got a bit too used to using the one in her bedroom."

"I'm very glad to hear she's recovering well. It was a frightening thing to happen, especially for somebody her age."

Hannah is so kind. She would have been well within her rights to demand to know what Mother was doing snooping around near her cottage. Her sweetness makes me bold.

"Can I take you out to tea?" I ask. "As a thank-you for helping Mother? I'm free now, if you are. I was going to drop a present round to thank you for what you did, but this would be so much nicer. Only if you want to, of course."

"I'd love to," she says.

I can't help smiling as she slips back behind the curtain to change. I realize how badly I wanted her to say yes.

"Will you be taking the dress?" the sales assistant calls.

"I'll think about it," Hannah says.

"Do you still want to try the blouse on?" the assistant asks me when Hannah emerges in her own clothes.

"What do you think?" I ask Hannah.

"I think it looks lovely, dear."

I finger the price tag. I shouldn't be buying clothes this expensive, even if they are on sale.

"I'll come back and try it on later."

"I can't guarantee it'll still be here. We don't hold items in the sale," the assistant says.

"It's a little expensive for me, anyway."

HANNAH AND I walk along the riverside path. A toddler is at the water's edge with her mother, or perhaps her nanny. They're feeding the ducks. The inside of my mouth is tacky and my heart is thudding.

I desperately want to ask Hannah about the night she left, but I feel as nervous as I did when I sat in the car in front of her cottage. I clear my throat and hope she can't hear the shake in my voice.

"I used to love doing that."

"You did," Hannah says. "You were scared of the swans, though."

"Was I? I remember being fascinated by them, but not scared."

"You were quite right to be frightened. I was pleased because it meant you kept your distance. They can break a man's arm, you know."

I thought it was Mother who told me that, but I must be wrong.

"Would you like to go to the Polly Tea Rooms? Like we used to?" I ask.

"That would be lovely."

The tearoom has hardly changed since we last came here. Cascading hanging baskets decorate the beams on the front of the building. Inside, the rooms are low-ceilinged and quaint and the staff are uniformed in black and white with frilly aprons.

"Our old table is free!" I say. "Shall we?"

"After you."

The table is beside a window with a good view onto the busy high street. We sit down and face each other. The years seem to melt away, then re-form, and it feels as if my heart has leaped into my throat, but still I don't feel brave enough to ask her outright about what happened. "Do you remember how we used to make up stories about all the people we saw walking past here?"

"So we did! You had such a wild and wonderful imagination. You loved your stories. If you weren't making them up, you were reading them. I remember those pony books you collected."

"What can I get you?" The waitress is hovering.

"The usual?" I ask. We used to order the same thing every time we came here.

"That would be lovely!"

"Two Earl Grey teas, a slice of lemon drizzle cake, and a cream tea." It feels strange to hear myself saying the words: another echo from another time. Hannah unfolds her starched napkin and smooths it onto her lap. The question I want to ask is burning inside me, but I feel as if I left my nerve in the dress shop.

"I'm very grateful for what you did for Mother," I say. Bland words. Cowardly. Why is it so impossible to bring up the past? How can her answer possibly hurt me more than leaving me already has?

"Anybody would have done the same."

"Well, I don't know about that. It was above and beyond to go to the hospital with her. Thank you."

"I would never have left her until she had her family with her."

I can barely concentrate on her answer. I take a deep breath. Come on, I tell myself, be a grown-up, pull yourself together and ask her now or you might never know.

"Hannah?"

"Yes, dear?" Her eyes look as deep and liquid as ever. So different from my mother's sharp green gaze, they brim with sympathy and encouragement.

"You don't have to answer this if you don't want to, but . . ." I pause and exhale sharply to try to steady myself. What is wrong with me? Just ask the question.

"What is it?"

"Why did you leave Lake Hall so suddenly when I was little? Was it because of me? Did I do something?"

"Oh, my dear, what makes you say that?"

"Mother told me you left because I behaved so badly."

"No! That's not true. Your mother and I argued that night after she was terribly harsh with you when you spoiled your dress. Do you remember the dress? She had chosen it especially for you and brought it from London. It was lovely."

"The blue dress," I say. "You hung it on my armoire. It was the prettiest dress I ever had."

"That's right. Your mother was widely admired for her very good taste. But unfortunately the dress got ruined. These things happen when you put small children in fine clothes, but your mother flew off the handle. She was incensed. Normally I used to bite my tongue when she chastised you because it wasn't my place to do anything else, but I couldn't help myself that night because she was so vicious with you. I felt she'd crossed a line and I told her so. It was a terrible mistake. She took it very badly. She told me to pack up my stuff and get out and refused to let me say goodbye to you. I appealed to your father. I apologized and told him I was desperate to stay, but he backed her up and there was nothing I could do. It hurt me so much to leave you, and they forbade me to write to you or phone you. They even threatened me with the law if I did."

I feel as if I've been punched in the gut. "They lied to me."

"I'm sorry."

"And they treated you so badly!"

"Don't be angry, please. I was upset and angry for a long time, but it's water under the bridge now. You and I are here. We're back together and we have so much to catch up on. If you confront your mother, she might forbid me from visiting Lake Hall or make it difficult for us to see each other. It would be a shame when we have such a wonderful opportunity to rediscover each other."

"Is that really what you want?"

She takes my hand in hers. Her skin is so soft. "It is. There's been enough upset, don't you think? We've all suffered. Let's leave it in the past where it belongs. I'd like to think it's even possible that your mother and I might be able to build our bridges."

I suppose it's the least I can do, considering how badly my parents treated her, though I would love to shake my mother hard until she comes clean about what really happened and make her apologize to Hannah. Grovel, even. That would feel more just.

"If you're sure."

"I'm sure. I'd sleep easier tonight if I knew this would stay between us."

"Then of course I won't mention it."

"Thank you. I knew you'd understand and I know I can rely on you. Shall I pour? It would be a shame to let the tea go cold. We should try to enjoy these lovely cakes. What I'd really like is to have a chat and hear all about you and Ruby."

She pours tea and spreads a neat layer of strawberry jam on her scone, followed by a thick blob of clotted cream. My mind is in chaos, racing to process everything I've just learned, and I keep thinking *Poor Hannah!* but I make an effort to say something lighthearted and normal.

"Didn't you teach me it should be cream first, then jam?"

"Well. Isn't that funny? I don't remember. I'm surprised you do."

I laugh.

"I can't tell you how nice it is to see your lovely smile again," she says.

Later, when we stroll out into the high street together, Hannah says, "That dress. The one you wore that night. It wasn't blue. It was green."

"Are you sure?" In my memory of that night, the dress is definitely blue.

"I remember matching the thread to it when the hem came

down. I chose one called apple green. Isn't it funny how little things like that stick in your mind?"

"I guess I'm wrong, then."

"Memory is a funny thing."

"You're right."

There's so much to think about when we've gone our separate ways, but the talk about the color of the dress sticks with me.

I could have sworn it was blue, but what difference does it make?

VIRGINIA

I'M STILL CONFINED TO BED. The wound on my head is healing nicely, but I'm suffering headaches and the muscles in my back spasm whenever I try to move. Getting to the bathroom is a slow and painful process, but I will not allow anybody to accompany me. It would be too humiliating.

On my bedside table there are containers of painkillers, and I have been taking them as instructed by the hospital. Jocelyn has taken on the role of bossy matron and polices me three or four times a day, watching as I swallow the blasted things down. They make me woozy and the wooziness frightens me because it means I can't closely observe what's going on in my own house.

I didn't think it was possible to irritate Jocelyn any more than I did before I fell, but I was wrong. She is perpetually snippy with me: angry that I went to Hannah's house and angry at my incapacitation and the work it's creating. She bustles about my bedroom with a frown and speaks to me as if I'm a child, tossing out scraps of information that seem curated to torment me.

"Faversham is selling a painting we used to own, but I just don't remember it. It's a vanitas. Very beautiful. I can't believe it was sold."

I wonder exactly what Faversham has told her. I feign sleep, but my mind roils with plans of what I want to say to him when I eventually get him on the phone. He will not hear the end of this.

Another thing she tells me—I don't know if it's at the same time:

"Did I tell you I saw Hannah in Marlborough the other day?" she says. "Mother? Did you hear me?"

"What of it?" I try to sound as if I don't care. I don't like the way Jocelyn is looking at me.

"I took her out to tea to thank her for looking after you when you fell. I never asked what on earth you were doing there anyway."

"Don't tell me you haven't been as curious about her as I have!" Attack can be the best form of defense. Jocelyn blushes.

"Well, she sends her love and best wishes." She speaks stiffly. I know her feelings about this woman she believes to be Hannah must be complicated. "And when you're better I think we should invite her to lunch so you can thank her, too."

This woman must not set foot in my house. She will not act on this stage again. I close my eyes and pretend to drift off because I want Jocelyn to leave. My frustration at my stupidity and my fear make my hands tremble. I roll onto my side, though it's a desperately painful movement, and I tuck my hands between my legs so she won't notice the bedcovers quivering.

"DR. HOWARD is here to see you, Mother. Are you presentable?"

Jocelyn opens the curtains. The daylight is gloomy and the tips of the oak trees are being violently yanked from side to side by a strong wind. It rattles the glass in the windowpanes. Jocelyn switches on the light. I move gingerly to a sitting position and she adjusts my pillows to prop me up, a little more roughly than I would like.

"Can you pass me my hand mirror and my lipstick? The pink one?"

"You don't need to put on lipstick for the doctor. Honestly! I'll bring him up."

How quickly we are at the mercy of others when we are unwell.

"Leave us, please," I say to Jocelyn when she reappears. The less she knows, the better. I must try to regain control.

Eric Howard puts his bag on the floor and drapes his jacket over it the same way he has done each and every time he has been to this house. He has looked after both Alexander and me since we married and first moved here. He is a very dapper man, only a few years younger than me. He looks at me kindly.

"Did they look after you in hospital? I would have come to see you sooner if I'd known."

"Very well, thank you, except that I've been prescribed all these damn pills and they're making me feel absolutely ghastly. I'm so groggy all the time."

He examines me and takes a look at my medication. "Naproxen and amitriptyline. It's a fairly heavy-duty combination. Side effects: confusion, depression, tiredness, and the feeling of being in a medicated state. Does that sound about right?"

"It's exactly right."

"How is the pain?"

"Barely tolerable. Is there something else I can take instead? Without the side effects?"

"You can try moving to over-the-counter painkillers, that would be the logical next step, but it might be too soon. Your head wound is healing well, but you still have some significant bruising and swelling."

"Better pain than confusion."

"You'll need to wean yourself slowly off the medication you're on now. Don't go cold turkey."

"I understand."

"It might be a bit soon, Ginny. Why don't you leave it a few more days? I'd be happier if you did."

He lingers, but neither of us speak. I think Eric Howard may have always been a little bit in love with me. I don't know that to be true. It's just a suspicion, one Alexander shared.

"It's nice to see Jocelyn again," he says. "She seems very well. I remember those bouts of tonsillitis she used to have."

Jocelyn never let me near her when she was ill as a child. I had to stand by the door and watch as Hannah held her hand while Eric examined her. I wonder if he remembers that.

"She grew out of it," I say.

"They usually do."

Ruby slips in while Jocelyn sees Eric out. "Mom says you have to have your pills," she says.

"Could you do me a favor? The doctor says I have to change pills. Could you go to my bathroom cabinet and get out a box that says *ibuprofen* on it, and also one that says *acetaminophen* on it and bring them here?"

She does as I ask.

"Now, can you get two pills out of the ibuprofen pack for me?"

She counts them out into my hand, "One, two," and I think of Hannah chanting a rhyme to Jocelyn: "One, two, buckle my shoe; three, four, knock on the door." Hannah had an encyclopedic knowledge of nursery rhymes. In later years I would think of each one as a lure she used to seduce my child further and further away from me. I longed to teach my daughter to count and to read myself, but by the time Jocelyn was old enough, she couldn't stand to be around me. She blocked her ears if I read to her, and she squeezed her eyes shut if I pointed at the pictures in her books. She only wanted Hannah.

"Thank you, darling," I say as Ruby passes me a glass of water. I swallow the pills. I'm desperate to get off the stronger ones. It has never been more important to have my wits about me. I have no idea what this woman who calls herself Hannah has been doing while I've been down and out. I hope I can stand the pain.

"Don't tell Mummy I've got new pills, will you?" I ask Ruby. "The doctor wants them to be my secret."

"Why?"

"Because medicines are private," I say. "Not everything is your mummy's business."

"Okay." She seems slightly doubtful but mostly untroubled by the deception and is quickly distracted when she opens a drawer of my dressing table. She's drawn to the relics of my glamour like a moth to a flame.

"Mom has a secret from you, too," she says. Her tone is idle, but my heart skips a beat. "Hannah sent her a new blouse. Mom saw it in the shop and couldn't afford it, and Hannah got it for her and sent it here. It's for work. It's nice, but not as nice as this." She turns around, holding one of my jeweled hair combs in front of her face.

"Are you interested in a trade?" I ask Ruby.

"What is it?" She loves to make a deal, just like her grandfather.

"I'll tell Mummy you worked on your maths puzzles up here with me if you let me borrow your iPad for half an hour."

"And can I wear this hair comb, too?"

"If you put it away where you found it afterward."

"Deal."

She fetches the iPad before sitting at my dressing table and trying out the hair comb. Once she's satisfied with how she looks, she raids my ring box. She puts on at least three of them and admires the stones from all angles.

I open the Internet browser on Ruby's iPad and go to the Google search page.

The gift of the blouse troubles me greatly. It's exactly the kind of move Hannah would make; even the idea of it seems to throb with danger. I don't know the size or shape of the danger yet, but I can sense it.

I try to marshal my concentration through the pain and medication. It has occurred to me that Hannah might have been able to survive a head injury, however bad it looked, and we might have mistaken her unconsciousness for death in all the chaos that night, but the head injury wasn't Hannah's only challenge.

I type a question: "Can you survive drowning?"

JO

"I WANT TO GO HOME," Ruby says.

It's three A.M. In just over four hours I am due to get on a train and travel to London for my first day at my new job. Ruby will spend her first day at her new school. The timing is bad, but Stan's mother has promised to take Ruby in for me.

Ruby stands by my bed wearing pajama trousers and a white T-shirt that was signed by all her friends on the day she left her school in California. I think I know what she means by *home*. It's not Lake Hall. It's the house on another continent we were both wrenched from.

"Come here, sweetie." I shove back the bedcovers. Ruby gets in and nestles. Her body is warm, but her feet feel like ice blocks and I wonder how long she's been out of bed. I touch her temple: that place where her skin was marshmallow soft when she was a baby, and so thin when she was born that I could see the shadows of veins. Its softness used to make me shudder sometimes. Tonight there is dampness on her temples and her cheeks.

"Tell me what's wrong," I whisper.

"I miss my friends."

"I'm sorry."

"I miss our house in America."

"I know. I do, too."

"And I miss Daddy."

"Oh, sweetie."

I let her cry. They say you should do that. You shouldn't tell a

child that her emotions are wrong. My mother never got that particular memo. Perhaps I'll make it her epitaph so I get the final
word.

Ruby's tears fall heavily and copiously. This is sadness, heavy
sadness, more sadness than a child should have to feel. It pains me
so much that I can't help her by bringing her daddy back.

The old-fashioned digital alarm clock on the bedside table says
it's 04:07 when Ruby finally sleeps. Her body is hot and my pillow is damp and I know I'm going to be awake for the rest of the
night—worrying about her, worrying about us, worrying about
Mother.

Dr. Howard spoke to me after seeing Mother. He's a gaunt man,
clean-shaven with a floppy quiff of snowy white hair. He smells
old-fashioned: of aftershave and antiseptic.

"How is she doing?" I asked.

"Very well, considering. You'll need to make sure she doesn't do
too much, too soon. She needs to give herself a chance to recover."

"Will she recover completely?"

"I don't see why not. She's robust for her age. But keep a close
eye on her."

He opened the door. Outside, stiff gusts of wind were hissing
through the beech trees and sending leaves tumbling. "I'm very
fond of your mother, you know," he said. "She's faced a lot of challenges over the years. She needs your support now." He nodded at
me and put his hat on firmly before closing the door behind him.

"Wow," I said out loud. I sensed a bond between Mother and
Eric Howard when I was a child; he was one of Mother's more
regular visitors at the house. I think Elizabeth was the only person
who came to Lake Hall more regularly than he did.

Mother will be fine, I thought. *She is indestructible.*

At five A.M. I ease myself out of bed, careful not to disturb Ruby.

She rolls onto her back and I freeze, holding my breath, willing her to stay asleep. I stay there until I'm sure she's going to remain peaceful.

I creep down the corridor to the bathroom. Mother's voice halts me outside her room. "Who's there?"

"It's me."

"Come here."

"I'm getting ready for work."

"Just for a minute."

I enter the room. The curtains are open. Mother is standing in front of the window watching the dawn break. "Do you hear that?" she says. I shake my head. "It's a tawny owl. Such a hollow sound. I couldn't sleep."

"Mother, my train's at . . ."

"I know when your train is. I wanted to wish you luck. Tell Faversham he needs to phone me. Be sure to do that, will you, please?"

"Get back to bed. You'll get cold." She shrugs my hand away when I touch her arm, so I watch impatiently until she's eased herself back into bed. "Anthea will be here at seven to do breakfast and get Ruby up. Please stay in bed and try to rest until then. Stan's mum will arrive at eight forty-five to take Ruby to school. Do you remember the arrangements?"

"Of course I do." She looks small and frail with the blankets pulled up to her neck.

"Where did you get that blouse?" she asks.

I don't want to tell her it's from Hannah. Not now. She'll only have something horrible to say about it.

"I had it in California," I say. "It's an old thing."

"I thought you didn't have anything suitable to wear to work," she says.

"I've got to go."

"You look lovely," she adds. I find the unexpected compliment far more disconcerting than her criticism.

"I'll see you later."

As I'm shutting the door, she says, "Can you ask Hannah something for me?"

"What?"

"Ask her if she remembers how she and I met?"

"Why?"

"I'm just curious to know if she remembers what I was wearing."

"Ask her yourself! Don't you think I've got enough on my plate?"

I close the door quickly and firmly. I can't deal with her being needy, too.

IT'S HARD to relax on the way to work, worrying about how Ruby is coping. I text her from the train.

How are you this morning? Sending all the hugs and kisses to wish you luck at school today

Her first reply is worryingly short:

Fine

I feel better when I get her next text a few minutes later:

Stan wants me to come to his house after school and see his new guinea pig.
Fine by me if Stan's mum says it's okay. I'll text her.

Stan's mum confirms she's going to pick them both up after school. I promise to call school and let them know of the change in arrangements for Ruby. I don't bother texting Mother to let her know about the change in arrangements because she's too out of it. I'd rather tell Anthea directly. Anthea has a mobile, but it's a dinosaur and she tells me she frequently runs out of data. It's safest to phone Lake Hall later, I think. I call when I come up from the Tube station, but Mother answers.

"Can you get Anthea for me?" I ask.

"She's gone out."

"When will she be back?"

"What do you need?"

"I'd rather tell Anthea."

"Do you think I can't pass on a message? Is the role of secretary considered too complex for me now?"

"Tell Anthea that Ruby's going to Stan's house after school, so she won't be coming home on the bus. I'll collect her from Stan's house on the way back from the station."

"I'll pass the message on."

"Write it down, why don't you?"

"Oh, I have no memory now, as well as no sense?"

"Do whatever you want, but make sure the message gets to Anthea."

I text Anthea to let her know of the new plans and I ask her to inform the school on my behalf. I'm confident this will be fine as Anthea is on their list of people responsible for Ruby. There's no way of knowing if my message went through, so I make a mental note to phone again later. Only Mother could make such a simple communication so fraught.

DETECTIVE ANDY WILTON

ANDY AND MAXINE GET OUT of the car.

"Ready?" she asks.

He squints at Lake Hall. "As I'll ever be."

They pull the cord at the door and hear the bell clanging inside the house.

"Perhaps we should have called first," Maxine says when nobody answers.

Andy doesn't reply. Maxine's right, but he didn't feel like giving Lady Holt any warning, not when she treats everybody as if they're beneath her. They ring again and just as they're about to give up, the door is answered.

"Can I help you?" The woman is in her late middle age and short of breath. She wears a housecoat over black trousers and sensible shoes.

They display their badges. "We'd like a word with Lady Holt, please, if she's available."

"She's not. She had a bad fall and she's laid up in bed."

"I said we should have called," Maxine mutters.

The woman twitches her nose and adjusts her glasses. "Is that all?"

"Do you work here?" Andy asks.

"I'm the housekeeper." She pulls herself up an inch and offers a rubber-gloved hand to each of them. "Anthea Marshall."

"We spoke with your mother recently. Would you be free to have a word with us, by any chance?" Andy says.

"Is it about that skull?"

"We'd like a bit of a general chat to help us get some background on the lake and the house and who has been here over the years. I expect there's not much you don't know? And if I'm honest, I could kill for a cuppa." Andy smiles his best smile.

She opens the door wider. "I might have a nice bit of fruitcake for you, too."

"You must be some kind of angel."

The fruitcake is too dry and the tea is so strong you could stand a spoon up in it, but Anthea talks as if she's been waiting a very long time for an ear to bend.

"Lake Hall used to be a good place to work, because there were lots of staff and everybody had their job, but it's just me and Geoff now. Geoff does the garden and I do the house, but there's too much work and not enough time by far. Just dusting the picture frames is a day's work. My mother was house-keeper here before me, and she didn't know how lucky they had it. The job was half of what it is now. To be fair, the house was busier then, with parties and whatnot. It's become a shadow of what it was, especially since Lord Holt died, God rest his soul. His own daughter didn't even come back for his funeral, you know, but she ran back here quick enough when she needed to, bringing her little girl. If you ask me, it's not healthy for a little one to grow up in a big house like this with just her mother and grandmother and me. She'll go mad, or get airs and graces like Her Ladyship. I'm not sure what's worse! And as if I haven't got enough on my plate, now they're expecting me to look after Ruby as well, even while her upstairs is still in bed and calling for me every five minutes."

Anthea nods toward a row of bells mounted on the wall. Each is connected to an antique system of ropes and pulleys and has the name of a room inscribed below it. She sips her tea and Andy takes the opportunity to get a question in.

"Do you remember hearing about a shooting party here? It would have been in 1984, at the beginning of the year. It might be memorable because a young lad from the village was hurt."

"Oh yes, that was in Mother's time. Everybody talked about it."

"What do you know about it?"

"Not much, because I was up in London at secretarial college at the time. Fancied I was going to be a city girl, didn't I? But it wasn't for me. I got so homesick. Anyway, I wasn't here at the time and Mum wasn't at Lake Hall, as I'm sure you'll have found out from her if she was talking any sense, because she'd just had an operation, but I do remember there was a fuss in the newspapers and Mum told me some journalists come to Downsley, but nobody talked to them. You wouldn't have. You stay loyal to your own."

"Does that include the Holts?"

"A lot of people in the village worked for them back then. You couldn't separate our families from theirs."

"What did people say in private?"

"In private, I heard there was talk that one of the men in the shooting party was drunk and did something stupid, but it was just talk. You wouldn't believe what the Holts got up to sometimes, but they did do things properly around the shoots."

"Did you believe the talk?"

"I don't pay any mind to gossip, especially what gets said after a few pints. There's always talk, Detective. I know you know that."

"I do."

One of the bells on the wall jangles sharply. "Hear that?" Anthea says. "That'll be her wanting something. I'd better be getting on if you don't mind. She won't want me talking to you, so best you don't mention I did if you come back here."

"One more quick question," Maxine says. "We heard there was a nanny who used to work here. Name of Hannah. She disappeared quite abruptly, I believe?"

"You don't need to be a detective to know that skull doesn't belong to Hannah Burgess!" Anthea says. She has a surprisingly loud laugh. "I have to admit it crossed my mind when they found it, because she's the only person disappeared suddenly around here, but it wasn't on my mind for long, nor anybody else's, because I heard Hannah's back in Downsley. She's even been round here apparently, not that I've seen her myself yet. Not everyone will be happy about her coming back, mind you. People used to say she thought she was above them. Coincidence she's back now, isn't it? I wonder if she's seen the piece in the paper about the skull. The village shop ran out of copies that day, you know."

The bell jangles more frantically than before.

"We'll get out from under your feet," Andy says. "Thank you for the cake. It was delicious."

In the car, Maxine says, "Next time we call first so we can actually talk to Lady Holt."

"I know." Andy cracks his fingers. "But it was an interesting chat. Anthea's not a happy camper, is she? Not that I'm surprised. But at least we won't be chasing down the nanny."

He remembers the photograph of her he saw in the newspaper, how different she looked from the Holts.

"We should talk to her if she's back here," Maxine says.

"Agreed. I bet she's got some dirt on them, especially if she had a crush on Lord Holt."

"Maybe it's nothing to do with them. Maybe the bloody gardener dumped someone in the lake."

"It's them," he says. "It feels like it's them because it's so bloody brazen."

"That's why I think it can't be. Who could stand to stare at the lake every day knowing what was in there?"

"They're not like us."

He turns on the ignition and puts his foot down. The tires spit gravel as the car pulls away.

JO

AT WORK, I HELP CLEMENCY unpack the vanitas in a private viewing room hidden at the back of the gallery. We spend a long time tweaking the lighting to show the painting off to best effect. As we work, I make an effort to try to get to know Clemency, but she shuts down my efforts politely and consistently until I reach the point where I wonder if she has a problem with my working here.

When the painting is ready, we both take a moment to admire it.

"Carpe diem," I say.

"What?"

"Seize the day. The message is loud and clear, don't you think?" I gesture toward the painting.

"I'm not paid to think," she says, and I wish I'd kept my mouth shut.

Faversham insists on taking me out to lunch to celebrate my first day. At the restaurant we're warmly greeted by the maître d', who obviously knows him. The decor is florid. A richly patterned carpet and velvet banquettes saturate the dining rooms with hues of gold and crimson, reminding me of decadent papal robes in centuries-old portraits. The white tablecloths are crisply starched and hang from the edges of the tables in extravagantly long folds.

Faversham orders oysters, followed by grouse for us both. "While it's in season," he says.

There's something I've been dying to ask him since our last conversation. "How well did you know my father?"

"Very well! We were at Eton together and went up to Oxford at the same time. He was at Queen's and I was at Balliol, but we were in some of the same societies, so we remained close and saw quite a lot of each other in town after graduating." By *town*, he means London, I think. Perhaps the City felt like a small town if you moved in their circles. They probably rarely left Mayfair.

"No, thank you, just pour," Faversham says to a waiter who displays a bottle of wine and offers to let him taste it. "I didn't see Alexander so much after he married your mother, of course, but she let him off the leash now and then."

"What exactly did he do?"

"Don't you know?"

"I know he worked in the City and he was the social secretary for the Burlington Club, but I don't know what any of it entailed."

When I eventually cracked and read Daddy's obituaries online, I was surprised to find there were some things I didn't know about him, including his position at the club. When I questioned my mother about it, she refused to discuss it. "He worked hard and played hard" was all she would say.

One of Faversham's eyebrows arches elegantly and he scrapes the underside of his chin with two fingernails. He unfolds his napkin and places it on his knee. "Do you like the vanitas?" he asks.

"It's exquisite."

"Do you remember what's in the lower right-hand corner of the painting?"

I try to visualize it. I see the skull, its teeth like broken shards of masonry, and a small bunch of grapes, lightly dusted with mold. There are some fallen petals curled at the edges and—of course!—a deck of cards in disarray, the five of hearts visible on top of the pile.

"Playing cards?" I say to Faversham. It sort of makes sense if he means my father had a high-stakes job in the City. Alexander

Holt certainly wasn't the type to have a boring job. He was a risk taker, everybody's hero, everybody's favorite. He would have had a job to match his status. "Your father is my priority," my mother said to me once. It made sense to me, even though it was hurtful. It reinforced my idea of him.

Faversham dabs his mouth with his napkin. "Darling," he says. The tease has gone out of his eyes and there might be something in them I don't wish to see: sympathy. "Your daddy was a professional gambler."

"What?"

"He discovered he was good at it at Oxford."

"I know he played. He and his friends gambled at home sometimes, but I didn't know he did it professionally. Really?"

I picture the square table at one end of the Blue Room, a length of baize rolled out and draped over it. After dinner, the chairs around it would fill with my father and his friends, dressed beautifully, and the baize would host decks of cards, heavy ashtrays, and cut-glass tumblers. My mother never joined in. She would perch in front of the fire, on the edge of the ottoman, smoking and watching.

Did a lot of money change hands at those games? It never occurred to me, because I never saw any. I remember one guest driving off into the night after a furious row, but I didn't link the two. I childishly assumed the adults played cards for the same reason Hannah and I played Happy Families or Snap: for fun.

"Look," Faversham says, "your father was employed by a high-end gambling club in Mayfair in order to help them attract a certain clientele. Clubs like the Burlington were struggling for money by the mid-seventies. They were no longer the exclusive preserve of the aristocracy because a lot of those people were flat broke, even if they weren't admitting it. The clubs needed the wealthy Arabs and the oil money they were bringing into the City as much as the government did. Your father was employed to be present at the club to host the new clientele—to entice them there, if you like. He wasn't the only one of our generation who did it, but he was the best at it. People like him, real lords, gave the illusion the old world was still functioning."

"My father was window dressing?" I feel a crushing disappointment.

"No. He was better than that. Like I said, he was very good at what he did. Oh, dear, I've upset you, Jocelyn. Please forgive me. It wasn't my intention to diminish Alexander. I thought you were aware of most of this."

"I'm sorry. I'm not upset by what you've said." It's a lie. My mind is racing as it rewrites what I thought I knew about my parents. I'm so tempted to ask Faversham more, but I daren't expose my ignorance. "It doesn't matter to me what he did, I just regret that I was so distant from him when he died."

"He regretted it, too, my dear. Very much."

Our food arrives and I take the opportunity to change the subject. "Why doesn't the Burlington Club send the vanitas to auction? Why do they want us to sell it?"

"I let them know that I already have interest from a potential buyer who has deep pockets."

His reply doesn't quite answer my question because an auction would give the club access to a number of buyers with deep pockets. He sees my frown.

"A discreet private sale has other benefits, as I'm sure you understand. The club won't want people to think they're strapped for cash and selling off their assets. It doesn't look good."

Faversham clearly hasn't wasted any time working his contacts, not that I'm complaining. The sooner the painting sells, the sooner I'll get paid. I raise my glass of wine. "To a successful sale. I look forward to meeting the buyer."

"And he's looking forward to meeting you," he says. "Chin-chin."

I keep a smile on my face and my tone of voice light, but I can't help feeling dirtied by our conversation and queasily oppressed by our surroundings. The glowing brass fixtures, the carefully placed mirrors reflecting reflections, and the trompe l'oeil murals all seem designed to confuse reality.

We started lunch late and Faversham insists on having three courses, so I don't check my phone until just after four P.M., when we leave the restaurant.

All hell has broken loose. My screen is filled with notifications of missed calls and frantic texts from Stan's mother. The first says:

Kids weren't at school when I got there to pick them up. Not answering their phones. Call me.

She sent it at 3:07 P.M.

I can taste my fear. I scroll frantically through the texts looking for the one telling me they're okay.

1978–79

IT DOESN'T TAKE LINDA LONG *to get used to calling herself Hannah, and Jean helps. Linda loves her new name. Hannah Burgess sounds much more special than Linda Taylor. There weren't any other Hannahs when she was at school, but she was one of three Lindas in her class.*

Hannah and Jean rent a room in a crumbling hostel in Montpelier in Bristol. Jean gets a job sweeping trimmings at a hair salon on a street where the buildings are painted in all the colors of the rainbow. One Saturday she goes to Woolworths and steals two of the brass curtain rings they stock for unmarried mothers to wear. "Let's pretend we're married when we go out," she says. At the pub, Hannah loves the role-play and flashing her ring finger at hungry male eyes, but Jean gets bored quickly and slips her ring off.

Hannah toys with the idea of trying to pass herself off as a Norland nanny when she looks for work, but decides it's too risky. She places an ad in the local rag:

EXPERIENCED NANNY NEW TO THE AREA LOOKING FOR
FULL-TIME WORK. REFERENCES ON REQUEST.

The phone in the hostel hallway rings that night. "I saw your advert," the man says. "My wife and I are artists and we have two feral sons. We need help."

Hannah is pleased when she turns up at their address. It's a huge house on the edge of Clifton Down, with stained glass in the hallway.

The boys are long-haired, argumentative, and undisciplined, but the room on offer is lovely, the pay is good, and Hannah is getting tired of sharing with Jean.

Jean has become increasingly needy since they moved. Hannah despises her friend's lack of motivation, whining, and petty jealousies. The room they share is too small, and the friendship is beginning to feel claustrophobic. Hannah finds it harder and harder to stop herself snapping at Jean, but she knows she must be careful. Jean is the only person who knows Hannah's real identity, and that's something Hannah doesn't want broadcast.

This job will give her the escape she needs.

Another plus is that the parents seem far too chaotic to follow up on references with any sort of attention to detail. Hannah reckons the letter she's doctored will suffice.

"I would love to accept the position," she tells them.

"Thank God!" the mother says. She bows her head in mock relief, and the silky ends of her headscarf pick up crumbs from the surface of the kitchen table.

"Sod tea, then!" the father says. He pushes their mugs aside and grabs a bottle of wine and three glasses. It's quite a fabulous thing to do, Hannah thinks, very racy. His shirt rises up as he reaches for the glasses. He's lean as a board and there's a line of black hair on his navel that disappears under the waistband of his jeans. She tries not to stare. He fills their glasses generously.

The wife is talkative and friendly, but Hannah doesn't approve of the way her blouse is undone, showing off the deep trough between her braless bosoms so even her boys can see it.

"You won't see much of me during the day," the wife says. "My studio is at the end of the garden. I adore it. It's so important for me to have space outside the house so I can eschew the domestic and concentrate on my work."

Best place for you, *Hannah thinks.* You can rot there with the compost.

"It's me who'll be under your feet," the husband says. "I work upstairs. But I prefer it. I'd go mad shut up on my own all day, and I like to hear the boys. Don't I, you monkeys?" He leaps up and fakeattacks the boys, chasing them from the room.

"Welcome to the family," the wife says and raises her glass. Hannah moves to chink her glass against it, but the wife doesn't notice and gulps down all her wine. "Right!" she says. She refills her glass to the brim. "Back to work! See you tomorrow?"

Hannah is left alone. She stands up. She's never had wine before. It's made her a bit tipsy. The younger boy appears in the doorway.

"My mummy's famous," he says.

"Is she now?" Hannah says. "I expect she's very busy, then?"

He nods. He looks shattered. He should be in bed by now, she thinks. These parents don't know what they're doing. Nanny Hughes would be appalled.

"Would you like me to read you a story?" she asks.

He curls up beside her on the sofa and puts his thumb in his mouth. The soles of his feet are dirty and his fingernails need cutting. She'll make sure he gets a bath before bed tomorrow. As she reads, she smells weed coming from a room upstairs. Neither parent reappears. The boy falls asleep before she gets to the last page.

HANNAH AND *Jean drift apart after Hannah takes the new job. It happens over a man. Jean falls hard for Arthur Wagoner. He's a clever, tense man who works at Rolls-Royce in Filton. Jean says he is going places. She tells Hannah she dreams of living in a brand-new home in Stoke Bishop with him. Jean wants Arthur badly, but when Hannah's introduced to him, she doesn't like the way Arthur makes Jean pay her way at the pub. It isn't the behavior of a gentleman. Hannah goes to their wedding and thinks Jean looked very thin in her knock-off Chloé dress. Next time she sees Jean, Hannah has to pay for their tea because Jean has run out of housekeeping money. Jean talks incessantly about her and Arthur's struggles to get pregnant, and Hannah notices the yellow shadow of a black eye under her concealer. It's an uncomfortable meeting.*

Soon after, Hannah gets a letter from Jean saying Arthur has a new job and they're moving to Surrey and hoping to start a new life there. Rather you than me, Hannah thinks. She finds she doesn't miss Jean at all.

At work, Hannah has her own challenges. She learns that the brothers need handling differently.

The younger boy, now five, is a pushover. He craves affection. After a year in the job, she must have run her fingers through his tousled hair hundreds of times, and the feel of his hand in hers is as familiar as her own little brother's was. She has a soft spot for him; she finds him so very malleable. The older boy, Peter, is more wary and not nearly as straightforward as his sibling.

Peter doesn't like Hannah right from the start. He makes her life difficult. To begin with, Hannah follows all of Nanny Hughes's strategies to win him over, but none of them work. Hannah never saw Nanny Hughes working with older children, so she thinks she should probably develop some strategies of her own. She decides to fight fire with fire: she tells a few lies about Peter's misbehaving to his parents, informing them that she has caught him lying on more than one occasion. They believe her. She has made herself indispensable by now. They let her decide what Peter's punishment should be. Being confined to his room works at first, but after a while it just seems to stoke his sullenness. She has to get more inventive. She confiscates some of his favorite things and bans him from watching the television.

When those measures fail to make Peter compliant, one day Hannah does what she's been itching to do for months: she pinches him. It's how she used to deal with her younger siblings. Hannah knows not to pinch hard enough to leave a big bruise. In the house she grew up in, you needed deniability, and she needs it here, too. She knows the most sensitive areas to target. The look of shock on Peter's face is priceless.

He tells on her, of course. His father is at the pub, so Peter runs out through the garden to his mother's studio. Hannah watches from the house, sees the white soles of his little feet as he crosses the garden and slams through the studio door. Not allowed. The mother asks everybody to knock before entering, and to do so only if it's an emergency. Hannah imagines Peter in there, red-faced, outraged, telling his tale of being pinched. He has such a strong sense of right and wrong, that boy. He is appalled by injustice. She imagines his mother's reaction. She will be addled from wine by now and bleary-eyed from staring at her ugly paintings. She will rear up from her daybed and say, "Fuck off, darling. Hannah would never do that."

Hannah is standing at the kitchen sink when Peter comes back inside. He looks like a kicked dog.

"Come here, please," she says.

He approaches, his head hanging. "Look at Hannah," she says. She puts a finger underneath his chin and lifts it until she can see the tendons stretched in his neck. His eyes slide to the side.

"Look . . . at . . . me," she repeats. With her other hand she finds a pinch of skin just under his armpit. She squeezes. His eyes meet hers. So much hatred.

"It's very simple, Peter," she says. "Naughty boys get what they deserve. If you behave, I won't hurt you. You have to accept that your mother does not want to care for you properly, and it's my authority that counts. Now go to your room. It's bedtime."

Later that night the husband arrives home as Hannah is heading upstairs with a cup of tea. She's wearing only a large man's shirt. She took it from a drawer in the house in Leeds before she left. His drawer. It is a reminder. Just like the two little porcelain kittens she has in her bedroom. She took those from the babies' room.

The look in the husband's eye is hungry, wolfish. He stares hard at her legs. His gaze moves slowly, deliberately upward, and she can tell he's savoring the feeling of imagining what's beneath the shirt. The answering tug inside her is powerful.

"Have I shown you what I'm working on at the moment?" he asks. He tries to sound jocular, but desire gives the sentence a thicker sound and a more dangerous inflection. She doesn't answer. She continues up the stairs and onto the landing. She hears him follow. To walk past his studio and onward to her bedroom, where the key can be easily turned in the lock before he reaches her, or not?

She reaches for the door handle flecked with paint. The studio is dark. Outside, through the skylight, Hannah can see the wife lying prone on the daybed in her studio at the end of the garden. All wined out. He doesn't turn the light on. He stands close behind her. Not touching. Not sure, suddenly? She turns and kisses him, just a grazing of the lips, a drawn-in breath.

"God, I've wanted to do this for so long," he says. It feels electric, that moment, and she thinks—hopes—he's too drunk to notice she's a virgin.

JO

THE TEXTS FROM STAN'S MUM are a real-time record of forty-five minutes of undiluted panic as she tries to find Ruby and Stan. My heart pounds as I read through them, even though I've already seen the one that simply says:

Found them. They are fine.

This was followed by another saying:

Call me.

Then:

You should know that Stan and Ruby took the school bus back to Lake Hall together. They somehow persuaded the bus driver to let them both on—goodness knows how—and when they turned up there NOBODY CALLED ME, and when I finally worked out where they were and turned up to collect Stan, they were unsupervised and GETTING OUT A KAYAK BESIDE THE LAKE WHERE A DEAD BODY WAS ONLY RECENTLY DRAGGED UP.

Her next text simply says:

Does your family have no boundaries?

I feel so ashamed. I call her. She sounds calmer but not much. I keep it simple and tell her I'm on my way now and am unbelievably sorry this happened and I will speak to everybody involved and phone her back once I've got to the bottom of it. Her response is frosty.

On the concourse of Paddington Station I try to speak to Ruby, Anthea, and Mother. As the train announcements drone in one ear, Ruby sobs and explains into the other. "We weren't going to take the kayak on the lake," she says, "we were only going to sit in it on the shore. I'm not *stupid*." I ask her to put Anthea on. Anthea tells me the convoluted and sorry order of events with muted fury and lays the blame firmly at Mother's door. Finally Mother says, "It's just a simple misunderstanding. Stanley's mother completely overreacted, and rather rudely, I might say. She shouted at poor Anthea, but it wasn't Anthea's fault because I didn't give her the message. The children were in no danger whatsoever."

The platform number for my train is announced and people begin to swarm toward it.

"I'll deal with this when I get home," I say. "Try and keep Ruby safe until then!"

WHEN I finally get home, I find Anthea sitting in the hall with her coat on and her bag beside her.

"You needn't have waited."

"I need to tell my side of things. I won't be blamed for this." She roughly wipes away a tear.

"Nobody's blaming you. I'm listening. What happened?"

"Nobody told me Ruby wasn't supposed to come back here. I met the children at the bus like you asked me to. Obviously I wasn't expecting Stan, but Ruby told me bold as brass that he'd texted his mum, who said it was okay, and he's nodding away beside her, so I believed them. Of course I would have phoned if I thought they were where they shouldn't be, but your mother never gave me the message they weren't coming here. And Ruby shouldn't have lied to me! It's not good enough asking me to take this extra responsibility on. It's bad enough defending your family in the village. Do you know what they're saying about the skull? People ask me about it all the time and I'm fed up. Picking up the pieces for you people is not my job."

"You're right. I'm so sorry." My heart sinks because this is partly my fault. I forgot to phone back to check Anthea had got my text message this morning.

"It's too much responsibility for me, looking after your mother and Ruby, too. And the police coming round here. I don't have time to do my normal job as it is."

"I'm really sorry. I'll make sure this never happens again."

I see Ruby lurking on the landing. "Come here," I say.

She throws her arms around me and buries her head in my neck. "What happened, Ruby? Why didn't you go to Stan's house? And how come the driver let you on the bus?"

Words spill from her so fast I can hardly keep up. "My name was on the bus list and Stan's wasn't, but Stan told the driver he was coming with me and the driver was new last term, so he thought it was okay because he knows Stan and Stan used to get the bus on Tuesdays, and he checked Stan got off with me and Anthea met us and Stan's mum was late anyway, so she wasn't even there and he texted his mum to say what we were doing but she never got it."

Another failure on my part. Instead of leaving it to Anthea, I should have phoned the school myself and told them Ruby's plans had changed so her name wasn't on the bus list. I bite my tongue to stop myself saying that this would never have happened in California where the school bus service is so much more organized. Only in Downsley, where everybody thinks they know everybody else.

"And the kayak? Tell me the truth."

"We only wanted to sit in it, I promise, but Stan's mum was really mad at me. She shouted really loudly."

She starts to cry and Anthea sniffs loudly, too. I don't know who to give my attention to.

"Anthea," I say, "I hear what you said and I'm so sorry you were blamed. It was unfair. Why don't you go on home and we'll talk tomorrow when everybody has calmed down?"

"I can't carry on like this. It's too much. Your mother needs more help than I can give her in the house, and that's when she's healthy."

"I understand. Perhaps it's better if we talk about it on Friday when I have a day off? Please? I could take you to lunch. Your help means so much to us all. I want you to be happy."

"I can't. I have my own mother to look after. It's not easy. It might be best if I say my goodbyes."

"I understand," I say. "But please don't decide anything tonight. Sleep on it."

She's too upset to say anything more, and when she walks to the door, I hold it open for her to leave. The tearful nod she gives me is horribly final. "I'll write to Lady Holt and explain," she says. "I don't want to leave her in the lurch, but there's only so much I can take."

"Ruby," I say once the door has shut behind Anthea, "lots of little things went wrong this afternoon. It's everybody and nobody's fault, but you must not change plans without clearing it with me. And you must not lie. Ever. Do you promise?"

"I promise. Stan's mum said he couldn't come here again."

"She was angry. I'm sure she'll think differently when she calms down."

"She won't. She was shouting."

"I'm sure she will."

"And people at school said I was a zombie that came out of the lake and that we murder people and throw them in there."

"Oh, sweetie. That's rough, but it's silly talk, you know that, don't you? I'm sure they won't be like that tomorrow. Okay? So I need you to stay down here while I talk to Granny. Put the TV on if you like."

I open the door to Mother's room, but it's dark inside. She's asleep. Or pretending to be. I creep back out into the corridor. Ruby gives me a fright.

"I hate it here!" she says.

I fold her into my arms. "This will all feel better in the morning," I say. "And I promise I will move us out of here as soon as I can. I promise you that. But we need to be brave right now because we need to make the best of things."

"If we move away," she says, "I want Granny to come, too, or she'll be lonely on her own."

I squeeze her tighter and hope it feels like love, unlike the band around my own chest, which feels like suffocation.

Later that night, when I can't sleep because it's all running around my mind too much, I check the Facebook page the mums in Ruby's class have set up.

A post from Stan's mum makes my heart sink.

URGENT. We need to review all arrangements for playdates after school. A system for informing school needs to be in place so we don't get scared out of our wits if other parents and/or the school bus driver are irresponsible.

It could be worse, and at least she doesn't name us, but I dread to think how many private messages she's got in response, asking what happened.

One thing I do know is that I have to make different arrangements for childcare, and the only thing stopping me feeling totally desolate tonight is that I think I'm going to follow my own advice to be brave and ask Hannah if she can help.

VIRGINIA

I OPEN MY EYES ONCE I'm sure Jocelyn has left the room. I can't stand to lie here and suffer the recriminations she surely would have flung at me.

In the end, no harm was done today. Ruby would not have gone out on the lake. She is too bright and sensible to have done such a thing. She adores her friend. The whole performance with the school bus was a simple mix-up. Today's parents are so terribly anxious.

My head aches, and pain grips like bony fingers in my neck and back when I move. It was perhaps too soon to ease off the heavy-duty painkillers, but I am determined. I turn onto my side with difficulty. Alexander watches me from the framed black-and-white photograph on my bedside table. How I wish he were here. I wish it with every tired, hurting bone in my body. The responsibility of keeping all our secrets alone is as painful and difficult to bear as my injuries.

I lie in a half state, neither awake nor asleep. Memories glow and fade like fireflies: parties, holidays, quiet times, moments of intimacy. These pretty memories feel like an indulgence before the inevitable moment when my thoughts turn sour and frightening.

When she was a child, our daughter belonged to another woman. This burden was heavier than a millstone around my neck. It broke me.

It was a Saturday night. We invited six guests to dinner. They arrived in the afternoon, so the drinking started early and the lines of coke came out before supper. I didn't partake. I didn't like to feel drunk or out of control ever, a result of years of habit in-grained as I watched Alexander at the card tables. One of us had to remain cautious, though much good it did us in the end. He found plenty of ways to gamble behind my back.

That weekend I stayed sober and insisted drugs be done behind closed doors. We had a child in the house, after all. I let the day staff go before dinner. I never minded serving guests myself, if it meant we gained our privacy. Walls have ears, after all.

Hannah stayed, of course. She was always there. She barely even took her days off. Her job was to keep Jocelyn entertained. Late afternoon, when our guests were already red-cheeked and very jolly, I asked Hannah to dress Jocelyn and bring her down a little earlier than planned, to meet everybody before the evening progressed any further.

I had picked out a dress for Jocelyn to wear. "She doesn't need to stay downstairs for long," I told Hannah. "A quick hello will suf-fice, and you can take her back to the nursery." I wanted Jocelyn to enjoy the moment. I loved to meet my parents' friends when I was a girl. It was special to come down in a nice dress and do a twirl and be allowed to try the tiniest sip of champagne.

I was also running out of things to offer Jocelyn that might please her—and goodness knows, I had tried everything I could think of over the years—so this was one of my last-ditch attempts.

"Of course, Lady Holt," Hannah said.

Now I wonder how she felt every time she answered so benignly. If she was reaching a peak of frustration of her own, it didn't show. Not yet.

I hear a phone ring. Not the landline. A mobile. A dull murmur as Jocelyn answers. She must be on the landing. I try to sit up. It is half past ten. Who calls at such an hour? Perhaps she is talking to somebody in California.

She says, "Hannah! Thanks so much for phoning me back. I'm so sorry it's late, but I'm in a bit of a fix because I think Anthea is going to leave and I didn't know who else to . . ." Her voice is cut off by the sound of her bedroom door closing.

I feel as if I've been punched in the stomach. Anthea is going and Jocelyn is going to invite Hannah back into our home. *Of course she is.* Where else would she turn for help looking after Ruby?

I glance at the containers of medication on my bedside table, Alexander's face staring from the photograph beside them. I could take them all and join him wherever he is. It's tempting, but I've protected my daughter for so long that I will not give up now.

We gave Jocelyn one of my pills on the night of the party. It was all we could think to do. We gave her a pill and hoped for the best.

"She's asleep," Alexander said when he came out of her bedroom. He looked like a man on the very brink of insanity.

"What did she see?"

He couldn't answer. He shook like a dog on its way to the vet. I held his head between my hands and steadied it, seeking eye contact, but he couldn't look at me. I slapped his cheek. "What did she see?" I shouted, though I shouldn't have. It could have been the thing that undid us. He put his hand gently over my mouth.

"Shh," he said. "It's okay, she's asleep." His pupils were pinpricks. Sweat stood out on his temples. The attic corridor seemed to close in around us.

While we talked, Hannah lay on the back stairs. Blood pooled beneath her head and matted her hair. Her eyes were shut and I was glad about that.

"Get a blanket," I said.

We rolled her in it and trussed her up like a joint, using the hand rope that had detached from the staircase wall when she grabbed at it. We carried her down the back stairs. I had her feet.

One of her shoes fell off and clattered down the steps, and her head lolled horribly against Alexander's chest. We took her body into the courtyard behind the kitchen and shut it in the coal bunker.

"We can't leave her there," Alexander said.

"We have to for now. We'll deal with it later. Go in, change your shirt, you've got coal dust and . . ." I didn't want to say *blood*, but it was smeared across him. "Speak to the guests. Tell them Jocelyn's not well and she vomited on you, but the nanny and I are looking after her. I'll join you as quickly as I can."

"We have to clean up the blood."

"That's what I'm going to do."

I climbed back up to the attic. I checked my clothes. They were immaculate, thank God. I took my dress and my stockings off, and got towels from the bathroom and shampoo. Jocelyn's fouled dress was on the floor, still reeking. Crouched in my underwear, I scrubbed the steps. I worked as quickly and soundlessly as I possibly could. When I reached the top I could see Jocelyn's bedroom door. She must not wake up. I stuffed the bloodied towels and Jocelyn's dress into the laundry bag in the bathroom and stood in the bath and washed myself with the shower attachment. The water was cold and I gasped, but it felt like punishment and it steadied me and reminded me to hold my nerve.

My breathing was calmer as I pulled my underwear and stockings back on and slipped my dress over my head. I looked at myself in the cracked mirror and took a deep breath. Alexander and I had committed to a course of action. There was no going back now.

Jocelyn's door was still shut when I left the bathroom. I opened it a fraction and peered in. She was a motionless shape in the bed. So small and vulnerable, such a little soul. It terrified me that I had no idea what was in her head now. What she might have seen and would not be able to un-see.

I walked down the stairs slowly and carefully. They were spotless. The rope handrail would have to be replaced. I put the laundry bag containing the bloodied towels and the dress in a dark corner beside the coal hamper. I couldn't bear to open it and look at the body.

The night was unseasonably warm, but I could feel a breeze coming off the lake. Light from the windows poured into the darkness. I needed to go back inside.

"Ginny! How is the little sick one?" Milla tripped into the hall as I was touching up my lipstick, her arms outstretched, trying to hug me yards before she reached me, cigarette dangling from fingertips.

"She's okay now. I think she must have eaten something bad. Hannah and I think she just needs to sleep it off."

"I do like Giles," she said. "You clever thing. How did you know I would?"

"Let me see—oh yes, it's coming back to me now. Right physical type, pots of money, recently single. Does that sound like you?"

"Love him already," she said. I had to support most of her weight as we reentered the Blue Room, but to be honest, it was a relief. It disguised the feeling of terrible regret that was threatening to come over me.

Alexander was in the wingback chair, looking out of the window. I hoped he had held it together.

"Dinner?" I said. "Sorry it's late."

Georgie heaved herself up. "God, I thought you'd never ask. I've drunk far too much on an empty stomach already."

Good, I thought. *The drunker, the better.*

Alexander got up as Milla detached herself from me and grabbed Giles's arm.

I watched Alexander approach. It was as if it were just the two of us in the room. There was so much in his eyes that I didn't want anybody else to see. *Come on,* I thought, *pull yourself together. It's too late for anything else now.*

I put my hand to the locket at my neck, the way I used to when I felt he was going too far at the card tables. He noticed. It was our secret signal, though he sometimes ignored it. I nodded to encourage him, hoping it was imperceptible to the others.

"Darling," he said, and as if from nowhere, a smile washed over his face, lightening it, brightening it. *Thank God.* "Will you do me the honor?"

I linked my arm through his. "I'd be delighted."

He placed his hand over mine and I felt the sweat on his palm and thought, *If we just keep going, we might get through this night.*

The memory sends a shudder through me, so violent that it triggers my pain and makes me moan. Once it has finally ebbed away, the thought that seeps into my head in its place is this:

When Jocelyn was a child, Hannah pulled the wool so far down over her eyes that all Jocelyn saw was a beloved nanny: fluffy, sweet, safe. If Jocelyn invites this woman calling herself Hannah into our lives, I cannot say what will happen because that depends on whether she is Hannah or not, and I'm still not sure. All I know for certain is that I feel very afraid.

DETECTIVE ANDY WILTON

ANDY'S PHONE RINGS AS HE'S driving.

Maxine picks up. "It's the lab."

"Can you put them on speakerphone?"

She hits the button.

"Anything to report?" Andy asks. "Or is this a social call?"

"Something to report, but you're not going to like it."

Maxine makes a face.

"What does that mean?" Andy asks.

"We extracted DNA from your Jane Doe, but it wasn't a match to anything in our system."

Andy's heart sinks. "What about a cause of death?"

"The best I can say is that the fracture may have been enough to kill her, but we can't be sure it was the cause of death. It's border-line in terms of the scale of it."

"Plan B?" Maxine asks when the call is over.

"Facial reconstruction. They can do it from the skull."

"How are you going to persuade the boss to pay for that?"

Andy pulls a copy of the local newspaper from the pocket in the car door and hands it to her.

"Page 4. There's another piece about the skull. Nothing speaks to the boss more than public pressure."

She scans the article. "Okay. Not bad. A few column inches," she says. "It might work."

"The story will only get bigger," Andy says, "if we release more information about the skull."

"And combined with the forensic information we have."

"Exactly. It's worth a try, because I'm not ready to let this drop."

JO

ANTHEA DOESN'T COME BACK TO work, but Hannah saves us. Hannah's reappearance in my life feels like the first bit of good fortune I've had for a very long time. When I ask her for short-term help with my childcare disaster, she says she had planned to be fully retired, but if she's honest, she's a little bit bored, so she could help out. Care for Ruby before and after school four days a week will give her just the stimulation she's been looking for but also plenty of free time. This is all provided Ruby likes her, of course, she adds. And she says she'd rather look after Ruby at Lake Hall. "Much more settled for her to be at home."

She named a price that was high, but I agreed to it immediately. I have no choice and I don't want to insult her by bargaining. I'll have to work out how to pay her somehow.

We muddle through the first day after Anthea leaves because Geoff agrees to wait at the school bus stop with Ruby. Hannah takes over on the second day.

I get a text from her as I'm getting off the train.

Ruby got the bus fine. Not happy but not unhappy either. I signed her reading report because I think you forgot. I hope you don't mind. I'm going to stay on a bit at the hall to make sure your mother gets up safely and do you want me to draft an ad for the village shop for another housekeeper? Hxxoo

I feel a huge swell of relief and gratitude. As quickly as everything fell apart, Hannah is making it better.

Thank you so much! That would be amazing. Jxx
Good luck today. Hxxoo

☺

I take a deep breath and let myself believe I might be able to make this job work.

Faversham requests that I join him for tea with the client who is interested in buying the vanitas.

"He wants to see my personal collection," Faversham says. "We share some of the same tastes."

Midafternoon, we walk to Faversham's place. It's an apartment on the first floor of a gracious building ten minutes from Cork Street. We climb to the first floor, and Faversham unlocks the door. Entering the flat is like going back in time. The place smells of cigarette smoke and old-fashioned aftershave.

The drawing room runs across the front of the building. Three tall, gracious windows overlook the street, and a grand black marble fireplace dominates one end of the room. Most striking, though, are the paintings and drawings hung on every wall from floor to ceiling, with barely an inch between their elaborate frames. Each one is of a nude or semi-nude woman, either lying on or draped in sumptuous fabrics. They stare out of the paintings and right at you, coquettish or openly inviting. They embarrass me.

Faversham invites me to sit and takes a seat opposite me, crossing his long legs. Red socks emerge.

"Your father detested my paintings," he says, gesturing at the walls.

"It's an extraordinary collection."

"Yes, I rather agree, but I think Alexander would have preferred a good military scene. Battleships at dawn—gunfire and glory."

"Perhaps. Or a portrait of his dogs."

"True. Yes, that might have been more his bag. He didn't have the Holt connoisseur gene, I think, but you do."

"Thank you." I'm flattered.

"Listen, I want to talk to you because the buyer for the vanitas is twitchy."

"Why?"

"Provenance. He wants proof of previous ownership."

"If the painting belonged to my family then it will be stamped. There'll be an *H* burned onto the back of the frame somewhere."

"It is stamped," Faversham says, "but he's being tiresomely cautious about the whole thing. He's looking for proof of dates when the painting was in your family's collection and proof of where your grandfather acquired it from."

The buzzer drones and Faversham tuts. "He's early."

Faversham greets the buyer flamboyantly and ushers him into the drawing room. Paul Mercier is wearing rimless glasses, an open-necked shirt with an expensive logo, black jeans, and brogues. We shake hands and he holds on to mine for a second or so longer than I would like, until his attention is caught by the paintings.

"Exceptional!" he says.

Faversham grins like a kid in a sweetshop. I stand a few paces behind them as Paul scrutinizes the paintings. I try to look professional but I feel uncomfortable.

"Can I ask what draws you to the vanitas?" I ask Paul. "It's so different from what I gather makes up the bulk of your collection."

I feel as if his gaze is pinning me to my chair and peeling the clothes from me. "What are the certainties in life?" he asks.

"Death and taxes, or so I've heard."

"Taxes are boring, but you're right about death. I'm surprised you don't mention love."

"Love is not a certainty."

"It's not a certainty that we will find love, but it's a certainty that we all want it, isn't it?"

"True."

"I already possess a large number of paintings which represent love. Like these. So I thought it might be interesting to go to the other end of the spectrum and collect on the theme of death."

I want to say: *Carnality isn't love. And amorous love is not the only kind of love.* But I don't. I am here to sell, so instead I say, "That's fascinating. Will this be the first vanitas you've bought?"

"The second; I bought one by Edward Collier a few months ago."

"What a fantastic choice." He must have very deep pockets.

"I gather the vanitas used to belong to your family."

"That's right. It was much loved by us all." I assume it was, anyhow. No harm for him to believe this.

"I heard everything in the Holt Collection was recorded in a catalogue of some sort?"

"Ah," Faversham says, "I'm afraid the Holt Catalogue no longer exists."

"What do you mean?"

"Some years ago my father put the catalogue in storage while his study was being decorated," I say, "and the storage area was flooded. The catalogue was destroyed. I'm so sorry you didn't know."

"I'm disappointed."

"I'm sorry. It was a great loss to our family."

"But you can get the photograph?"

I have no idea what he's talking about. Faversham clears his throat. "I was telling Paul that your father once mentioned to me that there was a photograph of you in front of the vanitas, taken when you were a child. Do you have any recollection of that? If we could find it, it would pinpoint at least one year when the painting was part of the Holt Collection."

"I don't recall it, I'm afraid."

"Could you ask your mother?"

"Of course. If it exists, we'll find it."

ON MY way home I read a flurry of texts from Hannah. They are wildly different from the ones I received from Stan's mum.

> Ruby safely home. She had a tumble when we got home (trying to climb the orchard wall again) & grazed both knees but otherwise fine. She's doing her homework now. Then we're going to bake brownies.

> I heard in the village Lottie Roberts from Mill Cottage is looking for work. I thought she might come for a trial as housekeeper? At least it'll help tide things over until we can find somebody you're happy with permanently. A permanent hire might take time because from what I've heard in the village not everybody is willing to work at the house with the situation with the police.

> We've had supper but your mother was sleepy, so I'll stay with Ruby until you're home. I think she should be supervised.

I reply that I'm happy with all that, and then text Ruby.

> How are you doing? How was school?
> *Fine.*
> I heard you hurt your knees
> *Only a bit. Hannah made a fuss. She said I wasn't big enough to climb the wall*
> If you fell, then she's right. Be safe!

*I literally just tripped when I was getting down off it. I can climb to
the top and walk along it fine. I've done it loads of times*
You have to be safe! It's a big wall. Keep away from it, please

I wait for a reply but none comes and I can picture her stubborn
expression if I pursue this now. I try another tack.

What else did you do at school?
Not much but I got a star for my English work.
Well done! Do you want a penguin, too?
Yes
🐧 xxxxxxxxx I'm on the train so c u soon xx

I sit back and close my eyes. The big question on my mind now
is how long I can keep paying Hannah to help if I don't make my
commission soon. She is not cheap, nor should she be, but I have to
work it out, because already I don't know how I'll cope without her.

VIRGINIA

MY LIFE WITH ALEXANDER STARTED for real the day he proposed to me, but it wasn't in the slightest bit romantic. He said, "So how about it, Ginny?"

"How about what?" We were in his flat in London, packing for my first visit to Lake Hall. My bag was stuffed with too many clothes. I was desperate to make the right impression.

Alexander jumped onto his side of the bed. We'd been seeing each other for a few months and I hadn't tired of him one little bit. We were mad for each other in all the ways you can be.

"Marry me," he said. "Will you?"

"Why should I?" I answered flippantly because I wasn't sure how serious he was.

He traveled across the bed on his knees, shoving my suitcase out of the way and onto the floor where my carefully packed clothes scattered everywhere. He was grinning. Everything he did was so intense. *He's definitely joking*, I thought. Part of me was relieved and part desperately disappointed.

Alexander reached into his back pocket and produced a small box. He held it between us and opened it. Inside, nestled in dark green silk, was a platinum ring with a single large diamond set in it.

"It was my grandmother's ring," he said. "She told me to give it only to the girl I truly love."

The moment felt so huge that I felt afraid of the ring. I could hardly bring myself to touch it. Alexander lifted it from the box and eased it onto my trembling finger. It fit. "Marry me?" he asked again, and this time there was no mistaking he was deadly serious.

"Yes," I said and I thought, *Don't hurt me,* because I knew he could.

Alexander studied my face intently. "That's why I want you," he said. "Because you're no pushover."

By the time we were well on our way to Wiltshire in the car, he had become flippant again. "I'm hoping Mummy will let us share a bedroom tonight if we're engaged," he said.

"Is that the only reason you proposed?"

"Naturally."

So it was that the first time I arrived at Lake Hall I was already engaged to be married to Lord Alexander Holt, and I knew the house would be mine one day.

How did I feel when I saw Lake Hall coming in and out of view as the windshield wipers worked at top speed to clear the rain? It was so different from the home I grew up in. I spent my childhood in a small but pretty manor house with whitewashed outbuildings in a wild place near Dartmoor, where purple heather tinted the broad horizon outside and books and warm chaos filled every room inside. Lake Hall intimidated me, and I felt an immediate sense of obligation, too. I sensed the loss of a thousand freedoms. I wasn't sure I was up to the task of being the future Lady Holt.

Alexander reassured me. "Don't worry," he said. "You'll take to it like a duck to water."

I suppose I did. I will see this house taken from me over my dead body.

THE WOMAN who calls herself Hannah is in my home, and she sounds just as Hannah used to. Every cadence of her speech is familiar to me as she bustles around chivying Ruby into her school uniform, giving her breakfast, checking that her bag is packed. What differs from my memories of how Hannah and Jocelyn were together is the way Ruby responds to her.

When Hannah says, "Eggs or muesli for breakfast?" Ruby says, "Porridge." No *please,* no *thank you,* just "porridge," articulated with dull sullenness. My Ruby keeps this behavior up for the entire hour Hannah spends with her. So far as I can hear—and you can hear more than you think if you lurk on the landing because sound travels in unexpected ways in Lake Hall—not one bright word leaves Ruby's lips.

I watch from Jocelyn's bedroom window when they depart for school. Ruby drags her backpack across the gravel until a word from Hannah makes her pick it up. When Hannah gets into the car, Ruby puts her backpack down and runs to the orchard wall. She scales it as nimbly as a mountain goat and starts to walk along the top, arms spread wide. Hannah's face is thunderous when she gets back out of the car to admonish Ruby. In return, Ruby gives her a look like daggers and walks slowly to the point where the wall slopes down a little. She steps carefully onto a ledge set into the wall and jumps from there to the ground. She lands safely, dust from the stones rising from her hands when she claps them together. She picks up her backpack and gets into the car with a triumphant look on her face.

That's my girl, I think. *Don't let them get you down.* I don't think Ruby likes this woman. Could it be that, unlike her mother, she senses trouble? Some children can be very perceptive.

Almost an hour after they've left, I hear a car, followed by the front door opening and shutting. I make my way to the window to check who it is and see the little car we've lent Hannah back in its space. She shouldn't be here when Ruby's not. That wasn't the arrangement Jocelyn made with her. I go downstairs. It's not easy because I'm still suffering moments of dizziness.

I find her in Alexander's study, and I'm pleased to see I startle her.

"Lady Holt!" she says. "Shouldn't you be in bed? You look cold."

This is the first time I get a good look at her close up. There are strong resemblances to Hannah in the eyes and the shape of the face, but is it her? It's impossible to be sure. We all metamorphose over thirty years.

"What are you doing in here? What's that in your hand?"

"This? It was on the floor." She's holding a silver letter opener with a sharp point. It was a present from me to Alexander.

"It's my husband's. Put it down."

"It *was* Alexander's," she says. "I know. But somebody has been absent-minded and left it on the floor. Was it Ruby, do you think? She's a careless child, I can see that already. This could do someone some harm if they were to slip on it." She places the letter opener on the desk with deliberate care.

"You are not to come in here without my permission. You shouldn't be in this house when Ruby is not."

"And you are not to speak to me like that."

"I beg your pardon?"

"You heard me."

She jostles me deliberately as she leaves the room, and I have to steady myself on the doorframe, trying to stay calm, although my breathing becomes rapid. I cling onto the furniture as I make my way to the safety of Alexander's wingback armchair and sink into it.

The game has begun, I think, and escalated quicker than I imagined. I do not have the advantage. She is in my home. She is contemptuous of me and not averse to insinuating that she might be dangerous. I still don't know if she is who she says she is.

I think about what I discovered on the Internet: that against the odds, it can be possible to fall into water and survive if you're unconscious because the shock of the cold water can revive you. The odds are vanishingly small, but that doesn't mean you can't be the lucky one. That's what they play for at the card tables and roulette wheel, after all.

Did I not check her pulse correctly as she lay on the stairs? Did I make a mistake in the heat of the moment? Could she have been alive when I heaved her body into the water?

ON THE night Hannah died, or the night I thought she died, I returned to the attic as soon as our guests had gone home or to bed and packed up her personal items methodically, until there was no trace of her. I made her bed up with hospital corners just the way she did. I did it all while Alexander broke down again, shivering and weeping, our daughter slept a narcotic sleep in the room next door, and Giles and Milla fucked drunkenly and joyfully in the guest bedroom below.

Later still, when all was quiet, Alexander and I retrieved Hannah's body from the coal bunker and carried it to the boathouse. He nearly dropped her. "Be careful!" I hissed.

"I thought she moved."

"She didn't move! How can she move?"

But maybe he was right. Maybe she did.

And if she did, what then? Did she wriggle from the blanket once she was underwater and swim to the island? It wasn't far. But we had secured the blanket around her well and I dumped her close to the island because the water is deepest there. Could she have surfaced amongst the gnarled tree roots and waited there, shivering and silent, until we had gone? If she did, she is made of tougher stuff than even I had feared.

If it is her. *If* it is.

. . .

I STAY in Alexander's study until I hear her leave. I don't know what she's been doing.

When she's gone, I return upstairs. The staircase has never seemed so daunting, my bed such a refuge. I take two more acetaminophen, resisting anything stronger. My prescription drugs remain on my bedside table.

I wonder if it would help me if Jocelyn and Hannah, or whoever she is, believe that I'm forgetful and confused because of the prescription drugs. I reach for them and remove the appropriate number so that anybody checking will think I'm still taking them. I try to crush them into dust so I can dispose of them without anybody noticing, but the pills are too small and my arthritic fingers make it too difficult. It was hard enough getting them out of the bottle. Instead, I take the box of tissues that's on my bedside table. I push the tissues aside and drop the tablets into the bottom of the box, one by one.

I might be a better adversary if no one believes I'm capable of it, and an adversary is what I need to be.

THAT EVENING, I feel more lucid. I telephone Anthea to try to persuade her back. If she is in the house, she can act as a buffer between Hannah and me, and be a witness to anything that might happen.

"Your job is still open to you if you want it. We value you very much and I'm very fond of you, I hope you know."

"Thank you, Lady Holt, but I'm decided now. I think it's for the best, especially with everything going on up at the hall. It would have been sometime in the next few years that I moved on anyway, so it might as well be now. I'm sorry if it leaves you in a fix."

"I hope you're not letting other people's silly talk about the skull persuade you away."

"No, I'm not."

"Is there nothing I can do to tempt you back?"

"I'm sorry."

"Very well. Please send my regards to your husband and your mother. You are welcome here whenever you want."

I put down the phone with a heavy heart. Everybody knows how hard it is to find good help, and Anthea was excellent. I feel a small sense of doom that the skull has contributed to her upset. This is a family matter, intensely so. I don't want it to taint our reputation in the village.

"Jocelyn!" I call, but there's no answer. It's so hard to get anybody's attention since Anthea left. Nobody responds to the bell. I wonder what would happen if I fell while I was up here alone. Would anybody hear? Would the Hannah woman come even if she did? I doubt it.

I make another glacially slow trip downstairs and find Jocelyn in the Blue Room on her laptop computer.

"If you frown at your screen like that, you'll get wrinkles," I say.

She doesn't look up. I don't want to sit, because it'll be painful and I'm not confident of getting up off the sofa without its becoming a humiliating performance.

"Could you please do something for me?" I ask. "I'd like to arrange a Fortnum's hamper for Anthea. Can you order for me online? Get a good one. I think her husband likes game pie, so that sort of thing, but not too many jams because she makes her own."

"Isn't that too little, too late?" Jocelyn has bags under her eyes. She shuts her laptop and yawns.

"Fine. I'll do it myself, then," I say. "I only asked because I wondered if you'd like to add your name to it."

She sighs. "Yes, I would. Okay, I'll do it. But I'll need your bank card. I don't think mine will stretch to a Fortnum's hamper."

"Of course. You know where to find it."

My back is aching. I've been standing for too long. "Was Ruby all right today?"

"Fine. Yes. Hannah is a godsend."

"And Ruby is happy with Hannah?"

"Of course. Why do you ask?"

"Hannah came back to the house today after dropping Ruby off."

"I know."

"I need to be informed. I don't want her here when Ruby isn't. And I don't think Ruby likes her!"

"Ruby's fine. It's not your problem, and just so you know, Hannah has arranged for a new girl to come and do a trial for the housekeeper position. She'll be here on my day off, so I'll keep an eye on her."

"It's not for Hannah to involve herself in recruiting for staff! She's taking an outrageous liberty."

"She suggested it and I agreed to it. Who else is going to do it? You're more or less bedbound still, and quite frankly I think we're lucky anybody is willing to work here at the moment."

"Didn't any of you think to consult me? This is my home."

"You haven't been well enough."

"I'm perfectly well enough to discuss hiring."

"But not to make a phone call to Fortnum's, apparently."

"Don't be snide."

"I'm just telling you what's going on."

"Well, I shall go back to bed then, if I'm considered so useless in my own home. I suppose it's only a matter of time until you start thinking of me as a burden?"

"Don't be silly."

"I'm not silly, Jocelyn. I am completely clear that it is unacceptable for Hannah to hire the people who work here. I won't have it."

"I can't stop her now, but I won't let her do it again without asking you. Okay?"

I nod. It's something, at least. I make my way out of the room because I can't bear to spend another minute in Jocelyn's company tonight. It is the past all over again: she and Hannah versus me.

"Mother, wait! Is there a photograph of me in the Belgravia house that shows our vanitas in the background?"

"Not that I recall."

"Where are the photo albums?"

I don't want her to look at the photo albums. There are gaps in her memory they might help to fill. I tucked the albums away on a high shelf when she and Ruby moved here, but I should have done more. I should have got rid of them when the skull was discovered. I'd like to lie and say they got destroyed in the "flood" that is also supposed to have destroyed the Holt Catalogue, but I can't because I'm too weak to fetch the albums down from the top shelf in the Blue Room and sneak them away.

"I forget," I say.

"You don't know where our family albums are?" She is so quick to read everything I say as evidence that I don't care about her, and never did.

"No."

She sighs heavily and rubs her eyes. "Mother, can I ask you something?"

"I'd like to get to bed."

"It's important. I wouldn't be asking if I didn't have to, believe me. I need Hannah, but I can't afford to keep paying her for long. Could you lend me some money to cover her wages? I'll pay you back as soon as I'm earning enough. It shouldn't be long."

"I can look after Ruby."

"No, you can't. We've been through that."

"I'll be perfectly fit in a few days' time and you can let Hannah go then. I've decided I'd like to provide all the childcare Ruby needs."

"Absolutely not. It's not going to happen."

"Why not?"

"So many reasons! Do I have to remind you what happened the other day? Do you know that kids at school are teasing her about the skull and about being posh?"

"It wouldn't happen if you sent her to the school I suggested. I will happily pay for that."

"Don't start on that again."

"Jocelyn, I need to lie down."

"Why won't you help me, ever?"

Sometimes she pushes me to my limit, but I will not crack. Better she resent me than know the truth. Since the night of the party, it has always been that way. "I won't give you money for Hannah and I won't discuss this anymore if you raise your voice at me. It's giving me a terrible headache. I'm going to bed. No, don't get up. I'll go on my own."

I hope she might ignore my words and at least follow me to make sure I climb the stairs safely, but she doesn't.

MY PAIN is a little better when I wake the following day. I come downstairs in the afternoon, but it's difficult to avoid being around Hannah. I invite Ruby to sit with me when she gets back from school. I offer to read with her, but Hannah forbids it. Ruby's face is like thunder.

I take myself to Alexander's study. I press play on his compact disc player. My finger shakes as I do. Unreliable digit. I haven't touched the compact disc player since Alexander died, so whatever I'm about to hear will be the thing he last chose to listen to. I sink into his armchair, into the soft dents his body made, an impression of him. I am swamped by it.

Violins and woodwinds create the impression of a wave cresting on a sparkling sunny day: a gently rising sound, which collapses onto a bright melody stirring to life beneath it. I know what follows: her voice. "The voice of an angel," Alexander used to say. "Who's that?" I would reply. "Me or your girlfriend?" By girlfriend I meant the singer. It was our little joke.

Alexander collected all her recordings. I can't remember the number of times I'd find him sitting here listening to her. He did it more and more often as we aged. It was a private pleasure for him—so many of his pleasures were—but a few weeks before he died, he asked me to sit with him. After the final notes of an aria, Alexander broke the moment with a question: "Was the body heavy?"

I drew in breath sharply. My fingers twitched and his closed more tightly around them, squeezing with just the right amount of pressure to make tears spring from my eyes. Not because it was painful, but because it was kind.

I said, "You know it was." I hated the intimacy of her head resting on his chest as we carried her down the stairs. I wouldn't have minded if the back of Hannah's head had bounced off every stair tread.

"What I mean is, how did you get her out of the boat?"

Is this what you think about every time you sit here? I wondered. *I bloody hope not.* "With difficulty," I said. I was not prepared to describe how I pulled, dragged, tipped, swore, panted, perspired. Not after all these years of keeping it to myself. I didn't want the body to make a splash, you see. I managed it because I was so much stronger then. I could never do it now. I curl and uncurl my liver-spotted fingers. They were slender and dexterous once, but now they are weak.

"I should have helped you," he said. He was right. I had to take Hannah's body out onto the lake alone because he had drunk too much by then. He would have been a liability in the boat.

Alexander may have lured me into his life with intense, promising eye contact, but that dwindled over the years. The crosshairs of his affection were nudged away from me whenever I took on the role of savior—though it wasn't through choice, I hasten to add.

I had to drag us out of the mire whenever we landed in it because Alexander failed to, but that sort of thing can bleed a man of pride, especially a Holt. Served to them with their first pappy meal is the idea that a peer of the realm should not have to rely on a woman. They are bred to believe in their own power. So those crosshairs left me behind and panned across a wider landscape, looking for easier targets, softer bodies, more compliant females, eyelash-flutterers. If a man wants a woman to be a mirror for his own achievements, he will look elsewhere if the purity of the way she reflects him becomes diminished. Foxed glass is never flattering.

I understand why Alexander loved the voice of this singer so much. It is ethereal. It betrays no effort. It offers purity, which can wipe the mind clean and transport you elsewhere. I breathe deeply and watch a squall roughen the surface of the lake.

The music stops abruptly, Alexander's girlfriend garroted just as her voice is soaring. Somebody has silenced her.

Hannah takes a seat opposite me. I try to wash my expression clean of any nerves I feel or calculations I might be making. I gaze at the fire tools. If I was strong enough and if I was sure this really is Hannah, I might be tempted to reach for the poker and put an end to this.

"The situation is simple," she says. "Alexander has paid me a regular sum of money, ever since I, how shall I say this, 'left your employment.'"

I don't move a muscle because if she reads my surprise it will give her the upper hand. I *cannot accept* that Alexander believed Hannah was still alive and never breathed one word of it to me. Why did he keep it a secret? For me? For Jocelyn? Maybe his poker face was better than I thought. Did he go to his grave with one more knife in his back than I believed?

Hannah keeps her tone as light as if we were discussing a mild turn in the weather. "I wish this arrangement to continue, but you should know that my silence has become rather more expensive than it used to be, certainly more expensive than the pittance your daughter is offering me to work here. And there is a back payment owed to me for the months since Alexander died."

She names two figures: a one-off and what she is expecting to receive monthly. Both are eye-watering. Of course they are. I quell a sudden fierce temptation to reach across and grab her wrist as if that would tell me whether this is really her. We are close enough that I could. I would only dig my fingernails in a little.

Instead, I place one of my hands upon the other as if posing for a portrait and I simply nod—a few more times than is necessary, hopefully just enough to indicate that I am listening and am possibly amenable to her suggestion. Better to acquiesce now and work out what to do later.

A twitch of annoyance contorts her lips. "I don't think I heard your reply," she says. She leans toward me and I feel afraid.

"Very well," I say.

"Good." She sits back.

"But don't you think you've had enough already?" I ask. It's worth a try.

She smiles. "What price silence?"

"And will you be handing in your notice once this payment is received?"

Beyond the lake, a flock of starlings bursts from the canopy of an oak tree, a scatter of black against the blue-gray sky. They form a murmuration: flexing and soaring, shape shifting. The geometry of it is capricious. The sight calls to mind a creature from a spirit world. Back from the dead, perhaps. Malevolent. Just like Hannah. Why isn't she answering me?

She stands and brushes the front of her trousers. I note the expensive cut and fabric. Has Holt money purchased this wardrobe for her? Undoubtedly.

"I won't be handing in my notice just yet," she says. "I'm enjoying the job too much. It's lovely getting close to Jocelyn again, especially as we were wrenched apart so suddenly all those years ago. We have a lot to catch up on."

"I'll double the money if you leave," I say. I'll do anything.

"I'll keep the offer in mind. Here are the details you need for my account. Alexander already had them, but this will avoid confusion." She places a slip of paper on the desk and restarts the music as she leaves, but there's no comfort in it now.

At least I know what cards she's holding. Not all of them, possibly, but some, and that's a start. It allows me to plan my response.

I gaze at the fire tools again. If this really is Hannah and money is not enough to persuade her to leave, I fear that ultimately she may be planning to repay the violence we inflicted on her with some violence of her own.

I shall have to be ready for it.

1979

HANNAH FINDS PAINT IN THE *most intimate places. When she takes a bath, she watches it soak off her inner thigh and bleed into the water. He has his hands all over her whenever he can. He wants to do it all the time.*

"God," he says when he comes across her alone in a room, "I cannot resist you."

She loves the attention, but the sex is disappointing. She reads saucy novels she plucks from the shelves downstairs, so she dreams of something gentler or more romantic. Instead, she is often left sore afterward and feeling as if she's been shaken up and set back down with everything not quite in place. But even though she knows he takes a selfish pleasure in her, she thinks it's worth it because she has him and his wife doesn't.

The boys are the same as ever. The younger one, ever more devoted to Hannah. Such a poppet. The gloomy, threatening swell behind the older boy's eyes is still there, though. She wonders if he guesses about her and his father. He's too clever for his own good. She likes to take him down a peg or two. Sometimes she sneaks his homework from his schoolbag after he's gone to bed and makes little changes to the sums in his maths book because he can't stand it when he doesn't get full marks. He cries with frustration. He's such a swot. She feels put out when he starts keeping his bag in his bedroom, but also challenged. Let's see which one of us is smarter now, *she thinks.*

The wife has started taking medication. "Happy pills!" she says tightly and brightly, gulping them down in full view of the children.

The pills are blue. Hannah barely visits her studio, but when she does, she notices the paintings are becoming sloppier and unfinished canvases are accumulating in stacks against the walls. The pills make the wife very relaxed. Hannah wonders if she could crush one of the pills, or half of one, and grind it up and hide it in the older boy's dinner. It might do him some good. Being so hostile all the time can't be healthy for him.

"How do you put up with her?" she asks the husband one night, weeks after she's had these thoughts about the pills, days after she first put them into action. By now she and the husband have been doing it for months, and Hannah's become brave enough to discuss his wife with him.

"That's easy," he says. "Everything belongs to her. If I want all this and access to the pots of cash in the bank, I need to stay with her. Even if she is a fucking zombie." He waves a hand around the room, and Hannah obediently takes in the high ceiling, the ornate plasterwork, the recently installed Italian chandelier, the rugs, the throws, the paintings, the fully stocked drinks cabinet, the television.

Ash from his spliff falls onto his leg. He rubs it into his jeans. He offers her a drag, but she shakes her head. This is news to her, that the wife owns everything. It changes things.

"Come on," he says. "What's the harm? You'll feel sexy."

"I have to check on the boys," she says. The wife is out for the evening, so they've been brave enough to fuck in the sitting room. She turned the keys in the boys' bedroom doors as a precaution. They're very good sleepers now that she's trained them, but she really should check on them. The younger boy is prone to bad dreams, and she gave the older boy three quarters of a pill tonight. Half a pill helped—he definitely mellowed out and there didn't seem to be any adverse side effects—but she felt he could use a little more. He's had a growth spurt recently.

She climbs the stairs nimbly. The husband was gentler with her today. He's been less rough lately, sweeter. On the half landing she glances through the window at the wife's studio. It's completely dark tonight, which gives Hannah pause. What if the wife didn't wake up one day? Didn't shuffle across the yard and into the kitchen smelling of incense and turpentine? What if her body just got colder and stiffer? What if she were dead? Who would get the house and all the money then? Who would get him?

VIRGINIA

I LISTEN BEFORE I OPEN my bedroom door. I want to know if the coast is clear. Hannah is coming and going at unpredictable times, and I hate not knowing whether she's in the house or not. I hear nothing, so I step out confidently—if she is here, I don't want her to think I'm skulking—but I step on something and my foot slips out from under me. I fall backward and my shoulder hits the doorframe. Back wedged against the frame, I slide down it a little but am just able to keep myself upright by grasping the edge of the gateleg table beside my bedroom door. I remain there for a moment, my chest heaving, until I am sure I'm all right.

I stoop carefully, mindful of dizziness, to pick up the offending object. It's a book of mine: *The Night of the Hunter.* I lent it to Ruby. Did she drop it here by mistake, or was it in the pile of books Jocelyn removed from my room? Or—and this thought nips like a nasty insect bite—did Hannah leave it here, hoping I would slip on it? Could she have? Would she have?

I place the book on the table and watch where I'm stepping as I go downstairs. I skip breakfast for the safety of my sitting room. I feel safe sitting down, and here, at least, I can keep an ear out for comings and goings.

I stare out of the window at the lake.

I won at most things, I think, until I became a mother.

Before I had Jocelyn, the prospect of motherhood was a heart-wrenching yearning, a delicious anticipation, but it became my greatest failure. Do you know how it feels when your child looks at you with eyes full of hatred? You feel as if your soul is being scraped out of you. I had so much love to give her, but she didn't want a single piece of it.

Alexander offered to pay for a psychiatrist so I could talk it through, but I refused. It was dreadful enough to live with the situation without the humiliation of having to describe it to a stranger. He also offered to get rid of Hannah. "Is she coming between you and Jocelyn?" he asked. I wondered that, too, and I was tempted to let her go, but in the end I was more afraid that without Hannah, things would be far, far worse because Jocelyn was so devoted to her.

How I wish I had now. But isn't hindsight a wonderful thing?

I NEED to arrange money for Hannah. I try to do it on Alexander's laptop, but there is a Kafkaesque rigmarole to go through to access our accounts online and I fail. I also try to telephone my branch, but that's just as difficult. I find myself in a cycle of electronic messages. I decide to call in at the bank in person. Elizabeth gives me a lift to Marlborough.

"Lady Holt?"

"Yes?"

"You are in Marlborough. You're at the bank."

"Of course I am."

"Oh, it's just that you said . . ."

I look at the young woman. Her customer service uniform is too tight. Was I speaking out loud without meaning to? "What did I say?"

"That you needed to be here to transfer money."

"And that's why I'm here. I told you that when I arrived."

She looks better when she smiles, at least, though it's perhaps less of a smile and more of a smirk.

"Is something funny?" I ask her.

"Mr. Parfrey is ready for you now."

The bank manager is a decent sort. We've known him for years. Anthea told me he'd had a hair transplant. I examine his head when he looks down and I believe she's right.

"I can find no recent trace of a regular payment to a Hannah Burgess from the account your husband held at this branch," he says. "This account has been running as normal, but I'm glad you're here, because there is a slightly delicate matter I'd like to discuss, with your permission. I haven't wanted to mention it before now, out of respect for your situation, but it does need attending to, I'm afraid."

"What is it?"

"Before Alexander died, he and I spoke about the necessity of making a substantial payment into this account. It has been overdrawn for rather longer than usual."

"How overdrawn?"

Parfrey tilts the computer toward me. The number in red runs to six figures. It's a shock. Alexander and I have often been in financial trouble. I helped him work out how we could save ourselves when it happened, but even so I left the day-to-day running of the accounts to him. His pride was too great to hand them over to me. I see now it was a mistake.

"I'm so sorry to ask," he says. "As you know, we had an understanding with Lord Holt, but unhappily things have developed in the banking world and I don't enjoy the autonomy I used to have when managing personal accounts. My head office takes rather a close interest these days."

He looks embarrassed, but I don't blame him. "Of course."

"Well?" Elizabeth says when I meet her afterward. She's holding a carrier bag fat with spoils from the art shop.

"I need to go to London."

JO

IT'S MY DAY OFF. MOTHER'S voice, needily high-pitched and saturated with self-pity, floats down the staircase. I think of it as a physical thing: the tendril of a climbing plant invading a space where it's not welcome.

"What?" I yell up the stairs.

"The new girl is not to go into my bedroom."

"Does that mean you're planning to clean it yourself?"

"Nobody goes in my bedroom unless I know I can trust them." She appears on the landing in a tweed skirt and a pale blue twinset. Pearls are in place and so is her black velvet hairband. Her highly rouged cheeks can't disguise her pallor, though. She looks exhausted, but she is insisting on traveling to London for the day.

"Are you sure you'll be all right today?" I ask.

"Quite sure, thank you. Elizabeth will assist me if I need it."

"What's that?" She's carrying a huge box.

"A hat. The feathers need replacing. I thought I'd drop it off at Lock and Co."

"Why? When are you ever going to wear it?"

"I don't see how that's any of your concern."

"You're unsteady on your feet anyway, why would you take that with you today? It's so bulky."

"Elizabeth will carry it."

Mother spends time in front of the mirror in the hall, curling the ends of her hair, smoothing her quiff. She pulls on a pair of red leather gloves, and as she does, she says, so quietly that I almost can't hear it, "I love her very much, you know. I love Ruby."

I'm so surprised that I wonder if I've heard her correctly. I've never heard her express love for any person except my father before. Property, artworks, theater, or clothing: that kind of thing she *loves. Adores.* People: never. She never told me she loved me, not once, and so I find I have absolutely nothing to say to her in reply.

She clamps a scarlet-gloved hand on my forearm and says, "Listen to me, Jocelyn. I am warning you: Hannah should not be caring for Ruby."

"Did you say my name, Granny?" Ruby interrupts us. She's wearing an outfit that's more suitable for the opera than for school.

"I did, darling." Mother hugs her and Ruby returns the embrace just as fiercely as she hugs me.

"Rubes," I say. "You know you have to get changed. And take Granny's rings off."

"Be a good girl, darling," Granny says. "And take care today." She kisses Ruby's head. Their arms are still around each other.

"Now!" I say.

IN THE car on the way to school I try to talk to Ruby.

"Is everything okay with you and Hannah?"

She doesn't answer. I try another question.

"Have you made any new friends I don't know about?"

She shakes her head. "Stan is my only friend."

"Any of the girls?"

"They don't like me."

"What? Why not?"

"Because I want to play football with the boys."

Football. A few months ago she would have said *soccer.* She's becoming a real little English girl. Of course I'm glad she's assimilating, but it's also another sign that our life in California is tethered further behind us than ever.

"Well, give it time," I say. "They're not being mean to you, are they?"

She shrugs.

"Ruby?"

"No. Not mean."

"What, then?"

"Nothing. I'm fine! You're making it sound bad, but it's not."

I can't get another word out of her. When I drop her off, she instructs me fiercely not to walk beyond the playground gate. I hover, watching, until she turns around and motions that I should leave.

On my way back to the car park I find myself walking behind a group of women. Stan's mum is amongst them.

"Clare, hi, it's Jo," I say. She stops and the others stop, too. She neither smiles nor introduces me, so I stick out my hand to each and every one of them and introduce myself. They are all mothers of kids in Ruby's class.

"Ruby would love to have Stan back to ours to play again," I say. "She's being looked after by her nanny now—you might have seen her around or met her—so anyway, my point is that there'll be no more confusion like last time."

The women exchange glances that look meaningful.

"What?" I say.

"Nothing," Stan's mum says. "We just noticed the nanny is quite old-fashioned, if you know what I mean." She says it as if it's an insult and rolls her eyes to drive the point home. One of the other women giggles. I'm not quite sure how to respond, so I plow on: "Well then, perhaps Stan could come over on a Friday, and I'll pick them up myself. It's my day off."

"I'm not happy with Stan being at Lake Hall. I'm sorry, but I'm just not," she says. "It's not a safe environment if you're not properly supervised." She doesn't even look slightly embarrassed about what she's saying, nor do her friends. I dread to think what they've been saying about us behind my back.

"I understand. Perhaps he'd like to come swimming after school or at the weekend or something like that instead?"

"Sure," she says, but it's lukewarm.

"I'll text you."

She nods and they start walking again, but the vibes they give off don't make me feel as if I'm welcome to join them. I stay a few paces behind all the way to the car.

I consider looking at the Facebook chat to see what might have been said online, but decide I can't bear to.

WHEN I get home, Hannah surprises me by turning up at Lake Hall with the girl, Lottie, who is having a trial as a housekeeper today. I thought Lottie was coming alone.

"You don't need to be here when Ruby's at school," I tell Hannah.

"It's fine. I said I'd organize this for you and I shall. You've got enough on your plate."

I don't argue. Being able to hand over any responsibility feels like a luxury. "You'll have to take some time off in lieu."

"Or you could just add the time onto my weekly hours, if that's more convenient."

I feel awkward about discussing the transactional part of our relationship. I know Hannah was paid to be my nanny when I was younger, but it never felt that way. To her credit, I grew up unaware of any financial arrangement she had with my parents. It's unavoidable now, though.

"Hannah, you should know that money is very tight. I can't afford to pay you for any extra hours. I'm sorry."

"Of course, I understand. I would have thought your mother might contribute, but that's none of my business. It's a shame because you need help if you're going to get back on your feet."

"The help you're giving me now is worth its weight in gold."

"It's my absolute pleasure. Who would have thought we would find ourselves here now? Ruby is such a delight."

"Thank you."

"You've been through such a lot, you two." She has a way of looking at me that brings down the emotional floodgates just as reliably as a word from Mother can make them go up. I'm embarrassed to find myself tearing up. I change the subject.

"What about you? What have you been up to? Have things been good for you?" It's crossed my mind that they might not have, since Hannah hasn't mentioned children of her own or a partner, but that might have been her choice.

"Oh, this and that. I worked for some other families, which was very rewarding. Then I had to care for my mother for a number of years. I've lived a quiet life, really. For a long time a part of me felt that I should have been here, with you." I feel myself getting tearful again. "Oh, dear," she says. "I didn't mean to make you cry. Happy tears, I hope, now we're all back here?" I nod and she pulls me close for a hug.

"I can see trouble," she says when she lets me go. Lottie is at the far end of the corridor, where she is supposed to be mopping the floor, but instead she's looking at her phone. "Young lady!" Hannah calls as she strides toward Lottie.

I haven't felt safe confiding in another adult since Chris died, but I think that might be about to change. Hannah's understanding feels like the first gentle touch in the aftermath of a brutal pounding.

VIRGINIA

VICTOR ELLISON IS STILL IN charge of our accounts at the bank in London. He's aged a bit, of course; he must be on the cusp of retirement now, which is a shame because he's a good man. He wears very decent suits and has perfectly white teeth. Alexander used to have most of the face-to-face meetings, but Victor and I have met once or twice over the years.

Victor pours tea and offers me a biscuit, which I decline, because it is too big. People almost never offer you anything suitably sized to eat these days, even at Coutts.

"I need to see all Alexander's monthly payments," I remind him.

"I've taken the liberty of printing out a list."

I try to locate my reading spectacles in my bag before remembering I put them on a chain around my neck today. Victor is tactful and maintains a beatific smile while I search. I don't wish to look a fool in front of him. This is business, and I take business very seriously.

I scan the list and find the payment to Hannah's account. It's a large outgoing monthly sum, and it's shocking to see it there in black and white. I show it to Victor: "How long has this payment been in place?"

He consults his screen. "Since electronic records started, certainly. To go further back, I'd need to delve into our paper files."

"No, that'll do. I need to increase the payment, and might I access my deposit boxes, too, please?"

"Of course, Lady Holt. But before we do, could we discuss the possibility of your making a deposit into your account? Your over-draft limit was exceeded months ago, and if you wish such large payments to keep going out without interruption, we might need to top it up."

"A significant deposit will be forthcoming, as usual."

"Are you able to advise me when?"

"Not precisely, but I expect within a month, or possibly two."

"You can't be more specific?"

"I'm afraid I can't. My word is good, just as Alexander's was."

Victor has a Cheshire cat smile. I wouldn't be surprised if he melted into the view of London's skyline framed by the picture window behind him.

"Of course," he replies. "But if the situation was to change, would you be so kind as to let me know?"

I wonder if he would have dared to ask Alexander to do the same. I don't dignify his request with an answer.

"I'd like to look at my deposit boxes now, if I may?"

He taps his pen on the desk one more time than is necessary, as if he is considering his response.

"We can go down right away," he says.

I OPEN my boxes in a private room. Victor lays them on a table. He gives me a key for each box and leaves me alone.

I open the first box. I take a pair of white cotton gloves from my handbag and put them on before I touch anything inside it. I followed the advice of others when I first packed this box and acquired special conservation paper. It contains no acid that could eat away at the drawings. The gloves will protect them from my own body fluids.

Removing the final layer of paper makes my heart beat faster.

It always does. Even though I've seen them many times before, I'm not immune to the excitement of handling brilliant, important works of art. These are not just any old drawings. These would make the heart of any auctioneer or art dealer palpitate with excitement.

There are over forty drawings in total. The artists who made them include Mantegna, Leonardo da Vinci, Titian, Rembrandt, and some lesser names. They represent our financial security—*my* financial security now that Alexander is gone.

Nobody outside the family knows exactly what the Holt Collection includes. I select one of the Italian drawings. It is attributed to the School of Leonardo. A drawing like this won't make a fortune, but its value isn't insignificant, either. I take it from the deposit box and place it in a hatbox I brought with me. An old lady on the streets of London might get mugged for her handbag, but nobody is likely to bother snatching a hatbox from her. The drawing fits nicely into the bottom of the box, between more layers of conservation paper I placed there earlier. The hat goes back on top.

I check my watch. I must not forget Elizabeth. She is around the corner at the National Gallery. She was planning to see the Mantegna and Bellini exhibition and had an appointment to root around in the archives. She's probably sitting at a table in the National Gallery café at this very moment partaking of coffee and cake without me.

I unlock the other box and glance inside. It contains a few bits of jewelry and a ledger: the Holt Catalogue, that marvel of centuries of carefully inscribed notes recording details of each and every work in the Holt Collection. I remove the catalogue. Elizabeth will want to consult it. I lift the hat and drawing and put the catalogue into the hatbox beneath them.

I lock the boxes and take a deep breath. At least I will be able to pay Hannah now. I believe that gives me some power over her. I pick up my bag and make ready to face the world again.

As I'm walking away from the room where the deposit boxes are stored, a young attendant runs after me.

"Lady Holt!" She's holding my hatbox. "Is this yours?"

"Thank you so much, my dear," I say. "I don't know what I would have done without that."

DETECTIVE ANDY WILTON

THE FORENSIC ARTIST INVITES THE detectives to the workshop where he re-creates the faces of the dead from their skulls. Three casts of skulls are mounted on stands and arranged at intervals along a generous worktable. Each is at a different stage of the reconstruction process. Andy and Maxine look at each one, wondering which is their Jane Doe.

The nearest skull has numerous small white pegs fixed onto the face, each neatly numbered. "To indicate tissue thickness," the forensic artist says. They move down the line. "We build up the facial muscles first," the artist explains as they look at a skull where layers of white clay have brought the skull partially to life. The final skull has a skin-like coating of shiny red-brown clay and hard plastic eyes. "Looks as if he or she has been out in the sun too long," Andy says.

"That's your Jane Doe," the artist says. "She's nearly ready. She just needs texture on her skin." He picks up a small piece of soft leather, presses it into the clay on one of her cheeks, and peels it back. "Deerskin," he says. "The impression stops her 'skin' from looking so taut. Do you see? Try it. I always think it's the moment they come to life."

Maxine has a go. Andy would rather not, but he peers at the web of fine lines and contours the imprint leaves on the clay. Their Jane Doe looks both stark and vulnerable. Her eyebrows are there, represented by scoring in the clay, but she is otherwise bald.

"She's got nice wide eyes and quite fine features, but no obvious distinguishing features," the artist says. "I'm quite pleased with how she came out. You get attached to them as you work."

"Could you ask her what the hell happened to her, then?"

"Ha! Well, wouldn't life be sweet if I could? Here, take a look at this. I need to finish her before I scan her into the computer, but this is another head we did. It gives you an idea of what I'll be able to send you."

The head appears in three dimensions on screen and he makes it rotate.

"We can add hair to the image very easily." With a few more clicks the head is transformed by the addition of shoulder-length brunette hair. The artist swaps the brunette hair out for long blond hair, then another, shorter style.

Andy asks for profile and full-face shots of his Jane Doe with a few different hairstyles and hair colors.

"We'll make sure you have a few different angles, too. I'll send them over first thing next week," the artist says.

"Thank you. Then we can take her out into the world and see if we can introduce her to any old friends," Maxine says.

"Or enemies," Andy adds.

VIRGINIA

THERE SEEM TO BE SO many more people on the Strand than there used to be. Elizabeth and I walk arm in arm, but we can barely progress for tourists swarming like insects with their telephones on sticks. It's hard going.

"I'm not going to make it all the way to the Courtauld," I tell her. "I'll wait for you in the Savoy." An idea occurs to me. "Can you phone Faversham for me? Invite him to meet you in the American Bar for a drink, but don't tell him I'll be here."

"Are you sure?"

"He's not returning my calls."

"You won't persuade him to let Jocelyn go."

"I can try."

The Savoy feels like a sanctuary. None of the staff recognize me now, which is sad, but to be expected.

I have many memories of evenings spent here, but a special birthday dinner is my favorite. I wore a red gown by Ossie Clark. It was full length, in scarlet, with bishop sleeves and a plunging neckline, and it was made from a divine figure-sculpting moss crepe. Of course I had to Sellotape my breasts in place to make the whole ensemble work, but nobody knew apart from me and the dress.

"A devilish dress," Alexander said when I emerged from the dressing room. "Absolutely devilish."

"Takes one to know one," I said.

He ran his fingers down the neckline. "Ravishing, darling."

He offered me his arm and we went downstairs. Every head turned as we entered the bar. We had a fabulous time that night, which was nice, because however promisingly our evenings started, they didn't always end well.

I sink into a comfortable chair and order a White Lady, my favorite cocktail. Why not? I watch the waitress as she weaves through the tables with my drink on a tray. Diamanté detail on the neckline of her svelte black dress and a figure to die for. Gorgeous creature. Feline.

"Does Jack Brabbage still work here?" I ask as she performs more theater with the placement of the napkin and the perfect orientation of the cocktail glass on the table in front of me.

"I don't think so," she says.

"Did you ever meet him?"

She shakes her elegant head.

"He was an institution himself," I say.

Jack. Dear Jack. He used to help me get my husband upstairs if Alexander had overdone it. *Will a room be needed, Lady Holt? It's no trouble. Would you like me to escort Lord Holt? Do you think Lord Holt would like his trousers laundered before morning? If you would like to call down when he's changed, I'll have them collected.*

Alexander, dead drunk, a urine stain blooming across his trousers, deposited on a bed. But oh, the discretion from Jack and this hotel! It allowed me to keep my chin up, just so long as we could pay later.

Elizabeth is here. Too soon.

"What's happened?"

"Bloody archive at the Courtauld is closed."

"Did you explain that you booked?"

"I can't make a scene."

"No. Of course."

"What are you drinking? I'll have one of those."

I order and she relaxes incrementally. It's like watching the feathers settle on a flustered hen. She glances around. "I think I'm a bit underdressed, don't you?"

"Nonsense." But she is, and woefully so. It has ever been thus. "Will the archive be open tomorrow?"

"Apparently, yes."

"We could stay the night at my club."

I kept a membership in town after we had to sell the Belgravia house. I chose a women's club purposely because I wanted it to be a place just for me. I was tired of playing Bonnie to Alexander's Clyde by then. I haven't been to the club for years, but I expect Elizabeth will fit right in. It's usually chock-full of bluestockings and Royal Academicians.

"Then we could have another cocktail." She raises her glass and we chink.

"And dinner somewhere fun?"

"That settles it then." She giggles. "I feel as if we're having an adventure."

Faversham arrives on cue, elegant in his trademark trilby and long coat, smelling musty with cigarette smoke, his cheeks cold from outside when we kiss.

"Virginia," he says. "What a lovely surprise."

"You can't avoid me forever."

"Apparently not. Are you going to tell me off?"

"You deserve it."

"Jocelyn's going to be very good at her job. She's a natural, like her father."

"I forbid you to involve her in the sale of any of our paintings. You have to let her go, and she mustn't know that you and I have spoken."

He leans forward and whispers. "She doesn't know the vanitas is a forgery."

"I know that, because she'd run a bloody mile if she did! She'd be absolutely mortified. The point is, I don't want her involved at all, whether she knows she's doing something illegal or not. She stays out of this."

"Illegality never bothered you in the past."

"My daughter was never involved before."

"I can't let her go until we've sold the vanitas. She's met the client and she was brilliant with him, so she'd be very upset if I told her I didn't need her now. And she might smell a rat. Thank you, darling." He waits for the waitress to leave us before turning up the charm. "Consider it, Ginny, darling, if we keep her on she could be such an asset."

"He's right," Elizabeth says. "If you think about it from a business point of view."

"She is not business! She is my daughter! You had no right to invite her to work for you without consulting me, and I don't thank you, Elizabeth, for facilitating it." My cocktail glass slips from my hand and falls, bouncing on the carpet, creating a puddle and a constellation of spatters. Elizabeth snatches the hatbox out of the way just in time and we heave a collective sigh of relief.

"Jocelyn's an adult," Faversham says. "You shouldn't hide so much from her. She might relish the opportunity to join us. Have you thought of that?"

"Stop it, Jacob. It's none of your business what I do or don't tell her. The fact is, you went behind my back to hire her and you're misleading her. She's a lamb to the bloody slaughter."

"If we get caught."

"We won't." Elizabeth has such misplaced confidence. She believes her forgeries are undetectable. It is the arrogance of the creator, but we all make mistakes sometimes.

I haven't finished with Faversham. "You shouldn't have done it, and you know it or you would have returned my calls. Alexander would be furious if he knew about this. Actually, he wouldn't be furious, he'd be devastated."

"Fine," Faversham says. "Calm down. As soon as this sale has gone through, I'll let her go."

"Thank you."

We sit silently as the waitress cleans up the mess.

MY CLUB has only one room available. It's a twin, but Elizabeth and I don't care. We recovered our equanimity after Faversham left. I believe her when she insists she had no idea Faversham was going to recruit Jocelyn after she introduced them.

We sit on our beds.

"I mustn't lie down," Elizabeth says. "Or I shall never get up again. Where shall we go for dinner?"

"I have no idea. It's been so long since I was in town." Twenty years ago, even ten years ago, I would have known exactly where I wanted to eat and I would have been able to get a table, but I am out of touch.

"Are you going to show me what you got?" Elizabeth asks.

The hatbox is on my bed. I ease the lid off and remove the hat and the conservation paper. Elizabeth extracts a pair of white cotton gloves from her own handbag and picks up the drawing.

"Oh, it's sublime," she says.

That's a good sign. "Can you do it?"

"Of course I can, but have you asked Faversham if he's happy to sell it so soon after putting the vanitas on the market?"

"He'll do it. He owes me." How mutually dependent we are, we three. "The catalogue is in there, too, if you'd like to look at it."

She takes it out and leafs carefully through the pages until she locates the entry relating to the drawing in the hatbox. "Lovely. Always helps me get a fuller picture, so to speak."

I lie down. I'm exhausted. "Darling, do you mind if we order room service and get an early night instead of going out? We could eat in bed and put the television on."

"Are you all right?" Elizabeth asks. For a moment I long to tell her everything, but you should never let one person know all of your secrets, even your best friend.

"I'm fine, just tired. I'm sorry it's so boring of me. Do you mind?"

"Not at all. It's been a long day." Elizabeth groans as she leans down to remove her shoes. "We're not what we were, are we?"

We order macaroni and cheese, summer pudding, and a good bottle of wine. "Doesn't this remind you of school?" Elizabeth says as we sit on our parallel beds, trays on our laps, bare feet tucked under eiderdowns.

"It does, rather." I wriggle my toes and feel a sensation that is almost like relief, because for once I have a few hours when I can let my guard down. Any moments when I can cease being Lady Holt and just be myself are vanishingly rare and all the more precious for it.

This is not an evening at the Savoy. It doesn't compare. But those days are over, my energy is ebbing, and I have to look after myself. I have a daughter and a granddaughter to protect. The thought of that is enough to turn my food into ashes in my mouth and plague my sleep with troubling dreams.

JO

RUBY HAS A FLOPPY-LIMBED, TIRED-TO-THE-BONE, end-of-the-week exhaustion about her when I collect her from school. It's worn her out, but she's happy, because she's been chosen to look after the class hamster for the weekend. We strap its cage onto the back seat, throw its food and other paraphernalia into the boot.

At home, we take the hamster upstairs. I've agreed to let Ruby keep the animal in her bedroom because Boudicca isn't allowed upstairs. It'll be out of Mother's way there, too. "Animals should not be caged" is a mantra she's been repeating since I was a child.

Hannah is still at the house.

"Thank you for being here today. How did Lottie get on in the end?"

"I think Lottie might be more of a liability than a help. Never mind. We'll keep trying. We could put an ad in the *Evening Advertiser.*"

"I don't know. They've been running stories about the body. I think we'd be in danger of getting people applying because they want to come and gawp."

"Well, maybe you're right. Let's both give it some thought."

She picks up her bag. I don't want her to go.

"Can I at least make you some supper tonight as a thank-you for everything? If you're not busy, that is. Mother is staying up in London for the night."

A smile lights up her face. "That would be lovely."

"I thought it was just going to be you, me, and Granny," Ruby says. She's in the doorway, scuffing her shoe on the flagstones.

"Don't be rude! Sorry, Hannah. I think she's tired." I shoot a disapproving glance at Ruby, but she flounces away.

"Sorry," I say again.

"Don't be! I know children."

"Even so."

"Ruby is grieving. This is a very difficult time for her. She's getting to know your mother, which might not be easy, and adjusting to a new family unit. It's understandable if she doesn't always cope with it perfectly. And having to get used to me represents yet more change just after she's lived through more than her fair share of trauma and upheaval. Ruby is a little girl in a strange place. The way your mother puts you down in front of her can't help when the one thing she's seeking is stability."

That's true enough. I hadn't thought of it. Hannah has insight into our family that nobody else ever could and the knack of knowing just the right thing to say. "Thank you for understanding," I say.

"You're welcome," she says. "I will make it my business to be your right-hand man so Ruby knows who she can rely on. She'll settle down soon if we get that right."

"She will, won't she?" Hannah offers such a lovely clear pathway out of the maelstrom we've been in.

"Of course. And on the subject of Ruby, do you mind if I ask you something?"

"Of course not."

"Don't take this the wrong way, but are you aware of everything Ruby is doing on the Internet?"

"I hope so! Why?"

"It's part of a wider problem, I think. Her behavior in general is a little furtive. She often sneaks off around the house and the grounds, you know that. She and I have had discussions about doing dangerous things: climbing trees, going far too high, and trying to walk along the orchard wall would be recent examples, and I heard about her and Stan getting in the kayak. Phone use is no different. There are hazards, as you know. I've got no proof, and I've not said anything to her, because I wanted to talk to you about it first."

"I haven't noticed anything." Though as I say it, I'm thinking: *But would I really know?* I wouldn't like to admit it to Hannah, but I'm sometimes grateful when Ruby is on her device, because it gives me a few precious moments when I don't have to parent her, and of course I don't always know *everything* she's doing. What parent can? "Do you think she's hiding something?"

"I wouldn't like to speculate. It could be something very minor. It could be nothing. But I thought I'd mention it so we can keep an eye on it together."

"Thank you."

Hannah yawns. "Sorry," she says. "I didn't sleep well last night."

"Is everything all right?"

"A few little things on my mind, but nothing to concern yourself about."

"Why don't you sit and let me make you a cup of tea," I say. "Relax."

"In just a minute, dear." She opens the fridge and takes out a bag of salad leaves. "First, I might take this up to Ruby. The hamster will love it."

THE CORK makes a satisfying pop as it leaves the bottle. I found the red wine in my father's cellar. Without Mother here, Lake Hall feels less oppressive than usual. It's like being able to breathe again after being in a stifling room.

"Not much for me," Hannah says. "I'm driving."

I pour a small glass for her and a large one for me. The wine is a dark blackberry color, the label on the bottle dusty. I've already fed Ruby, so it's just Hannah and me dining together.

"I hope we're not drinking something very special," Hannah says.

"I hope we are! Why not?"

She raises her glass. "Cheers. Now tell me, how is work going?"

"Very well. Loving it. Which reminds me, do you remember a photo of me taken in the drawing room in Belgravia? It would have been when I was little."

"Goodness! That's going back a bit! I remember a frightful fuss one afternoon when you had to miss a trip to the London zoo because your mother wanted to have a portrait of you. You were about five or six at the time."

"She forced me to wear a frilly dress I hated."

"No, dear. You've got that wrong, I'm afraid. You loved the dress. You said the frills made you feel like a Spanish dancing lady. But you hated the hairband she made you wear. It left red marks behind your ears."

"That sounds about right," I say, although I'm really not sure. So many of my memories are shadowy things. I think I remember feeling small in a room full of adults and the white pop of the camera flashlight and its electronic wheeze as it charged up again and I was told to "SIT STILL." Such sibilant words if somebody spits them at you. When you're a child, it can feel as if they wrap around you and tighten. They can feel like your fear of the dark.

"If it's going to be anywhere, it'll probably be in one of the albums," Hannah says. "I don't know where they are now, but your father used to keep them in his study. Do you need a hand looking?"

"If you don't mind?"

"I'll join you in a moment."

I find the albums on a top shelf in the Blue Room. The fire is already lit. Hannah must have done it. How thoughtful.

"Rubes!" I call upstairs. "Do you want to look at some old photos with me and Hannah?"

She appears on the landing.

"Can I go on my iPad? Stan said he might be allowed to Skype." I would insist on her coming down if it wasn't for Stan. I badly want her to be able to mend that relationship. "Sure," I say. "Say hi to Stan from me. I'll show you the photos another time."

"More wine?" I ask Hannah when she joins me. "I'd like another. Join me? You could stay over. I'll lend you anything you need."

"Well, I wouldn't like to . . ."

"Please. I'd love it if you did."

"Well, thank you. I'd love to."

"Excellent! I'll bring the wine through. No! You sit. I'll get it."

When I return, she has stoked the fire and it flickers, burnishing the room. She's turning the pages of one of the albums. "Brings back so many memories," she says. "Look at your father in this one."

My father is in the garden in tennis whites, looking very young and smoking a cigarette as he chats to friends by the net. Mother is with him, in a chic tennis dress.

"Is that his cigarette case in his pocket?" I say. The photograph is grainy, but you can make out the distinctive decoration on the top of the case where it protrudes from the pocket of his shirt.

"He was never without it, was he?" Hannah says.

"Never. Everything was more glamorous then, don't you think? Even tennis."

"They were certainly in a world of their own."

We look through the photographs. Some are familiar, some not so much. After I'm born, Hannah and I feature little, my parents often. Hannah and I appear mostly in snaps of birthday tea parties or of the first day at school. Hannah points at one picture where she's sitting on a picnic rug with me. The cake in front of me has two lit candles on it and I'm wholly absorbed by it. There's a toddler sitting beside me with a woman too old to be his mother. The chubby legs of another are visible at the edge of the shot.

"The little boy was called Simon. That's his nanny, but I forget her name," Hannah says.

Some garden chairs have been arranged a few feet away from the rug. My mother is sitting in one of them. The photograph has caught her chatting conspiratorially with two friends. They have proper drinks and cigarettes. They are in another world from those of us on the rug. Not one of them is looking at her child.

"Who took the picture?" I ask. "Was it my father?"

"Oh, no. He never made it to your birthday parties. It would have been Marion. I made the cake, though. She wasn't happy about it because the kitchen was her domain, but I insisted."

"That's so nice."

There are many pages of photographs of my parents looking posed and glamorous against ever more exotic backdrops, even as they age. They have film-star quality, but as we turn the pages, I can't help thinking of Faversham and what he said about my father, and how his own apartment reeked of moral laxity as if it were a varnish rubbed into every surface, buffed in places but in others decayed into a crystalline dust that felt as if it settled on my skin while I was there. I believe my parents' lives had a similar quality back then.

The more recent pictures, from when I was a teenager, only at home during holidays from boarding school, confirm it. They remind me of things that made me uncomfortable: a gaze from one of my parents' friends that rested on me too hard and for too long; a jack of hearts found on the baize-covered table in this room the morning after a party, creased and still damp at the edges where somebody had licked cocaine off it; a mother who often would not get up until midday; a father who wore dark shadows under his handsome eyes and developed a habit of pushing his hair back, over and over again, like a tic.

"You've got a thousand-yard stare," Hannah says.

"Sorry. I was just thinking." These are memories I'm not ready to share just now. They make me more determined than ever to remove Ruby from this environment. That life might have been years ago, but behaviors and attitudes linger like dust motes and I see them in my mother still, in her arrogance and the judgments she makes about others.

The photograph of me posed in front of the vanitas is hard to find because it's not where it should be chronologically. We've almost given up when we reach the final album, which mostly contains photographs from the 1990s, but we find it there, loose, tucked into the spine.

In the photograph I'm sitting in a formal chair, upholstered in deep green velvet, in front of the fireplace in Belgravia. I'm wearing the frilly dress I remember and the headband Hannah remembered, and I'm staring at the camera blankly. It's a weird feeling to be disconcerted by your own expression, but I am, a little.

"Mrs. Grump," Hannah says.

"Wasn't I just? Do you remember that painting?"

In the photograph, the vanitas is hanging over the fireplace behind me, just as Faversham described.

"I do. Not one of my favorites, I must admit. Too gloomy."

"It's for sale. We're selling it at the gallery."

"What a shame."

"Daddy gave it away years ago, apparently, but the person buying it wants proof it was in our family collection before that."

"Why on earth?"

"It avoids doubt as to whether the painting is genuine."

"Oh," Hannah says. "I see."

We both look again at the photograph.

"Well," she says after a moment, "it's probably time for bed."

"It was very special to revisit some memories with you."

"We had such happy times, didn't we? I didn't envy your parents at all, for all their jet-setting. You and I had everything we wanted here at Lake Hall."

"I totally agree. And it was always better when they weren't here."

"Well, you did love to see your daddy. You were very possessive of him, do you remember?"

"I remember looking forward to seeing him."

"You used to squeeze between him and your mother and push her away if they tried to embrace."

"Did I? I don't remember that at all."

As we gather up plates and wineglasses, I think of how the photographs have made things shuffle in my head once more. I've seen things I hadn't remembered quite right and other things I had forgotten completely. It's a strange sensation to see yourself somewhere doing something you would not have remembered otherwise.

"Did I always have such a poor memory?" I ask.

"Well, I wouldn't expect you to remember things from when you were very little, but I suppose you did have a bit of a poor memory. Mostly it meant you lost your stuff all the time. Do you remember when you didn't give in your signed permission slip for the school trip to the ballet because you lost it? You must have been a bit older then, about six. You phoned me from the school office. You were sobbing so hard I could hardly hear what the problem was, but when I got it out of you, I rushed down and signed a new slip so you could get on the coach. I used to say if you were a dog, you'd forget your own tail."

She laughs and I laugh with her, although beneath it, I feel uneasy. Perhaps I'm a little drunk. The wine bottle is nearly empty and I think I've had more than Hannah.

Let in by that little feeling of agitation, the exhaustion of the previous week arrives and hits me like a freight train. It's definitely time for bed.

In the minutes before I sleep, I open the Internet browser on my phone. I'm curious to see whether Hannah has an online presence. She's been muted about what she's been up to since she left our household, but I'd love to know something about her personal life.

I have no luck, though. I can't find a single thing about her. She doesn't have any kind of social media or other presence. So far as I can see before the effects of the wine drag me into a deep sleep, Hannah is invisible online.

VIRGINIA

THE WEEKEND WAS QUIET AND blessedly free of Hannah. London exhausted me so I rested and played board games with Ruby. I observed her carefully, but she seemed okay, so I didn't ask about Hannah. I don't want Jocelyn to accuse me of turning Ruby against her. Ruby wanted to know where the Lake Hall gargoyles were to be found, so we went on a hunt outside to find them and she photographed each one. She has a very good eye. She also showed me how to take a selfie.

I cheered her on as she walked along the top of the orchard wall. "Well done, darling! No, don't jump down where you usually do. Go farther along and see if you can get onto the pear tree from there. I bet you can!"

I know Jocelyn and Hannah are having a fit about Ruby doing things like this, but she has an adventurous spirit and it needs to be nurtured, not crushed. Life requires bravery.

This morning Hannah returned to Lake Hall after dropping Ruby off at school once again, and I felt as if her presence cast a dark pall over me.

"What are you doing?" I asked. "I told you you shouldn't be here when Ruby's at school."

"The girl we tried out on Friday was no good, so I'm still recruiting for your new housekeeper. I need to organize an advertisement and I have no Wi-Fi at home." Her tone is one of unimpeachable efficiency. I remember it well.

I am sorely tempted to demand she leaves my house this instant because this is so impertinent, but I must pick my battles. Once she has her money, there's no reason for her to stay here, so I'll let her pretend to be a part of this household in the meantime. It'll be easy enough to get rid of anyone she appoints if I need to.

"The money will be in your account by the end of the week," I say. "It's all arranged."

"Good," she says. "I'll be checking."

"Be it on your conscience."

"And what about your conscience? I can't imagine how you felt when they discovered the skull. When I read about it, I thought, Lady Holt must be feeling very nervous about this. Didn't you feel better when I returned, so you knew the body wasn't me? Though that must have been very surprising. And confusing."

It's so hard to maintain my belief that this might not be Hannah. So often I find myself thinking about her or talking to her as if it really is her, and I can't help myself now. "Don't taunt me. We both know you would have trouble proving what happened."

"Would we?"

"It's your word against mine."

"No. It's my word and Alexander's word against yours."

"What do you mean?"

"When I first made contact with Alexander to let him know I'd survived, I recorded our conversation and Alexander described exactly what happened. I have the whole thing on tape. It was so fresh in his mind, it was as if he'd just been waiting to unburden himself."

"I don't believe you." But she looks so calm and sure that part of me does, even though I wonder, if this isn't Hannah, *How can she know this stuff?* If it really isn't Hannah, it must be somebody Hannah knew, because this woman knows so much. Layers of confusion settle like ash. "You will leave when you have your money." My voice is shaking.

"You will have to wait and see."

"I want you out by the end of this week. As soon as the money is in your account and not a moment longer."

Her response is a cruel and bitter smile. She's the duckling who never grew into a swan. The most dangerous kind of adversary.

"I have things to do," she says. "Would you mind?"

I can't stay in the house with her, so I go outside. Geoff is mulching the roses. I join him, though I don't have much stamina for it.

Geoff shovels the mulch and I form and pat it into little mounds around the stem of each rose.

"You're getting wet," he says after a time. It has begun to rain: a fine, cold drizzle. He offers me his arm and we move up the slippery bank and stand under an oak tree. Its canopy forms an almost perfect circle above us, the tracery of its branches complex and dense.

"Celestial oak," I say.

"That it is," Geoff says. "Smoke?"

Years ago, before I was pregnant with Jocelyn, I used to sneak into the gardens and smoke a cigarette with Geoff. Talking to him reminded me of my father, a man who loved the land and farmed it for a living. I haven't shared a smoke with him for over thirty-five years, but I think I shall.

"Why not?"

I watch Geoff prepare our cigarettes: two wafer-thin papers, two meticulously laid rows of tobacco. He hunches over them to shield them from the rain.

As we smoke, we see Hannah open the back door and vigorously shake out a rug.

"She never used to clean," Geoff says. "Got herself all uppity about it."

"You're absolutely right. I'd forgotten." Hannah threw a blue fit when I asked her to cover for our housekeeper once, insisting it was beneath her position to do housework that wasn't related to the nursery. We watch as she stands at the back door, rug in hand, and contemplates the lake before going back inside. She doesn't see us.

"Can I ask you something?" I say.

"Fire away."

"Do you think Hannah is different from how she used to be? I mean significantly? Not just the usual aging."

He removes a piece of tobacco from his tongue. "Not that I've noticed," he says. "But I haven't had much to do with her. She never liked me back in the day, so I don't see why she would now. I probably shouldn't say it, but I always thought she was a bit soft on Lord Holt."

He's right, but I don't confirm it. It's not a conversation I wish to have with anybody. I wonder what else he noticed.

"Ruby would like to plant a rose of her own," I say.

"Good time now. It can go in bare-rooted."

"Which variety do you think she'd like?"

"I'd let her choose if I were you."

"Of course."

Smoking is making me feel a little woozy. I drop the cigarette and crush it beneath my shoe. Geoff picks it up before I can. We retrace our steps down the bank, my arm through his again. My feet are soaked. I shall need to change my tights when I get in. I turn toward the house. Rain has blackened the stone on the tips of the parapets and the side of the chimney stacks, as if tar has been poured down them.

"Lady Holt," Geoff says.

"Yes?"

"There's talk in the village about the skull."

"I expect there is."

"People said it was Hannah at first, and there's other rumors going round now, but it'll die down. Not everybody pays mind to it. I want you to know that, in case you hear about it."

"Thank you, Geoff." I feel ridiculously grateful to him. I hadn't realized how much in need of an ally I felt.

He begins to dig again. The rasping, rhythmic slice of his shovel fades by the time I reach the courtyard. I try to get into the house via the boot room, but the back door is locked. I can't see anybody through the window. I go around the front and find that locked, too. The car that Hannah uses isn't here. She must have gone. The wet and cold have got through to my skin and I start to shake. I ring the bell, but there's no answer. I go back to the rose garden, but Geoff has packed up and gone, too.

I have no choice but to wait on the front porch of my own home, cold and shivering, like an abandoned dog.

DETECTIVE ANDY WILTON

ANDY HAS TO DUCK TO avoid the fronds of wisteria as he reaches to knock on the door of the cottage. It's picturesque and generously sized. The front garden is densely planted and overgrown. Autumn flowers vie for space with the collapsed carcasses of summer blooms.

"Elizabeth Fuller?" he asks when the door is opened. He knows this woman is an old friend of Lady Holt and was expecting someone equally uptight and difficult. Elizabeth Fuller speaks with the same cut-glass accent as Virginia Holt, but she couldn't be more different. She's warm, jovial, and apparently haphazardly dressed in a large sweater over patterned trousers, with a bright, clashing scarf at her throat and another holding her hair back from her face.

She shows Andy and Maxine through a narrow hallway into an informal, light-filled room at the back of the cottage, which doubles as both kitchen and sitting room. The walls are crowded with prints and watercolors, all bursting with color.

Andy can see another building at the end of the garden.

"That's my studio," Elizabeth says. "Where I dabble. Have a seat. Sorry about the mess."

The table is cluttered with a basket of vegetables that look freshly pulled from the garden, art magazines, the remnants of breakfast, and an articulated life-size wooden model of a hand. Andy picks it up.

"It's an artist's model. I use it to draw from. I call it Max Klinger's glove," Elizabeth says. "You can move it if you like."

"Max Klinger?" Andy doesn't get it. He moves the fingers on the hand so it's doing a thumbs-up.

"Doesn't matter. He's an artist. It's a private joke, probably funny only to me."

She pushes aside the clutter on the table to make room for the teapot and mugs.

"Could we talk about your friendship with Lady Holt?"

"I've known Virginia for donkey's years, ever since she met Alexander. I grew up with him, running around the countryside. She and I became friends immediately. She was my kind of person."

"Were you closely involved with the Holts after their marriage?"

"Absolutely!"

He gets his phone out. "I'm sorry I don't have a good quality printout of this yet, but would you mind looking at a photograph of a reconstruction of the skull we found at Lake Hall?"

Elizabeth peers at the image and manipulates it on-screen. "It's rather difficult to tell, even if you zoom in. Very skilled work. Aren't they clever to do this? I don't think I recognize it, although . . . No. I don't think so."

Andy's little surge of hope dies as quickly as it was born.

"We'd also like to ask you about an incident that happened at a shooting party the Holts had, in the winter of 1984," Maxine says.

"It's no good asking me about that," Elizabeth says. "I don't shoot. I don't like it. I'm far too much of an animal lover."

She glances at the threadbare sofa, where a black cat is nestled between the cushions in a shaft of sunlight. As if on cue, it stretches, flexing its claws. Maxine reaches out to stroke it.

"I wouldn't do that," Elizabeth says. "She looks cuddly, but she's far from it."

She lifts her glasses and peers once more at the photograph of the skull. "If I were to say this resembled anyone I've seen at Lake

Hall, it would be Nanny Hannah, but as I'm sure you know, she's alive and well and still working for the Holts."

In the car, Maxine says, "What did you think?"

"Harmless old biddy. Nice and friendly, which makes a change from Virginia Holt."

"Amazing how you can 'dabble' and still afford a beautiful cottage like that."

"These people don't know they're born."

JO

PAUL MERCIER, OUR CLIENT FOR the vanitas, has come to the gallery to see it. He is pleased to be shown the photograph I found and requests a copy. He stands a few feet back from the vanitas and his eyes rove the painting's surface. He doesn't step any closer, even though the detail in it begs to be examined, and he remains silent until Clemency asks in tones as hushed as a librarian, "What do you think?"

"It's exquisite. Yes. I'm very pleased. It'll do nicely." I'm surprised when he starts to put his coat back on. It all seems too perfunctory.

"Is everything all right?" Faversham asks.

"Yes, absolutely. I'm afraid I'm due at an appointment. Can I call you later and make a time to formalize the arrangements?"

I tense a little. I need to be involved in the negotiations. I've done my research: in recent years, Rachel Ruysch still life paintings have sold at prices well into six figures. My commission is fifteen percent. That's money I could very much use.

"Of course," Faversham says. "My dear chap, of course. At your convenience." I sense he and Clemency are as surprised as I am by Mercier's sudden departure. I think we were all expecting him to linger longer over his new purchase. Faversham shows him out graciously.

Clemency and I watch from behind the window. "How do you think that went?" she says.

"Good," I say. "Except, do you think he really loved the painting?

I mean it seemed to mesmerize him for a few moments, but I didn't feel like he fell in love with it. He didn't even smile."

"He may be buying for investment."

"I got the strong impression the rest of his collection hasn't been built that way. Faversham says he talks with real passion about it. Yet he said almost nothing about the vanitas. It really surprised me."

Clemency seems irritated. "It's not for us to question why he wants the painting; I hope you weren't thinking of doing so."

"Of course not!"

"Good! You can't expect clients to feel what you feel. It's business."

Clemency leaves the room abruptly and I feel chastised. I'm new to this, I know that, and I'm probably too idealistic, so perhaps I'm judging the situation in all the wrong ways, but even so, something about it feels a bit grubby.

FAVERSHAM SENDS me home early. "You might as well, darling. We don't need three of us here for the rest of the day."

I spend the train journey in my usual reverie of "if only." If only I could rewind life and be in my home. Our home. The one I shared with Chris. I want to hear him say something that makes me laugh and to share fierce, uncomplicated little child hugs with Ruby.

When I arrive at Lake Hall, I find Mother in the porch, hunched and shivering. She's soaking wet. "I'm locked out," she says.

"How long have you been out here?"

"Ages."

"What happened?"

"Your woman, your precious Hannah, went out and locked all the doors. She knew I was in the garden. She knew it."

"I'm sure she didn't. You never tell any of us what you're doing. She will have assumed you were inside. Where was Geoff?"

"He'd gone, too, by the time I looked for him. Ruby and Hannah should have been back by now. Where are they? Where has Hannah taken her? The bells struck five ages ago."

"Mother, relax! Let's get you in. Ruby has swimming on Monday. You know that. Have you been smoking?"

"Don't question me as if I am a child!"

"Then stop behaving like one!"

Mother's clothes are dripping, but even so she walks up the stairs with a ramrod straight back and raised chin. She tries to be so unshakable, but her skirt is clinging to the back of her legs and I can see the shape of her backside. Her blouse is so drenched it's see-through. As she turns on the half landing, I see her bra and the fallen contours of her breasts.

Hannah is mortified when she and Ruby return. "I'm so sorry. I thought Virginia was inside. She told me she was coming in for a nap, so I locked the doors. I didn't want to leave everything open if she was asleep."

"It's her own fault for not communicating with you," I say. "So don't feel too guilty."

"She's elderly and she got wet," Hannah says. "I don't want her to catch a chill." She bustles around the kitchen warming Mother some soup and cutting and buttering bread. "I'll take this to her and apologize," she says. "And make sure her fire's on."

Once Hannah has left the room, Ruby whispers, "I don't like her."

"Don't like who?"

"Hannah."

"Why not?"

"Can Granny look after me?"

"What's wrong with Hannah?"

She pauses, as if not sure what to say at first, then says, "She won't let me go on my iPad."

"Oh, you mean she sets boundaries and sticks to them?" I laugh. "That's good for you, believe it or not. Give it some time, sweetheart, you'll get used to her. It would mean a lot to me if you could try."

Ruby looks at me with a gaze that seems older than her years, but she nods. "My tummy hurt at school today."

"Did it? Is it better now?"

She nods. "Can we have ice cream later?"

"Can't have been that bad a tummy ache, then!" I say, but she doesn't see the funny side. "Yes. You can have some ice cream later."

"Good. Because *she* said I couldn't."

"Well, I'll tell you what: why don't you and I watch *SpongeBob* and eat ice cream together before bed. Is that a good plan?"

Ruby nods, though it's lackluster. She gets her homework out and spreads it across the table. I shift closer to her and she leans into me until it feels almost as if we're one person.

We're still sitting that way when Hannah reappears and pauses in the doorway. "What a lovely sight," she says. "Bless you both. Your mother is fine. She's warming up in her sitting room."

"Thank you so much." I don't know what I would do without her. She is so much more than a practical solution to my child-care requirements. She knows me, knows us, and having someone around whom I can trust is the most extraordinary feeling.

"I will say I don't think this would have happened if your mother wasn't so reluctant to communicate with me," Hannah says. "It would be helpful if she could let me know if she's going out. If we can all pull as a team, it will be possible to make this house run like clockwork and run safely."

Hannah puts on her coat and picks up her bag. I should probably get up to see her out, but I can't bear to move from Ruby's side. I plant another kiss on the top of my girl's head while she's in the mood to let me. She isn't always, these days.

"Good night," Hannah says.

"Good night," I reply as the wind blows the back door shut hard behind her, drowning out my response. Rain and sodden leaves spatter the doormat. I wonder for a moment if Mother has upset her more than I realized.

I watch Ruby's pen move across her exercise book.

What if Mother wasn't here? I wonder. What would that be like? If I could do things on my own terms, with the support of somebody like Hannah and in Mother's absence, would I be happy to stay at Lake Hall with Ruby and make our new life here?

Ruby stops writing and looks up as if a thought has just occurred to her. "It's Granny's house," she says, bringing me back to earth. "She can do what she likes. Hannah shouldn't tell her what to do."

"It's better if we can all work together, don't you think?"

"We should do what Granny says, not what Hannah says."

"You have to do what you're told by Hannah," I say. She doesn't reply. Her head bends over her homework for a few more minutes, before she thinks of something else.

"We forgot to take the hamster back today."

"You didn't take him this morning?"

"You didn't tell Hannah we had to."

"You could have told her. Rubes, you need to start taking responsibility for things like this. That's kind of the point of being allowed to look after the hamster."

She pouts majestically and I drop it because I don't want to sour our evening.

"I'll get him now and bring his cage down," I say. "That way you won't forget him tomorrow morning."

There are drops of water and damp footprints on the stairs and landing carpet. They trail along the corridor to Mother's bedroom, and surprisingly, they go farther, down the corridor and around the corner. I follow them into Ruby's bedroom. They stop in front of the hamster's cage. The cage door is open and Twiglet is nowhere to be seen. After some frantic searching, I find him cowering beneath a bow-fronted chest on the landing. I can see his oily eye, but I can't reach him and the chest is too heavy to move.

Ruby and I try to entice him out. We place food on the carpet and wait. It doesn't work. Ruby runs downstairs and gets a broom while I keep watch. We slide it carefully underneath the chest to dislodge Twiglet and he makes a break for it. Ruby tries to catch him, but he's too fast. He scuttles past us to the end of the corridor, but Boudicca is there, lured by the excitement and cheeping noises we've been making to coax the hamster out. Boudicca's ears are pricked. She lunges for Twiglet and grabs him by the head.

"Boudicca!" I scream. She flees downstairs with Twiglet in her mouth as fast as her arthritic legs will carry her. Ruby and I hurtle after her. Mother is standing at the bottom of the stairs. "What on earth is going on?"

"Boudicca's got Twiglet!" Ruby shrieks.

Mother's eyes narrow as Boudicca makes the turn from the half landing on to the final flight of stairs. She grabs the dog's collar in a surprisingly deft move. "Boudicca," she says. "Drop!"

The limp hamster falls into her hands. Mother takes a look at it and shakes her head. "I'm sorry, Ruby darling," she says. She turns away from Ruby and breaks the hamster's neck in a clean motion.

"It was the only kind thing to do," she says.

Ruby takes the hamster's limp body from Mother and I let her hold it for a moment or two and stroke its head. There's blood on its neck where Boudicca's teeth did some damage.

"Rubes, I need to take him, I'm so sorry."

"Why? In a minute."

"No. Now." Blood is smeared on the front of her school shirt.

"Where will you put him?" Her eyes are brimming.

"Let her hold him. It's only a bit of blood," Mother says.

I snap. The row is awful. Mother vehemently denies touching the cage in spite of the damp footprints in front of it. I make her come upstairs and look at them.

"Try to deny it!" I shout. "The evidence is right in front of you!"

"Hannah did it," she says, and my rage feels like a white, shimmering thing.

"This being the Hannah who taught me how to care for my pets when I was a child? The Hannah who just brought you hot soup because you were stupid enough to get locked out? The Hannah who is saving my skin right now? Can't you climb down off your high horse just for once in your life and acknowledge that you are not perfect and not better than everybody else?"

"You have no idea."

"No, I don't! Because my life hasn't been as tawdry or selfish as yours!"

While we argue, Ruby sits on the bottom step and cradles Twiglet and Boudicca looks on hungrily and afterward I feel ashamed I let that happen.

RUBY AND I bury Twiglet in the rose garden, lit by the torch on my phone and a shaft of light from an upstairs window.

"Rubes," I say as we stand in front of the tiny grave, where she has placed a handmade marker, "let's not tell school about Boudicca."

"You mean about Boudicca eating Twiglet all up?"

"I don't think your teacher needs to know that happened. We can just say we found Twiglet dead in his cage."

"Why?"

I put my arm around her shoulder and pull her closer. "Because sometimes, my love, it's better if people don't know the exact truth."

"Did Granny really let Twiglet out of the cage?"

"I don't know, darling, but if she did, it was by mistake and she forgot. She's not quite herself at the moment. You and me and Hannah have to look out for her."

"Can the doctor make Granny better?"

"Maybe. I'll phone him and see what he says."

"I want Granny to be better."

So do I.

I think I do, anyway.

1979

HANNAH IS GETTING ON SO *well in Bristol she can hardly remember being Linda anymore. She writes a letter to Jean and tells her friend all about the affair she's having with the husband. She's bursting with excitement about it. She writes that they don't just fuck anymore. Sometimes they have a glass of wine together, or a coffee during the day. Once they went together to the younger boy's school play and somebody mistook them for a couple, which was funny. They snuck in a quick curry on the way home. The wife was away and the boys at a friend's house. Hannah feels they're really getting to know each other.*

The letter is returned to her with a curt note from Arthur Wagoner. Jean left him, he says. He has no idea where she has gone. She is a liar and a monster and was a no-good, pathetic attempt at a wife anyway and he never wants to hear her name again, so can Hannah please not write. Hannah is shocked, but also pleased that Jean has got away from him. He had the charm of a ferret. She wonders if Jean will write to her or if this means they will lose touch permanently. She finds she doesn't really care if they do or they don't.

One day the husband tells Hannah his wife thinks the older boy should go to boarding school.

"He's not happy," he says, and he sounds upset about it, as if it's his fault.

"Boarding school will be good for Peter," Hannah says and she thinks, Good riddance to bad rubbish.

"They're not nice places," he tells her. "I went to a horrible one."

"I'm sure they're not all like that."

She feels jubilant when the term starts and Peter leaves, taking his enormous trunk, his exorbitantly priced school uniform, and his stroppy attitude with him. He's got a face like a smacked arse as he's driven away. She stands and waves madly at Peter along with his brother and his mother. He stares at them through the back window of the car, his face like a pale little moon.

The younger boy is still delightful and as faithful to her as a puppy, and the wife spends so much time in her studio indulging in wild fits of painting mania or swooning depression that she hardly bothers them at all.

Hannah does special things for the husband: making cakes, slipping a homemade lavender sachet in between the folded clothes in his chest of drawers, serving him a Cinzano when she's dressed in a French maid's outfit. Saucy, he says. He has only one sip of his drink before he's all over her.

She also takes little tributes to the wife: a small nosegay of flowers cut from the overgrown borders, a cup of tea, angel cakes. The cakes and tea are her favorite. The wife has a good appetite. "God, I'll be as big as a house!" she says whenever Hannah turns up with another offering, but she stuffs her face anyway.

She doesn't notice when Hannah begins to crumble pills into her food. Hannah is very careful at first. She thinks of it as experimental. She'd got rather good at numbing Peter, so why not his mother? Why not see what happens? She can't vouch for how many pills the mother takes on her own, though. That's her business.

One night the wife doesn't appear in the house all evening. Hannah peers out of the kitchen window toward the studio. There are no lights on. That's unusual because she knows the wife hasn't gone out. She feels a flutter of panic but steels herself.

She checks her watch. It's late. The husband is out, but due back at any moment. The little boy is asleep upstairs.

She hears the key turn in the front door lock and she's about to go and meet the husband in the hall and tell him she's concerned when she hears a voice.

"You have such a massive house!" It's a young voice, a woman's voice. Hannah freezes.

"Shh," the husband says, and the woman giggles. He must have warned her to be quiet, Hannah thinks. It's the giggle of a woman who knows she's being snuck in.

"We could have a drink in my studio, if you like," he says. "I can show you what I've been working on."

"Love to."

The stairs creak as the two of them climb. Hannah creeps into the hallway and stands out of sight. The woman climbs with a wiggle to her backside. Her hair is so long that the tips of it play on her buttocks. The husband is walking up behind her, transfixed. He's a dirty man. Hannah covers her mouth with her hand and stays there, frozen, as they go into his studio. The door closes behind them and Hannah creeps up the stairs and onto the landing.

She waits there, still as a statue, and she hears it more quickly than she expected: the rhythmic squeal of the springs on his chaise longue, getting faster and faster, and the muted grunts and cries of secret lovemaking. She waits until the pace has picked up so fast she knows he'll have a vein popping out on his temple and she throws the door open.

"Seb," she says, her eyes glittering. "I think there might be something wrong with your wife."

While the husband and wife are at the hospital, she packs her bags. The younger boy sleeps through it all and she goes to him and kisses him on the forehead. "Gorgeous boy," she whispers. "I'll miss you."

She creeps downstairs with her bag. The wife's parents are sitting in the kitchen, white with shock. Hannah made them tea, but neither of them has drunk it.

She leaves the house without their noticing.

On the coach to London she sees her own face in the window and is captivated by the sight of her tears glistening on her cheeks, her reflection warped and colored by the shapes and lights outside.

She has a notebook on her knee. Normally she uses it to make lists and note down important reminders. She turns to a fresh page and writes, as neatly as the motion of the vehicle will let her: He must be faithful to me. I must be his number one woman. *She underlines each sentence twice and draws a heart around them. Who, she wonders as the hum of the drive lulls and calms her, easing her disappointment and replacing it with thoughts about what's next, who will my sweetheart be?*

She knows what he'll be: he'll be rich. But who will he be? Images converge in her mind: men she knows, men she's observed in real life, men she's seen on TV and in films. They assemble and form a collage of leading men, any one of whom could be just right for her. As she falls asleep, she smiles. It's not until the following day when she's settling into her new lodgings that she remembers Jean, and realizes that this means they've lost touch forever.

JO

I BEGIN TO RECOGNIZE FACES at the train station. Every morning it feels as if we are a little band of brothers waiting for the 07:12 service to London, dressed in our city clothes and looking out of place at the no-frills country station, which is no more than a small, musty waiting room nestled between two exposed platforms.

A canal runs parallel to the tracks a short distance away and attracts the gaze of more than one sleepy commuter each morning. It's usually picturesque, but one morning, shockingly, we see a moorhen pecking relentlessly at the head of her weakest chick as the others bob around her.

A text from Hannah pops up as the train pulls into Paddington Station.

> Just wondering, did you remember to talk to Ruby about her
> Internet use?

Oops! I think. I've been loosely monitoring Ruby's Instagram feed and asking about her chat-room use sporadically, but I haven't done anything more. It went out of my head.

> *Planning to do it this weekend.*
> Don't forget!
> *I won't!*
> Would you like me to remind you?

That's unnecessary, I think, and I feel a twitch of irritation, but to be polite, I reply.

Yes, please. That would be great.

You've got a head like a sieve! But don't worry, I've got your back!

"YOU LOOK cheerful." Faversham is sitting in Clemency's spot in the back office when I arrive. He looks too big for her desk.

"I'm feeling cheerful," I say.

"Excellent!"

"Where's Clemency?"

"She has a migraine."

I start to take off my coat. "Keep it on!" Faversham says. "Monsieur Mercier, our esteemed client for the vanitas, wants to know more about the painting. Which is tiresome. Could you do me a favor, darling, and pop over to the Witt Library? See if you can unearth anything?"

"Isn't the photograph I provided enough? I thought we were at negotiation stage."

He sighs. "Yes and no. The client wants to know if there's evidence of where the work was before your grandfather purchased it. I'm willing to indulge him for a little longer because he's not quibbling about price. Yet. Any more fuss from him and I'll tell him I've got another buyer positively frothing at the mouth to get it."

"I haven't been to the Witt for years," I say.

"Enjoy, darling. Enjoy it in all its fusty, dusty glory."

For all his seedier qualities, Faversham does make me laugh sometimes.

THE WITT Library is in the basement of the Courtauld Institute of Art. I navigate the route down from memory, nostalgic for my time there.

"Area of interest?" the librarian asks as she issues a reader's card.

"Dutch. Eighteenth century. Still lifes."

"Popular this week," she says. I figure it's a librarian joke and smile. She glances up at me over a pair of reading glasses with screamingly bright rims. "Third stack, end of the row on the left. We close at four."

The library stacks are filled to capacity with green box files, identical in size but varying in tone. Rachel Ruysch has a cardboard folder dedicated to her work, containing around forty pictures, mostly black-and-white photographs. I begin to sift through them. The images are organized by date, and in the middle of the stack I spot the vanitas. The discovery makes my heart leap a little. It's a small clipping from an art journal, an exhibition review of a show at the National Gallery in 1964. It mentions our painting in the text: "A notable vanitas from Ruysch, on loan from the Paul König Collection."

I take a photograph of the clipping and put it back in the file. Next stop: the National Gallery. I Google "Paul König" as I walk through Trafalgar Square. Wikipedia has a short entry, which tells me König began his art collection when his friend, a Jewish art dealer called Michael Roth, sold his stock to König right before he escaped from Germany. Roth was never heard of again. König, it is implied, got a very good deal on the collection.

At the National Gallery archives I get politely but firmly stonewalled because I haven't made an appointment. I schedule one for Monday.

"Never mind," Faversham says when I tell him this as I'm showing him the photograph of the clipping I found in the Witt Library. "This alone is a splendid discovery. Why don't you join the client and me for drinks later and we can share this in person?"

"I'd be delighted," I say. It's easier with Clemency not here. I can show my hunger for this sale.

"Are you rubbing your hands together, Jocelyn?" Faversham asks. "In an overt gesture of enthusiasm for moneymaking?" His eyebrow arches perfectly.

"No."

"Liar!"

"How dare you! I never lie!" I say in mock outrage. "I just forget sometimes."

I PARK at the Coop in Pewsey on my way home. Hannah has asked if we can meet for a quick drink at the pub. She says she wants to talk to me about something. The Coop is closed and only a handful of cars remain in the car park. The lighting is poor, damply white against the black country night, weakly outlining the long grasses whose roots nibble away the broken edges of the hardstanding.

As I step out onto the high street, I see Hannah at the cash machine on the other side of the road.

I'm about to call out to her, but her expression stops me. She is staring intently at her balance slip. I hang back as she removes her card from the machine and puts it back in. She presses a few buttons, then takes the card again before moving on. I know I shouldn't look as I pass the machine, but I can't help myself. There's a new message slip dangling from the receipt outlet. I take it. It says, "No available funds for withdrawal."

I catch up with her in the pub, making sure to arrive a few minutes after she does.

"Can I get you a drink?" she says.

"No. These are on me. I insist." I have almost no money, but I reckon it might be more than Hannah has.

"How are things?" I ask when I sit down.

"I wanted to talk to you about the hamster incident. I know you and Ruby believe it's your mother who left the cage door open, but I thought you should know that Ruby left it open the evening before. It was just an oversight and no harm was done because Twiglet didn't escape and I explained to Ruby how important it is for her to pay attention. I'm not saying she left the door open a second time, or that she lied about it, but I thought you should know she'd been careless once before."

"She promised it wasn't her and there were wet footprints everywhere. It had to be Mother."

"It's not for me to say what actually happened, but Ruby does lie sometimes, I believe, and that's normal for a child of her age, but I think you and I need to watch out for it and stop it becoming a habit, if only because some of the things she does are risky, like climbing on the orchard wall. As you know, she's already fallen and hurt herself once, and thankfully it was only a graze, but she's like a moth to a flame with that wall. She can't seem to keep away from it, even though I've warned her of the dangers. At that age they're convinced they're immune to injury, but we all have our clumsy moments, including Ruby."

"You're right. Chris, her dad, used to encourage her to be adventurous, and it does shred my nerves sometimes."

"One slip is all it would take."

The thought sickens me. Hannah puts her hand on my arm. "Don't look so worried, dear. We'll work on creating some stability in her life and make sure she understands her boundaries. You and I will manage that between us and it'll enable Ruby to manage her grief and her impetuousness. I do believe one feeds the other. Then she'll flourish, you'll see. Now, if you'll excuse me, I need to visit the little girls' room."

I nurse my drink, thinking about Ruby, until I feel a tap on my shoulder.

"Anthea! How are you?" I don't think I've seen her looking this relaxed before.

"This is my husband, Alan," she says.

I shake hands with a benevolent-looking man.

Anthea delves in her handbag. "I've been meaning to bring these back," she says. She hands me a large set of keys. "Master keys," she says. "For all the rooms at the hall. I'm sorry I didn't leave them when I left."

"It's no problem. Thank you." I put them into my bag.

"Police found out who that body is yet?" she asks.

"Not so far as I know."

Alan pipes up. "That lake's tainted now, then. You'll not want to go near it, let alone on it. You couldn't pay me to dip a toe in it."

A man sitting at the bar has been earwigging. "Probably not the first or last person to die in there," he says. "The Holts aren't a nice family. Never have been and never will be. We all know that's why you left, Anthea. You probably feared for your life. You Holts won't find another housekeeper from round here."

Hannah is on her way back from the bathroom. She slows as she hears what he is saying.

"I beg your pardon?" she says. "What are you implying? Have some respect for this young woman, who by the way is wonderful, and also for her family, who have done so much for people around here, and while you're at it, you might want to have some respect for the poor soul who died. Disgraceful to sit there and mutter about people. What have you ever done you're so proud of?"

Anthea and Alan look embarrassed and say a muted goodbye. The man swivels back around to stare into his pint glass. As Anthea and her husband leave, Anthea and Hannah acknowledge each other with a tiny nod.

I clear my throat. "Thank you," I say.

"You're welcome. That kind of idle gossip makes my blood boil. Nobody deserves that."

"No," I say. "It's hard to try and stay immune to it. Anyway, how are things at Hillside Cottage?"

"I've been enjoying it very much, but I've had a bit of bad news today. I shouldn't burden you with it."

"Why not? Tell!"

"The owners want me to move out so they can start renovations earlier than planned. The thing is, I'm not sure if I'll be able to find anything so close to Lake Hall, and I'm worried I can't afford the upkeep on my car. It's been costing me a fortune."

"You mean you might not be able to work for us?"

"It's a concern. I don't know where I'll end up."

An idea occurs to me. A big idea. I'm nervous about voicing it, because it might be too much, too soon, but I ask myself what I've got to lose.

"How would you feel about moving into Lake Hall? You could live rent free and I could keep paying you what I'm paying now. The only difference would be that you might take on a few extra hours of work here and there, in return for the rent. It would help me enormously to have another capable adult living with us."

"I won't do cleaning, though."

"No. I understand. Mother will still want to recruit a housekeeper. It would just be an extension of your nanny duties, and you can have use of the spare car whenever you wanted it. What do you say? I'd love it if you'd consider it. You could have your old room upstairs or take your pick on the first floor."

"It's far too generous an offer. I feel I should contribute something extra financially, but in all honesty I'm not sure I can."

I'm warming to this idea by the minute. She's broke and I'm broke. This could be the perfect solution. "You're absolutely not allowed to consider it. You'd be helping me raise my daughter in the best possible way. That's the very best thing I could possibly have in return."

"Might I ask what your mother thinks of this?"

"She doesn't know. I've only just thought of it, but she'll have to accept it."

"I don't want to cause a rift between you two."

"If anything, you'd probably be stopping me from killing her. It would make life so much easier."

Hannah smiles faintly.

I hope it means she's about to be persuaded. "You would be saving my life. Just the way you always did."

"Then I can't think of anything I'd rather do. It would be so special to be back in the heart of the Holt family. A new opportunity to contribute to the next generation."

"Wonderful. I'd be grateful if you didn't mention it to Mother for now. Just until I've found the right moment to tell her."

VIRGINIA

ELIZABETH PHONES TO TELL ME the police came around to her cottage. "My heart skipped a beat when I answered the door," she says. "But they only wanted to talk about your skull. I told them nothing, obviously, because I had nothing to say. But I'd been practicing sketches for our little project, so I had to hide them under piles of vegetables and the detective even picked up the model of the hand I was working from. Can you imagine? The subterfuge! It felt very Roald Dahl. And let me tell you something else. They showed me a photograph of the skull they reconstructed. Have you seen it yet?"

"No."

"It had a little bit of a resemblance to Hannah. Or so far as I could remember her. Extraordinary!"

"Are you sure?"

"Not a hundred percent. Probably not even sixty percent. There was something, though. Maybe just the way they'd aged it, shape of the head, that sort of thing. Silly, because it can't be her, can it?"

"No," I say. Once I put down the phone, I wonder about this. Elizabeth could be mistaken, but what if she isn't? I need to see the photographs for myself, but I can't phone and ask to see them. It might look suspicious. I'll have to wait for the detectives to bring them to me.

I feel very low and the call hasn't helped. I still feel humiliated by the saga with the school hamster. How dare Jocelyn accuse me of opening the cage door when I did nothing of the sort? It must have been Hannah.

I keep to my bedroom and my sitting room as much as possible when she is in the house. I feel confused about her because I don't know whether to hope this woman is really Hannah or to hope that she is not. I just want her out of our lives. I phone my bank to see if the transfer has arrived in her account and they assure me it should have done by now. Yet she has said nothing. She turns up as she used to and avoids being alone with me.

I think a lot about the past.

The morning after Hannah died, or maybe didn't die, Alexander and I debated whether to wake Jocelyn up or wait until she woke naturally. I was all for waking her, because I wanted to be the first to know if she remembered anything about the night before, but Alexander insisted it was better if we didn't. It would be more normal for her to wake up alone, he said. If we woke her, she might think something was odd even before she discovered Hannah was gone. Also, Marion might notice we weren't behaving normally. Better to behave the way we always do, and hope for the best.

I agreed, but I felt sick to my core as we waited for Jocelyn to wake up. We had to spend time with our guests, but were lucky we could blame our shaky hands and dysfunctional attempts at conversation on rampant hangovers. Our guests were suffering from their own.

In the end, Alexander was right. His tactic worked a treat. Jocelyn woke alone and discovered Hannah's disappearance with all the shock of somebody who remembered nothing of the night before. She bothered Marion with it before she came to us. She said nothing about the previous evening. She remembered nothing. It was bloody miraculous.

My only regret is how harshly I broke the news of Hannah's departure to Jocelyn. I told her that Hannah left because she had been such a horrible child. I was thinking on my feet and it wasn't a good thing to say. It left a scar. But it did help to make Hannah's departure a final one.

I just wish I hadn't seen the light go out of my daughter's eyes at that moment. You don't forget something like that. You never stop regretting it.

We left Lake Hall for our London home as soon as our guests had gone and we took Jocelyn with us. I was terrified staying in Lake Hall would trigger her memory.

Jocelyn threw stupendous tantrums from the moment we arrived in London because she missed Hannah. She had a million questions I found I was too exhausted to answer. I went to my room, shut the door and curtains, took the phone off the hook, and got into bed.

I needed to think.

I was determined I would not let Hannah's death destroy me, or us. As I lay in my bedroom, I thought about it. I interrogated how it had happened and why and my feelings about it. I would never deny to myself what had happened, I thought, or try to minimize it. I would be brave enough to stare the terrible and profound nature of it in the face, but I would do that silently and stoically and I would move on as best I could, because we did what we did because *we had no choice.*

You have to protect your family.

After a few days of my being in bed, Alexander, out of desperation, announced that if I didn't get up and help him with Jocelyn he would get in beside me and remain there for as long as I did. He was as good as his word. He held me for two days straight. He rose only to see to Jocelyn; then he came back to me.

Jocelyn appeared and disappeared in our bedroom doorway while he held me, her eyes like dark pennies, strangely quiet. Alexander moved her dollhouse to the landing outside my bedroom door, and she played with it for hours. I listened to the games she made up. The baby in the dollhouse had a nanny she loved and a mother who wasn't very nice. She said nothing about anybody being hurt on a staircase.

The phone downstairs rang and rang, and the doorbell, too, but Alexander ignored both to be with me. On the third day my body ceased shaking and my thoughts became repetitive. There were no new insights to be gained, not while I was lying in bed, anyhow. I was where I was and it was time to try and live. I had a daughter to look after.

I got up and opened the curtains and saw that London looked just the same as ever. It had been oblivious to our torment all along. It was seething with life and it was time for us to reenter the fray.

"I think I'd like some breakfast," I said. The room smelled sour. My legs buckled. I hadn't eaten more than the bare minimum for days. Alexander supported me as we went downstairs. He made me hot buttered toast and tea. I stared at our courtyard garden where the walls were painted white and the ivy looked darkly green against them, and I let my tears run freely. He ran me a bath afterward and washed my back. We spoke very little.

Over the next week, we rebuilt ourselves as best we could, testing incrementally our ability to cope with public interaction, to see friends. We did quite well. It helped that we were in it together. Jocelyn watched us quietly and never approached either of us without coaxing. By protecting her, we had severed her from us. If I had entertained fantasies of winning her over in Hannah's absence, I began to realize they were just that: fantasies. Jocelyn was withdrawing even further than before and I could do nothing to stop it. I coped with it by thinking it was the price I would be willing to pay to protect her from what happened.

RUBY AND I make biscuits. I am, at least, still allowed to mind Ruby alone for an hour or two sometimes, though I suspect Jocelyn and Hannah exchange texts about my competency. I wonder how it's happened that I find I need permission to do things in my own home.

Ruby knows what she's doing. She calls the biscuits cookies, of course, in the North American way, but I rather like it. It makes them sound exotic. We couldn't find any chocolate chips, so we're making Anzacs, which will do very well.

Ruby chats sweetly and I watch her working the dough. It feels almost shocking how intimate I find the time I spend with my granddaughter. I haven't experienced this sort of closeness since I was a child myself, living at the heart of my own family.

"I'll expect your resignation within twenty-four hours," I said to Hannah when she left earlier. I followed her out onto the drive. She had been evading me, I'm sure, and she looked strangely smug, as if there is something she knows that I don't.

"I'll think about it," she said, but the look on her face was sheer mockery. She put up her umbrella and I had to step smartly out of the way to avoid being hit by it. She didn't need an umbrella. The car was only a short distance away. I nearly fell.

"I can't believe you're still driving that old Land Rover," she said. It was parked on the drive. "Hanging on to memories of Alexander, are you? I hope you drive it more safely than he did."

"What do you mean?"

"Everybody in the village used to complain about how he

hurtled down the lanes. They probably say the same about you. The Holts own the roads, right?"

"I don't know what you mean." Though she's correct. Alexander drove too fast.

"You want to be careful, you know," Hannah says. "Old Land Rovers can be very dangerous if they're not properly maintained, very unreliable. You wouldn't want to lose control. It could happen so easily in a vehicle like that. What if the brakes were to fail? And here's a thought: I wonder who would miss you if you were no longer with us?"

It was unmistakably a threat. I thought immediately of the book I tripped on outside my bedroom door. As soon as I could, I asked Geoff to check over the car and he assured me all was well, but even so, I felt badly shaken and can't forget it.

I calmed down eventually, though. I still feel afraid, of course, but I must be rational and stick to my plan. What other choice do I have, really?

Money is a powerful persuader, and I believe my best tactic is to try to use it to get rid of Hannah even if it bankrupts me. Better to lose everything than to have Hannah in our lives. I have made the payment and it's her move now. I ask myself repeatedly what more she could require from us if she has the money she wants. There is nothing else for her here, not now that Alexander has gone.

Ruby arranges little balls of biscuit dough neatly on the baking tray, and I make sure she slides it into the oven safely.

"Granny," she says. We have the mixing bowl between us and two spoons to scrape up the leftover mixture.

"Yes, darling?"

"Can you teach me 'A Sailor Went to Sea'? Everybody at school laughed because I didn't know it."

It's a simple childhood game where you clap in a pattern with somebody else, including crossing hands and other variations, and you do it in time to a rhyme you both chant. Ruby masters it in seconds. It's not difficult. We do it faster and faster until I'm laughing too much to keep up with her. Her sleeve has fallen up her arm and I notice something.

"You've got nasty bruises on the inside of your arm, darling. How did you get that?"

She folds her arms and her lips disappear between her teeth. She's thinking about what to say. I wait. I won't pressure this child. Her trust is a spark I wish to nurture. Before she decides how she's going to answer, we hear Jocelyn calling "hello" from the hall. Ruby, quick as a darting kingfisher, puts her finger to her lips and pulls down her sleeve before Jocelyn sees.

Jocelyn storms in like Poseidon himself, cross because I haven't got Ruby to bed on time. The frown on her forehead is so deep and her mood casts such a pall that she might as well be throwing thunderbolts or making oceans rage.

"What are you doing making biscuits at this time of night? You're supposed to be getting her to bed, Mother. Have you done your homework, Ruby?"

Such a sharp tone, and so many questions. They make the warmth in the room disappear and the dough in the bowl, which was so full of promise a moment ago, suddenly seems claggy and unappealing. Ruby's face falls. She looks the way Jocelyn used to when I entered a room: all the joy gone. It tears my heart.

"It's my kitchen," I say. "I shall sit in here if I want to."

Ruby scoots to the edge of her chair so her leg is pressing against mine. "I asked Granny to make cookies with me," she tells Jocelyn. "Like you and me used to."

"Well, Granny mustn't get too tired and nor must you."

How joyless my daughter can be sometimes. "I'll be in my sitting room," I say. "Ruby?"

"Yes?" She looks upset, but I must leave it to her and Jocelyn to sort this out.

"Come and give me a kiss before bed, won't you?"

No fire has been lit in my sitting room today, so I turn on the electric bar fire and pull a rug over my knees. I must look like a proper pensioner. How Alexander would laugh. Ruby slips in a little later. She plants a kiss on my cheek and slips her hand beneath mine.

"Is that a diamond on your ring?" she asks.

"It is. You see how it twinkles? That's because of the way it's cut. And do you see it has a yellow tint to it? That makes it very rare. It first belonged to Grandpa's mother. It'll be yours one day."

She smiles and feels the cut edges of the stone with her finger. She looks tired.

"Ruby! Teeth! Come on!" Jocelyn barks from the corridor.

"You must do your teeth, darling," I say. "You don't want to get fillings."

"I always do." Fibber. I know she doesn't. Her toothbrush is often dry when it should be wet. I can't let her go without asking a question. It's the reason I wanted to see her before bed.

"Ruby. The bruises on your arm. How did you get them?"

She glances toward the corridor. Jocelyn has bustled off somewhere.

"It'll be our secret," I say.

"Hannah did it," she says.

"Ruby, you must tell your mummy about this."

"I don't want to."

"Why not?"

"You promised you won't tell."

"But this is something she needs to know."

"It wasn't Hannah, it was an accident. I did it when I fell off the wall the other day."

"When did you fall off the wall?"

"When Hannah was looking after me. Mom knows about it already. Hannah texted her."

Jocelyn calls again and Ruby leaves the room, watching me as she does. She's trying to assess whether I believe her about its being an accident.

I don't.

JO

A MORNING OFF. I TAKE Ruby to school myself and she is very quiet. We've already argued about her packing a long-sleeved top in her bag for PE. "Won't you boil in that?" I asked. "Why don't you wear a T-shirt?"

"It's cold in the gym."

"Okay then, but can I ask you something?" I've been meaning to broach this since Hannah mentioned it.

"What?"

"Did you accidentally leave Twiglet's cage door open once? Not the night he got out, but before that?"

"No."

"Are you sure?"

"I didn't! I'm not lying!"

"Okay, don't get excited. It's okay if you did forget once. I'm sure it was an accident. You can tell me if you did."

"It wasn't an accident because I didn't do it! Only you lied about Twiglet because you told school he died in his cage and nobody in my class believes me. They keep asking if I murdered him and put his body in the lake!"

I pull into the school car park and stop the car.

"That's a horrible thing to say. Would you like me to come in and speak to the teacher?"

"No. They only did it one day."

"All right," I say. "I'm sorry. I'm sorry I mentioned about the cage and I believe you. Let's just take a few minutes so you can calm down before you go in." Her chest is rising and falling dramatically. "I've got some good news, if that helps."

"What?"

"I've asked Hannah to come and live with us. I think it'll make life much easier and calmer for all of us."

"I don't want her to!"

"Why not?"

"I don't like her."

"I think if she moves in, it'll help. It'll be more consistent for you. You'll always have somebody there for you."

"I like Granny! I don't need anybody else!"

"Granny is too fragile right now to care for you properly. I know she doesn't seem like it, she seems pretty strong, but it was only a little while ago she couldn't get out of bed. If anything were to happen to you while she was looking after you and she couldn't cope, I would never forgive myself. I've asked Hannah to move in because I'm trying to make sure you're well cared for just like I was."

Ruby slumps farther down. "You're always at work."

"You know I don't have a choice. We need money."

Her arms are crossed tightly across her midriff. She looks more angry than upset now. I wish I'd never mentioned Hannah moving in. I should have picked a better moment, but I was hoping she'd be pleased. I can't understand why she's so violently against the idea.

"I don't feel well," Ruby says.

"What's the matter?"

"I'm really tired."

"Ruby! I'm tired, too! We're all tired! *Tired* isn't a good enough excuse not to go to school."

Now I've made her cry. It's a crappy feeling. I undo my seat belt, get out, and open the back door of the car. "Shuffle up," I tell her, and I climb in and give her a hug. She flinches but I ignore it. "I'm sorry we had a disagreement. Do you feel well enough to go into school and give it a go? If you still feel bad in an hour or so, you can see the nurse and I'll come and collect you."

She nods but keeps her head bowed. I kiss the top of it. "Okay. Go on, then. I love you."

I watch her until she's safely through the school gates. She doesn't look back once.

In my late-night correspondence with my mom friends from California, they have been telling me their girls are being difficult in similar ways. They start to grow up young now, is the consensus. Hormonal changes are beginning, and they can be the tip of a long blade that might gradually cleave mothers and daughters apart. I think of Hannah's advice that I must remember Ruby is still grieving. I know she is, of course she is, but it doesn't always make it easy to control my own temper.

Ruby stays on my mind all morning. I decide I need to plan something for us to do together. A day out, maybe. It occurs to me that we haven't been texting much lately, so I send her one.

Heya. Love you to the moon and back. And penguin does too. Just saying. 🍪 🖤 🐧 xxxxoooooooxxxxx

She doesn't reply, even at break time. I hope all this means is that they're being strict with phone use at school.

I take a look at her Instagram feed to see what she's been posting, mindful that Hannah has been nagging me to monitor this stuff more closely. The latest post is a photo of one of the Lake Hall gargoyles. I smile because it's a great picture, but my smile fades when I read the caption: "When your nanny looks this bad and acts even worse." The hashtag is "#evilnanny."

DETECTIVE ANDY WILTON

ANDY TURNS THE PHOTOGRAPHS OF the reconstructed face over one by one. Lady Holt and her daughter both look at them carefully, but neither shows any emotional reaction. Steely, the pair of them, he thinks. He's not sure it's blue blood in their veins so much as antifreeze.

Lady Holt picks up one of the photographs. She puts on a pair of reading glasses and studies it. Andy watches her closely.

"Whoever this is, she has a very bland face," Lady Holt says.

"I'm sorry about my mother," her daughter says. "She has no tact."

"That's all right," Andy replies. "Nor do I. Do you recognize her?"

The daughter takes a closer look at the image her mother is holding and shakes her head. "No. I don't think so. If I ever met her, I have no recollection of it."

VIRGINIA

THE FACE IN THE PHOTOGRAPHS was not Hannah Burgess.

The features were similar to Hannah's, but it wasn't her. The chin didn't protrude enough, the way the eyes were set was wrong, and the nose was too refined.

This means I have no idea who the body in the lake belongs to, but it really is Hannah Burgess who is in my home, caring for my granddaughter. There is no longer any doubt.

Hannah is a schemer. Her motives were never simply financial. She wanted my husband, too.

She still wants money, that much is clear, but what else?

There must be more, because why else would you hurt a child, the way she has hurt Ruby?

Does she want an eye for an eye?

A tooth for a tooth?

A new little girl in her power, to replace the one she lost?

Another body slipped into the lake's waters, sinking quickly just the way hers did?

My plan to buy her off feels like sand slipping through my fingers.

1979

FINDING A JOB IN LONDON *is harder than Hannah imagined. The size and pace of the city disorients her, and she quickly discovers the fancier nanny agencies won't take her on because she lacks pukka qualifications. Her references and experience aren't enough for them. You'd think every other nanny was Mary bloody Poppins, the way they shake their heads and look at her after perusing her résumé.*

Using her savings from the Bristol job, Hannah rents a room in Vauxhall and gets a few hours of work a day at the New Covent Garden Market. It means a three A.M. start, but she doesn't mind the hours spent unpacking flowers before the rest of London wakes. She enjoys market life: the daily banter, the scalding watery coffees, the bacon butties that make her fingers oily. Hannah doesn't integrate very well, though, because her coworkers seem coarse to her. They remind her of her own family. She gets to know a few of the florists who are regulars, and she learns to barter with them and watch for their tics and tells as they negotiate.

What Hannah looks forward to most is seeing the brides and grooms. The posher florists bring them to the market to choose their wedding flowers. The happy couple are always bleary-eyed, unused to the early start, but glowingly loved up: walking around arm in arm, their misty breath blending as they lean in for a kiss. Hannah loves to see that. She loves the way they dream and how they want everything to be perfect for their big day. Feelings of jealousy and longing swell inside her when she watches them. Hannah dreams of choosing her own corsage. She knows exactly which flowers she wants in it.

Sometimes Hannah gets to take home a bunch of flowers for free:

whatever hasn't sold and can't be kept until tomorrow. She arranges the stems in front of the drafty narrow window in her bed-sitting room. It blocks the view of a busy high street. She misses the views of the Clifton Down in Bristol, and the big sky.

She sticks at the market job, though, because it's not unpleasant and it pays the rent. She likes the fact her shift ends at eleven A.M. because it gives her time to hunt for a nanny position.

In her spare time, Hannah walks the city streets, taking it all in with the unflinching gaze of a cat. She learns the neighborhoods one by one, paying attention to who lives where and how they live. She often gravitates back to the fancier areas, where she wanders down streets lined with beautiful white houses, admiring the glossy black railings fronting them, the immaculate window boxes and bay trees like lollipops framing grand front doors. She loves that the houses look so solid, permanent, and gracious.

On fine days Hannah goes to Hyde Park or Holland Park and watches the Norland nannies with their charges. She swings beside the children in the playground, feeling the wind in her hair as she goes higher and higher, and she eavesdrops on the nannies as they chat. Mostly they bitch about their employers and kids. One of them is a little older than the rest; she reminds Hannah of Nanny Hughes because she loves to give advice. "You should never stop learning," Hannah overhears her say one day. Hannah feels a little thrill because she thinks, That's what I'm doing, listening to you. Even though I'm not working as a nanny yet, I'm learning.

By the time Hannah gets a job offer, her hands have become coarse from the market work. It's not a permanent position; it's temporary cover for a nanny who has to have surgery. "But it's a foot in the door somewhere," Sandra from the agency says. Everything about the agency and Sandra herself is tired around the edges, styled in the 1950s when London is on the cusp of the 1980s.

The agency is situated above a corner shop on a neglected street in Pimlico, where the stucco is peeling away from the facades of the houses and the windows are grubby. Hannah signed with them because they were the only agency with a decent address that would have her. Observing the chaos they worked in, she didn't think they would be too exacting about references, either. Not that she hasn't got an excellent one from the husband in Bristol ("our youngest son was devastated when Hannah moved on; she was an absolute rock; she organized our household with extraordinary efficiency"), but it pays to be careful.

From the moment she starts the new job, Hannah doesn't like Casper, the boy she's supposed to look after. He's five years old and only ever a moment from messy tears. When the tears escalate into a tantrum, the pitch of his voice sets Hannah's teeth on edge. She knows there's no point trying to reform him because she won't be there long enough, so she decides she'll have to tolerate him mostly, and perhaps improve him a little, in the time she has.

Casper's mother doesn't work, so the three of them spend their days crammed into the family's small flat together. Hannah never meets the husband. He works abroad, the mother tells her. Every time Hannah tries to assert some discipline, the mother intervenes and says Casper should do what he wants to do because he must be free to express himself. The mother says she doesn't like to hear the word no. "Yes, Mrs. Deacon," Hannah says. She develops an itch to slap both mother and son.

Two days before she's due to leave the job, Hannah's patience snaps. The mother has gone out and Hannah is sitting on the toilet seat in the cramped bathroom while Casper bathes. Normally she would kneel on the bath mat and engage with the child, perhaps play a game, make him giggle. That's what she used to do with the younger boy in Bristol. Instead, she stares at the back of this child's weedy shoulders and feels blank. She is just counting time until her contract here is over.

Casper fishes a large water pistol out from under the bathwater. He laboriously fills it. He breathes heavily as he concentrates. When it's full, he shoots at Hannah, and the jet of water inscribes a pattern on the front of her shirt. It looks like a dog has peed there.

"Casper! No!" she says, but he does it again. "That's enough!"

This time the jet of water scores a pattern across her face. She opens her mouth to chide him more forcefully, but he shoots again and water fills it. As she chokes and spits, he shoots once more. She stands up. He tries to fire again, but only a few drops dribble from the end of the gun's barrel. It's empty. Hannah smiles. She puts her hand on his head and pushes it under the water. When he struggles, she steadies him with a hand on his shoulder. He's surprisingly strong. She counts to five before releasing him.

"Oh! I'm sorry, my love," she says when he's stopped screaming and his little rib cage doesn't expand and contract so violently. "Did some shampoo get in your eyes? Shall we rinse your hair again?" She reaches toward him.

"No! No, no, no, no!"

She can't help smiling at the fact that no has suddenly become his favorite word. "Don't tell your mummy you slipped under the water, will you?" she says. "Because if you do, the police will find out and they'll say she's a bad mummy and they'll put her in jail and you'll never see your mummy or your daddy again. Okay? Casper? Casper! It's polite to answer."

Casper nods, then shakes his head, desperate to give her the right answer. She's grateful he's such a stupid child—a brighter five-year-old might challenge her. She checks on him later after bedtime and he still looks stricken even though he's asleep.

Casper remains as good as gold for the last forty-eight hours of her contract, and Hannah is grateful to be able to move on without another incident. She is a bit spooked by how quickly her temper snapped and how close she was to keeping the boy's head under the water until the last silvery bubble rose from his mouth and the light went out of his eyes. It keeps her awake at night for a night or two after it happens, and she thinks, I must be careful. I must be more careful than I have been. This will not happen again.

As she reflects, she decides the experience of looking after Casper was a good lesson for her. In the future, there must be something in it for her, in any job she takes. Something more than a paycheck. She must like the child or one of the parents, at the very least, and she doesn't want to live anywhere so cramped and unattractive again, or work for a mother who is always hovering.

Under her bed at home are some magazines she stole from the doctor's waiting room. When she can't sleep, she grabs one of her favorites: Tatler. *She loves to read the gossip about the aristocracy and look at photographs of them. Sometimes their homes are pictured, too.*

This is what I need, *she thinks as she turns the pages for the umpteenth time, her eyes lingering on her favorite pictures:* I need a family with class; people who know how to behave and how to live. *It's almost a physical thrill for her, the sight of the beautifully dressed men and women draped over furniture or over one another, with their special double-barreled names and titles.*

How she would love to have one of those men for herself.

JO

WORK HAS BECOME RESPITE FROM home while I count the days until Hannah moves in.

Telling Mother that I'd invited Hannah to live at Lake Hall went down about as well as when I told Ruby.

"Over my dead body," she says.

"That's not fair, I need the help."

"I offered you help." Her hands trembled, but I felt no sympathy, only anger that she would make this about her.

"You can't do it, Mother! It's not a part-time commitment. Ruby needs consistency and I need reliability. You were happy enough to let Hannah bring me up."

"I overrule you," she says.

"You can't. This is happening. It won't be for long, I hope, because Ruby and I will be gone from here as soon as we can afford it."

"Ruby should have a family member looking after her."

"So what was good for me isn't good enough for her? You are unbelievable."

I expect the argument to escalate and I'm braced to defend myself further, but she takes a deep breath and looks at me with a peculiar intensity.

"Jocelyn," she says. "You must listen to me."

"What is it?" I feel a flutter of fear.

"There's something I need to tell you, something Ruby told me: Hannah is hurting her."

"Hannah is hurting Ruby?" This is the most outrageous thing

Mother's ever said. How low will she stoop to get her own way? "I can't believe you would say such a thing. Hannah wouldn't hurt a fly. She never lifted a finger to me in my life. And Ruby would have said something to me if that were the case."

"Darling, I swear this is true. I swear it on my life. It's happening."

"You're confused."

"You must act. If you don't act, I shall."

"Stop it. Enough. It's an outrageous accusation. I thought better of you. I have to go to work now, but we'll talk about this tonight. In the meantime, you should get used to the idea that Hannah will be living here."

I SIT on the train and think about what Mother said. I can't believe it's true, but it's the sort of thing you can't get out of your head. Once said, it can't be unsaid.

My reaction is still disbelief, though. Out of Hannah and Mother, only one of them treated me roughly when I was a child, and it wasn't Hannah. Mother is trying to smear Hannah. It's appalling and I know Ruby would have said something to me if it were true.

At work, I throw myself back into my search for proof of provenance of the vanitas. I feel part detective and part treasure hunter, and I love it. I wonder how many drawing-room walls the painting has hung on over the years and how much human drama it has witnessed in its various homes. I would be fascinated to know every detail, but I'll settle for finding what I'm looking for. Once I'm at the National Gallery archives, it doesn't take me long.

The document is in the catalogue from the exhibition that included our vanitas. It's only a slim pamphlet listing the paintings, with small black-and-white images of each, but it provides a more complete provenance of the vanitas. Before my family and the Paul

König Collection owned the painting, it apparently belonged to the Johannes Hofkes Foundation. The pamphlet makes a lovely addition to the paper trail I'm putting together. I photograph it and leave with a smile. The sale commission feels closer than ever.

I also begin to wonder if I can do even better. Perhaps I could extend the paper trail back to the Hofkes Foundation. A quick Internet search tells me the foundation still exists today; I'm hopeful they might have records.

I walk back to the gallery. London looks fine and crisp in the sunshine. Shadows rake Piccadilly. The trees beside St. James's Church have lost their foliage, and milky sunshine falls through the lattice of boughs, dousing the market traders and their stalls below. The shops will be putting up their Christmas displays soon, I think, and I wonder if I can afford to take Ruby away for a few days once I get paid. Perhaps Hannah would like to come with us. It would be so nice for all three of us to spend time together. I try not to think about what Mother said about Hannah and what I'm going to do about it.

At the gallery, Clemency is cleaning glass.

"I found the exhibition catalogue!" I say.

She keeps polishing and doesn't turn around. "Very good."

"Is Faversham in?"

"Nope."

"Oh." Deflated by her flat response and by Faversham's absence, I try not to feel hurt. "I was thinking I should contact the foundation who owned the vanitas before the Paul König Collection bought it. The more we know, the better, right?"

Clemency turns to face me. Her hands are blackened from the newsprint she's been using to shine the glass. "I don't think that's necessary. Let's see if the client is satisfied with what you've already got."

"Is something the matter?"

"Nothing's the matter."

She moves on to the next painting. She squirts glass cleaner onto a duster and rubs it gently over the glass. I refuse to give up because I think this is important. "I'm going to ask Faversham about it, because I really think we should give the client everything we can find. I mean, this is history, art history. If I can put together a package of proof of provenance now, it will stay with the painting forever and become a part of its story."

Clemency's shoulders sag. "Do you have any idea how pretentious you sound?" she says. My shock must be easy to read because she softens her tone. "Look, can we sit down? There's something I think you need to know."

She looks so serious I'm afraid I'm in danger of losing my job. I take a seat. "I'm so sorry if I crossed a line. I'm trying to do my best."

She sits opposite me. "I'm sorry to say this," she says, "very sorry. But things here aren't what they seem. Faversham is involved in forging artworks. He has been doing it for well over a decade."

"What?" Of all the things I might have expected her to say, this would never have occurred to me. It's extraordinary. "How?"

"There are a few different methods involved. It's complicated and I can explain it all in detail, but what you need to know is that Faversham works with your parents and also with Elizabeth Fuller, your mother's friend. Elizabeth creates the forgeries. Your family art collection is used to give them context. Faversham's reputation as a connoisseur means the fakes can be released onto the market alongside the genuine stuff he does sell. Their favorite method is to create new drawings, usually Italian Renaissance, and claim a Holt Collection provenance to give them validity based on the information in the Holt Catalogue."

"But the Holt Catalogue was destroyed in a flood."

"Is that what they told you? They were lying, I'm afraid."

I'm almost speechless with shock, but I have so many questions. "What about you? Are you part of it?"

"This is why I want to tell you about it. They involved me in their forgery scheme without my knowing. They made a criminal of me, and they are doing the same to you. The documents you 'discovered' in the archives? Those were planted by Elizabeth. Paintings aren't the only thing she can fake. She is very, very good at what she does. One of the best forgers of all time, I suspect."

It seems everything I thought I knew has been wrong. Everything. Including my opinion of Clemency. "I thought you didn't like me."

She shakes her head. "It wasn't you. It was what they were doing to you."

"And the photograph of me as a child with the vanitas? Is that real, or did they fake that, too?" That they might have tampered with my memories is particularly disturbing. Have I been living in a house of cards?

"I don't know about the photograph and I'm so sorry to have to tell you any of this. I know it must come as a huge shock, but I think you have a right to know what they are doing and involving you in."

"Here I was thinking I was discovering these amazing things."

"It's a potent thing to believe you're making a discovery. I know. I used to feel the same. It sickens me now when I remember how excited I got."

"Why are you still working here?"

"Once I discovered what was going on and what a stooge they'd made of me, I had three choices: leave and not breathe a word about what I knew; leave and turn them in to the police, which would implicate me; or join them and profit. I had no money. I was in debt, so I joined them, but you don't have to. I'm telling you this because I want to give you a chance to get out before you are in too deep. I never had that opportunity."

"What makes you so sure I won't go to the police and turn all of you in?"

"It's your family." She's so sure of this it brings a resigned smile to her face. She doesn't know me as well as she believes. I need time to think.

"Can you tell Faversham I had to go home?"

"Of course, and call me if it's any use to talk."

"Thank you," I say. "It was unbelievably brave of you to tell me."

"I'm sorry you had to hear it and sorry it had to be me to say it. I hope I've done the right thing."

"You have."

I leave the gallery and walk briskly away from Cork Street until I find myself deep in Green Park. I feel suffocated, sullied, and very angry. I'm angry with Faversham, but most of all I'm angry with Mother and Elizabeth. How dare they manipulate me like this? I had to come home to Lake Hall because I needed a refuge. I wanted as little to do with Mother as possible, but I tolerated her trying to get her claws into Ruby and I made an effort for both their sakes even though I felt as if grief were chewing holes through me. To find out that I have been entrapped in something illegal by my own mother makes me burn with outrage. If I was caught, my ability to raise my own child would be compromised. It's an unthinkable betrayal.

I head for Paddington Station. I feel absolutely murderous.

1980

HANNAH DECIDES IT'S TIME TO *treat herself to a tour of Buckingham Palace. She has saved up enough money and is bursting with excitement. She gets off the Tube at Piccadilly to enjoy a walk to the palace and a look in the shops, but they all seem to be staffed by unsmiling men and women who glance condescendingly at Hannah.* You're no better than me, *she thinks.* You're just shop assistants, *but they make her feel small.*

For all that she's tried, her life hasn't moved on in the way she wants it to. She still works at the market because nannying opportunities have been almost nonexistent. She's beginning to hate this city with its displays of wealth and success that she can't access. It's time she considered her options.

On her way toward The Mall, she spots a sign on the other side of the street that makes her stop in her tracks.

Jennifer Mirren: A Retrospective

It must be an exhibition of the Bristol mother's paintings. She can't believe it. She crosses the street and enters the gallery. Opening the door sets off a jangling bell, but nobody comes. The room is only half hung with paintings. Many others are stacked on the floor, still swathed in Bubble Wrap. The ones that are already hung are as bad as she remembers: they look like somebody squeezed shampoo all over the canvas.

"Hello?" she calls, but there's no response. She approaches the desk, on which neat parallel stacks of cards and envelopes wait for

somebody's attention. She picks up the card on the top of the stack. It's an invitation to the private viewing in ten days' time. "Champagne and canapés," it says. It is inscribed to Lord and Lady Alexander Holt. She wants one, but she'd better not take that one. Those people sound well known. She riffles through the stack and comes across one inscribed to some woman called Charlotte Phillipson. Not so posh. She can hear footsteps, so she puts the card into her handbag and slips out of the gallery.

For ten days the private viewing occupies her thoughts. She finds she's even looking forward to seeing the Bristol husband again. She peruses her dog-eared copies of Tatler *with closer attention than ever, especially the society photographs, and in particular any spreads that feature exhibition openings. She looks at what the women are wearing and finds herself a dress she thinks will do in Camden Market and steals a scarf from Liberty to wear with it. She remembers the wife in Bristol, her artsy authority. She puts the outfit on and practices looking confident in front of the mirror.*

On the night of the opening, she approaches the gallery with a pounding heart, but she needn't have worried. The woman at the door is preoccupied with kowtowing to a beautiful couple when Hannah arrives and doesn't even check the name on Hannah's invitation. She just adds it to a wedge of cards she's holding and waves Hannah in.

The husband from Bristol is roaring drunk, but he recognizes her immediately.

"God! Hannah! Long time no see!" he shouts. He unsticks his hands from the waist of another woman and plants them low on Hannah's back as he hugs her. "You look absolutely edible!" he says. "Did somebody get you an invitation? How marvelous that you're here!"

He stands too close to her as he fills her in on the news: the younger boy was hit very hard by his mother's death, he's had a few problems, and the older boy was devastated, but he's actually been doing better and he's back at home. They have a new nanny. His own painting is going very, very well.

"What about you?"

"I'm between jobs," Hannah says.

"Oh, that is the most splendid coincidence. My cousin is looking for somebody. London and Wiltshire. Virginia!"

A woman turns. She is pregnant, quite far on, and she looks ravishing in a gauzy dress with silky panels over a nude body stocking. It accentuates and gives some modesty to her bump all at once. It's a far cry from the maternity smocks Hannah has seen other women wear. She is tall and undeniably elegant but not conventionally pretty. Her face is too strong and compelling for that. Even so, Hannah feels sick with envy.

"My cousin," the Bristol husband whispers. "I'd be bloody tempted if she wasn't, I tell you."

Virginia is sweet and not at all as fierce as she looks. "I wasn't sure I wanted a nanny," she says. Her hands smooth her dress over her bump. Men watch her. "I've been resisting it because I wanted to raise her myself, but now Alexander has finally persuaded me to hire some help, I've left it so late it's impossible to get somebody good."

"How do you know it's a girl?" Hannah asks.

"I don't. But I'm longing for a daughter!"

How amazing to be so certain that just thinking about what you want might make it come true, *Hannah thinks. What kind of person believes that?*

"I happen to be free earlier than expected," she says. "The family I'm working for are moving abroad." It's a lie, but she'll deal with the consequences later. She wants this job badly. She can tell these are quality people, and they have a country home. It's more than she dared dream of.

"Perhaps this is serendipity!" she adds because she thinks Virginia would like the idea of this being an amazing, fortunate thing to happen, and she sends a silent thank-you to Nanny Hughes for teaching her the word.

Virginia laughs. "Perhaps it is! Well, would you be free to pop around to our house and have a chat this week? We're not far from here."

"Of course!" Hannah says. "It's so important to see if we like each other and can work together." She sends another silent thank-you to Nanny Hughes for that little gem.

"Wonderful! Though I think we're going to get along fine. Why don't I introduce you to my husband? Alexander!"

Could this be Lord and Lady Holt? Hannah wonders. Her heart patters even faster, as if baby fingers are drumming on the inside of her rib cage. Alexander Holt extracts himself from a conversation when his wife calls. He is absolutely ravishing. He is the type of handsome Hannah has only ever seen in a magazine or on a cinema screen. He is so beautiful she can hardly bear to look at him when they are introduced.

"Hannah is a nanny and she might be free to help us with the baby. She looked after Seb's boys in Bristol." Virginia leans into him when she talks to him. Her lips almost graze his cheek.

"Hannah's absolutely marvelous!" Seb says.

"Do you have any experience with babies?" Alexander asks.

"I looked after a pair of twins."

"For how long?"

Virginia lays a hand on her husband's chest and Hannah feels a stab of jealousy. "Darling, I'll arrange for Hannah to come and see us this week and we can interview her then. Let's not ruin her party. Can you give her our address?"

He reaches for his inside pocket and extracts a slim gold and blue cigarette case and a few cards. The cigarette case goes back in *smoothly, and he retains a card. He borrows a pen from the girl at the desk and writes down their address and a time they agree for Hannah to come for an interview.*

Throughout the rest of the evening, and even the fuck she settles for later that night with a city boy so drunk he struggles to find his own flat after the taxi has dropped them off on the King's Road, Hannah cannot think of anything other than Alexander. She grips the card he gave her even while the city boy has his hands all over her. "Lord Alexander Holt," the card says. "Social Secretary. The Burlington Club." He's the one, *she thinks.*

Every muscle in her body already aches for him and every cell in her body tells her that she will never do better than him.

He's the one she wants.

VIRGINIA

HANNAH IS MOVING BACK INTO Lake Hall to care for Ruby. History is repeating itself. I don't know how to warn Jocelyn strongly enough that I fear the outcome could be violent. Violence against whom, I don't know yet, but I expect Hannah does. She always did plan so well.

I want to go out today because I can hardly bear to be here, but I'm nervous of using the Land Rover. I get as far as taking it for a little spin on the drive and testing the brakes. They seem fine, but what if Hannah has tampered with something else since Geoff checked it over? I can't ask him to look at it again. He'll think I've gone mad. I lose my courage and slink back into the house like a dog with its tail between its legs.

When Jocelyn gets back from work I try to talk to her again about Ruby's bruises. She won't have it. She is seething with rage, spitting tacks.

"I'll speak to Ruby myself," she says. "I don't want to hear another word about it from you. We have something else to discuss."

Clemency has spilled the beans about the forgeries.

"I didn't want to involve you," I insist. "It wasn't my idea."

I want to explain to Jocelyn that it was her father who got us into this mess in the first place and Faversham recruited her without my permission, but she won't listen. Her angry tirade is unstoppable and directed at me entirely: I am the bad seed from which everything ugly and terrible in her life has grown and this is just more proof.

It leaves me reeling.

It wasn't my fault. I became complicit, I'll admit that, but Alexander started it.

I first learned about our financial situation one night when Alexander and I sat together in the garden. Where the tips of the oaks met the dusky sky, it was densely blue. I saw the silhouette of an owl on a fence post. It was surveying the stubble in the fields. We could hear the occasional small splash from the lake and snippets of a lullaby drifted from the attic windows where Hannah was putting Jocelyn to bed.

Alexander winced. "Isn't she too old to be sung to every night?" he asked.

"Hannah insists it's part of Jocelyn's routine. She says . . ."—and here I couldn't resist making my tone a little bit nasty as I mimicked our nanny—"'A song and a story make a happy bedtime.'"

"I don't suppose we can ask Hannah to attend singing lessons?"

I sniggered. Alexander had made strong gin and tonics, and alcohol always warmed up his sense of humor.

"Or, failing that, ask her to close the window?" he added, but that wasn't funny.

"It's too hot for Jocelyn, darling."

"It was just a joke."

"I'm sorry."

I was touchy about Jocelyn's care and felt a pathetic eagerness to assert my maternal instincts whenever I could. It was pointless, because by then Hannah was making most of the decisions and I nursed the knowledge that my daughter loathed me. I couldn't remain blind to it when each day brought me more proof. I had come to believe I was abhorrent. What else could I be if my own child hated me so much?

Alexander looked up at the open window of Jocelyn's room. "Let's take a walk," he said.

"Now?"

"Now."

"Where are we going?" I kicked my shoes off and followed him barefoot across the lawn.

Alexander pushed the boathouse door open. The wooden dingy idled against its mooring and the oars lay tidily within it. A match flared as Alexander lit a small paraffin lamp. He took blankets from a chest and shook them. He laid them on the deck beside the boat. I felt as if my whole body was clenched. We had not been intimate for many months. The light from the lamp was kind to him, hiding the shadows under his eyes. It had been a long few weeks of parties and work for him. We had come to the country to recuperate.

He seated himself and I sat beside him. I edged close so our thighs were touching. I turned to him. I put my hand to his cheek and his fingers closed over mine. I turned my face toward his and closed my eyes, but intimacy wasn't on his mind. "Ginny," he said. He moved my hand from his cheek. I opened my eyes. "I have something to tell you."

I was desperately disappointed. What more could a marriage wish for, especially a marriage as high stakes as ours, than for our desire for each other to be still felt after all these years? I composed myself quickly. You do best not to let disappointment show. Men don't like it.

Alexander pushed the boat away from the deck with his toes, and caught it as it drifted back. The sound of lapping filled the space, and the water sent flickering waves of reflected light across the walls and ceiling.

This was the rhythm to which I learned we were in danger of losing everything.

Alexander told a gentleman's tale of spiraling debt and loans offered by suited and booted young bankers who were at first ecstatic to be invited to share a table at the Burlington Club with Lord Holt, but less keen to be on first-name terms with him once their membership had been seconded and accepted and Alexander was in default on repayments of the loans they secured for him.

Alexander told me our accounts were empty and all his credit cards were maxed out. He said he'd sold a drawing from his grandfather's collection at auction for what he had subsequently discovered was a woefully low price. It was Faversham, his old school friend, who had spotted the sale of the drawing and confronted Alexander as to why he'd let it go. Once he learned what had happened, he insisted Alexander tell me what our situation was.

So here we were. Alexander retched at the end of his story, as if there were a hair ball of shame in his throat. Was I tempted to leave him? Never. We had come too far together, and we had a child. Her face may have scrunched with distaste every time she saw me, but she loved her daddy very much.

I took other routes to resolve things. First, I went to the doctor.

"Mother's little helper," Eric said as he wrote the prescription.

"Wife's little helper might be a better description," I said, but I wished I could have taken the words back, because Eric looked at me in a curious way.

I didn't take too many, though, just enough to get me through those first hard weeks. Then I told Alexander I'd been talking to Elizabeth and we'd had an idea.

Faversham, Alexander, Elizabeth, and I hatched the forgery plan to save Lake Hall and the art collection for Jocelyn with enough profit generated along the way to keep everybody happy. The plan worked beautifully until Faversham overstepped the mark and involved Clemency. And now he has sucked Jocelyn in, too. And I am being blamed.

Jocelyn finishes her diatribe by telling me I am poisoning Ruby.

She has observed our closeness, she says, and it's unhealthy for Ruby because I am a dishonest person. She makes it sound as if every overture I have made to my granddaughter is no more than a strange sorcery, made in a caldron, designed as a hex. Her words cut so deep I fear my strength will drain from me and puddle around my feet. I bow my head and wait to hear the door slam behind her when she goes.

In the silence she leaves behind her, I fight back tears. Jocelyn thinks nothing of planting a fresh blade in my back every single day, and I feel weaker with each one, but I must continue to try to defend her past and her future, and that is the end of it.

JO

I TALK TO RUBY AT bedtime, when we're away from Mother's flappy ears. It's the conversation you never want to have with your child. I trust Hannah implicitly and I don't want to do this, but I have to, just in case. When Ruby's all tucked up with her book, I sit on the side of her bed.

"Can I ask you about something you said to Granny? You told Granny that Hannah had hurt you. Granny said there was a bruise on your arm."

She pulls up her sleeve and reveals two bruises. They are fingerprint-size and probably a few days old.

"Can you tell me how you got them?"

"It was an accident."

"What kind of accident?"

"I don't know."

"Are these the only bruises? Are there more?"

She shakes her head and pulls up her other sleeve. Her arms look perfect otherwise.

"I need to know what happened, poppet. It's important."

"Why?"

"Because you told Granny that Hannah hurt you and that's a very serious thing to say."

"I didn't tell her that."

"You didn't?"

"I don't know why Granny said that. I think she got mixed up."

"So how did you get the bruises?"

She shrugs. "I don't remember. At school, maybe. We played dodgeball at break and some of the boys got a little ball and threw it really hard. They got told off."

I question her gently a little more, but that's the line she sticks to and it's plausible, I suppose, so I quit before she gets upset about it. It stays on my mind, though. It's because the bruises are on the inside of her arm.

Like so much else that's happening at the moment, I'm not sure what or whom to believe.

I LIE in bed. It's too early to sleep, but I'm avoiding Mother who is roaming the house downstairs. I try to read, but I can't concentrate on my novel. The bruises on Ruby's arm are still bothering me. I can't get them out of my head, but it's different from before. I can visualize her bruises, but whenever I do, I also see a different arm, another's girl's arm. It's my arm and it's bruised, too.

The memory is unexpected and unfamiliar. I recognize it in the way you might an old object you need to dust off before you can identify it properly. I know what I'm remembering is the night of my parents' party, the night they told Hannah to leave, because I am wearing the dress, the one I remember as blue, even though Hannah has assured me it was apple green. The dress is definitely blue in my memory, so I wonder how reliable that makes it? I don't know the answer, but reliable or not it's both vivid and powerful.

I'm in the garden with Mother and her friend Giles and some other people. They all have drinks. Mother looks beautiful. I'm hot and sweaty because Giles is daring me to do things as fast as I can.

"No!" Mother says when he dares me to attempt a cartwheel. I'm not a very acrobatic girl. Mother gets up from her chair on the terrace. She kneels down beside me and smoke from her cigarette makes me cough. "We don't show our knickers to our guests," she hisses in my ear. "Stop making a spectacle of yourself."

"Don't be such a spoilsport, Ginny!" Giles shouts. "Come on, little one, cartwheel, please. Or perhaps a backflip."

Mother shakes her head, but I feel defiant. I can do a cartwheel and I'm enjoying being the focus of Giles's attention. I step away from Mother and give it my best shot.

"Jocelyn!" she warns.

"Marvelous! More, please!" Giles claps energetically.

I do another and another and I'm getting hotter and the cartwheels are getting messier, but I keep going. I'll show them how many I can do. Out of breath after five or six, I stop and check for their reaction, but they've stopped watching, even Giles. I call him to look at me. I don't care if it's rude.

"Jocelyn!" Mother turns. "Stop shouting! In fact go back inside this instant!"

I run as fast as I can and do another three cartwheels in a row right in front of Mother and Giles, but on the final one I slip as I land and slide across the damp grass and into a huge dog turd on the edge of the flowerbed. Mother doesn't notice the turd until she pulls me up. Her nose wrinkles and she freezes, but it's too late. The poo is all over her, too, smeared across the yellow and orange folds of her dress and caked on the beautiful beads that dangle from its neckline.

Giles laughs. Head back, loud laughing. I know Mother is very upset because she loves her dresses, but she laughs, too, and says, "Oh well, it was a toss-up between this and the check Galliano dress anyway, so now I get to wear both."

"God!" one of her friends shouts. "I'm so jealous! How did you get your hands on that? You're always ahead of the bloody game."

"John's a friend," Mother says. "Come on, Jocelyn. Time to go in."

Inside, she grabs my arm and hits me sharply on the backs of the legs, one, two, three slaps, hard ones, each delivered faster than the last, and I scream because it hurts and I think more are coming, but Hannah appears and Mother stops. "What's happened here, then?" Hannah says, and Mother shoves me toward her.

"Where the hell were you?"

"Lord Holt needed assistance finding something."

"Well, I wish he'd bloody well hurry up. I can't deal with her on my own. Make sure this doesn't happen again."

The backs of my legs were slapped red but that faded quickly. Where Mother grabbed my arm, her fingerprints left a row of bruises. Just like Ruby's.

It's a troubling memory, just as the bruises on Ruby's arm are, and almost as troubling is why I haven't remembered this until now.

VIRGINIA

JOCELYN HAS TAKEN THE DAY off. She says she can't face Faversham until she has had time to think. I'm determined to make another effort to talk to her. My impotence is tormenting me. I wait for her all morning because she doesn't reappear after dropping Ruby at school. We are beyond the point where we communicate our movements to each other out of courtesy and she's not answering her phone.

Late morning I take a walk outside. Boudicca ambles with me. I notice that Jocelyn took the Land Rover this morning, unusually, and my heart skips a beat. What if Hannah tampered with it and Jocelyn has gone off the road in an "accident" that was meant to happen to me? I walk to the end of the driveway, but the only vehicle to pass is a tractor. I return to the house and pace the perimeter of the outbuildings.

I walk beside the orchard wall. I've been thinking of it as "Ruby's wall" lately, since she's taken to climbing it. I run my fingers along the wall as I walk, feeling the outcrops of stone where she lodges her feet to get a purchase on it until I reach the ledge she likes to jump from.

It's about five feet from the ground, a lovely bit of golden stone, wide and solid. It's been set into that wall since it was first built. It's rock solid.

I touch it, smiling as I think of Ruby leaping bravely from it, and it moves. I grasp it with both hands and find I can easily shift it from side to side. It's a death trap. I look at the ground beneath it. There's a small dusting of mortar there. Did I create it when I wobbled the stone or has somebody scraped the mortar away deliberately? It's hard to tell, but I'm seized with terror. It's one thing for Hannah to make threats to me, but what if she has decided to target Ruby?

I hear the gravel crunch from the front of the house. I hurry around. I must tell Jocelyn about this immediately. She has backed the Land Rover up to the door of the house and she doesn't acknowledge me when she gets out of the car. In the back I see a suitcase and some bags.

"What's happening?" I ask.

"It's Hannah's moving-in day." The look she gives me dares me to object. I don't, but I feel another surge of anger and fear. *Open your eyes!* I want to scream. *I love you. I am not the threat!*

Hannah emerges from the passenger seat before I can say anything. I must hold my nerve until I can talk to Jocelyn alone.

"Well, I expect that'll make life much easier for you both," I say. "I'll help you with the bags." I reach for the handle of a suitcase.

"No, no!" Jocelyn puts her hand on my arm as if I am some kind of hooligan in need of restraint. "It's too heavy."

"Take your hand off me!"

"It's too heavy for you!"

"It is not!" I refuse to stop now that I've started. It's humiliating. I yank on the suitcase handle and she's right, it is too heavy for me, but I've pulled it too far out to push it back and it plummets to the ground before I can take my hand off the handle, yanking me off balance. I put out my other hand to break my fall.

I don't hear the sound my wrist makes when I break it, but I feel it as an absence of something, a moment of intense calm before a scorching pain radiates up my arm.

Hannah and Jocelyn help me to the bench and I collapse onto it.

They tower over me, absorbing the light. I hold my wrist against myself. I don't want either of them to look at it or at me. I am ashamed.

Hannah's face is a picture of fake sympathy and concern, but my daughter looks at me with contempt. To her I am an old fool.

She is so wrong, I think as the pain intensifies and I bend over my wrist. She needs to leave behind the anger she has nurtured since she was a child and see through the veils of falsity Hannah is shrouding us with. She needs to be so much more than this. It's our only hope.

THREE

1982

TWO-YEAR-OLD JOCELYN IS STANDING UP *in her crib when Hannah comes to her. The little girl is pleased to see her nanny. She bounces up and down, fingers gripping the bars. "Careful," Hannah warns. "Don't bang your head!"*

Hannah lifts Jocelyn from her crib and lays her down on the changing mat. When she's put a clean nappy on, she offers Jocelyn her two index fingers and the little girl grips one in each hand and pulls herself up into a sitting, then standing position with Hannah's help. "Heave!" she and Hannah chorus as she does. Jocelyn laughs.

Hannah decides to try something. She's done it before. She's been doing it with Jocelyn since she was a baby. Hannah smiles broadly at the little girl and Jocelyn's own smile widens until she's absolutely beaming. Hannah changes her expression, turning down the sides of her mouth, slackening the muscles in her cheeks and letting sadness well into her eyes. Jocelyn reacts instantly. She stares at Hannah and her own smile fades and her features fall. Hannah keeps completely still, staring at the girl, until Jocelyn's chin begins to quiver and tears well and then spill.

"Oh, Jocelyn!" Hannah says, snapping back into happy mode, smiling again. "I'm sorry! Nanny Hannah felt a bit poorly for a minute, but you cheered me up by caring about me." She showers kisses on the little girl until Jocelyn is giggling again. "Now what do you say," Hannah asks, "shall we put your dress on and go and join the party?"

Jocelyn smiles sweetly as they head downstairs. Hannah bounces her on her hip as they go. "Bouncy, bouncy," Jocelyn says. Jocelyn is wearing a pale pink corduroy pinafore and Hannah has expertly pinned her silken hair so it frames her face. She looks like a little doll. Everybody will love her. Hannah checks her watch. The balloons won't appear for another hour. She knows the timings exactly. It's important, because Jocelyn hates balloons since one popped in her face.

The summer fete has just opened. People arrive at Lake Hall in large numbers, eager to see what's behind the ancient gates. Lord Holt and young Geoff, who helps in the garden, work together guiding cars into a field to park. On the lawn, village ladies serve tea and cordial, filling empty ice cream tubs with change. Locally made crafts, watercolors, and homemade cakes are displayed in stalls and on tables, and cuttings raised from the Lake Hall gardens are on sale under an awning attached to the side of the barn.

Hannah oversees Jocelyn closely as they make a tour of the stalls. She also keeps a weather eye on Virginia Holt's movements. Virginia looks every inch the part of the lady of the manor in a tweed skirt belted to show off her slender waist, a white shirt with the collar upturned, and a tweed hat with feathers angled sharply from the brim. Around her neck is a platinum chain from which a heart-shaped pendant dangles, the diamonds and emeralds within it sparkling even when the sun disappears behind the clouds. It's an heirloom necklace Hannah has spotted in a portrait of a previous Lady Holt. She knows it must be worth a fortune. She itches to wear it herself.

At three-thirty Hannah and Jocelyn stand at the sideline and clap as Lady Holt awards the prize for best-looking mongrel at the dog show. At four o'clock, Virginia moves as planned toward the makeshift platform, supported by straw bales, where the brass band plays a too-slow rendition of "Jerusalem" and the gusty wind whisks the sound off and away over the cornfields. Once the final note has been held for a patriotic length of time, Virginia mounts the platform, where a microphone has been positioned for her. She taps it and it squawks. "Hello. Can you hear me?" Her voice booms and she has the attention of most of the visitors. "Very good!" she adds. "Please do gather round." Her smile is gracious.

"Look at your mother!" Hannah says to Jocelyn.

"Mother," Jocelyn says. It's a statement: informative, nothing more. She's perfectly content to stay in Hannah's arms.

Hannah uses her elbows to get herself and Jocelyn to the front of the crowd. If Jocelyn reached out, she could touch her mother's boots. Some women have assembled on either side of Virginia. Each holds a bulging black bin liner and wears a sweatshirt emblazoned with the logo of a local children's hospice.

"Thank you so much for coming here today," Virginia says. Hannah peers over her shoulder to see if Alexander is watching his wife, and sure enough, she spots him at the back of the crowd, arms crossed, entirely relaxed, as if he has all the time in the world to admire a very fine possession. Hannah wishes she hadn't looked because her emotions rise so fast, and so sharply, and take so long to recede afterward. Jealousy of Virginia and the desire to possess Alexander Holt are a fierce ache in every fiber of her body.

"We are very grateful for the help of all of our volunteers, without whom this event would not be nearly as splendid," Virginia says. The crowd loves her. Jocelyn feels heavy on Hannah's hip. She shifts the little girl onto her other side.

"And now we have something very special to celebrate. Even before we opened the gates of Lake Hall this afternoon, our Women's Institute met their fundraising target to build an extension that will provide a much-needed family room for parents of sick children at the Joseph Cares Hospice. Can you join me in a big round of applause to congratulate them?"

The clapping is loud enough to startle Jocelyn. Hannah notices the ladies with the bin bags are beginning to stir. It's time.

"Want to go to Mother?" she asks Jocelyn. "And see all the lovely instruments?"

She reaches out and taps Virginia's knee. Virginia moves her leg back. Hannah taps again, and this time she gets Virginia's attention. She holds Jocelyn up. Virginia's smile freezes. She shakes her head almost imperceptibly. Hannah pushes Jocelyn out farther. The child looks uncertain, but Hannah says, "Be a good girl for Hannah! Let Mother have you for just a minute. Then we'll get you an ice cream." Jocelyn is now so far aloft that Virginia has no choice but to take her daughter. As she does, the crowd says, "Ahhhh."

Virginia can't clap now she's holding Jocelyn but she resurrects her smile. She looks like a model on the front of Country Life. *Jocelyn stares down at Hannah, who makes encouraging faces. It doesn't work. Jocelyn goes limp and holds her arms out to her nanny. Virginia heaves the child higher in response, rucking up her shirt. "And now," she says, "let's release the balloons!" Her free hand gestures to the skies, and Hannah takes a step or two back into the crowd as the ladies with the bin bags rip them open to release two dozen pink helium balloons into the air.*

Jocelyn's scream has a thread of pure terror running through it. She bucks vigorously to escape the balloons and her mother's arms. Virginia almost drops her. Hannah watches her try to admonish the child firmly, but there's no saving Virginia now: Jocelyn is hysterical. Being cross with her is only going to make it worse. Virginia looks panicked and profoundly embarrassed.

Hannah counts to ten before she makes herself visible again and takes the distraught child from her mother, by which time Virginia is humiliated and Jocelyn is fighting tooth and nail to get away. Everybody is watching.

VIRGINIA

JOCELYN DRIVES ME TO THE hospital in the Land Rover. Every pothole on the road feels brutally jarring, even though Jocelyn is driving carefully. My wrist is aflame with pain and my head pounds. I fear we'll go off the road in this car, but I daren't mention Hannah's threatening comment about it. Jocelyn won't believe me.

There is so much to say that's urgent.

"Hannah loosened the stone ledge," I say. "On the orchard wall. It's the ledge Ruby jumps from and she'll hurt herself very badly if she tries to do it again. You must tell Geoff to fix it."

"Stop it," she says.

"Listen to me!"

"Are you going to tell me that Hannah pushed you over just now, too? Is everything her fault?"

"You must check the stone ledge."

She shakes her head in disbelief.

"I'm serious, Jocelyn. Promise me you'll do it as soon as we're home."

"Okay, I promise, if you promise me you'll be civil to Hannah."

I keep my mouth shut.

"Mother!"

"Never."

I see another pothole ahead, but this time Jocelyn doesn't decelerate as we approach it. My whole body shakes as I brace myself against it. Did Jocelyn see it, or not?

I don't dare think about the answer to that question.

DETECTIVE ANDY WILTON

ANDY CURSES AS THE GRAND door shuts behind him. He shakes his shoulders, as if ridding himself of a foul garment, and surveys the scene in front of him.

The police archivist finally sent the original file relating to the shooting. It was disappointing. Mostly it told Andy what he already knew. The only useful thing it yielded was a partial list of names of some of the guests who took part in the shoot. Andy has just spent a frustrating twenty minutes being stonewalled by one of them. It was a total waste of time.

To his right, giant topiary yews emerge from a dense, low-lying fog that plagued the drive down into the valley this morning. To his left, beyond a tennis court with a sagging net, is a view that extends for miles across the county. Crows caw from their treetop nests.

"What's wrong with these people?" he rages. "They live in a fucking time warp. There are ways to tell us he doesn't remember this woman without patronizing us. I'll bet he's lying through his teeth as well. I'd bloody love to take him down a few pegs."

"Him or the entire aristocracy? Good luck with that, mate. And for what it's worth, I think he was telling the truth." Maxine's phone rings. She answers and wanders away as she talks.

Andy gets into the car. He's impatient to leave. He decides to turn the car around while he's waiting for Maxine. He reverses and hears a thump. He gets out of the car and takes a look. He's backed into one of the low columns flanking a carriage arch. He's knocked a chunk of stone out of it and dented the rear bumper of the car.

He glances at Maxine. She hasn't noticed. He gets back into the car and moves it forward. If there's no reaction from anybody in the house in the next minute or two, he thinks, he's not going to say anything. He can claim the car got bumped while it was parked somewhere. Under any other circumstances he would take responsibility, but these people don't deserve it and he's not going to give them another chance to look down their noses at him if he can help it.

Maxine jogs back to the car. He reaches over and opens the passenger door for her from the inside. She's pumped.

"Good news," she says. "They've got a familial match on Jane Doe's DNA. You might get to bring down the establishment after all."

1985

"WELL, LOOK WHO'S HERE!"

Hannah recoils. The woman's in a state: homeless, at a guess; the skin on her face raw and red from street life; and possibly drunk. Hannah feels Jocelyn's hand tighten around hers and out of the corner of her eye she sees the little girl's face turn up to hers, seeking reassurance.

"You don't recognize me, do you? It's me! Jean! It's Jean!"

So it is.

"How are you, Jean?" Hannah asks. She tries to erase the disgust from her expression. Jean stinks. She has greasy hair and wears a horrible dirty parka with a ripped orange lining. Her eyes are pinprick small.

"Oh, you know. Not so good. Things have been hard. I was homeless for a while, but I'm in a hostel now. Got to give credit to Dave for that. Dave's my boyfriend." She points to a man propped up against a bench, passed out.

Jean takes in Hannah's smart outfit and the child. She makes an effort to straighten herself up a bit and smiles at Jocelyn. "What are you doing here, then?" she asks.

"We're going to McIlroy's," Jocelyn says. "We need to get something from the haberdashery department."

Jean snorts. "Ooh, the haberdashery department! How posh are you? Fuck me, Hannah, she's not yours, then? Landed on your feet with a good job, have you?" She leans down toward Jocelyn, who recoils and takes a side step into the folds of Hannah's coat. "What's your name then?"

"Jocelyn Camilla Frances Holt. I'm nearly six."

"And where do you live, Jocelyn Camilla Frances Holt?"

"I live in Lake Hall near Downsley."

"Do you, now? Oh, you're a laugh and a half, aren't you? Eat your dinner with a silver spoon, do you? What's that?"

Jocelyn shows her the cover of the book she's carrying. "I've read it two times already," she says.

"Pony Princess," Jean says, reading the title. "Have a pony of your own, do you? I bet you do."

"We should go," Hannah says. She doesn't want Jocelyn to tell her father that Hannah knows homeless people. Not when things are starting to feel promising between them.

Jean is still focused on Jocelyn, her dirty face getting closer to the child's.

Hannah pushes Jocelyn behind her. "It was nice to see you, Jean. Take care."

"Can you spare me some change?"

"No. I'm sorry. I don't have any on me. We've got to go."

As they walk away, Jocelyn asks, "Who is that lady?" but Hannah doesn't answer. She strides as fast as possible, pulling Jocelyn along, until the sound of Jean's shouting, "Don't forget your old friend! Don't fucking forget Jean!" can't be heard any longer. She forgets about the incident until Jean turns up at Lake Hall three weeks later.

JO

AT THE HOSPITAL, WIND IS whipping so hard across the car park I'm afraid it will blow Mother over. I fetch a wheelchair. Hunched in it, she looks ten years older. I think of the accusations she's been making and wonder if she might be losing her mind.

She's seen by the same doctor who treated her last time we were here.

"Been in the wars again, Mrs. Holt?" she asks.

"Lady Holt," Mother replies. I cough, reminding her of her promise not to patronize people here, and she glances at me and shuts up. They X-ray her, put her wrist in a cast, and give her more heavy-duty painkillers. Her pallor stays ghostly throughout.

"How are you feeling?" I ask in the car home. "More comfortable?"

No answer. I put the radio on. It's *The Archers,* her favorite show, but she turns it off.

"You must listen to me," she says. Her voice is weedy. "About Hannah hurting Ruby. Nothing is what you think it is."

I hit the brakes and pull the car into a roadside parking area. The valley that's been our family's home for hundreds of years is laid out below us.

"Hannah didn't hurt Ruby. Ruby is ten. She doesn't always tell the truth."

"It's the truth! I know it is."

"How can you be so sure? Why would Hannah do that to her? Why?"

"I saw the bruises."

"I saw them, too."

"And?"

I know I had my own small doubts about Ruby's explanation for her bruises, but all I can think of right now is my memory of the slaps and bruises Mother inflicted on me.

"Nothing," I say. "I'm not discussing this with you."

I restart the car.

LATE AFTERNOON, I put in a call to California, hoping against hope that things might be looking up financially so I can tell Faversham to go to hell.

The news is bad. Chris's business partner is somber and apologetic. "I'm so sorry. I should have called you," he says. "It's not good news, and I've been trying to think of a way to break it to you."

I'm at my bedroom window, feeling the ache in my toes as they curl on the cold floor, listening and trying not to bite the inside of my mouth so hard in case it bleeds.

"I couldn't save the business. I'm so sorry. It was impossible to go on without Chris, and I had no choice but to close it down. I fought hard, Jo. I promise you. I fought as hard as I could, but we've lost everything."

"All of it?" I whisper. "I heard from my solicitor that it was going to be difficult, but I didn't know it was over."

"Yes, I'm so sorry. I don't know what else to say."

I want to offer him sympathy in return because he's financially ruined now, just as I am, but there is really nothing I can say.

"YOU LOOK dreadful," Hannah says.

I want to be near my daughter while I process the news about the business. Ruby is sitting at the table with a slice of lemon drizzle cake and a hot chocolate. There's a green felt-tip line on the collar of her school shirt that wasn't there this morning, and it reminds how very young she still is. I kiss Ruby on the top of her head and she pulls away. Hormones, I tell myself. It's normal.

"Did you do some artwork today?" I ask.

She shrugs.

"Yes, or no, Ruby? I asked you a question and it's polite to answer." My patience is already stretched so thin it's a struggle to maintain an even tone.

"Yes."

I wait for her to say more, but it's not forthcoming. She pushes her half-finished hot chocolate away. "Can I go to the toilet?" she asks.

"You don't need to ask permission, you're not at school now."

Ruby glances at Hannah before leaving the room, and I don't much like the way she does it, but I don't call her out on it. "Pick your battles," my mom friends have been advising in our online chats.

"Jocelyn, I'm worried about you," Hannah says. She puts a hand on my forehead and I close my eyes.

"I'm fine. It's been a long day, that's all."

"Your mother's behavior was very startling this afternoon. I'm concerned about her state of mind. She seems to have become so impulsive."

"Impulsive, paranoid, and that's just the start of it. You have no idea. I hope I never have another week like this."

She looks at me as if she can read my mind, and she probably can. She always used to be able to. "I'm here if you need me, dear."

It is always the kindest words that release your feelings. I feel as if I have to off-load something or I'm going to explode. I tell Hannah everything Clemency told me.

When I've finished, she clears her throat and says, "Oh my dear. What a devastating thing to learn about your own mother."

"Mother *and* father."

"Yes."

The way she glances at me, swiftly, appraisingly, unguardedly, provokes a small and unexpected flutter of fear. Have I gone too far? Would Hannah report Mother to the police for this? I have just weaponized her if she was ever to fall out with Mother again, and suddenly I'm not sure how clever that was.

"Hannah," I say, because I'm desperate to backpedal somehow, but she starts speaking at the same time.

"I think this has come as a huge shock to you, and it's a very serious thing. It's also a family matter, so it's very important that you keep it to yourself while you think about what you've learned and until you decide what to do about it. Have you told anybody else?"

"No. Just you." Relief courses through me. Of course Hannah will not betray us. She will support me. This is good advice. She always knows the right thing to do.

"Keep it between us, then. You've done nothing wrong." She squeezes my hand.

"Who's done something wrong?" Ruby speaks from the doorway. Hannah keeps her hand on mine until I move it, feeling awkward in front of Ruby. I don't want Ruby to think of me as the child, needing comfort. I must be strong for her.

"Nobody, darling," I say.

"Someone's ears are flapping," Hannah says.

"Is it about Granny?" Ruby asks. How long has she been there?

"No, no. It's nothing to do with Granny and nothing for you to worry about."

"I don't feel very well."

"Again?" She doesn't look well. Hannah makes to stand. "Don't worry. I'll go," I say. I fold Ruby into my arms in the doorway and she collapses onto me a little. Her head rests on me as we walk upstairs.

"What's wrong?" I ask. "Tummy ache? Headache?"

"Tummy ache and so tired," she says.

She gets into her pajamas while I turn down her bedcovers and she snuggles under her duvet.

"Mom," she says.

"What is it, sweetie?"

"I saw Hannah in Grandpa's study. She was looking in his desk drawers."

"Perhaps she was looking for something."

"I think she took his cigarette case."

"Oh, Ruby. Really? Did you see her take it?"

"I saw her hold it."

"That's very different from seeing her steal something."

"I think she did steal it."

"Sweetheart, be very careful about what you're saying. Did you actually see her take the case from Grandpa's room?"

She shakes her head.

"Then she was probably just looking at it, don't you think?"

"I don't know. My tummy hurts." Her face scrunches up in pain, but I can't tell if she's doing it for show or for real.

"You need some sleep."

I think I can guess at what might really be bothering her: "I miss Daddy, too, very much. All the time," I say. I think Hannah's right: grief is at the root of Ruby's behavior and her poorliness. It has to be.

"It's not because of Daddy," she says.

"Then what is it? Tell me."

She pulls the cover until it's right under her chin.

"It's her," she says.

"Who?"

"Hannah."

"What's wrong with Hannah?"

"I don't know."

"Is it just that it's funny getting used to Hannah being here or is it something else? You can tell me anything, you know, anything at all."

She gazes at me, eyes watery but as wide and pure as when she was a baby and I was the center of her world. "It's okay," she says. She blinks. She yawns and curls up like a little dormouse in its nest. Her eyes close. She looks so very small and vulnerable.

"Things will get better soon," I whisper into her hair. "I promise."

VIRGINIA

I HAMMER ON THE WINDOW to get Geoff's attention. We meet at the back door.

"Please could you check the stone ledge on the orchard wall?" I ask. "I think it's unstable. And can you come and tell me directly what you find? Don't talk to anybody else about it."

He returns some time later. "Lady Holt," he says. I have to force my eyelids open. He stands awkwardly in the doorway of my sitting room in his socks. I've almost never seen him in the house.

"It was loose," he says. "I've fixed it up nice. It's solid as a rock now."

"Did somebody loosen it deliberately, do you think?"

"Couldn't say." I'm grateful he doesn't seem to judge me for asking the question, as Jocelyn would. Geoff is the very definition of loyal. "It could have been Ruby using it to stand on that loosened it."

HANNAH COMES to me when Jocelyn is out. When I return to my sitting room after visiting the lavatory, she is there, sitting in my seat.

"Sit," she says.

I don't think I have any choice but to obey her. I sit carefully. My wrist is throbbing and I feel quite faint.

She smiles. "I believe you were still holding out hope that the body in the lake was mine."

I refuse to answer.

"Jocelyn told me about the forgeries."

My heart sinks. Of course she did.

"I was worried," Hannah says, "that this place was looking a lit-tle run-down. I thought money might be tight, but this scheme of yours, I have to admit, it's genius. Did you think of it, or Alexander?"

"Don't you dare speak his name."

"Nicely," she warns. It's a word she used to say to Jocelyn all the time: *Play nicely, do it nicely, nicely is better than nastily.* It makes my flesh prickle.

"Whoever thought of the scheme, I applaud them," she says. "The coffers will never run dry, will they, if you're clever about it? I've done a little research. You've got your forger, you've got your so-called connoisseur to authenticate and sell the pictures, and you've got a mighty collection of artworks in the family to give you be-lievability."

She's right. Everything we have done has been carefully weighed up and planned meticulously.

"I want in," Hannah says. "I want you to involve me in this scheme and in the profits, but I also want security. I want the Holt Catalogue. I know it didn't get destroyed. Give me the catalogue and give me a share, and you'll have my absolute discretion in re-turn. I think I could be useful to you, actually. You could perhaps do with a little old lady who has 'discovered' a painting in her attic and wants it valued. Can you imagine the expression on the face of some old codger at Sotheby's or Christie's if I turned up with a dusty old master?"

This can't happen. She can't work alongside us. Jocelyn is allow-ing her to embed herself more and more deeply in our lives. We will never be free of her.

"I shall speak to the others involved," I say.

"Don't take too long about it."

"I understand." But I'll take as long as I can.

"Excellent," she says. "Well, no rest for the wicked. I've got to think about what Ruby might want for tea."

I want to implore her not to harm Ruby, but I daren't. I am afraid that it will encourage her to target Ruby more if I say it. I hold the words back but my self-control is fractured enough that I let something else slip out: "Don't ruin Jocelyn's life."

I regret it as soon as I say it.

"Why on earth not?" she asks. "When she ruined mine?"

There it is. She has shown her cards, finally: money is sweet, and she'll take as much as she can get, but revenge is sweeter for Hannah.

At least I have clarity now, and in the midst of the constricting terror it makes me feel, I find my fighting spirit is still there because an idea occurs to me. It arrives fully formed, a small flame that won't be extinguished. I have always been a problem solver. I have dug Alexander and me out of more trenches than you would believe. I am not beaten yet.

"Jocelyn will never willingly take part in the forgery scheme," I say. "Unless you ask her to. She'd see me behind bars before she would help me. I disgust her and you know that, because you encouraged it."

She considers this. "I suppose you might be right. Well then. Leave it to me. And I know I can rely on your support."

I maintain my composure until she's left the room. I stare out of the window at the lake. I have a plan, but its weakness is that I can't undertake it alone. Jocelyn will have to help me, but right now I am the furthest I have ever been from being able to persuade her of anything.

The pain in my wrist is dreadful, increasing by the minute and making me feel nauseous. I'm going to have to give in and take some pills. Upstairs, my wrist makes it too difficult to get my new medication out of the foil packets, so I turn the tissue box upside down and shake it to release the pills I stored there. They tumble out onto the bed and I take one of each. I try to gather the others up to replace them in the box but there aren't as many as I think there should be. I shake the box again. It's empty. I look at the pills I've gathered. There are definitely too few.

I must count them, I think, because something is amiss here, but I must lie down first.

WHEN RUBY sits with me later, I say, "Promise me you won't go on that wall or do anything else I would normally let you do. Nothing dangerous. Promise me that, darling, please? Just until I say you can?"

"I won't," she says. She looks the picture of innocence and good behavior, but how can I trust her?

1985

HANNAH IS WALKING THE HOLTS' *dogs: Jed and Bijou. Hannah is harsh with Bijou because the doe-eyed golden spaniel was a gift from Alexander to Virginia, but she favors Jed, the latest in a line of black Labradors Alexander has owned since he was a boy. He gets all the treats. They walk up Lake Hall's driveway, where the gardeners are sweeping beech leaves into large piles, and turn onto the footpath running through the woods.*

She sees a woman walking unsteadily toward her from the direction of the village. Hannah takes in her unsuitable clothing and footwear before their eyes meet. With a sinking heart she recognizes Jean, who looks even more raddled by drink than the last time Hannah saw her.

"Fuck me!" Jean says. "You're a sight for sore eyes. I thought I was lost. I've come to see you!"

"I'm working," Hannah says. "It's not a good time. You should have phoned first."

"What are you doing?"

"Walking the dogs, then I've got a bit of shopping to do." She hasn't, but she doesn't want Jean to think she can come back to Lake Hall.

Jean's shoulders sag and she sighs. "Well, can I walk with you? I'm knackered, though, so we'll have to go slowly."

They tread a path surrounded by dense foliage, which drips with rainwater from an earlier shower. A pheasant crosses the path ahead and the dogs give chase.

Jean walks at a toddler's pace, protesting more than Jocelyn used to when she was that age. Hannah's contempt for Jean grows with every complaint she makes. Her list of woes oscillates from immediate concerns (wet feet, desperate for a cigarette, doesn't know how she's going to get home because she spent all her money on the bus ticket over here) to longer-term issues (skint, rejected by her boyfriend, disowned by her family, and the bastards at the benefits office are threatening to cut off her support). Hannah listens without responding and marches onward until she feels a tug on her arm. Jean has stopped.

"I was thinking," she says. "Can you get me a job? We could be together again."

Hannah is horrified. All she can think is that Jean would drag her back to the gutter, just when she's lifted herself somewhere to be proud of. Just when she's certain she's caught the eye of Alexander Holt.

"I don't have any say in that kind of thing," she says.

"Can't you put in a good word at least?"

"It wouldn't make any difference."

"You're a bitch, Hannah Burgess."

Hannah feels her patience stretch. "Go home, Jean. You're out of order."

"Fucking the husband yet?"

Hannah blushes. She can't help it. "You need to go. Now."

"What if I was to come to the house and tell them that you aren't really Hannah Burgess? What if I was to tell them you was Linda Taylor, pretending to be somebody else, and you wasn't a trained nanny after all?"

Jean plucks at Hannah's sleeve and Hannah jerks her arm away. She has way too much to lose for Jean to snatch it from her now.

"Go," she repeats.

"I haven't got any money. I'm just trying to go straight. Have a heart."

The dogs are working the undergrowth in ever-decreasing circles. Hannah can glimpse farmland between the trees now. We're close to the lake, *she thinks.*

"I can drive you home if you come with me, but I can't take you in the house," she says.

"I'm not getting in the car until you promise you'll put in a word for me. Or I swear I'll do it: I'll come here in my Sunday fucking best and go right up to the front door and tell them you're not who you say you are."

"Does anybody know you're here? Can they come and fetch you?"

"Nobody. I'm on my own."

"Let's walk back to the house," Hannah says. "Come on. I'll see if the housekeeper's there, and if she is, I'll introduce you, but that's all I can do."

"Really?" Jean says.

Hannah nods. "Really."

After they've walked a few paces Hannah slips her foot in front of Jean's. Jean falls forward onto her face, her drunken mind too slow to tell her arms to break the fall. Hannah hears the sound of the breath leaving Jean's chest and wastes no time putting her knee between Jean's shoulder blades and wrapping the dog leads around Jean's neck and pulling them as hard as she can for as long as she can, holding her own breath as she does so at first, but then breathing, once, twice, three times. She keeps on inhaling and exhaling as she holds the leads as taut as she can until her arms shake from the effort and the breath goes out of Jean's body and it stops bucking. Eventually, pain in Hannah's arms forces her to release the leads. She climbs off Jean and looks at her. She thinks Jean might still be breathing weakly, but it's hard to be sure. Hannah finds a rock and brings it down on Jean's head more than once.

When she stops, everything seems completely still around her. The dogs watch her from a distance. Jed whimpers. Hannah is sweating and her adrenaline is surging. Jean will never stand between her and Alexander Holt now.

As her high subsides, logistics begin to trouble her. Jean is facedown in the muddy leaves and Hannah can't leave her there. She considers her options, then sets to work.

It's not easy dragging Jean through the woodland, but luckily Hannah has only fifty yards to cover. At the edge of the woodland she steps through the barbed-wire fence separating the footpath from the grounds of Lake Hall. She pulls Jean through after her and makes a safer gap for the dogs to step through.

The gardeners are still at the front of the house where smoke rises from their pyres of beech leaves. Hannah is able to fetch a wheelbarrow from the walled garden without being seen, and she manages to get Jean's body into it. She wraps Jean's head in her coat first, so the blood doesn't stain the barrow. She pushes it down the incline, which is trickier than she imagined because the front wheel wobbles, but she gets to the boathouse. She retrieves the key from under a rock, unlocks the door, and pushes the wheelbarrow in. She manages to tip the body into the little boat that's moored there without overturning it. She looks at Jean lying in the boat. Good riddance to bad rubbish, *she thinks. She'll return after dark to sink Jean in the lake. The gardeners and housekeeper will be gone by then, and the Holts are in London. It'll be just her and Jocelyn.*

It'll be hard to sink the body, she knows that, but she reckons she can find some rocks to weigh it down.

What a terrible tragedy Jean's disappearance will be, *Hannah thinks*, but only if somebody misses her, and it sounds as if there's not much chance of that.

JO

I PHONE FAVERSHAM AND TELL him I know about the forgery scam. I cut him off before he has a chance to launch into excuses or explanations and tell him I need a couple more days off to deal with Mother. The truth is, I need more time and space to think everything through.

There's a pause on the other end of the line before he says, "Of course. I completely understand."

"I'll be in touch."

"Don't leave it too long."

"I'll take as long as I need."

"Of course you will. And you should. But you should also know that ours is not the only good vanitas on the market, and our client is an impatient man." The barefaced cheek of him, and he's not finished yet. "This is not a crime in the way you might be thinking of it. Our client will have his painting."

"Not the one he thought he was getting."

"It looks identical and it has the right documentation. If he isn't any the wiser, he will enjoy it the same way he would the original."

"I'll call you in a couple of days."

"Very well. But, Jocelyn?"

"Yes."

"You are very good at your job. Please, remember that. It has been a joy working with you, and I would love to continue to do so. I mean that absolutely sincerely."

He hangs up and I'm left feeling somewhat astounded. I'm still angry, of course, but part of me believes him. I shudder. *Don't let yourself be swayed by a compliment,* I think. *Words are cheap, especially if you are the sort of person to whom other people's lives are cheap.*

WHEN I go out to get the car, I remember Mother's talk about the ledge on the orchard wall being unstable and I decide to check it. It's rock solid. I can't move it a millimeter. I don't know what she was fussing about.

At school, the playground's heaving and I scan the throngs of children for Ruby.

"Excuse me, are you Ruby's mum, by any chance?"

"I am."

"I'm Kate. Jacob's mum." I must look blank because she adds, "Jacob's in Ruby's class."

"Oh, okay, it's nice to meet you."

She's smartly dressed and has a baby in a very expensive stroller. *Oh, crap,* I think, *please don't ask me to sell raffle tickets or put up a stall for the school fete because I haven't got time.* I want to integrate, but not like that, not yet. I can't resist glancing over her shoulder so I don't miss Ruby.

She picks up on my agitation. "I won't keep you. I wanted to apologize in person for what Jacob did to Ruby."

Now she has my attention. "Apologize for what?"

"He's lashed out at her once or twice. He's . . . a bit . . . troubled. He's being assessed at the moment because . . . anyway, I won't bore you with the detail. I'm so sorry about it."

She is tearing up, and now I see beyond the sharp clothes, the gym-fit figure, and the thick layer of makeup, noticing the dark shadows under her eyes and their puffy rims.

"What did he do?"

"Didn't the school tell you?"

"No."

"They said they'd left you a message. I'm sorry. I thought you knew."

I check my phone. There is a message I must have missed. It's from Ruby's teacher. She's asking me if I've got five minutes to come in and have a chat at collection time.

"What did he do to her?"

"I'm so sorry." Tears are brimming and spilling now. "He hit Ruby and he pushed her. The teacher has spoken to him. The headmistress and his dad and I will, too, and he won't ever do it again, I promise. I can't tell you how sorry I am."

"He hurt her?"

"Yes. I'm so sorry."

"*Jacob* your son hurt her?"

She nods. Her baby starts to cry, too.

"Thank you!" I say. "For the apology. I appreciate it. I mean that. I'd better go and find the teacher. Please don't worry about it."

She looks surprised. I suppose she was expecting me to be gunning for retribution, but a bit of rough-and-tumble amongst classmates, quite honestly, doesn't even come close to the idea of an adult hurting Ruby, let alone that that adult should be Hannah, or, and this has occurred to me, my mother.

Ruby's teacher is in full-blown grovel mode and the headmistress has been roped into the meeting, too. I am practically relaxed as they assure me they've done everything in their power to address the problem and that they'll remain ultra-vigilant to ensure it doesn't happen again.

On the way back to the car with Ruby I say, "Sweetheart, I'm sorry this happened. It must have been absolutely horrible. But it's very important you understand that next time it happens you must tell an adult immediately."

"I did," she says. "I told Hannah."

"Hannah would have told me," I say.

"I'm not lying!"

"Are you sure about that? Are you trying to get Hannah into trouble because you don't like her? Now would be a really good time to tell me if you've said anything that might not be true."

She kicks at the ground, dislodging some moss from the crevice where the pavement meets an old stone wall, and squashes it with the toe of her shoe.

"Ruby?"

"I didn't lie."

"Do you remember telling Granny that it was Hannah who hurt you?"

"It was Hannah who pinched me. Jacob just pushes me sometimes."

"Ruby! You just said it was Jacob who hurt you and I've heard the same thing from Jacob's mother, your teacher, and the headmistress. And he's admitted it, too. Come on, Ruby, what's going on? It's very wrong of you to point the finger at Hannah."

"They both hurt me!"

"You mustn't lie!"

"I'm not lying! Why won't you believe me?" She looks fit to burst. Before I can reply she throws her backpack to the ground and takes off at full pelt down the lane.

I race after her because the pavement extends only about another fifty yards before the lane narrows and is solely for the use of traffic. I catch Ruby by the hood of her coat just as she's about to run around a blind corner. A van appears from the other direction, horn blaring, and I push Ruby back into the hedgerow. I'm so scared and angry I could slap her. Instead, I hug her fiercely. "Ruby," I say over and over again into her hair. "It's okay. I love you. Let's go home. Let's talk about it at home."

"I don't want to."

"Why not?"

"Because she's living there now."

"Ruby! She is not the problem."

AT HOME, Ruby disappears to her room with her iPad. Mother is blotto on her bed, fully dressed.

I'm relieved to have some respite from them both. I find Hannah in the kitchen. "Long face on Ruby," she says. "Is everything all right?"

I tell her about the bruises that Jacob caused and about Ruby's running off after school.

"Goodness!" she says. "I should have noticed she was hurt. I feel terrible."

"You weren't to know. She was hiding it from us."

"Poor little soul. It's a big secret for a small person to carry on their own."

"I know. I feel guilty, too."

"You shouldn't. You're doing all the right things and you can't be perfect. Ruby needs to know she's loved and she needs stability and we've got that covered between us. I think it's only a matter of time before she settles down and becomes more docile and every-thing will feel better then. Grief can be slow to heal."

I watch as she rubs flour and butter together, with sticky, pow-dery fingers.

"What are you making?"

"Crumble. For Ruby. She said she'd like to try it, and if she does, I'll teach her how to make it."

"That's nice."

"I hope you won't mind me mentioning something?"

"What?"

"Ruby was a bit upset because you promised you would help her with her English homework, but you didn't."

"Oh no! I don't remember saying that." My maternal guilt, after a hiatus of maybe a few minutes, returns with a vengeance.

"I heard you say it, dear."

"When?"

"It was after you brought your mother back from the hospital, so it's understandable you forgot."

"I'll help her tonight."

"The work was due in today. Don't worry. I helped her."

"Do you think I'll ever get the hang of this single working mother thing?"

"That's what I'm here for. How are you feeling about work now?"

"I don't know yet. My best option is probably to move on and try to find work at another gallery."

"Won't you need more experience for that?"

"Probably."

"I'm happy to talk it through if you need to. I think the key is not to do anything hasty. There! I think this is done."

I watch her sprinkle the crumble mixture over a dish of prepared apples and blackberries. It reminds me of so many meals she and I shared in the nursery when I was little.

"You know, one thought I had," Hannah says, "was that it might help you if you had the Holt Catalogue in your possession. That could give you some influence over the others, don't you think?" She puts the crumble in the oven.

"It's a thought," I say.

"Probably a silly one."

"No. Not necessarily."

. . .

I THINK about Hannah's suggestion while I tidy Ruby's bedroom. She's lying in bed, listlessly tapping at the iPad.

"You could help me, you know," I say.

"When I've finished this game."

"No. Now."

"Two minutes."

She has bags under her eyes, so I relent. It's an interesting thought that possession of the catalogue could give me some influence. I hadn't thought of turning the tables on the others, but perhaps it's possible. It's certainly tempting.

I have an armful of Ruby's clothes when we hear Mother scream. I drop the clothes on her bed and we rush out onto the landing to find Mother near the top of the stairs, gripping the banister as if her life depended on it.

"What's the matter?" I ask.

"I tripped. Somebody loosened the runner at the top of the stairs." She points with a trembling finger at the edge of the runner. I examine it. It looks a little rucked up, but no worse than every other carpet in this place.

"Hannah did it," Mother hisses. She staggers. She's holding the banister as tightly as if she were in a tornado. She looks quite mad.

"That's nonsense! You cannot say things like that. Ruby, go to your room!" I can't have Ruby hearing this stuff.

I guide Mother back to bed and she lies down, chest heaving. Her eyes shut but her mouth stays open. If it weren't for her breathing she'd be a facsimile of a corpse.

"I know every inch of my home; there is no ruck in that runner," she says after a while.

I pick up the painkillers from her bedside table. "You're bombed out on pills, Mother. You need rest. You have to stop this crazy talk."

"That's another thing," she says. "The pills."

"No. Nothing more now. Please. Get some rest."

I shut her bedroom door and lean against it. Ruby is lurking. "What are you doing?"

"I want to see Granny."

"Let Granny rest now, and Ruby?"

"What?"

"I don't want you to mention Hannah holding Grandpa's cigarette case or Hannah hurting you or anything else like that to Granny."

"I promise," she says. The fight has gone out of her for once, which is a relief. I don't want her to stoke up Mother's feelings about Hannah.

"Thank you," I say. I kiss her forehead. The shadows under her eyes look really dark now, but I think it's just the gloom in this corridor exaggerating them.

I leave her in her room and go down. I want some time to myself. I'm having one of those moments when it's very hard to stop myself fantasizing what life would be like if it was just Hannah, Ruby, and me at Lake Hall. How much easier it would be to have a future here without Mother.

THE FIRST place I search for the Holt Catalogue is my father's study, because that's where it used to be kept. I look through each and every one of his shelves but I don't see it. I search his desk drawers, too, but it's not there, either.

At a loss as to where to look next, I stand at the window and take in the view of the lake and the grounds.

The lake's surface is undisturbed enough to reflect a sky where towering clouds have massed so densely they resemble an unearthly citadel. By the near bank, fallen leaves float below the surface of the water, decaying. What a horrible place to end your days.

What did my father think as he stood here? I wonder. He must have done so often. I lean against the window and look up toward the nursery bedrooms in the other wing of the house, remembering the view of this window I saw from Hannah's room. There's not such a good view in the other direction because the parapet obscures the bottom half of her window. She would have been able to see a lot if she looked down, but not vice versa. It's a disconcerting thought. Nobody wants to be spied upon.

I search the desk drawers one more time and I remember the cigarette case. I didn't notice it when I was searching for the catalogue and I can't find it now. Was there truth in Ruby's accusation that Hannah took it? Or perhaps Ruby has taken it and she's casting blame once again. She has been a bit of a magpie around Mother's jewelry. I've had to make her take off one of Mother's rings before she leaves for school more than once. Or perhaps Mother took it. She's been sounding less stiff upper lip and more maudlin when referring to my father lately. Perhaps she sought out the case and took it to get some comfort from it.

I rub my eyes. I feel restless, confused, and too tired to continue searching for the Holt Catalogue now.

In the Blue Room the fire is lit and the photograph albums are stacked up on the ottoman. I pick one up. I'm curious to see if there are any more photographs of our Belgravia house. I want to know if Mother and her gang somehow forged that photograph of me in front of the vanitas. Did we ever own the painting at all?

I leaf through the books slowly, but I don't find another picture of our dining room in Belgravia, even though my heart skips a beat when I find two pages of one album stuck together. I prize them apart. They're pictures we didn't see before: a few are of my parents' dogs and two are of my mother. My father must have taken them. Mother's in her bedroom here at Lake Hall, holding up two different outfits to show him. She looks flirtatious and there's a heap of dresses on the bed behind her. I remember how they used to pile up as she tried them on. Dressing always was an art for her.

On the top of one of the piles is a dress I remember because it's mine: it's the dress I wore on the night Hannah left. I recognize it immediately because it was such a big deal that night. I peer at it because one detail is off. I remember the dress as blue, though Hannah assured me it was green. The dress on the bed is blue, so am I mistaken in thinking it's mine? I'm not. It's quite obviously a child-size dress. It's definitely the one, and I think how strange it is that Hannah was so insistent I'd remembered it wrongly.

I close the album, feeling uneasy. The dress isn't the only thing Hannah has insisted I've been wrong about and that bothers me suddenly, amidst all the other things I'm finding I've misremembered. It's not so much the fact that she's repeatedly called me out on little things I've forgotten, but the way she's implied I can barely remember anything correctly. I don't think I have that bad a memory, or I didn't always. This photograph of the dress proves me right.

DETECTIVE ANDY WILTON

"RAY WAS A WRONG 'UN," she says to the detective. She gazes out of the window as if it's the Taj Mahal she can see out there, not an overgrown privet hedge. Her skin is folded and yellow, sagged under her eyes in crescents.

The DNA from the Jane Doe is a partial match to Ray Palmer, a man with a rap sheet longer than his arm. He's deceased. Andy and Maxine are with his widow.

"We're wondering if any female members of Ray's family went missing? It would have been during the 1980s."

Maxine is standing in the doorway. Andy wishes she would sit down with him, but she's uncomfortable about being here. "It smells of death," she whispered in the nursing home foyer.

Andy doesn't mind it a bit. He's sanguine about death. His view is, you fight hard to get to wherever you can before it happens, because the rest is out of your hands and all credit to the old folks for getting to a decent age. Plus, he likes oldies because he reckons you tend to get a straighter answer from them because they've been around the block. Unless they're Lady Holt, of course, with her manipulative ways.

The woman beside him is from the opposite world. The most expensive item in her room is an old-fashioned travel alarm clock, the foldout kind with a faux-leather case torn at the edges where it meets the tarnished metal. She is as warm, welcoming, and open as Lady Holt was cold, patronizing, and opaque.

"Jean went missing," she says. "Ray's niece. Ray's brother, Jean's dad, was just as bad as Ray. Knocked them all around. Jean took off one night. She had the chutzpah to get away. A few years later, as soon as she dared, because he would knock her for six if she so much as mentioned Jean's name right after she left, her mum traced her to Leeds and then to Bristol, but it was too late to find her because she'd moved on from there as well. No trace of her after that. Might have been she got married or went abroad. I've often thought about Jean. I had an idea she might have made something of herself. I'd hate to think she came to a bad end."

"What's Jean's full name, darling?" Andy asks.

"Jean Grace Palmer. The Grace was after Grace Kelly. I remember her birthday, too, because it was the same as mine: 2 July. Except she was born in 1957 and I was born in 1937. Ever so spunky she was. Probably would have been better if she wasn't. Do you know what happened to her, Detective?"

"Call me Andy," he says. "I don't know what happened to her, but I'll be back if I get any news. You'll be the first to know, I promise."

He knows he should leave right away, but he stays and talks for a few more minutes because he can't bear the thought of her sitting there alone after he's gone, staring at that awful hedge, her only company memories of a missing girl who came to a bad end after all.

Maxine calls into the office as he drives.

"I want every bit of information you call pull on a female called Jean Grace Palmer. Date of birth 2 July 1957. She's our Jane Doe."

JO

I SHUT THE PHOTO ALBUM. Perhaps I'm too tired to think about all this now.

Hannah puts her head around the door.

"I'm just popping to Pewsey before the shops shut," she says. "Is there anything you need?"

"No. I don't think so."

"Have a think. Are you sure you haven't forgotten anything?"

"Yes, I'm sure." I think I am, anyway. I smile as she leaves, and when she's gone, I let my expression and my shoulders slump.

I climb the stairs wearily, feeling guilty about what I'm about to do. I don't want to snoop in Hannah's room, but I don't know how else I'm going to set my mind at rest about the cigarette case.

The leaded windows on the landing look as dark as the sky outside. A few drops of rainwater have seeped through one of the joins and run down the inside of the glass. I see the taillights of the car Hannah uses disappear up the drive.

There's a dim light coming from under Ruby's bedroom door on the first-floor landing and a brighter glow from the back stairwell at the far end of the corridor. It looks like a beacon and I feel as if it's beckoning me up.

When Hannah moved in, she decided to take her old room up in the attic to maintain some privacy, and as I make my way toward the stairwell, I find my curiosity is piqued. I want to prove to Ruby that she's wrong about Hannah's taking the case, but I also want to know how Hannah's living up there.

I'm careful as I head upstairs. The treads are so worn and slippery, each one dipped in the middle. I know Hannah's out, but I still feel trepidation as I approach her bedroom door. This is an invasion of both her privacy and her trust. I turn the handle and push, but the door is locked. I try the entrance from my old bedroom but that's locked, too. Why on earth does she feel she has to lock her room?

I crouch down and peer through the keyhole. I can't see much, but my heart quickens when I glimpse the dim silhouettes of some of her personal things. The sight of her empty room on the day she left me imprinted itself on my mind so deeply that it feels surreal to see her stuff back in there.

I feel even more determined to get in now. I go downstairs and search the drawers in the kitchen dresser for the set of master keys Anthea returned to me when I met her in the pub. I find them easily and scoop them up into my palm. I jog back upstairs faster than I usually dare.

My hand shakes as I try several keys in the lock before I find the right one. When it turns easily, I inhale sharply and open the door cautiously. The hinges squeak as I step in. I turn on the light.

The room is as clean as a new pin and as spartan and tidy as I remember Hannah always kept it, but there are touches of luxury I wasn't expecting: a towel beside the hand basin too thick and fluffy to have come from Lake Hall's airing cupboard, a dressing gown on the back of the door that feels as if it's made from silk. The label confirms it.

There are more familiar things, too, in particular a pair of porcelain kittens on the mantel shelf: Siamese cats, in a playing pose. I loved Hannah's porcelain kittens when I was a child. I coveted them. I could have sworn the kittens she had then were white with black socks and noses, so these aren't quite as I remember them, but then what is these days?

It feels very strange to be in here. Incredibly familiar, but altered. The feeling I have is of being in a museum of my own childhood where the things that have been preserved aren't quite right. I've stepped back into the past, but I don't feel immersed in it, I feel removed from it. I'm a spectator.

I sit on the stool in front of Hannah's vanity table and realize I can't search this room. It would be very wrong of me.

This vanity table is such a contrast to Mother's opulent setup downstairs. The mirror on Hannah's dressing table is small and foxed and badly lit. A hairbrush and comb are neatly lined up parallel to each other on the chipped painted surface, a simple face cream beside them, nothing more.

I should go, I think. I'm aware I won't be able to hear Hannah's car from here if she comes back, and I'd be mortified if she caught me snooping, but I don't move. I want just a few more minutes to understand better what I'm feeling.

I look in the mirror, noting the years on my face since I last sat here. Hannah used to do my hair as I sat in this chair, and I used to watch her get ready sometimes. "Do you want to see me put my face on?" she would ask, and I would hand her each item as she needed it. I asked Hannah to put makeup on me, too, occasionally. It was one of the quiet ways I got back at my mother. I never let Mother make me up however often she offered. I only wanted Hannah to do it and I used to stare at myself in the mirror as she worked on my face. It was mesmerizing.

"That's the thing," Hannah used to say as she brushed powder on my cheeks. "With makeup you can change who you want to be and what people think of you." What an intoxicating idea that was.

There are two drawers in the vanity table. I open the first one and find Hannah's cosmetics neatly arranged there just as I expected. My face is free of makeup today. I pick up Hannah's lip liner and draw carefully around my lips with a dark, sumptuous red. It's the color I loved most when I was little. I add some lipstick, using a little brush to apply it neatly and carefully, keeping within the lines, just how Hannah showed me all those years ago. It feels heavy on my lips.

I consider my reflection and reach for the eyeliner. It's easy to fight the part of me that knows I shouldn't be doing this, because there's a more insistent part that doesn't want to stop. Is it so wrong to want to reconnect for just a few minutes with the way I used to feel before Hannah left?

I try to re-create exactly what she used to do when she made me up. I paint black lines above my eyes and taper them at the edges of the lids.

"You have to put extra on your lashes because they're quite thin," I can hear her saying. "So we need a steady hand with the mascara. Layer over layer, that's the idea. Look up."

I would hold my breath as she worked and keep my eyes as wide as possible, trying not to blink. I pick out a black mascara from the drawer and apply it in gentle strokes until I have long, full lashes.

I look at my reflection. My skin is very pale.

"You can pinch your cheeks to get color into them," Hannah would say, "but it's nicer to have a bit of blush."

When she'd put the blush on me, she used to stand back and survey her handiwork. "There!" she would say. "What a pretty little doll you are! Hannah's little dolly."

I search the drawer for blush but I can't find any, so I open the other one. It gets stuck when it's a little way out. I wiggle it, but it won't budge. I yank the drawer, but that doesn't release it.

I try to slip my hand into it. It's difficult because of the angle. My fingertips explore the space and brush against the object that's stopping the drawer from opening. It feels shockingly familiar. I contort myself so I can shove my hand farther in. I scrape the skin on the back of it and it hurts, but that only makes me more determined. I ignore the pain and push my hand in until my fingers are able to close around the object.

I know what it is. It's something that shouldn't be here.

Gently I work my fingers farther around it, hoping I'm wrong, but the textures and contours are just as familiar as I expect them to be. The feel of this object is part of my muscle memory and I know how to grasp it, so it dovetails with the shape of my hand.

It's my father's cigarette case.

Barely remembering to breathe, I ease the case out of the drawer. When I've freed it, I hold it to my pounding heart.

I feel absolutely anesthetized, too numb to move.

In the mirror I see the face of Hannah's little doll grown old.

Between my fingers I see the glow of the Fabergé enamel on the cigarette case and the dull glint of the gold wearing the patina of my father's touch. This case does not belong to Hannah. She has no right to have it, so why is it here?

I stare at my reflection, transfixed by it. I am a grotesquely made-up version of myself, distorted like everything else. Which is the real me? This painted creature or the woman beneath the mask?

I no longer know whom or what to believe.

The door opens behind me and I see my daughter's reflection in the mirror, her face hovering behind mine, round as a coin, with bright cornflower-blue eyes. Unblemished.

I don't want her to see me now. I don't want her to become me.

"Get out," I say.

She goes.

I look back at my reflection and now all I see is my mother.

DETECTIVE ANDY WILTON

"I WANT TO TALK TO the nanny," Andy says. "She was working at Lake Hall at the time of the shooting party and apparently she's back. She's about the only person who's not a hundred years old by now. If we can link Jean Palmer to the Holts or their associates, we're a step closer to getting some answers. We should take the photographs out further, too. I want to try and get one of them in the newspaper, along with her name, etc."

"I've made progress putting together a wider list of friends and associates of the Holts from that time," Maxine says. "We could show them the photographs, too."

"We'll get to them, and we've got to hope they won't be such absolute . . ."—he whispers a curse word because the boss is walking through the office—"as the last guy we interviewed, but let's concentrate on the staff first. They're more likely to break ranks. You can't tell me everybody who worked for the Holts is going to stay loyal to them. I don't believe it for an instant. Wouldn't Virginia Holt get your back up if you had to care for her child?"

He reaches for a printout of the original *Evening Advertiser* article he found in the library and points to the woman in the photograph who is holding the young Jocelyn Holt.

"Just look at them all together," he says. "Doesn't that just scream trouble to you?"

Maxine takes it from him.

"It is weird," she says. "You're standing right there with your husband, but another woman is holding your child."

"Exactly!"

"But isn't that a normal upper-class thing?"

"It's not normal, though, is it?"

She looks again. Everyone is smiling, but the smiles aren't reaching their eyes. Even in a bad printout of a grainy photograph you can tell that there's more tension than warmth in this little group.

"You're right," she says.

"Let's get some background on the nanny and set up a face-to-face interview next week."

He's got a proper photograph of Jean now, given to him by her aunt. It was taken just before she left home. It's a great addition to the skull reconstruction photographs. In it, Jean is younger than she would have been when she died, but she has a spark in her eye. She looks full of life and fun. You get a sense of the person she was, and that might help jog some memories.

JO

RUBY'S INTERRUPTION SHATTERS MY REVERIE. I wipe the makeup from my face with sharp movements, disgusted at myself. I stuff the tissues in my pocket.

"Mom?" Ruby must still be lurking outside the door.

"Yes."

"What are you doing?"

"I'm putting something away for Hannah. I'm just coming. Go downstairs."

"Hannah's home."

For a moment, I'm undecided whether to bring the cigarette case with me or not. Is it better to have it and know it's safe or leave it so Hannah won't know I came into her bedroom? I decide to bring it. It's too precious to lose. It is ours, not hers.

Ruby's waiting on the landing. She watches me lock the door with trembling hands. We hear footsteps echoing sharply on the back stairs. I don't want to confront Hannah now, not in front of Ruby, not until I've thought about what I want to say.

I beckon Ruby down the corridor away from the stairs, my finger to my lips. I open the door to a tiny room packed full of stuff covered by dust sheets. I recognize the silhouettes of objects I used to cherish: a dollhouse, a tricycle.

I usher Ruby in and close the door as quietly as I can just as the footsteps reach the top of the stairs.

"Mom?" she says after a few moments. Her eyes are bright. She's not sure why we're in here, but she's enjoying the subterfuge.

"Shush!"

I pray Mother won't start calling for us and I pray Ruby can keep her mouth shut. We stay where we are, silent and still for more minutes than I can count, and I start to feel stupid hiding in my own home, and a bit ashamed. I consider sneaking out, but I don't dare in case Hannah emerges. Her room is between the room we're in and the top of the stairs. I'm afraid she'll see through any excuse I might make as to why we are up here.

After a while the silence and darkness feel deep and enveloping. Our eyes adjust and I watch Ruby pad about the room and lift the edge of the dust sheets to inspect what's beneath.

Hannah must have taken the cigarette case, but why would she want it? Why the case in particular? If she'd taken any other object, I would find it easier to compute and easier to forgive. Perhaps she needed money; perhaps she's in a worse place financially than I thought. But this cigarette case, it didn't just belong to my father, it *is* my father. She knows what this case would mean to me. How dare she?

When we finally hear Hannah's door open, then shut, and her footsteps on the stairs, Ruby goes for the door, but I hold her still for a moment or two more. I want to give Hannah enough time to get all the way downstairs.

"Ready?" I whisper after a short while.

We slip from the room as quietly as we entered it and I close the door, leaving the draped relics of my childhood behind us. We descend the stairs in our socked feet, cautiously. The corridor downstairs is empty. Ruby looks as if she's about to ask me what's going on, but I can't answer her questions just now.

"Can you go and check on Granny, please?" I ask.

"Can I read to her?"

"Yes, whatever you like."

"Were you looking for the cigarette case?"

"Go to Granny."

I need to be alone.

I sit on my bed in my room and look at the case.

I should know what to say to Hannah and what to do, but instead of the clarity I'm searching for, there's nothing but shock and uncertainty swimming in a pervasive blankness.

DETECTIVE ANDY WILTON

"HER NAME IS JEAN GRACE Palmer," Andy says. "And her body turned up in the lake at Lake Hall in Downsley. Forensics tell us she died in 1984 or thereabouts. Her family hadn't seen her for ten years before that, and we haven't been able to trace anybody who spent time with her in the eighties. If you could give us a bit of space in the paper to run her picture we'd much appreciate it. I might be able to slip you something in return, down the line."

"Can I link it to the Lake Hall case?"

"I don't see why not, but don't run it before Monday, will you?"

"Send it over, then," Dennis Westcott says. "I'll see what I can do. A mysterious skull could make for a better front page than the roadworks on the magic roundabout, which is all I've got to run with at the moment and all I will have unless Swindon pulls off a miracle victory in the game. Hope never dies. See you in the Wheatsheaf tomorrow night?"

"Yeah, probably." If his girlfriend will let him, but he's not stupid enough to admit that. Dennis would die laughing.

"All right, son."

"Cheers, Dennis."

"Well?" Maxine says after he's hung up.

"Next week. Possible front page."

"Nicely done."

"Did you make the appointment with the nanny?"

"Not yet. I tried, but no answer. I'll try again tomorrow."

"Don't let it slide. I've got a feeling about her."

JO

HANNAH IS UP BEFORE ME making porridge for Ruby. I wake feeling foggy and upset. Any sleep I got was far from restful and more disturbing than anything. As I tried to make sense of discovering the cigarette case in Hannah's drawer, my thoughts gathered, then swirled, as impossible to tame as a tidal swell.

If Hannah has noticed the cigarette case is missing from her room, she doesn't say anything; nor do I. I need to broach it with her, I know I do, but every time I try to work out how, I draw a blank because I can't think of a way to do it that won't feel like a confrontation. I can't confront Hannah. It's not who we are to each other. Or not who we were. Who knows, now.

"Did you look for the Holt Catalogue yesterday?" she asks as she passes the golden syrup to Ruby.

"No, but I will." I don't want to tell her the truth. I am bitterly regretting telling her about the forgery scheme now that I'm unsure if I can trust her.

"What a fascinating document it must be."

"Absolutely."

"How's your mother this morning?"

"I don't know. I haven't seen her."

"She's fine," Ruby says. She's made a pattern with the syrup on her porridge.

"Are you all right, dear?" Hannah ignores Ruby and looks at me with a gaze that I feel might pierce right through me and intuit every thought I'm having.

"I'm fine." I get up and turn my back to her on the pretext of checking Ruby's schoolbag.

"Are you sure?"

I nod. "I'll take Ruby in today, I've got to run some errands afterward."

I put the cigarette case in my handbag before I came down this morning. I want to keep it near me.

"Last night, what were you doing in Hannah's bedroom?" Ruby asks as we set out.

"Sweetheart, we will talk about this, but not now, okay? We'll talk this evening, I promise."

We pull up at an intersection where the visibility is poor. I crane my neck forward to check for traffic. I avoid meeting Ruby's eye.

I do know I have to ask Hannah about it, even if I can't bear the thought of it. Hannah can't be allowed to take my father's things, especially not this thing. And there's a chance she has a good explanation, I remind myself, though it's hard to imagine what that might be.

When we get to school, I walk Ruby to the playground. She trips on the curb as we cross the road and I grab her by the hood of her coat to stop her falling.

"Are you okay?"

"I'm tired."

"You need to look where you're going."

She shrugs and pulls her coat tighter around her neck. It's a cold day and the wind is playing with the tips of Ruby's hair. Her lips look blue.

"Are you all right, darling?"

She nods. "Bye." She ducks away before I can plant a kiss on her.

"Jo?" One of the mothers catches up with me beside the car. "A few of us are going for coffee in Marlborough. We've got room for one more if you'd like to join us?"

She points to her car where two women are gathered and another is approaching them. I recognize Stan's mum. She meets my eye. I smile, but she doesn't return it. The look she gives me is borderline hostile, and I'm not in a good place to deal with it.

"Thank you so much," I say to the woman who invited me. "I'd love to come another time, but I've got an appointment this morning."

As soon as I get in my car I feel ashamed of myself. I should have gone with them. It was an opportunity to meet the school mum tribe, and in a village as small as this, there is only one tribe. I watch them drive away and smack the steering wheel. When will my life be normal? I could drive after them and ask to join them, but I don't even have the courage to do that.

I unclip my handbag and peek inside. My father's cigarette case nestles amongst all the usual mess. I had planned to go to Marlborough and kill some time so I could think, but I don't want to go now, because I can't face running into the coffee mummies. I'm not ready to go back to Lake Hall and face Hannah, not until I've worked things out, and there's no way I'm telling Mother about this yet. She's only going to react one way.

I take the cigarette case out of my bag and open it. I inhale its old-tobacco smell. It takes me back to my father's arms, the precious moments I used to long for when he would envelop me in a hug or turn the full beam of his attention onto me. They made me feel as if I might burst with happiness.

I snap the cigarette case shut. I know where I have to go.

It's a short drive. After five minutes winding through lanes I pull into the small parking area. The village church is nestled in a dip in the landscape on the edge of Downsley.

I follow a path through the gravestones. The cigarette case is in my coat pocket and I grasp it tightly as I walk. The gravestones punctuate a sloping yard and the same few family names repeat on many of them amongst the spreads of lichen. The graveyard is exposed to the elements and I feel the full force of the sharp wind. I get some respite from it only when I reach the Holt mausoleum.

Our mausoleum is on the side of the path in a prominent position. It's by far the grandest structure here. The door is flanked by fluted columns and two stone angels mounted on pedestals. The angels genuflect, facing each other. In prayer or in deference to the generations of Holts buried here? It looks like both. Carved into the front of the pedestals beneath them are the names of generations of Holts.

I haven't visited my father's grave before. I've avoided it, and it's a shock to see his name engraved beneath the others. It looks so final.

I touch the letters of his name and find myself weeping for the years when I kept contact with him to a minimum because being close to him meant being close to Mother and I couldn't stand that, weeping because Ruby never got to meet him, and weeping for how much I loved him. I loved him so much it hurts to think about it. He was my daddy and it was Mother's fault that he and I never had the relationship we should have. On the pedestal there's a space beside his name where hers will be carved one day. They will lie together forever. It doesn't seem fair. It makes me feel bitter. Everything would be different if it were her name already there, instead of his. Everything would be better.

"Jocelyn! I thought it was you!" The vicar strides toward me, his robes billowing. "I don't wish to interrupt a private moment, but I couldn't help noticing your distress. Can I help? Or would you rather be alone?"

"No, thank you, I'm fine. Actually I must be going." I don't want to share my thoughts with him or have him watch me cry. He's a gossip.

"You know where to find me if you need me."

I have no small talk to ease my way out of this comfortably. I try to step around him, but he turns and falls in beside me. "Have you seen these?" he says.

To the side of the mausoleum, in a large marble urn, is a fresh and extravagant bunch of flowers.

"Who put these here?"

"I assumed it was your mother."

"My father hated lilies."

"Oh, dear. I'm sure he would have appreciated the gesture, anyway."

I can't understand why these are here. I'm certain Mother would never have put lilies beside his grave, which means somebody else must have done it. Somebody who didn't know him quite as well as Mother did. My hand closes around the cigarette case. *Could it have been Hannah?*

"I must go," I say.

The vicar stands at the church gate and watches me leave. I drive with hands clenched on the wheel. On a sharp bend, the Land Rover swerves unexpectedly and my heart pounds as I manage to right it and barely avoid crashing into a ditch. I slam the brakes on so hard it stalls.

When I've recovered myself I restart the engine and carry on, taking more care. I feel sick with nerves. I need to go home and ask Hannah about the cigarette case.

I STEP into the hallway at Lake Hall determined to find Hannah immediately and ask her outright, but I'm ambushed by music. It's like walking into a wall of sound, and for a powerfully disorienting moment, it's as if my father is still alive. The music's coming from his study, just as it used to throughout my childhood. The voice of his favorite soprano is unmistakable. Her voice soars exquisitely in an aria, the sound rising like an elegant trail of smoke, curling around the moldings above the paneling.

His study door is ajar. I push it farther open and see Mother in the wingback chair facing the door. She is cradling her wrist. She sees I'm about to speak and gives her head the tiniest of shakes. I push the door open wider. Hannah is sitting in my father's chair, behind his desk. On the desk in front of her is an old ledger. The cover is plain apart from a handwritten title: "Catalogue of Works of Art in the Holt Collection."

"Look what your mother found!" Hannah says.

"Well, that's wonderful," I say. The sight of Hannah behind my father's desk makes me very uncomfortable, and the atmosphere in the room feels strange and wrong. I glance at Mother, but she's staring out of the window. Her chin is raised and the tendons in her neck are taut. Something has happened.

"I understand your reluctance to join the forgery scheme your mother told you about," Hannah says, "but I think it's time to speak plainly. Take a seat." I hesitate. "Take a seat, Jocelyn, please!"

I ease myself into the chair opposite her. She is talking to me as if I'm a child.

"I know you don't want to be part of this scheme and I under- stand that, but I believe you're making the wrong decision," Han- nah says. "So I've had an idea and here's what we're going to do. Turn down the music, please."

I reach for the stereo and turn the music off. The silence feels oppressive.

Hannah pulls something across the desk in front of her. It's an old-fashioned cassette player.

"Don't!" Mother says. It's more of a groan of pain than a word.

Hannah smiles. "Hush, Virginia! Now, Jocelyn, I want you to listen to this carefully."

My mother's head sinks low. Hannah sits back in my father's chair. My unease is building. "What is this?"

Hannah puts her finger to her lips. I hear a few minutes of scrambled white noise followed by a voice. It's my father's voice and it conjures up his presence as if he's right here with us in the room. It's shockingly clear.

"Is it really you?" my father asks.

"Yes," a woman replies. "It's me."

"You!" I say to Hannah. "Shush!" she says and turns up the volume. The recorded conversation swells to fill the room. It hurts so much to hear my father's voice. Mother still won't look at me.

My father says:

> How is it you?
> *Do you mean, "How does a dead person come back to life?"*
> You were in a very bad way when I last saw you.
> *You always were the master of understatement, Alexander.*
> And we were so worried about you after you disappeared.
> *Do you mean after you threw my body into the lake?*

I listen in sickened silence. I can't believe what I'm hearing. My father, a murderer? Or he tried to be? He can't have succeeded, because Hannah is here now. Unless this isn't Hannah? But that can't be true.

I look at Mother again, but she remains completely still and her face betrays no surprise. The conversation develops. Hannah toys with my father as he tries and fails to maintain his composure.

> *Did you never love me, Alexander?*
> I love Virginia.
> *Even when we were together?*
> I don't think I'm going to answer that.

"I can't listen to this!" I stand up. I am devastated, sickened beyond measure. My father would never have had an affair with Hannah, would he? Not Hannah. She was mine. He was mine. They didn't belong to each other. For Hannah and my father to be together would have been unthinkable, a betrayal of everything I believed in.

And my father would never have harmed another person, would he?

I turn to Mother again, but she still won't meet my eye. I think of the cigarette case in Hannah's drawer and the fresh flowers at his grave that Mother would never have put there.

"Listen!" Hannah says.

As the tape keeps rolling, I hear Hannah tell my father she wants money from him in return for her silence over what happened that night. He tries to argue, becoming more distraught and then pleading as Hannah's voice hardens.

> *If you don't pay, I'll tell everybody what happened.*
> Tell them it was me.
> *Doesn't your daughter need you?*
> No. I'll take responsibility for everything, put an end
>   to it.
> *Then where would I get my money? I'd have to ask*
>   *Virginia. Perhaps I'll just tell everyone the truth.*

No. Please.

I could tell them Virginia pushed me.

No.

His voice cracks.

> *Who pushed me, Alexander?*
>
> No. I won't say it.
>
> *Then I shall. It was Jocelyn who pushed me. What a nasty little temper she turned out to have. I was not expecting it. You saw it. She pushed me deliberately. She wanted me to fall.*
>
> No, she didn't. You know it was an accident. Jocelyn pushed you, but she didn't mean for you to fall down the stairs.
>
> *Yes, she did. She saw her beloved daddy with me and she couldn't bear it. She wanted me dead.*

Hannah pauses the recording and looks at me so closely I feel as if I have been flayed. Mother has covered her face with her good hand. I kneel in front of her chair.

"Is this true? Did I push Hannah down the stairs?"

She shakes her head. It's a tiny movement. She's still covering her face.

"Tell me! What happened?"

"We thought she was dead," Mother says. "I checked her pulse."

"They dumped my body in the lake," Hannah cuts in. "As if I were no better than trash. An inconvenience. The fall knocked me unconscious. You gave me a very good shove, you know. I didn't think you had it in you, you being such a dull child. A disappointment to all of us, wouldn't you agree, Virginia?"

"Shut up!" I say. "Let Mother tell me!"

I take Mother's good hand and pull it from her face. "What happened?"

"Your father was having an affair with Hannah and you walked in on them after your bath. Do you remember? You had to bathe after you ruined your dress?"

I shake my head. I remember the bath, but nothing after it.

"The sight of your father and Hannah together shocked you very much and you became distraught. You pushed Hannah. You pushed her and she fell down the stairs, but it was an accident, darling. You didn't mean to hurt her. You were only trying to separate them."

"You weren't there, Virginia!" Hannah says. "You meant to do it, Jocelyn. You meant to kill. After all, you're just a typical Holt in the end. You thought I wasn't good enough for your daddy, so you pushed me down those stairs and you wanted me to die."

"You were seven years old!" Mother says. "No child that young has the intent to kill."

"I know what I saw in your eyes," Hannah says.

Shock pulsates through me. I am confused, appalled, disbelieving. Horrified. I am also searching my mind for some kind of memory of this, but there's nothing there. Nothing at all. I feel Mother squeeze my hand.

"Do you want to know how I survived?" Hannah asks. "When I came round, I found myself in the coal bunker, all trussed up like a bird ready to roast. My head was so painful it felt twice its normal size. I felt dizzy and sick. I had to work hard to loosen the ties enough to free myself, but when I did, I found I couldn't get out of the bunker. They'd locked it. I shouted for help. Screamed for it, but nobody heard me. I had to calm down and try to think what to do. Can you imagine how that felt? Should I wait for them to come back and try to talk them out of whatever they planned to do with me next? That risked them finishing what you'd started. Should I try to attack them when they returned? I was weak, hurt, and bleeding, my head injury was significant, and there was nothing in the bunker I could use as a weapon, especially not against two of them. So I decided to play dead. I wrapped myself back up as best I could, so they'd find me as they left me, and I waited to see what they were going to do with me. If I was to put up a fight, I thought there must be better places to do it than the coal bunker. And all the while, Jocelyn, there was one thing I didn't forget. What kept me strong was the thought that I would have my revenge one day on that spoiled, entitled, miserable little girl who had everything she could ever want but didn't think I was good enough for her daddy.

"Of course your parents were in such a panic when they came to get me they didn't notice the ties weren't precisely as they'd left them. I'd made a good job of it. After I was dumped in the lake, I let myself sink. They had tied weights to the end of the cords I was bound with. They meant for me to stay at the bottom of that lake. The water was so cold. I hadn't had time to take a very deep breath, but I stayed under for as long as possible. It was easy to free myself when I couldn't hold my breath any longer because I had retied the cords loosely. I surfaced as quietly as possible, but I was lucky your mother didn't see me. She could have. I took a breath and sank back underwater. I swam toward the island and I waited there for as long as I could bear to before I swam back to shore. And do you remember, Virginia? You'd left a bag of clothes in the boot room for the jumble sale. I stole them and you probably never noticed. I left Lake Hall in dry clothes, your clothes. I took my wet ones with me, too. I didn't want you suspecting I'd survived. I didn't know how far you would go to hunt me down and finish what Jocelyn started."

GILLY MACMILLAN

"You thought I'd killed her?" I ask Mother.

"Your mother covered up for you because you were a murderer. And, you know, we mustn't forget the skull in the lake. Who else did you get rid of, Virginia? This wasn't the first time you'd dumped a body in there, was it? All of you are born murderers. The Holts dispose of whomever they choose to, when it suits them. Other people are expendable to you. It's disgusting."

Hannah's words are vile. I try to block them out and focus on Mother. I want her to tell me what happened. "I don't remember this. Any of it."

"We gave you one of my pills," Mother says. "We hoped it would obliterate your memory, and it did."

"All of which is to say," Hannah says, "that I own you. I own you both, just the way you used to own me, and unless you want me to talk about this, you will accept that I am now a part of your life here. If you don't accept it, I'll tell the police everything I know."

"And have them know you're a blackmailer?" Mother asks.

"If it comes to that, it's a small price to pay for the justice I deserve, don't you think? I'll be a blackmailer, but you'll both be worse. But I hope it doesn't come to that. I trust the two of you can find it in you to agree to my proposal. It would be such a shame for Ruby, wouldn't it, if a police investigation were to be started?"

She pushes a button on the cassette player and the cassette pops up. She extracts it.

"I have made copies of this," she says. "Before you think destroying it will solve your problems."

She slips the cassette into her pocket and stands. She straightens her skirt and picks up the Holt Catalogue. I am too stunned to do anything other than stay on my knees in front of Mother and watch her go.

It's not until she's left that the spell of all the horror she's shared is broken. The intimacy of being so close to Mother feels unbearable suddenly. I need space. I snatch my hand from Mother's and back away from her. I feel as if I can hardly get enough air into my chest to breathe.

"Mother," I ask. "Is it really true?"

"Darling, I'm so sorry. We never wanted you to know."

VIRGINIA

THE PAIN IS SEARING. I try to ignore it, but it's impossible. Every word Hannah spoke worsened it, as if it were a punishment for everything.

"Does your wrist hurt?" Jocelyn asks. It's the first thing she's said for what feels like hours and her voice is hoarse. She has been slumped and almost silent in the chair opposite mine since Hannah left us, only throwing out the occasional question. I have answered with a heavy heart, confirming what neither of us wants to know.

"Hannah hurt me," I tell her now. "She wanted the catalogue. I didn't want to give it to her."

Hannah is not a particularly strong woman. I am taller and probably as fit as she is, but it's not difficult to cause pain to somebody whose wrist is already broken.

"What did she do?"

"It doesn't matter. It'll pass."

"Do you want a painkiller?"

"No. I mustn't." Though I'm not sure keeping a clear head can help us anymore, not when I have no idea what to do. As Jocelyn tries to process what she has learned, all I am able to feel is that I am a complete failure. I had one thing to protect my daughter from—the knowledge of what happened that night—and I wasn't able to.

As far as what to do about Hannah goes, I am absolutely at sea. I no longer have a plan. I can't think of anything that might help us.

"How is it that I don't remember what happened?" Jocelyn asks. "Not any of it?"

"Trauma. Medication. A combination of both. People suppress traumatic memories, darling. It felt like a gift to Daddy and me. We couldn't believe our good fortune. But you didn't mean to hurt Hannah. Let me make that clear."

Jocelyn looks so dazed. I can see she is going to have to take everything in bit by bit, but I wish it wasn't so. We need to do something, and for the first time in my life, I'm afraid I'm going to have to rely on somebody else to think of it.

I look at a photograph of Alexander. *I'm sorry,* I think. *I'm sorry I couldn't protect Jocelyn. Hannah won in the end.*

Jocelyn, Ruby, and I are as vulnerable to Hannah as a fox to the dogs. I might have hoped I'd be canny enough to make the chase last longer than this, long enough to outwit her even, but there's nowhere else to go now. It's the end and she's right: we belong to her.

"Darling, can you help me up to my room? I feel very faint."

We climb the stairs slowly. I lean heavily on my daughter. I feel pain. I feel the weight of this family's history around us. I feel guilt and failure intertwine within me.

Hannah is at the top of the stairs.

"Golly!" she says. "I hope the two of you are going to pep up because I've had an idea. I think the three of us should have dinner together. Not a kitchen supper, a proper dinner in the dining room with everything looking lovely, including us. Wouldn't that be nice? We can plan what we're going to do going forward. I've done a bit of research and I've got lots of ideas for our little art scheme."

Jocelyn and I pause on the landing. I am a little breathless. Hannah is smiling. She is glorying in this. It is vile.

"Well, what do you think?" she asks.

"Yes," I say. "It would be lovely. Leave it with me."

"Shall we say drinks at eight in the Blue Room? Dinner afterward?"

"Of course."

Jocelyn's grip tightens around my arm, making me flinch, though she doesn't notice. Once we're in my bedroom, she whispers, "I won't do it."

"We have no choice," I say. "What else can we do? There is Ruby to think of."

I sit on the side of my bed. I want nothing more than to lie down and sleep. I feel something underneath my hand. It's one of my pills. I put it on the palm of my hand and show Jocelyn.

"I was stashing my painkillers in the tissue box," I say, "because they were so strong I didn't want to take them anymore. I got them out again after I broke my wrist, but some were missing and I think Hannah might have been slipping them to Ruby. Ruby's changed since Hannah arrived here. She's so tired all the time now and she used to be so vital. And listen, I think Hannah might have been doing the same to you when you were a girl. We only realized after she was gone, because we found bottles of pills when we cleaned out her room."

Jocelyn stares at me as she listens. It breaks my heart to see her so shattered. All I can hope is that it means she will be on my side now. "How can we stop her?" she says. I see she's making wild, desperate calculations in her mind, trying to find a way out of this, but I already know it's impossible. For now we must bear it. Hannah is capable of physical harm. This morning showed me that.

"We have to do what she wants for now," I say. "It's the safest way."

She shakes her head, but I pick up my telephone and dial a number I know by heart.

"Hello," I say when a familiar voice answers, "this is Lady Holt. Do you happen to have a nice piece of venison you could put aside for me? Or a rack of lamb would do. And would you be a dear and send someone to the house with it? I have a surprise guest tonight and I'm rather up against it."

When I put down the phone, Jocelyn is staring at me as if I'm mad.

"We have to do this, darling," I say. "She'll expect a good dinner."

She shakes her head. A tear falls, tracking down her cheek, then dampening the surface of my bedspread. She says, "I don't know how to cook venison and you can't do it with your wrist."

"Don't worry. I'll tell you what to do."

This will be a good meal. It will make Hannah think we are taking her seriously.

I have no better idea.

JO

MOTHER AND I WORK TOGETHER in the kitchen. I collected Ruby from school in a trance. I can't remember a single thing she said in the car or since we got home, but she didn't seem to notice. She's excited by the sight of Mother and me working together and eager to help.

Mother gets out her wallet of Sabatier knives. She explains the function of each one to Ruby and shows her how to slice carrots on the diagonal.

"They look much more elegant that way," she says.

Ruby works carefully, but my heart is in my mouth as she makes each slice. She's so young and the knife is so sharp.

When I drain the potatoes, a cloud of steam billows in front of the window. As it dissipates, I see Hannah outside, walking around the side of the house. The back door opens.

"What a lovely sight this is!" she says. "I'm so looking forward to our dinner." She carefully removes her headscarf and I see she's had her hair done.

Ruby looks from my mother to me. "Who else is coming to dinner?" she asks.

"Just us, darling," Mother replies.

"But you said I could have sausages."

"You can," I say. "The dinner isn't for you."

"It'll be very boring," Mother says. "You won't enjoy it."

"Yes," Hannah says. "I agree. But there might be evenings when I'd like you to join us, Ruby, because it'll be good for you to learn some better manners. Don't you agree, Virginia?"

Mother's reply sticks in her mouth at first, but she recovers enough to say something, which is more than I can manage. Hearing Hannah speak my daughter's name terrifies me to the point of muteness. "Yes," Mother says, "it's a good idea to develop gracious manners. Ruby, darling, I think it's time we laid the table. Would you help me?"

When they've left the room, Hannah says, "Doesn't that food smell nice already?" She surveys the prepared vegetables. "Did you forget I don't like broccoli, Jocelyn? You can put that away."

I put my knife down and replace the broccoli in the fridge.

"What's the time?" Hannah asks.

"Half past six." I can hardly get the words out.

"Perfect! I think I'll go and have a bath. I'll see you for drinks."

In the dining room, Ruby is laying everything out under Mother's instruction.

"I can't do it," I say.

"And we can't reach the good candlesticks," Mother says. The look she gives me warns me not to break in front of Ruby. I open the cabinet and take the candlesticks down. They're heavy. The crystal droplets hanging from the rims quiver after I've placed them on the table.

"Look at these!" Ruby says. She shows me the tiny silver spoons that go with the saltcellars.

"Very delicate," I say.

"So cute!"

"And look at this!"

She hands me a silver napkin ring. It's my father's. His initials are engraved on the side of it. I sense Mother watching me, and when I look at her, she looks away.

"We won't use this one," I say. "Not tonight."

RUBY IS happy to go to bed early.

"I want to have dinner with you and Granny and get all dressed up," she says. "But not with Hannah."

"I understand."

She yawns. "I'm tired."

"You look it. You can go on your iPad for half an hour and then read for a while if you want, but turn out your light before half past eight, okay? I'll come and check on you later."

She gives me the sweetest cuddle. "I liked making dinner with you and Granny," she says. I'm too choked up to reply.

I pause at the doorway for a long moment before I leave her. "Good night," I say, but she doesn't hear because she already has her headphones in. I close her door firmly behind me and lean against it. I love her so much. The thought that I've put her in so much danger is unbearable.

I CHECK on the food and spend ages looking through my clothes. I will not wear the blouse Hannah gave me and I have nothing else suitable.

I watch the clock. It's coming close to eight and there are still hors d'oeuvres to prepare, though I'd rather choke than eat them with Hannah. I feel like her servant, but I suppose that's the point.

I go to Mother's room and find her struggling to get into a dress. She hasn't done her makeup yet and she looks vulnerable, pale, and old.

"Can you help me?" she asks. She's chosen a dress with wide sleeves, but even so the cast on her wrist makes it difficult to get on. I help ease her into it and do up the zip at the side for her.

"What about you?" she asks. I'm wearing my dressing gown.

"I don't know what to wear."

"Shall I help you?"

"Do we have to do this?" I have never felt so helpless.

"I think we do. And you can do it, Jocelyn. You can get through it." She doesn't look as sure as she sounds. "This is the first time you've ever let me dress you," she says, and that hits me hard. It's almost the most wounding thing I've heard today, because for the first time I allow in the thought that Mother made an effort to get close to me on so many occasions, over so many years, and I rejected her every single time. Because of Hannah.

How much damage must that have done?

Mother pulls open the doors to both her closets. The clothes are hung in crowded rows, and many of the dresses and jackets are wrapped in dry cleaner's plastic. Boxes of shoes are stacked neatly beneath them. It's a shrine to fashion.

"Let me see," she says. "I've always thought green or blue suits you best." She riffles through her dresses and plucks one out. "You'll look wonderful in a—"

She doesn't get to finish her sentence because the door opens. Hannah peers around it. "Here you are!" she says. "I wondered where you'd both got to. Are you getting ready together? That's so sweet. Do you mind if I join?"

She's wearing the dress I saw her trying on in Marlborough and more makeup than I've ever seen on her. She is also wearing a pair of drop diamond earrings that belong to my mother and belonged to my grandmother before her. They're a family heirloom. I feel sick to my stomach.

Hannah's eyes light up when she sees the clothes in Mother's wardrobe.

"Goodness! What an embarrassment of riches these are. I had no idea. Well, perhaps I did. Now, where are some of my favorites?"

She pushes Mother aside and riffles through the clothes roughly. Mother can hardly bear to watch.

"What's the matter, Virginia? Are you worried I'm not good enough to touch your clothes?"

"No," Mother says. "But some of the dresses are museum quality and need very careful handling."

"Is that right?" Hannah says. "Would this be one of them?"

She yanks out a dress and holds it up against herself. "How do I look? I was thinking maybe I would prefer to wear one of your 'museum quality' dresses tonight. Would that be all right with you, Virginia?"

She pulls more dresses from the wardrobe, ripping tissue wrapping and dry cleaning plastic from them, dropping some on the floor at her feet, flinging others onto the bed or across the vanity table.

Mother and I can do nothing other than stand and stare as the dresses fall around us and the sound of the plastic settling is like a gentle exhale, the last gasp of breath from our lives as we knew them. I feel as if Hannah isn't going to stop until she's emptied the cupboards of every last dress, but she pauses suddenly.

"This one!" she says. "I wore it once, Virginia. Did you know that? I took it from your wardrobe and tried it on. It wasn't the only one I tried on, but it was my favorite because I saw how Alexander looked at you when you wore it. I have to say, I looked sensational in it. In fact, why don't I try it on now and you can see for yourself?"

Hannah wriggles out of the dress she's wearing and stands in front of us in her underwear. It's silky and lacy and I look away. She works hard to fit into Mother's dress. As she leans over to pull it up, the beading catches on a few strands of her hair and she has to yank it free. I hope it hurts. She struggles to get the dress over her hips, thighs, and belly.

"Zip," she says once it's on. I pull the zip up, but it's not easy.

The dress is too tight. Watching the beautiful fabric stretch over Hannah's skin is disgusting. I can't wait to pull my hands away.

"You always were fatter than me, Hannah," Mother says, and I feel Hannah stiffen. I get the zip done up and step back.

Hannah admires herself in the mirror, turning this way and that, striking a pose. "It looks just as I remember. But you know what was better than wearing this, Virginia? Do you know when I really felt like you?"

Mother can only stare at her. There are two high points of color on Hannah's cheeks. She is glorying in this.

"It was when Alexander was inside me," Hannah says.

"Stop!" I say. "That's enough."

"That's not for you to decide, dear."

"Please. We're going to do what you ask."

"You know, I might have more faith in you if you weren't so furtive, Jocelyn."

"I don't know what you mean."

"The cigarette case. I presume it was you that took it, unless it was Ruby. You can fetch it for me now, please. I'd like it back tonight."

"It's not yours."

"Jocelyn," Mother says. "It's fine. Get the case."

"It's not fine. Even if my father was having an affair he was ours, too. He didn't just belong to you. He was my daddy."

"Did you know he used to let me drug you so he and I could meet in my bedroom at night?"

"No! That's not true. Mother?"

"I don't know if it is or not, darling. I'm sorry."

"It's not true!"

"You slept through so much. We were a very passionate couple," Hannah says.

"He would never have done that." I can't stand the thought of it.

"Of course he would. He did it all the time. And it was because he didn't care about you. He never even wanted you. He always wanted a boy, and do you know what? I was going to give him one."

Her words build up, each one another little point of pressure around me.

"Alexander was such a gentleman, though," she says with unbearable relish, as if he was made for her and her alone, "that he never would have let you know how much he despised you. He never tired of telling me, though. How we laughed about you. So earnest you were, so serious, so desperate to please me. He thought it was pathetic. You bored him. Poor little Jocelyn Holt, loathed by her mother and her father, but really, who could love you? You disappointed your father in every single way possible. Such a plain, dull little girl on the outside, and inside you were nothing better than a revolting, entitled, murderous little bitch."

She turns back to the closet. "Now," she says, "shoes. Isn't it lucky we're the same size, Virginia?"

I look at her ugly back where I pulled the zipper up. She is just flesh and bone underneath my mother's dress, nothing more than doughy flesh and breakable bone. How dare she say these things? Her words are pure poison. The pressure around my head feels immense and I can't take it any longer. She means to destroy me, my mother, and my daughter. Something breaks inside me with absolute finality.

I snatch a dry cleaning bag from the bed and wrap the ends of it around my hands until there are only a few inches of it left. About the width of somebody's face. Every part of me is seized by a burning anger. Every part of me wants to end this.

Hannah's not as tall as me and not as strong, and I reach her before she has a chance to react. I throw the bag over her head and pull it across her face, twisting my hands so the plastic is as tight as I can make it, wrenching her backward. She loses her balance. I pull the bag tighter than ever and her knees buckle and her arms flail as she tries to escape. Already she can't breathe. I hear it. As she inhales, the plastic seals her mouth.

I sink to my knees so I can keep the pressure up and pull her with me. The muscles in my arms and neck and shoulders are screaming, but I keep pulling and twisting the polythene around my hands. Now I can see her face beneath the plastic and I watch her suffer and it feels so good. She makes a terrible noise as she tries to breathe, she fights hard, but she doesn't last long because the layers of polythene are taut across her mouth and nose, suctioned there in a perfect concave *O* where she's sucked them in, stretched obscenely tight but not breaking.

She's losing this fight, and I want to be the last person she sees before she dies. Her eyes are stretched wide open as if she's trying to draw oxygen in through them out of sheer desperation. I look right into them until she stops blinking and it feels as if it isn't long, as if it doesn't take long at all, though I don't know how long it is because I'm panting and trying to draw breath myself, and then I'm sobbing, and Mother puts her hand on my shoulder and says, "She's gone. Jocelyn, you can let go now. She's gone."

It's hard to release her. I want to keep the plastic tight forever. I want it to punish her for everything she's done to us, but I start to shake when Mother touches me.

When I unwrap the polythene, my hands look bleached in places and ridged red in others. I'm transfixed by the sight of them. I hear Mother saying my name and saying other things, but I can't take it in. I can tear my gaze away only when the phone starts to ring.

DETECTIVE ANDY WILTON

IT'S ALMOST EIGHT-THIRTY ON FRIDAY night when he rolls out of the pub. They went for a few jars at five and time ran away from him. He hasn't eaten anything and he didn't turn up to the spin class he was supposed to be doing with his girlfriend. He has six missed calls from her and two very narky messages. He's listening to the end of one of them when his colleagues emerge from the pub behind him. The door swings wildly in their wake.

"Andy! Mate! Are you coming for a curry?" Their breath mists in the cold air. "Maxine's meeting us there."

Maxine has been out all day at a training course and hasn't responded to his texts.

"Yeah, I'm coming." He starts up the street to join his friends—big, fit lads, all of them. He bloody loves them. He pulls the collar of his coat tighter around his neck to keep the chill out and sparks up a cigarette. He knows in that moment that his new girlfriend is not going to last beyond the weekend. If she hasn't dumped him by tomorrow morning, he'll be dumping her.

Maxine is already seated with a pint of lager in front of her. She keeps up with the lads.

"Don't ask!" she says. "The course trainer made us lock our phones up. It's been a long day, but I've got some good news for you."

"Interview with the nanny?" Andy asks.

"No, but I'll do it first thing on Monday. I promise."

"Is that your country house case?" one of the lads asks.

"Yep. We've got an ID off of the DNA. The family claimed not to recognize the images we got from the skull reconstruction, but we've got a proper photograph now. I want to show it to them and see if they react to the name."

"There's more," Maxine says. She hands him her phone and he reads an email from a colleague:

Background check has thrown up something very interesting.
Hannah Maria Burgess d.o.b. 7 November 1957 actually died
1 February 1973, aged 15. She died of self-asphyxiation.

"The nanny isn't who she said she is," Maxine says.

"Holy crap," Andy says.

"You should phone the family now, let them sweat it over the weekend," his colleague suggests.

"You think?" The beer has fuddled him.

"Don't," Maxine says. "That's ridiculous. It's too late and you've had too much to drink."

Andy's got to admit it. He's tempted by the idea of aggravating Lady Holt on a Friday night.

Maxine sees it. "Don't! It'll just piss them off and we need to see their reactions. It's totally unprofessional."

"I'll just make the appointment," he says. "I won't tell them anything." He steps out of the restaurant and finds a quiet spot at the end of a filthy alleyway. He calls Lake Hall.

"Hello?" It's Virginia Holt. Not difficult to recognize that voice.

"Mrs. Holt, it's Detective Andy Wilton here."

"It's very late to be calling." She doesn't sound quite as sharp as usual.

"Yes. It's important, though." She's not going to get an apology out of him.

"What is it?"

"I'd like to come and see you on Monday morning."

"See who?"

"You, your daughter, and the nanny."

"That won't be possible." Is he imagining it or does her voice sound shaky, as if something is off?

He's pacing as he's talking and he's about to ask if something is wrong, but he trips on the curb and has to save himself.

"Hello?" she says. He leans against the wall and shuts his eyes. He's an idiot because he's too drunk to be doing this. He can see his mates inside the curry house. They're beckoning him to join them. He needs to eat. He can't get the better of Virginia Holt when he's pissed like this, and he has to shut it down now.

"Nine o'clock Monday morning. I expect you all to be there. It's important."

It takes him a few stabs of his finger to end the call.

VIRGINIA

I REPLACE THE HANDSET ON its base on my bedside table.

Jocelyn is staring at me but not seeing me. She's in shock. It's what happened to her father when Hannah "died" the first time.

"Who was it?" she asks.

"Nobody. A wrong number." She doesn't need to know.

"You shouldn't have answered."

"Yes, I should."

Hannah lies motionless in the middle of my bedroom, wearing my dress. My other garments are collapsed in jeweled and beaded silken heaps around her; the wrappings that were protecting them strewn everywhere. The polythene bags and sheets of tissue paper whisper and rustle around my feet as I leave the room. I feel as if I'm wading through them.

I open Ruby's bedroom door as quietly as possible. Her light is off. I approach her bed. She is facing the window, her iPad on the pillow in front of her, earbuds tucked into her ears. I have pretended to be asleep on many an occasion, and I search her face for signs that she is still awake, but her body is relaxed in a way that convinces me and her breathing is deep and regular. I don't think she heard a thing.

I back out of the room and shut the door. I lean my back against it and take deep breaths. I know what to do now. I don't feel helpless any longer.

Jocelyn is hunched on my bed. She is looking across Hannah, over her, as if the body isn't there. I sit beside her, taking care not to touch her. Shock is an unpredictable thing.

"Darling," I say. "Listen to me. What's done is done."

Her eyes flit toward me and then away.

"Jocelyn, there are things we have to do now and I can't do them alone. I need you to help me. Then we need never think or speak of this again."

She blanks me. I feel a flutter of apprehension. Her father was like this, but I knew better how to get through to him.

"Jocelyn. Jo."

Nothing. She shuts her eyes. I lean toward her and enunciate my words clearly. "Listen to me carefully. Ruby cannot find this body here. If you don't help me now, there is a real possibility that she will. Now, come on!"

She moves robotically, but at least she moves.

We take the dress off Hannah. I open Alexander's wardrobe and reach for a garment bag. I got rid of almost everything of his after his death, apart from the things that had value to the family. In the bag is a military greatcoat one of his ancestors wore. I remove it. It's a huge, heavy garment. It smells of mothballs. The bag is very sturdy and a little longer than Hannah.

Jocelyn lays the bag out on the floor and we roll Hannah onto it. Jocelyn tucks her limbs in and starts to drag the zip up, though it's difficult.

"Wait!" I say. "Take off the earrings."

She unclips my diamond earrings from Hannah's ears. She zips the bag completely closed. We check the corridor and drag the body out and down the back stairs so we don't have to go past Ruby's room. I can't carry my end on the stairs, not with my wrist as it is, so I let Hannah's head thump down, just as we should have let it do the first time.

We get the body to the lake, treading a path that both of us know so well that the sliver of moonlight is all we need to guide us. The body flattens the damp grass as we drag it. The pain in my wrist feels white hot, but I don't let it distract me now.

We are both panting by the time we get to the shore. Jocelyn drags the kayak from the boathouse. It is for two people. She will have to take the body out alone.

"We have to weight her down," she says.

"I know what to do. I read a book where a body came up in a fishing net. Somebody had slit the stomach to stop it bloating and floating up." The book told me something I wish I'd known the first time we sank Hannah's body, because I suffered terrible nightmares in the aftermath where I imagined her body resurfacing, even though we'd weighted it.

"Fetch my knife roll," I say.

She nods. She's focused. "And you thought I read too many crime stories, darling," I say.

She makes her way up the lawn and disappears into the house, her silhouette framed by the light from the boot room door. I watch Ruby's bedroom window, afraid that at any moment her light will come on. It's freezing out here, but I bear it and hold my head high, alert for noise and disturbance.

Jocelyn returns with the knife roll.

"Unwrap it," I say.

She unfolds it so we can see each knife stored in its own soft pocket. Not all are there, because we have been using them, but there's one that will be perfect. I select the ten-inch knife that I know to be very sharp. I unzip the suit bag so Hannah's soft abdomen is exposed.

"Look away," I say, but Jocelyn doesn't.

I wedge the knife between the cast and my fingers on my bad hand and clasp my other hand around it. I plunge it into Hannah's belly as deep as it will go. I do it twice more, in different places.

The sound it makes is terrible and the sight of the flesh parting beneath the blade is awful. But there is no blood. Hannah is truly dead this time. Jocelyn retches and staggers away, hands on her knees. She coughs and spits, and strings of bile hang from her mouth. I kneel and wash the knife in the lake. I manage to zip the bag back up with my good hand. I have almost forgotten the pain in my wrist now that we're so close to finishing this.

"Jocelyn!" I say. "We have to get on with it. If Ruby were to hear us and look out . . ."

She wipes her mouth, straightens up, and glances at Ruby's window. All is dark as it should be. The tawny owl cries in the woods as we move the kayak to the edge of the lake and heave the body onto it. We push the kayak out a little and I steady it while Jocelyn packs some stones into the suit bag with the body before zipping it back up again. You can't be too careful.

Jocelyn gets into the kayak. She is shaking more than I am. The bottom of her dressing gown is sodden.

As she paddles out onto the water, I watch every stroke she makes, even though the cold chills me to the bone and clouds obscure the moonlight intermittently.

She stops paddling when she's near the island. I can't see her properly now, but I can hear her. I exhale deeply when I hear the splash that means the body has hit the water, and I remember the sight of the ripples slowly subsiding all those years ago when I did the same.

As Jocelyn paddles back, the moon whitens the edges of the undulating waves in the kayak's wake, but otherwise all is calm and Ruby's bedroom light remains off.

IN THE boot room I shut the door and take off Jocelyn's dressing gown. I wrap her in a long down coat of mine and lead her to the

Blue Room. The glasses are still on the side where we placed them ready for our drinks with Hannah. The ice in the champagne bucket has melted. I turn on a corner lamp, feed the fire, and fetch an eiderdown, which I place over her. I pour a neat whiskey for Jocelyn and one for myself.

"Drink," I say. The alcohol scorches my throat.

She drinks. Her mouth contorts.

"We tell nobody what happened," I say.

She nods.

"We tell nobody what happened because we must protect Ruby. If this gets out, everything Hannah wanted will come to pass and I can't allow it. We can't allow it."

She sips again. She takes the whiskey better this time. Firelight flickers across her face.

"Yes," she says.

JO

MOTHER WANTS CHEESE ON TOAST for lunch. Ruby grates the cheese and Mother grills it one-handed.

"Where's Hannah?" Ruby says.

Mother looks at me. I shake my head. I can't say it.

"She left," Mother says.

"Forever?"

"Yes."

"She's never coming back?"

"Never."

Ruby looks shocked at first, then hugs my mother and me in turn. She beams.

I can't eat.

"THE DETECTIVE phoned," Mother says. "I forgot to mention it. He wants to visit us on Monday."

"What did you tell him?"

"I had to agree to it. He was insistent."

"No."

"I think we have to do it, Jocelyn."

"We can't."

VIRGINIA

"JEAN PALMER," THE DETECTIVE SAYS. "Jean Grace Palmer."

He has a new photograph to show us. He says it's of the woman whose skull they reconstructed, and he puts it down on the table between us just the way they do in television shows. I don't recognize her. She doesn't look like anyone I know or ever knew.

"No," I say. "It doesn't ring any bells."

"What about you?" the female detective asks. She has such sharp eyes.

"No," Jocelyn says. "Not for me, either."

She sounds steady. Good.

"Where's your nanny?" the female detective asks.

"I'm so sorry she can't be here," I say. "It's rather embarrassing, but she's moved on. She left unexpectedly in the middle of the night on Friday. She gave no notice and no forwarding details, and we have no idea where she's gone. She did the same thing to us once before, years ago. We're very upset about it."

"Really?" the female detective says. She and her colleague exchange a glance.

"The thing is," Detective Wilton says, "we believe that your nanny might not be called Hannah Burgess. From our investigations we have ascertained that a Hannah Maria Burgess, of the same date and place of birth, actually died on 1 February 1973, when she was fifteen years old."

The shock on Jocelyn's face looks as genuine as mine feels.

"Could you tell us exactly when Hannah disappeared from your house the first time?"

"Nineteen eighty-seven," Jocelyn says.

"You have a good memory," the female officer says as she notes it down.

"You don't forget something like that. I was very fond of her and I was devastated when she disappeared. It was as if she'd gone up in smoke."

"And what brought her back into your lives so recently?"

"She just turned up on our doorstep," I say. "Bold as brass."

"Did she say why?"

Jocelyn shakes her head. "No. Not really. Something about making a fresh start after caring for her mother. That's all."

"She was a very private person," I say. "We respected that."

"Do you mind if we have a look in her bedroom?" Detective Wilton asks. "It might be useful if we could find something that we could get a DNA sample from."

"She cleared her room out, but you're welcome to see it. Her DNA must be all over this house."

"Are you aware of anything missing from the house that didn't belong to her?"

"No."

"Can I ask how you broke your wrist?"

"I fell. At my age, it happens."

Jocelyn shows them upstairs and I follow. I pause on the landing because I've had a thought. In my wardrobe, I find the dress that Hannah was wearing when she died.

I take it downstairs and wait in the hallway.

They come down soon enough.

"She cleaned out good and proper, didn't she?" Detective Wilton says.

"She'd had practice. She's done it before. I was thinking while you were upstairs that you might get some DNA from this dress. I

lent it to her last week. She was asking if she could borrow something to wear to a party, so I offered it to her to try on. The beading always catches my hair when I put it on, so perhaps it did the
same to her."

He takes it from me, scrunching it clumsily in his big hand.

"Careful! It's couture."

The female officer takes the dress from him with a smile and
lays it across her arm. "Thank you," she says. "We'll take care of it."

They swab the inside of our cheeks to eliminate our DNA.

Jocelyn and I watch them drive away.

"You could have given them the earrings," she says.

"They're for Ruby."

JO

"ARE YOU PICKING ME UP today?" Ruby says. She's bouncing around me. She's so much better and less tired now. She is happy.

"I'm taking you to school, but Granny will collect you. I'll be back late, after bedtime."

"Are you going to London?"

"Yes."

"Can you buy me a Ouija board?"

"No."

"Stan wants one."

"Then Stan can ask his own mother to get him one."

After dropping Ruby at school, I spend the morning in Elizabeth's studio, planning with her and Mother, then take the train to London for a dinner with Faversham and a client.

The detective phones as we arrive at the restaurant.

"Excuse me a minute, I should take this."

I stand under the awning where winter hanging baskets drip with ivy, and I watch cabs hustle for curb space as they disgorge well-dressed passengers.

"How can I help you?" I ask.

Detective Andy Wilton is no less economical with words than he was when I first met him. "We got a familial match from the DNA we took from your mother's dress. It's been a bit of a long process trying to track people down to interview, but we think we've ascertained that the DNA belongs to a woman called Linda Taylor."

"Really?"

"Linda Taylor was working at the house of the deceased Hannah Burgess's brother for a time, so we assume that's where she got the idea to steal Hannah Burgess's identity. More importantly, we have been able to link Linda Taylor to Jean Palmer— the body in your lake—because they shared a residence for a while."

"Does that mean what I think it means?"

"Nothing is certain yet, but what I can tell you is that it makes Linda Taylor, aka Hannah Burgess, a person of interest with regards to the death of Jean Palmer."

"You think Hannah might have killed Jean Palmer? And then come back here after the skull was dug up? Why?"

"One thought is that Jean Palmer might have threatened to expose Hannah's real identity, causing Hannah to lash out at her. I can't tell you why she came back, but she could have read about the skull resurfacing and returned to keep an eye on what was happening. It's not uncommon for perpetrators to try to insert themselves into an investigation. It can give them an illusion of control. Certainly we don't consider it a coincidence that she disappeared a second time once we had identified Jean."

"Because she was afraid you might link her to Jean?"

"That's a possibility we'll be looking into."

"Oh my god."

"And we will be doing everything in our power to track her down, so please don't worry about that. Will you contact me immediately if you hear from her?"

"Of course we will," I say. "Do you think she'll come back?"

"I imagine she's long gone, and we'll do our best to find out where."

"Thank you so much, Detective. I can't tell you how much we appreciate you keeping us informed."

I call Mother to tell her the news.

I GET home late to Lake Hall, but Mother has waited up for me. She's gleeful. "They'll never think to look for her back here," she says. "Not now. I can't believe it. Who would have thought it?"

She pours us a drink each and hands me a glass. "Chin-chin," she says. "Here's to an end to it. Finally."

"Cheers," I say.

I'm totally unprepared when she tries to hug me. I flinch. Our cheekbones clash and I pull back. I can't help it.

She steps away as if she's been burnt.

"I'm sorry," I say.

"I understand."

"It's just . . ." I don't know how to finish my sentence. Mother goes to touch my face but stops herself.

I move forward and put my arms around her.

"I'm sorry," I say. "It was just a little souvenir from Hannah."

ACKNOWLEDGMENTS

Helen Heller's input shaped this novel and its characters from the first word to the last. Thank you for making it such a blast to work on.

Enormous thanks to my editors, Emily Krump in New York and Emily Griffin in London, whose insightful notes and generous support improved the book immeasurably. Very warm thanks to Julia Elliott and Becky Millar and also to Shari Lapena for being such a sharp-eyed and generous early reader.

I appreciate deeply the support of Liate Stehlik at William Morrow and Selina Walker at Century & Arrow. Thank you both.

Sales, marketing, publicity, and production teams are crucial to a book's success. I am extremely thankful to Jen Hart, Lauren Truskowski, Molly Waxman, and Kaitlin Harri in the United States; to Sarah Harwood, Sarah Ridley, Natalia Cacciatore, and Linda Hodgson in the UK; and to everyone else who works on my books. Special thanks to Elsie Lyons for the stunning cover design.

The folks at HarperCollins Canada must get a special mention. Thanks to Leo MacDonald for your support (and your inspiring photography), to Sandra Leef for everything you've done for my books, and also to Mike Millar and the rest of the awesome team in Toronto.

Warmest thanks to Jemma McDonagh, Camilla Ferrier, and all at the Marsh Agency for everything you do. I appreciate it mightily.

Thank you to the editors and publishers who translate my books internationally, and to the teams who work with them. I am very grateful to you all, and it's been so nice to meet some of you face-to-face this year.

I am lucky to work with such talented and lovely people.

Booksellers, bloggers, reviewers, fellow authors, and readers are all part of the generous and supportive community who make my job such a pleasure, even on a bad day. Thank you all.

On the home front, thank you to the two retired detectives who generously give me their time and advice on all things police related. We didn't get a chance to discuss this book, but I'm making a lunch reservation for the next one! Any mistakes or liberties taken with police procedure in the novel are mine alone.

To my writing partner Abbie Ross, Annemarie Caracciolo, Philippa Lowthorpe, and other friends near and far, thank you for your generous encouragement. It was inspiring to work alongside Laurie Maffly-Kipp, Rachael Gilmour, and Heiderose Gerberding at Gladstone's Library.

To Sean Burrows, Nick Lear, Jrae Davis, Ben Shepherd, John Hewer, Brett Marsden, Jake Burrows, and Richard Banister, thank you for building me a new office during the time it took to write this book.

My family has been incredibly patient during the writing of this book. Jules, thank you for the omelettes and red wine. Rose, Max, and Louis, thank you and I couldn't be more proud of you.

ABOUT THE AUTHOR

GILLY MACMILLAN is the bestselling author of *What She Knew*, *The Perfect Girl*, *Odd Child Out*, and *I Know You Know*. She grew up in Swindon, Wiltshire, and lived in Northern California in her late teens. She worked at *The Burlington Magazine* and the Hayward Gallery before starting a family. Since then, she has worked as a part-time lecturer in photography, and she now writes full time. She resides in Bristol, England.